PREY SILENCE

by

Sally Spedding

Magna Large Print Books
Long Preston, North Yorkshire,
BD23 4ND, England.

British Library Cataloguing in Publication Data.

Spedding, Sally
   Prey silence.

   A catalogue record of this book is
   available from the British Library

   ISBN   0-7505-2636-X
   ISBN   978-0-7505-2636-4

First published in Great Britain in 2006 by Allison & Busby Ltd.

Published in Large Print 2006 by arrangement with
Allison & Busby Ltd.

Magna Large Print is an imprint of Library Magna Books Ltd.

Printed and bound in Great Britain by
T.J. (International) Ltd., Cornwall, PL28 8RW

Stone fermette (Quercy style) to restore.
Big potential in quiet friendly hamlet.
Convenient all amentics.
Six hectarcs grazing.
Private sale. Telephone B Metz.
(0033)05 61 47 05 40

READERS' PROBLEM PAGE

I've heard from ex-pat friends in Paris that French red tape is horrendous for anyone hoping to set up in business in France. We intend opening a B&B in the Vendée. Can any of your readers give us some practical advice on this?

James Dowell by email

Our family has just moved to an idyllic barn restoration in the Charente, but are increasingly perturbed by the froideur of the locals toward us. We are learning French as quickly as we can and our son attends the local École Primaire. Has anyone any similar experiences? What are we doing wrong?

Gill Marr, Soljuste

URGENT. Two black cockers missing near Lodève. Please contact Live France if seen.

Grieving owners, Nick and Jenny Green by email

My wife and I learnt from friends in Deux-Sèvres that the French will shoot anything that moves. We are understandably very anxious for the safety of our cat who'll be moving to the Ardèche with us next month. What are other readers' experiences?

M Porter, Essex

My Packard Bell pc simply won't function here. Do I have to buy a French make?

Susie Taylor, Béziers

Our second home has been burgled twice in the Dordogne (near Souillac) and we now seek reliable British keyholder/security personnel in that area.

David Farrar, Epsom

We have just found our dream home in the Quercy region near Cahors, and would like to be put in touch with local artisans who would do the renovations, including the installation of a new septic tank. All suggestions much appreciated.

Tom Wardle-Smith by email

Help! Tics everywhere. We have lost three precious dogs to these pernicious pests and now feel we can't subject any more pets to the suffering they bring. Any specialist vetinerary advice most welcome.

Nancy Lodge, Agen

Live France

PROLOGUE

Not a sound except for the eagles' bark high up on the Fer à Cheval as they hunt for life, any life to sustain them through the rest of the winter's barren months. But hunger will soon drive them from this arid rocky plateau to those few abandoned dwellings nestling in its shadow above the hamlet of St Sauveur. Here, the once-sheltering roofs have long fallen in on themselves and tumbled heaps of stone wall lie strewn on the scrubby ground.

A solitary predator alights on the smallest, least derelict *fermette* and, exchanging one darkness for another, breaches a hole between its dishevelled tiles. In the farthest, dampest room carved out from the rock itself, his beak strokes the soil like a metal detector, but it's not metal that he finds. Instead, something far more nourishing. His amber eye fixes on the tiny prize before snatching it aloft, and by the time the local church bells have ended their midnight chime, he has flown clear of the hovel, higher and higher into the freezing night...

CHAPTER ONE

Tom Wardle-Smith followed his own shadow up his neighbour's driveway feeling the impossibly smooth gravel under his shoes, noting the shaved grass on either side, the neat beds of miniature narcissus and green-budded tulips, all serving to slow him up, reminding him what he and his young family were about to leave behind. The springs, summers, autumns and winters amongst the Scots pines and chestnuts which everyone on Berris Hill Road possessed at the ends of their gardens. The sheer material ease of life in Surrey. The convenience of everything, from takeaway aromatic duck to repeat prescriptions for Prozac. (Not for him, you understand. For his wife, Kathy.) The companionable but non-intrusive neighbours, the House Watch Scheme that he'd help set up last autumn before he'd spotted Hibou in the *Live France* Christmas edition. A wreck of a *fermette* deep in the Midi-Pyrénées.

He paused. Could hear music pulsing from the Simiston's house – a frequently upgraded version of his – boasting two extensions and a heated outdoor pool where, on summer evenings from his upper windows, he could see Una Simiston breasting the turquoise water, length after length, while her husband's drinking progressed, slackening his body on the sun lounger.

And this, now, on Friday 22nd March, 2002,

was the farewell party.

Tom glanced back at the rear of his own newly rendered home which had just netted three hundred and fifty grand in a sticky market. Its whiteness gleamed in the sunshine; its leaded windows prettily reflecting blue, enough to trigger another tug of regret. What the hell was he doing? he asked himself yet again, because now there really was no going back. Yesterday in Chertsey had not only been Completion Day on the sale, but also when Right Move removals were paid their interim balance. Soon the Puris, a Sikh family from Totteridge, would be enjoying the power showers, the integral dishwasher, and they already had plans for the kind of conservatory that Kathy had always wanted.

Her hourly mantra about why hadn't he waited to see how things panned out at work once his goddamn awful boss had gone, now stuck in his brain, while the kids' loyalty was less constant, veering from one parent to the other like some skiff on a stormy sea.

By the time he reached the Simiston's front door, a knot of panic had lodged in his stomach and, if he searched his soul, he realised the real reason for it being there was that wherever he and she holed up, she'd probably still be the same. Overprotective of Flora and Max, plus a raft of compulsive cleanliness disorders from skirting boards to light bulbs and loo seats. But maybe, he'd reasoned during the signing of the *compromis de vente* in Cahors, a different environment with its slower pace of life, good food, good wine, would

11

change her back to the woman he'd once fallen in love with. Funny, spontaneous, addicted to his own special brand of foreplay...

When had they last done it? he mused, ringing his neighbour's bell. When he'd first talked about living in France; living the dream. Just before the Prozac had started. Six months ago. Jesus Christ, was it that long?

'Tom. Great to see you.' Ben Simiston interrupted his calculations by holding his front door open as wide as it would go. What more hint was needed that Tom's desk-bound job as IT consultant with Prestige People had done his body no favours? Just then, under Simiston's gaze, his leather jacket seemed to cling too tightly, his belt to invade his stomach. He breathed in to lose a few inches while the music subsided.

'Johnny Halliday. Just for you.' Simiston's breath was neat whisky.

'Thanks.'

'All set to go then, are we?'

'Yep. Once the *Carte de Séjour's* arrived.'

'They like their bureaucracy, do the frogs. You'd never guess they'd had a revolution.'

'It's been less than I thought, actually.' Tom glanced around at the expensive tat which, to him, looked like typical Show Home stuff. Money can't buy good taste, he thought, suddenly needing a drink.

'Kathy seems OK about it. That's half the battle.' The former BA executive gave him a knowing look, before leading the way along the parquet hallway into a huge lounge where most of the residents of Berris Hill Road clustered around a heaving buffet table. Una had been busy, Tom thought ungratefully. Una, the perfect wife.

'*Bon voyage!*' said someone.

'*Arrivederci,*' another.

'Cheers,' Tom wheeled out his six-teeth IT smile, and made his way towards his kids, who were busy trying to poke each others' eyes out with a cocktail sausage apiece. Then he noticed Kathy standing by the pink-quilted bar looking more like an upright corpse than someone about to embark on an exciting journey. Her apple juice lay untouched in her glass, her gaze fixed on what, he couldn't fathom. The word catatonic came to mind.

He only had to nudge Max for the burly nine-year-old to stop his antics and look up at him with those huge calf-like eyes. No words, just a look. A man's man already, he guessed, who'd got the measure of his school bullies. Flora too, backed off to push a pizza triangle into her mouth.

'So, when can we all come and sample your delightful abode?' Ben Simiston overfilled his wineglass.

'Once the *fosse septique*'s in. That's priority.'

A ripple of amusement passed through the gathering, yet Kathy was scowling. At least she's alive, thought Tom bleakly, taking the first gulp of the less than chilled Chardonnay.

'Surely there's some new law coming out that all private drainage has to change to mains?' Simiston added, clearly revelling in his superior knowledge.

Tom forgot to swallow. The vendor, a sculptor

13

in St Sauveur, hadn't mentioned anything about that. In fact, in retrospect, he'd been pretty low-key, full-stop.

'And where *is* this particular crock of gold, might I ask?' Simiston went on, topping up his glass. 'You've been remarkably hush hush so far.'

'Really?' Aware of all eyes now on him. Including Kathy's. 'Oh, just a short drive from Cahors.'

The neighbours then began to chip in. Everyone, it seemed, had something to say.

'Isn't that where Blair was seen brown-nosing with Chirac?'

'Interesting reds there.'

'Who? New Labour?'

'The wine, stupid!'

'And what about the porcelain and the foie gras?'

'Poor geese. That's what I say. Just imagine a day in the life of...'

'Nonsense, darling. That really is anthropomorphism gone mad.'

'And so have we.' Kathy's voice cut through the chatter like a cleaver. 'This is all Tom's idea.'

Colour burned his cheeks. Even the kids looked subdued.

'I've had to give up my nice little job at the surgery, my own car...'

'Chin up, Mrs W-S,' jollied the architect from number 21, responsible for both enormous extensions which formed a Spanish style courtyard beyond the window. 'Think of the scenery, the bloody history for a start. All those wonderful old buildings that they leave to gently rot...'

'I know, I know.' She wasn't looking at Tom nor

anyone. 'But this project's going to gobble up all the profit we've made here, all our savings, and supposing...'

'Supposing what?' Tom challenged her, aware that the knot of panic in his stomach was now a leaden boulder. He emptied his glass and looked round for a refill. Aware too that Johnny Halliday was now Françoise Hardy. A rare vocalist whose CDs made his daily trip to work bearable.

'That it all goes wrong.'

'Oh, come on,' Una slipped a well muscled arm around her neck. 'You've got Tom.'

'Exactly.'

Suddenly *L'heure bleue* grew louder and several neighbours began to sway their Daks-covered hips. Country Casuals and Jaeger all on the move.

'And the kids, don't forget,' the hostess gave them an indulgent smile.

'Yeah,' Flora said, then burped. 'I can have a pony.'

Tom bit into an anchovy vol-au-vent. It was too bitter. He wanted to spit it out on the immaculate carpet. He wanted out. OK, this was a nice neighbourly thing for Una and Ben to do, but he felt like a zoo exhibit. In fact, all four of them were on public display, dropping their guard, revealing too much.

'You can have *ten* ponies,' he said loud enough for all to hear. 'After all, we'll have six hectares to play with.'

Someone whistled.

'D'you know what that would set you back here?' The architect's lips were wet from his Pimms. 'Two bloody million.'

Another gasp, and Tom felt better. But not for long.

'A dicky bird's just told me your bonuses have gone down the pan,' Ben Simiston refilled his glass and winked at him. 'Job's not what it was, eh?'

'Job's fine,' he lied, glad for a chance to avoid his eyes. 'Need a new challenge, that's all.'

'Give the buggers the finger, say I. By the way, you getting any kind of deal?'

Tom hesitated. This smart-arse would find out anyhow.

'Can't grumble.'

'Thirty? Forty? Fifty?'

Nothing to lose. Go on man. Talk it up...

'Treble the fifty.'

Simiston's drink slopped over the rim of his glass. His bottom lip hung open in sulky surprise.

'Nice work, old son,' he patted his arm. 'Be interesting to see if they reappoint...'

Tom stared after him as he sauntered away to the food, his thoughts interrupted by Max trying to speak through a mouthful of crisps.

'I won't miss old Minging,' he announced.

'Your teacher's name is Mrs *Hem*ming.' Kathy corrected him, taking his and Flora's hands and heading for the door. On the way, she stopped to thank the Simistons and those neighbours not too busy gyrating to notice her. 'I think these two need an early night.'

A murmur of farewells followed the threesome out into the dusk, and just then, Tom felt as if an ice-pack had settled around his heart.

'She'll soon get used to the idea,' a man's voice

made him jump. The architect was behind him, lighting a cigar. 'Women always do.'

Tom didn't stay to agree or disagree. All he could think of was Kathy turning the kids against him, just when he needed them most. At least he had a week to build whatever bridges he could; paper over the ever-widening cracks before irrevocably crossing the water.

'Ben and Una have our new address,' he finally turned to face the busy room. 'And if ever you're passing there'll be a bed and a decent bottle.' That was the bit he was good at. Speiling the speil. Why he'd lasted so long at Prestige People. But it was now time to cast off that particular snakeskin and once the waves and handshakes had subsided and the Simiston's front door closed behind him, the cool March night crept under his clothes and seemed to chill even his bones.

CHAPTER TWO

Six days later, while the four Wardle-Smiths were bedding down for the night in a Campanile Hotel outside Bordeaux, Samson Bonneau, veal farmer of St Sauveur, was shielding his eyes from the glare as he entered the Café de la Paix in Loupin's main street; the nearest watering hole for ten kilometres. He'd heard about the place, of course. It was notorious for drug dealing and other sins of the flesh, and after his own Belette Farm's gloomy rooms, this first visit was proving a shock to his system. And the noise... Holy Mary, it was worse than the bells of his local church. Worse than any racket made by his suckling heifers at losing their calves straight after the first colostrum feed.

Still, this was by way of a celebration not for any Dutch courage. He owed it to himself. He was here to get pissed, away from the beady eyes and the clucking tongue of his mother. To congratulate himself on his cunning enterprise designed to bring a certain someone down to size.

He smiled at the brunette working the till, but she promptly busied herself by stuffing a pile of paper napkins into a wire holder on the counter. Normally he'd have reacted to this rebuff. But not tonight. He must be invisible, one of the crowd, to savour all the more sweetly his revenge on Bernard Metz his neighbour in St Sauveur. The sculptor, who'd inherited Hibou and its six hectares from his mother, had finally put it up for sale last autumn, only to sell to English vermin for two hundred thousand euros. Double what he himself had offered during the years it had lain empty. Double what he could have lain his hands on. Veal calves or no veal calves.

Yes, he thought, having found a table at the back of the room and ordered a large bière blonde. What a difference the next few days would make.

Metz had humiliated him in front of everybody. Metz would be punished.

The young waitress returned to him, pushing her way through the crush of bodies near the bar to deliver his beer and the bill. For a second she was hemmed in against his thigh, and the touch of her body sent a jab of desire to his cock. He

18

wanted to pull her on to his lap and slip his fingers between her legs, but in an instant she'd moved away and he had to make do as always, with a hand in his pocket. Deep and to the point.

After ten minutes, he ordered another beer, already feeling as if its foamy head had, by some alchemy, transferred itself to his brain. Then, at nine o'clock, it was time for whisky.

Bonneau stared absently at the busy door while his planned timetable rolled backwards and forwards in his mind. Not quite the moveable feast this might suggest, but rather the cementing of order of play. The sculptor was now in Albi until tomorrow afternoon. Some commission or other. Doubtless more of his special brand of blasphemy. He could see it now. So the first move must be early tomorrow. And a Good Friday it should be, too. He smiled to himself and a man at the next table grinned yellow teeth as smoke snaked from his nostrils.

'Someone's happy,' he leered. 'What's your secret, *hein?*'

'Bitches.'

'Pardon, *monsieur?*'

Bonneau didn't reply, instead pushed back his chair and stood up, immediately colliding with that same waitress.

She blushed as he felt her breasts against his body. Small, pointed, with a hint of nipple through her blouse. Neat little handfuls, he thought. Just like Musset's pair. The tart. He wondered where she was now. Still in Limoges most likely. Maybe found herself another meal ticket. Another older man. However, in his book, that didn't make any difference to her situation. None whatsoever. She'd pleasured the man who'd betrayed him, and if she ever showed up again it would be the biggest mistake of her life.

The waitress backed away as he headed for the door, his head a stew of lust and longing, of drink he couldn't handle, wondering how best to proceed with his plan.

'*Revoir monsieur,*' called out the girl by the till. But it was his turn to snub her now, and he let the door bang shut behind him.

As he approached his old Transit van parked outside in the Rue Voltaire, he thought of the loaded rifle hidden under its front seat. Four rounds left and, until his next visit to the gunsmith in Gandoux, not difficult to wonder how they might best be used. He knew the sculptor had entrusted his precious bitch to his neighbour, Georges Ninon. Easiest thing in the world to entice her with a big fat bone out of her kennel and into his van. And that would just be the start. Besides, he could always check up on the senile old fart at Evening Mass, just to make sure all was well.

He climbed into the driver's seat and pulled the old weapon from its hiding place, letting his fingerless gloved hands play along its cold barrel. Letting his thoughts wander to eight hours away when the serious fun would start.

CHAPTER THREE

From: <LSF@wanadoo.fr>
To: <nb.musset©aol.com>
Sent: 28 March 2002 21:30
CC: Paul Ormonde
Subject: Bonneau

Number 8,

Re our last meeting. Time's up for our friend and, as Cahors is in your patch, we're counting on you to be at the Aujac abattoir tomorrow. Step one, remember. We mustn't scare him off. According to Rufin, he's due there @ 1500 hrs. Half an hour before it closes. Keep your phone switched on and be sure to take your camera. Expenses as per usual.

Do *not* put yourself at risk. Do *not* go to the farm and, remember, no loose talk. That's an order. Ring me later. Am in office till 19.00hrs. Map attached. Good luck.

Paul.
Lose this message!

Natalie Musset shivered as she stared at her computer screen, aware that the temperature in her small ground floor apartment in Boisseuil near Limoges seemed to have plummeted to below zero. The dilemma now facing her seemed to drain her heart of blood.

In your patch?

I don't think so. Not any more. But how could Paul know that that particular era of her life, begun over a year ago, had now ended? She'd never told him. Never told anyone, in fact. Hurt is like a bruise. A private matter. Hers alone.

She bit into the side of her thumb till it stung, a childhood habit never outgrown. Surely there was someone else who could go instead of her? she wondered, aware of a headache kicking in. Surely he'd understand if she cried off? The longer she stared at his message, so the mix of guilt and confusion grew in her mind. Who the hell could she confide in? Whose advice could she seek? Her two best friends had gone to Greece for the holidays. Her divorced parents? Forget it. Jacques Musset was thousands of miles away in Quebec, probably skiing somewhere, while her mother based in Southfields, London since Natalie enrolled as a student at Limoges University, was too busy to ever be at home. No point in even trying to ring her.

Damn.

She thought back to the 2nd of September last year in St Sauveur – one of her rare visits – when she'd waited by the *boulangerie* van to buy *brioches* for breakfast for two. How a shabbily dressed old lady who'd introduced herself as Madame Bonneau of Belette Farm in St Sauveur, had tapped her on the shoulder and begun the weirdest one-sided conversation that she, Natalie, had ever heard. It was as if she was suddenly the priest inside the confessional box, and this poor old girl, the sinner. Suspicious and fearful of her son. Troubled by his greedy and cruel veal farming methods and the way he kept her short of money – short of everything, in fact – and so absorbed had she been in her misery that she'd ordered two baguettes from the vendor instead of one without the money in her battered old purse to pay for them.

'Here, let me settle up,' Natalie had offered, but before she could dig out the necessary coins, that extra loaf was swiftly returned to the baker.

'Thank you, but it's only me and my son,' she'd said, her bottom lip trembling and it wasn't until much later that Natalie realised his mother had never called him by name.

Back at university, she'd used the staff room's Minitel to access all the animal rights organisations she could. The League of St Francis was the only outfit who'd shown any interest in her reported story about the calves, so she'd joined them in October as a trainee investigator. At the time she had been too inexperienced to be given the case, but now here it was, like a freak wave hitting her in the face. Six months from that first phone call to them. Six months in which her life had been turned upside down and, despite the veal calves' plight, she'd sworn never to revisit that unlucky area near Cahors again.

But location wasn't the only problem.

Trust Paul to spring this on her when she'd mountains of final year English coursework to mark. Had he forgotten so quickly about the demands of being a university lecturer in 2002? He'd been one himself not so long ago, until the animal rights work had taken over with his promotion to Operations Leader in Clermond Ferrand.

She diverted her gaze from the screen to flick through her students' translations of twentieth century English novels, yet her thoughts were firmly elsewhere. In particular, Belette Farm, where last November, even an experienced League worker from Perpignan had chickened out of his obligations. And who could blame him, given what else she'd learnt about its sole male occupant?

OK, so it was flattering that her Leader felt she was up to the job, and right then flattery – any flattery – was in short supply. She should gulp it down before it evaporated altogether. And why? Because, in a nutshell, she'd been dumped by a man she'd loved too much. A man who'd made her feel worth far more than the hundred or so students who annually passed through her hands in the Humanities Department at Limoges. Who'd treated her as his muse, his soulmate. Even dedicated a series of wax maquettes to her, one of which later became the bronze Magdalene sculpture for Villefort's main church.

Bernard Metz of St Sauveur.

Never again would she pose in the nude. Never mind trust anyone wholesale.

Now she, Natalie Bridget Musset aged thirty years and one month, was as high and dry as a solitary reed in a parched riverbed. Apart from the legacy of never having made it to the *Grande École* and then on to the *ENA* as her mother – particularly her mother – had always wanted, she'd flung herself at the artist whom she'd met in June 2000 at a final year ceramics show at her university. A man whose touch, whose supreme confidence in himself and his abilities had literally snatched the breath from her throat. To him, wood, flesh, metal seemed one indivisible whole. Materials to be treated with subtlety and tenderness. Why else had she walked on air for that year and two months? Waited for his calls and emails whenever she was away during term times, and spent too long deciding what to wear for their holiday nights out in Périgueux and Montauban. Overspending her meagre salary so she wouldn't be found wanting. Being what he'd desired her to be and, above all, keeping her parents in the dark.

The void he'd left, with no one remotely comparable to take his place, soon filled with lingering doubts which festered and multiplied as a new academic year began. Had there been another woman? Was he married, maybe with kids somewhere? Had a hidden past caught up with him? Was he really a closet gay who couldn't hack women any more? Or a bi, needing a change? And because he'd never answered her calls or emails begging for an answer, these possible reasons for that rambling email he'd sent her on the 3rd September, flowed thick and fast like the Vienne after rain. If she'd lived more locally and had had more time, she'd have spied on him, found out his server password, followed him wherever he'd gone. But she'd had to work, to pay her way in life. Been forced to let it go.

Would she be tempted to hang around his place now? she asked herself, curious as to what her subconscious reply might be. To glimpse that

25

dark glossy hair with a hint of grey above his ears? The strong fit body and eyes of flecked honey? Above all, those hands which had delivered her to heaven and back?

No. Not in a million years. If she saw him again, she'd probably kill him. And what about those lonely sleepless nights in Boisseuil, wondering how she might do it?

Her eyes then rested on his earliest wax figurine for the Magdalene – barely six centimetres high – which separated her dictionaries from other tomes on a shelf over her desk. A kneeling pose, hands outspread in a gesture of what, she'd never been sure. Anyway, it was the one the Bishop had chosen for the church in Villefort, and she'd meant to chuck it out straight after the rejection. Now it bristled with stuck pins. One for each month of Metz's desertion. The best she could do in the circumstances.

She stared at the screen, shivering yet again, realising that his passions – for her, for his work – had devoured all hers. And could this email now be her salvation? A chance to prove herself. To fight the war against animals cruelly reared and transported live for human consumption. And for what? For supermarket shelves to be ever full. A ready meal just a hand's stretch away?

At secondary school in Wimbledon, where she'd shared a flat with her mother, she'd donated most of her pocket money to various animal rescue centres. Often denying herself the latest pop record or make-up. Running the gauntlet for being different. Wearing less than trendy clothes. Being too hard up to go out at weekends. No wonder as a consenting adult with self-esteem still in short supply, she'd fallen headlong into Metz's rough and ready arms. His intoxicating world.

Even he'd not had a good word to say about Samson Bonneau. A hypocrite and bigot, in his opinion, who'd nearly cost him three valuable commissions because of his complaints to those in high places. And as for his poor mother and that dump of a farm, stuffed with numberless crated calves, they were surely cursed since the day he was born.

But neither were her students simply numbers and, if her marking wasn't submitted on time, or was inaccurate, their lives, although not ended on some bloodied floor, could be changed for ever. A fail meant the dole queue along with the rest of out-of-work France. There was no alternative. Yet the League of St Francis' activities had taken up most of her weekends since she'd joined them in January and already her Department Head had received a complaint over an unmarked essay.

In that stringent and competitive academic world, one slip-up could be one too many.

She attacked her thumb again, making it bleed. Should she reply to Paul or not? Tell the truth or lie? Pretend she was away, or that his request had been accidentally deleted? Could she say her mother was ill and needed her around over Easter? The longer she deliberated, so the number of excuses multiplied, and the more she realised she just wasn't a good liar. To herself or anyone else. Besides, she stared out at the sliver of moonlight between her curtains, what about the animals she was supposed to be protecting? How could she let them down? Or indeed, her Leader, whose middle name was surely Persuasive.

Again she flicked through the mound of files by her elbow and immediately saw syntax errors which she couldn't leave. Wrong dates; misplaced footnotes, which her beady-eyed professor would spot immediately.

Having boiled a kettle and made herself a mug of instant black coffee, she settled down with a corrective red ballpoint, oblivious to the minutes slipping by. Only when next door's dog began to wail, did she realise that almost three hours had passed and it was now eleven thirty. Time for its owner to leave for his late shift at the tyre factory. However, this eerie, strangulated sound grew louder and louder, so that when she squeezed her eyes shut, its din became the clamour of un-stunned sheep before the halal and shechita knife. The roar of horses in transit – all squeezed up, trampling one another to near-death, bruised and bleeding. Their noses torn. Their legs broken.

She replaced the cap on her pen. That had decided her and, having switched off her computer and stored her students' work in a neat pile, she emailed Paul Ormonde that she'd be making an early start tomorrow. She then turned back the duvet on her bed, thinking how the two other regional team members – science teachers from Figeac – were probably in the sack somewhere. She'd seen signs of it when the three of them had been waiting near the *autoroute* at Brive for the Polish foal transports to come through. They'd huddled too close, kissing and fondling each other, so that when the Cracow truck had loomed up out of the wintry darkness in the Relais lorry park, it was she who'd risked injury or worse by confronting the driver and asking to see his documents.

Natalie undressed and slipped her nightshirt over her head, aware that this next venture was possibly more dangerous than tangling with some Polish peasant who had a neat line in hunting knives. And not just because it would mean her being on her own.

At seven o'clock next morning, in the bedside lamp's weak glow, she extracted the *Bison Futé* road map of the Lot region from her desk drawer. Next, all her biking gear – black leathers, helmet and goggles, Fujifilm camera plus a five-inch fold-away hunting knife in its leather case with NBM embossed on the front. Her father's latest Christmas present. He'd been living his own life near Quebec since she was eight, and it was a photo of her family during a long-ago skiing holiday at Les Angles that kept her going when times got rough. She in a red woollen hat, squeezed between her parents. Three laughing mouths. Arms interlocked as if for ever against a backdrop of pure white. Her theory being that if this particular image stayed in her wallet for long enough, those arms might one day interlock again. Just as in her dreams, until that same laughter would wake her to the reality of being fall-out from a broken home. Despite her close bonds with her mother, it was with Jacques Musset, her father, that she'd had the most rapport. Knowing when he'd phone to share a joke; generally give her spirits a lift. Even if his architect's job was pissing him off. Or the love life wasn't happening. Just like now, for her.

As an afterthought, she then filled her remaining pockets with a pack of radishes and two spare pairs of briefs, before slipping out through the front door of 6, Rue Gironde, finally kitted out for the rigours of a harsh frosty morning, with her knife deep inside her jacket pocket.

Her prized Suzuki 900 motorbike, bought second-hand as a present to herself after Metz had abandoned her, leant against the house wall on a strip of chunky gravel. Its chrome felt like ice under her fingers and already a frosty film covered the saddle. Natalie wiped it with her sleeve and slotted her hands into her wind-proof gloves. She unlocked the machine and wheeled it some way along the quiet street before straddling it, opening the throttle and engaging first gear. As the melancholy bells of various churches tolled eight o'clock, she cruised past the hospital and the telephone exchange, then, with the engine's echoing growl loud enough to stir all the dead in the neighbouring cemetery, she followed signs for the A20 heading south. However, no sooner had she reached the toll, a ripple of panic made her slow up and consider turning back.

The veal farmer must have known from local gossip that she'd once been Metz's lover. But would he still recognise her? If so, this particular mission could put her in more danger than ever.

CHAPTER FOUR

Good Friday afternoon was bitter cold under a sunless sky. Beyond the service station's play area a copse of larches still lay where they'd toppled almost five years ago, cradled by the crowns and lower branches of more sturdy survivors – oak and beech – and casting an eerie weave of shadows on the hard dry ground.

Samson Bonneau, who'd endured yet another night of his late grandparents' faces hovering like a pair of bloated communion wafers over his bed, tutted to himself at this ongoing municipal negligence as he checked over his transporter's green cover and tested its many padlocks so that his live cargo of Easter veal was both safe from prying eyes and unable to escape. It was time this unwelcome pair of relatives gave him some peace and a full night's sleep. Time also that these unsightly dead trees were removed.

Five years had passed since that Atlantic storm had scythed through the hedgeless farmland of Charente Maritime and the coastal pines of the Landes before powering south to be trapped by the Fer à Cheval's limestone shield. For two days this force had circled round and round, seeking out the smallest flaw in the works of both man and God. A loose nail here, a spindly sapling there. An elderly man on the bridge high over the Florentin river: his father, Albert Bonneau whose half-drowned body had shaped itself to the rocks below, and who, after a week of searching by the local *gendarmerie,* was only identified by a sodden *permis de conduire* accidentally left in his pocket.

Since then, his only son had learned to be more careful. More attentive to detail. However, none of that mattered now, because so far, things had gone to plan. A warm sensation suffused his whole body as he stared down at the foliage beyond the deserted play area. He daren't go and look at his handiwork. That would be foolish in the extreme. His gaze then fell upon *La Croix,* as it was known, but, unlike the cross of *Gethsemane,* fashioned from palm cedar, cypress and olive, this was solid steel, locked three metres deep into concrete. Love-child of artisan *métailliste* Bernard Metz, his neighbour in St Sauveur, this contraption born of flame and the man's sour sweat, made a surreal centrepiece amid the fallen trees. Ox-blood rust had already devoured both its main prop and cross-bars now wavering in the minimal breeze as if some unseen entity possessed them.

Despite his written and verbal protests, Metz had persevered with this sacred tau design, the kind once associated with St Anthony the Great, but Bonneau had always thought this particular bastardised version an overpriced monstrosity, a blasphemy even, just like the Magdalene in Villefort church.

Some locals claimed it was unsafe. That a warning notice was needed after the Mahfooz twins from nearby Gandoux had both fallen during play and suffered concussion, and little Annie Paul's pelvis had broken. But still children come from far and near to twine their limbs around those two iron chains dangling from the cross-bar's ends and which, through the night wind's lonely hours, chime their own eerie tune.

Now it was nine-year-old Max Wardle-Smith's turn to charge into the play area, and Bonneau climbed back inside his cab to watch him from behind its murky glass. Red shorts, blue socks, curly blond hair.

He darted from one toy to the next with all the pent-up energy of a youngster constrained in a car for too long. Finally the lad mounted the blue plastic train, his chubby legs gripping its engine as it lurched from side to side under his weight on its matching coloured spring, until suddenly he spotted The Cross, in shadow nearer the undergrowth. Was it for playing on? he seemed to be asking himself as Bonneau noted the puzzled frown on the big forehead.

'Ye-esss!'

With a whoop of pleasure he deserted the train and leapt towards one of the sculpture's iron chains, clinging tight as he began to circle the central prop. 'Wowee!' he shrieked, kicking up grey dust with his shoes.

Anglais, thought Bonneau.

He re-tuned his radio to TF1 to hear yesterday's racing results in full and banged his hand on his knee in disgust at L'honneur de Dieu's poor showing at Auteuil. His scowl was not for the squeamish. That well-fancied horse had failed to recoup any of the money he'd withdrawn from the bank only yesterday to pay for new aluminium

33

calf crates.

Merde!

'Flora!' The boy suddenly yelled out. His face too had changed. Crumpled in pain because his thumb was caught fast in one of the chain links and was hurting, turning more blue by the second. 'Flora!'

The lorry driver switched off his radio and left the cab, careful not to let his door slam behind him. He made his way down the scrubby slope towards *La Croix*. A man used to tricky terrain, his boots threw up small stones which trickled down on to the tarmac below, while across his path like a dark oblong, lay the public phone box's shadow.

Upon seeing him, the boy's mouth opened in surprise then fear. So like his calves as they heave their feeble sides against the metal crates. A look which binds all creatures together as powerless victims.

'Who is Flora?' Bonneau asked him, practising his basic English, learnt from library tapes since he knew the sculptor was selling his *fermette* to the Anglais.

'My sister. Where is she?'

'Wait. I help.' He soothed as he removed his fingerless gloves and slipped them into his boiler suit pocket. With one swift movement, he freed the boy's rust-coloured thumb from the chain. The young flesh felt soft and new against his and, for a brief foolish moment he wanted to take the whole hand in his, to savour it a little longer. 'You eat a bon bon?' he asked instead, but like a Charolais steer, the boy lowered his curly head and bolted away from his rescuer, deeper into the hinterland of gorse and bramble beyond the play area. His little cries became the call of crows startled from their black nests as Bonneau slunk back towards his cab cursing all foreigners. Cursing their souls.

CHAPTER FIVE

The bells. Always too many of them, thought Liliane Bonneau as she smoothed down the cracks in the waxed tablecloth for her son's early evening meal in the farmhouse's one large room, which housed a kitchenette in its dark window-less corner. She'd often complained about their noise to the *Mairie* in Gandoux – especially the Mary Bell which struck at dawn each day – only to be told each time that any reduction in that holy intrusion might bring bad luck to the few remaining inhabitants of St Sauveur.

But what more bad luck could there be in such a place? she mused as she positioned two place mats bearing pictures of St Joan on horseback at opposite ends of the wormy table. Besides, it was as if there was now no part of any hour free of their gloomy reminders that we are born to suffer and die, like her son's motherless calves trapped in their tiny crates, covered in excrement and hidden from view behind Belette Farm's midden mountain.

Six months' manure lay stacked up like two Mont Blancs in the first field and behind the farmhouse itself, whose adjoining barn, in true Quercy style, also lay under the building's main roof. Whenever the east wind blew into the hamlet and ricocheted off the Fer à Cheval – that towering wall of rock behind the church – they delivered a stench so vile, that her latest meal would reappear unbidden in her throat.

She then deposited a bottle of *pastis* in the table's centre, but because it felt ominously light in her hand, she held it up against the room's one window to confirm her worst fears. It was almost empty, but what could she do? The nearest bar and supermarket was at Loupin, some ten kilometres away And she'd never learnt to drive. Never been allowed to...

A solution – the Menthe. Of *course*. Why hadn't she thought of that before? There was still an unopened bottle of the sticky green stuff that her in-laws, Jean and Christine Bonneau, had bought that last Christmas they'd all been together. Before their cadavers had played host to the huge summer flies of 1965 and 1967, when that particular aperitif had been all the rage and graced most local tables. However, since both their deaths there'd been precious little to celebrate, so the thing had languished in the cellar, stuck to the damp wooden shelf by its own treacly liquid, the colour of Belette Farm's one pond.

She took a torch from the cupboard under the sink and opened the door to the cellar. It immediately slammed shut behind her the moment she stood on the topmost stone step, and she let out a little scream as her slippered feet misjudged its depth and the torch fell from her grasp, clattering to the bottom.

Her nails clawed the powdery walls as she too slipped further down the steps into the reeking gloom that extended below the barn. Samson's place, where she wasn't allowed. Ever. Maybe because just above her head, beyond the cobwebs and the crumbling plasterboard, four thousand tiny hooves pattered out an existence too dismal to dwell upon. Barely born, some would never even open their eyes. She knew that from the one surreptitious peep she'd taken into their quarters last summer when their pitiful cries of separation from their mothers had brought her from her warm bed. So the next day had dawned and waned without her having any part of it. Bruised just like them. Punished all over her body for being a witness.

Shortly afterwards, Mademoiselle Musset, whom everyone knew was sharing the sculptor's bed, had commented on her black eye while queuing by the *boulangerie* van up near the church. Her kindly touch, the seemingly genuine concern the young blonde had shown, which Liliane hadn't received from anyone else since Albert's death, made past and present miseries flow unchecked from her lips. It hadn't mattered to her what the girl did with the man during her university holidays, or that her hair was the same colour as a tart in TV's *Châteauvallon* series – she'd left Liliane in no doubt that she was someone for whom cruelty in any form was an abomination.

'Please don't tell anyone what I've told you,' Liliane had begged her afterwards, clutching her still-warm baguette. 'My life at Belette will be

37

hell otherwise and I've nowhere else to go.'

'Of course not, *madame*,' the young woman had reassured, but, as Liliane had watched her walk away towards Metz's house she knew that her revelations might well prove to be the second biggest mistake of her life.

In the cellar's disorientating darkness, she managed to right herself at last, aware of stinging pain at the backs of her legs. But nothing would prevent her now from finding the precious Menthe and, after minutes of frantic searching her fingers closed thankfully around its damp glass body

Voilà.

However, her relief was short-lived, for when she retrieved the torch its shattered bulb tinkled ominously against the plastic shield. Broken. She groped her way back up the stairs then realised that the cellar door was stuck fast.

'Help!'

She hit the door first with her free hand and then, without thinking, the bottle, which with a sickening sound, suddenly cracked along its length, causing the minty contents to ooze down her pinafore and gather round her feet, trapping her in a pool of fear.

Her trembling fingers felt for the rosary beads around her neck but, despite her supplications, no one came. Why should they? The calves in the barn above were making too much din for her little voice to be heard. Besides, Marcelle Victor, widow and nearest neighbour in the Impasse des Troubadours, was visiting her daughter, far away in Brittany.

She choked back old tears stored too long in

her own personal well of grief and, while her son watched out for the English boy's reappearance at the play area, she sat down in the liquid mess and began to weep.

CHAPTER SIX

Samson Bonneau still waited. Checked his watch for the third time. Eight minutes had passed since the *petit Anglais* had run off. Was he lost in that undergrowth? Had he found something? If so, would he try to disturb things? Upset the plan? Behind him, his livestock was growing more restless, threatening to split the specially reinforced and costly material that covered the truck. It was the same with each trip, as if they *knew* the end was near. But for him, this last sortie before Easter would mean a bulging wallet to recoup his recent losses, and perhaps a few delicacies for his dinner plate.

He'd give the boy five more minutes.

The Daf's chassis began to sway making his newspaper slide to the cab floor, yet that boy's earlier fear was still fresh in his mind. How he'd glanced back at him as he'd run away. But he, Samson, had done the right thing by not following him into that wreckage of trees. Anyone might have seen him. The boy himself might have screamed blue murder. No, thought the farmer, aware of his hungry stomach growing hungrier, that would have been one risk too many.

Especially now. After what had happened.

He then extracted his lunch from the glove box, tore the foil wrapping open and lowered his nose to sniff the contents. This ritual never changed and, as usual his mother had placed two slices of rye bread around a chunk of cheese, and added a small brown onion. But this time his nose told him something wasn't quite right. The rye bread smelt different. Slightly musty, damp even. What was she thinking of? he scowled to himself, throwing the last sandwich out of his cab window. She was never that careless. Never *allowed* to be.

He'd just returned his fingerless gloves to his huge hands and was screwing the foil up into a tight hard ball, when suddenly he spotted a movement in the play area.

At last.

But this time, that same lad was careering towards the service station as if he'd seen a ghost.

A smile crept along Bonneau's mouth. Good. He knew exactly what had startled him in that wilderness. This was after all, *his* homeland. A land where he'd worked and prospered all his life. Now it was slipping away, bought by dirty foreign money.

He sighed. If only there were more gruesome sights like that in more of the region's woods and beauty spots, the rest of the creeping foreign hordes who were making full and noisy use of the new *péage* might turn round and go home.

Fat chance. He jettisoned the foil ball out of his cab window in disgust, thinking again of Metz. Where were the man's principles when he'd signed the *Compromis de Vente* and then taken the

Anglais' contaminated euros to his bank in Gandoux? Worse, what would the country's saviour Joan of Arc make of it all if she were alive now? At least Le Pen was gaining votes in all regions, especially Languedoc Roussillon. Foreigners out. Spongers and breeders out, while to his mind, all *musulmans* and *beurs* should be castrated then shipped back to north Africa.

Another thing, Bonneau mused, observing yet more Easter tourists arriving into the service station behind him, these pale incomers from over *La Manche* only wanted to eat at McDonald's or Buffalo Grill. Moreover, a recent survey in *Le Figaro* revealed a mere four per cent were prepared to eat French horse and two per cent any veal. So his viewpoint was entirely vindicated. Such parasites were his enemies.

He belched, then with a filthy bloodied fingernail, prised out stray rye grains from between his teeth before restarting the Daf's engine. He guided his rocking truck past the fuel pumps and the various skinny little *noirs* with their buckets and windscreen phlanges poised to waylay the tourists, past the *toilettes* to where a few picnicking families huddled round the rustic wooden tables at the rear of the *boutique.*

He slowed up, because one family in particular held his attention and, peering more closely through his dirty windscreen, he recognised not only the brown Volvo with a table strapped to its roof, but also that same fair-haired lad being comforted by two adults. The couple who'd paid the hamlet a fleeting visit at the beginning of the month and had agreed to buy Hibou from Metz.

41

Incomers who'd arrived a week too soon. Who'd snapped up what should have been his.

Unlike the other picnickers nearby, this four-some wore lightweight clothes as if summer was already in full swing, and Bonneau glimpsed their shop-bought baguettes, a Thermos flask and a crumpled outspread map. The boy, how-ever, was shaking his head at the offer of food, but the girl stood at the edge of the terrace, her cheeks stuffed with bread, jumping up and down as if in some disco or other.

Bonneau blinked at the sight. Another little *poule* he thought. Just like someone else not so far away at the *péage* toll, who needed to be taught a lesson. He crashed the lorry's gears yet again. Yes, that's what he'd do. If he couldn't have Hibou, then neither could they. He would find whatever means he could to drive them away.

Merde encore.

The blond boy was pointing at him, but thank-fully no one paid him any attention. Bonneau drove off the slip road still keeping them all in sight in his off-side wing mirror.

They were packing up now, calling the girl to heel as he rejoined the A10, wondering why Metz hadn't mentioned these two brats to him before, and why they'd not accompanied the two adults on their first visit to St Sauveur. Maybe they were not important enough to them, and that premise offered up such tempting possibilities, his concen-tration lapsed and a white Giraud transporter nearly hit him from behind as his speed suddenly dropped.

The Daf turned off at exit 57 and Bonneau saw one tart after another working the booths. Students, probably, but decent ones from good homes didn't work during the holidays. They were too busy with study to risk failure, which meant this lot were probably earning cash for abortions and drugs. The Lord knew too much of that particular plague was leaking into the Lot via the English, the Dutch and their depraved Belgian neighbours. He deftly crossed himself, for several other unholy thoughts had re-entered his mind. And then another.

He looked for the red-haired girl he'd seen on his last two trips and, having spotted her, swung his truck towards her booth. He noticed her skin as white as a Charolais' belly; her breasts encased in black wool, protruding above the hatch's edge.

'Cock-tease whore,' he murmured, handing over a collection of coins, letting her fingers briefly touch his. 'You'll get your comeuppance one day. Mark my words.'

'Fuck off, *monsieur.*'

Bonneau smiled again. He liked seeing bitches like her get riled up. Serve them right, he thought, finding first gear and disengaging the handbrake. The sound this made was like old bones. Old *dead* bones, and it spoilt the moment. His window slid up. But the girl's painted eyes were on him and, as he revved away, all he could see now in his rear view mirror was her staring face. Her pale hand pop-popping in and out of the booth.

The Aujac abattoir would be closed in half an hour and it was crucial he wasn't late. Normally

43

it stayed open until 8pm on a Friday, but Vendredi Saint was different. And there'd be no re-opening until the following Wednesday. By that time his calves would have been ten days old instead of seven, with the meat darkening and the price dropping accordingly.

The road away from the toll narrowed to a single lane and he cursed for the second time that day as a motorbike kept its place in front, not letting him pass. Another loose woman he judged by the rider's blonde pony-tail sticking out from under her crash helmet. That made three so far on this holy Friday.

'*Allez!*' he yelled at the motorcyclist who was still holding him back. 'And go to hell while you're at it.'

Her number plate ended with 68. Haut-Rhin. In his book, another mistake. It was a region of traitors and collaborators. Where France had first sold her soul to the Boches. His fist stayed clamped on the horn as suddenly he began to edge past her machine, grazing its rear wheel, forcing her across the still frosty verge and down into the deep gulley beyond.

'*Merci, Dieu,*' he whispered to himself, hitting 90, 100, 120 kilometres an hour over pot-holes and a camber so steep in parts it nearly toppled the truck over. Samson gripped the wheel. Only ten minutes left but nobody wanted bruised meat, least of all the Italians. He had to be careful. Through Aujac, a dismal hamlet of low concrete-rendered dwellings stickered with Front National posters of popular candidate Nicolas Grazes, then a steep right turn just past the public drinking fountain.

The hill took him towards the familiar large black corrugated building whose entrance was obstructed by a steel barrier and Berthe Vervins' bulk filling the little booth to the side of it.

'*Ça va?*' she enquired automatically as she pressed her fat thumb on the button for the barrier to open. It sounded like she had a cold.

'*Oui. Ça va.*' He avoided her little foxy eyes for she of the brown coat with moleskin collar was the feared '*Gestapo.*' The abattoir's front 'man' with always too many awkward questions for the local farmers and known to turn away stock on the slightest whisper of malpractice. She was also abattoir owner René Rufin's sister-in-law.

She gestured for him to park to the right of the main entrance and left her post to stand on tiptoe by his cab window. He noticed a bald patch at the crown end of her head and couldn't help wondering how this God he prayed to every Sunday could make certain women so ugly.

'We've been hearing things about you,' she began, and wiped her runny nose along her coat sleeve. 'Not good.'

He composed himself even though he felt as if a bullet had just struck his chest.

'Who from? *What* things, *madame?*'

'Too much chloramphenicol in your stock, for a start. We'll need the vet to check your load over.'

'The *vet?*' He felt his colour begin to rise. His fists clenched inside their black woollen gloves.

'He's not back from Villefort until the middle of next week, so I suggest you call here again with those calves next Thursday. And keep them off that antibiotic. If the general public learn that it

45

disrupts the production of human blood cells, we're in trouble.'

'I'm not going back to St Sauveur with all this lot,' he protested. 'Besides, by then they'll be no use to anybody.' His tone darkened. 'Listen, you. I've got a living to make. An old mother to keep.' He nearly added, 'useless mouth' as he swung open his cab door, leapt to the ground and, with the truck's engine still running, began unlocking the tarpaulin's padlocks.

Berthe Vervins, not known for her lack of courage, placed her bare hand on his, preventing him from unlocking any more.

'My brother-in-law's coming. I suggest we wait for him.'

He pushed her away and glanced towards the entrance where the door into the abattoir was sliding open on to a wide darkness. He sensed that bedroom smell again, when bloated black flies had swiftly congregated on his grandfather's eyelids. When that skin of his had resembled a map of blue rivers...

On hot summer evenings he'd lie on the double bed where his grandparents had both conveniently breathed their last. In an hour he could be back on that same bed again with his lustful fantasies, trying to ignore that strange sweet and sour smell which, like Jean and Christine Bonneau's spectral faces, had obstinately hung in the room since that summer of 1967, and which no electric fan or the shaking out of his bedclothes seemed to disperse...

'Bonneau, eh?' René Rufin's voice preceded him out of the hangar. When he finally moved into the daylight, the farmer noticed the man's

46

white overall was more bloodied than usual. Its buttons strained over his paunch. Prospering, evidently, he thought, with a rush of envy. 'How many have you brought in today?' the owner asked, extracting a stubby pencil from above his left ear and a grimy notebook from his pocket, from which black carbon paper fluttered to the ground like a charred leaf.

'Fifty-two. Seven days old. Every one.' He eyed Madame Vervins. 'So who's been making trouble for me round here?'

The woman leant towards her brother-in-law, and whispered so Bonneau couldn't hear, then, as another truck revved away from the far side of the building leaving a pall of dust in the air, she waddled back to her booth.

'Mmm.' Rufin's mouth was a tight line as he began to write.

'What's *mmm* supposed to mean?' Bonneau fixed on the man who'd held his livelihood in his hands for nearly a quarter of a century and so far hadn't let him down. By now the calves were squealing. Not a good sign. 'Look, I asked you a question.'

'I have to be careful, *monsieur.* We're inspected too, you know, and if I'm seen to be slaughtering stock unfit for...'

'*Unfit?*' The word boomed from Bonneau's throat, his partially gloved fists tightening. 'Are you referring to my animals?'

'You tell me.'

Bonneau reddened. 'This lot's the same as you've slaughtered for me before. Soft white meat, with not a trace of iron. And only the best

47

colostrum in their gut. Perfect, I'm telling you. Come and look.'

Both men walked over to the truck.

'Try Percues,' was all Rufin said once he'd peeped under the cover. He returned his pencil to his ear.

'It's closed. You know that.'

Rufin spat on the ground near Bonneau's boots and strode off into the slaughter area where the sliding door closed tight behind him.

The farmer stumbled over to the booth by the barrier where Berthe Vervins had ended a call on her mobile and was now locking up. The metal grille at the front crashed guillotine-like on to the ledge. The racket caused more squeals of terror from inside his vehicle.

'What have you been saying to him?' He wanted to wrap his hands tight around that flabby neck of hers. 'I've a right to know.'

'Your beasts have rights too, *monsieur*. Don't forget.'

'This is illegal. I'll report you both.'

'I don't think so. Now, if you'll excuse me...' The little woman pocketed the booth's keys and bustled past him towards her Peugeot, parked alongside the breeze-block building.

It was then that Bonneau realised that on the sly, she'd let the barrier down so his lorry was trapped in the yard. He followed her as she squeezed her bulk inside the small saloon then banged his fist on her car roof.

'How can I leave here to try Percues? Tell me!'

Madame Vervins' plump face looked up at him through the car window as she locked herself in.

'That's the idea, *monsieur*. You can't. When Monsieur Rufin's ready, he'll make a decision. So, I suggest you wait.'

With that she executed a nifty three-point turn and headed for the barrier. He ran to block her way. But she was too fast, her face set in grim concentration. He swore after her as the car skimmed under the horizontal steel pole with a centimetre to spare and disappeared down the hill.

Still cursing, he lumbered past his rowdy truck, aware of calf scour eking out from under the tarpaulin and, despite the chill afternoon, felt sweat under his clothes. He headed for the abattoir and hammered on its automatic door, bellowing out Rufin's name.

Suddenly he stopped as the familiar growl of a motorbike grew louder behind him. He stopped, spun round to see that same, black Suzuki appear. So he'd not disabled its rider after all. Seconds later, he recognised the young woman in matching leathers who sat astride it.

Natalie Musset. Well, well, well.

What in God's name was she doing here of all places? Had Metz sent her? Did she know of his plans? His early morning expedition? He watched her bend low on her machine as it passed under the barrier and came to a halt just yards away from him. Judging by the way she just sat there waiting for him to make the first move, this clearly wasn't a social call.

CHAPTER SEVEN

After twenty long minutes it seemed as if Liliane Bonneau's gabbled stream of Aves, Paternosters and Glorias had finally paid off. She'd managed to shove the cellar door open and emerged somewhat unsteadily into the farm's small hallway. Then, having removed her wet bedroom slippers, she tiptoed through into the tiny kitchenette at the far end of the main room to wash her feet in a chamber pot once used by Albert's parents, Jean and Christine Bonneau. A cluster of pink roses lay in the middle of its crackle-glazed base, and old Jean who'd survived his wife by two years, had often joked about pissing on the floribunda.

In fact those were his very last words before Liliane had found him dead in his bed the following morning. The newly qualified Docteur Craval had written *Sudden Respiratory Failure* on the Death certificate. The same for Christine, and neither Post-Mortem examination had challenged his view.

After this, and despite still having three men to lean on at the farm she often yearned to join them.

She eyed the wall clock nervously. Having barely any Ricard was bad enough, but now no Menthe either. The words 'dead meat' sprung to mind. Samson's threat to the gypsies who'd come calling at the farm last summer, now sent a glut

50

of shivers through her body as she began cleaning herself up then finished setting the table. The yellowed glass cruet, the extra-large mottled knife and fork for her extra-large first and last born son who, to her mind, given his crimes, should be re-baptised as Death.

Liliane returned to the cutlery drawer in the old dresser and found the one souvenir of her own baptism – a spoon given to her by an aunt eighty years ago and now all she could manage to eat with since most of her teeth had gone. Its curved end had worn so thin it sometimes cut her lips but the looped silver handle was perfect for her arthritic fingers.

She always kept it at the front of the drawer to save herself clattering through the tarnished heaps of fish knives and serving spoons handed down through the Bonneau family from before Robespierre's Revolution. After which, prosperity had reigned instead of the king.

She turned the precious spoon over, knowing full well that the copperplate engraving of her name underneath had completely rubbed away and no amount of longing to see it again would bring it back. Such is life, she thought, wondering why Samson was now half an hour late and why she'd heard his van leave and return before dawn that morning. She turned the heat down under the rabbit casserole so the pink meat wouldn't toughen and add to his other likely complaints.

Then, as always, she glanced over to where her dead husband's pipe still rested on the small table next to his armchair. His summer hat with the broken weave along its crown perched on one

51

of the padded leather wings. It was as if he might return to the room at any moment to claim these cherished possessions, and tell her he'll be back again after milking.

For five o'clock had always been dairy time at Belette Farm, even when older brother Eric had taken charge after the war. The huge white cows with their swollen udders would gather by the field gate before processing into the cool clean *laiterie*. They'd nudge Albert's body with their curly foreheads as he'd opened its door for them, then, once inside, stand as still as the statues in the church while both brothers guided the rich frothy harvest into their silver pails.

In those days, when the summers had seemed longer and the winters less harsh, Samson would patiently bottle-feed any orphan calves with colostrum expressed from other nursing cows. Although not yet in his teens, his education began and ended at Belette, the nearest *école* being too far away in Gandoux. He knew exactly when to draw this first-milk from the teat, making sure there was enough both for the natural calf and the other dependant. He knew also how to gain trust from these dumb but powerful creatures and they soon followed him everywhere – even as far as the farmhouse's back door.

Once Belette had specialist milking machinery, he grew skilled in the use of pulsators, pressure gauging, rubber tightening and the like, and his nurturing techniques for newborn vulnerable calves were envied by other less prosperous farmers in the Commune.

However, as the years passed, she became

increasingly puzzled as to why, once her son's own bones had fully grown and dark downy hair begun to smudge his face like charcoal, no *petite-amie* ever appeared at Belette. Maybe he was shy with the opposite sex, she'd reasoned at the time. Maybe no one pretty enough for his tastes had come along. But to her way of thinking – and these were concerns she never expressed to Albert – there were pretty girls everywhere. One only had to visit the Bastille Day celebrations in Loupin and Gandoux or attend catechism classes in any of the local churches, where the Nellys and Amélies were brought by cart and tractor, to see that she was right.

But on April 1st in 1980 when Samson was thirty-six and still single, her puzzlement about his lack of interest in the opposite sex grew into gnawing suspicion about a completely different matter.

The strange and sudden disappearance of his uncle, Eric Bonneau. The man who'd inherited Belette from his father Jean. It had been a day of storms with lightning shooting through the indigo sky behind the church, and thunder so deep it seemed as if the world itself was falling apart. Albert had left early for the bull market over at Loupin and still hadn't returned by the time Eric had taken to his bed straight after milking, complaining of a migraine. She'd left a cup of water within his reach then closed his shutters tight to keep God's anger at bay outside. He'd seemed fast asleep, his mouth set in a wistful smile, while his bare feet, which had borne him well for sixty-one years, stuck out from the ends of his trouser legs.

Their unexpected whiteness had startled her,

so had the delicacy of the underlying bones. She'd even been tempted to run her fingertip along them to check they were real and living, unlike that alabaster Paschal lamb carved by a young Bernard Metz, which Père Julien had used to decorate the church that Easter.

Afterwards, at seven o'clock, having changed the sheets on the other beds and picked a swede from the small *potager* near the *fosse septique*, she'd finally prepared supper and called out to her brother-in-law that it was ready. There'd been no reply so she'd sent Samson to wake him up, only to see him re-appear moments later, shaking his damp head.

'He's gone,' he said.

Those few words were to change life at Belette for ever and, once he'd flung her torn waterproof at her, she'd joined him for a search outside in the wet dusk.

Still gripping her metal sieve, while her stomach churned with fear, Liliane had followed him on a tour of the farm and its environs.

'Not the first time Uncle's wandered off,' Samson had reminded her, having checked the barn and shone his torch over the glistening white cattle huddled under the nearby oak trees. 'Remember his little trip to the Causse de Framat last month and what Docteur Craval said about his Alzheimers? He'll soon be back, *Maman*, you'll see. Besides, why else had our front door been left open?'

But Liliane knew even then that all these reassurances had been too glib, so she'd stayed silent with her doubts and the stomach pain which plagued her every time she thought of it.

After a rain-sodden hour they were just returning to the farmhouse door when Albert's trailer swept into the rear yard, sending plumes of dung spray from its wheels.

She could tell immediately he'd been drinking and his reaction to Eric's absence was merely an angry dismissal. However, once the newly purchased Charolais bull was installed in its dry quarters, Albert had calmed down and telephoned the *gendarmerie* in Gandoux. Their response brought little comfort. Following a family shooting in Cahors, no spare police were available until morning.

That evening, supper was forgotten and, as the pork shoulder cooled in its own fat and the storm abated, so did the mystery of Eric's vanishing grow. And by dawn, after no sleep for her and her husband, this bleak void nourished suspicion and conjecture. It was Albert asking the questions she dared not utter. Who might have wished Eric harm? And if he'd really had enough of hard work, the financial insecurity, and just walked out, why hadn't either Liliane or Samson guessed something was wrong, or heard anything of his leaving? After all, Eric was even taller than his nephew, with an even louder voice, a heavier tread. Above all, the man was a great letter writer. Yet there'd been no note left behind. Not a word. And what were everyone's exact movements after he'd retired to bed that day?

Her lips trembled as she recalled this the first of her husband's many interrogations. But, as spring warmed into a summer which cooled too soon to a frosty autumn, these unresolved questions rippled out from Belette into the whole community. In Albert's eyes, most inhabitants were now suspects.

As Christmas came and went there was still no body to grieve over, no grave to visit, and without such tangible reminders of his presence, she and Albert, who'd now inherited the farm, continued to exist in an unresolved limbo. On rare occasions some stray *gendarme* would call, but never with any fresh evidence, or anything new to add, and this lack of any progress affected Albert to a degree which, in hindsight, she'd never fully grasped. He'd even attempted to dredge the farm pond and dig where the wild boar had disturbed the ground in the furthest field in search of his dearly loved brother, but to no avail.

So, while Samson continued to tend the milking herd, and battle against ever-decreasing profits, the farm's books became her responsibility, together with the laundry and cooking. Albert would set off every day, whatever the weather, to search for Eric. Sometimes he'd be accompanied by Bernard Metz who at the time was living on his own, or by others he could trust such as old Joseph Flamand and his wife. But still without success.

No longer did he rise with the church's Mary Bell to clean out the barn or spread the middens' dung over the cattle crop land, so Samson brought in a local youth to do the work. He'd paid him less than the going rate, but at least let him sleep in the house.

However, after just six months the milk production ceased altogether, the herd and machinery were sold. It wasn't profitable enough, he'd said. No one was drinking the stuff any more. The young French were on low-fat diets while some professor from Lyons was claiming that humans weren't meant to drink cows' milk in any form – skimmed or semi-skinned – that the prospects for the Republic's health were alarming.

Therefore, Samson's new plans for extra tender baby veal created *his* way, quickly and in great numbers went unopposed.

It was clear that Albert didn't care any more. And what could she, a mere woman have said to change things? Even Père Julien at the local church suggested at Confession that she focus instead on putting food on the table for her menfolk and leave notions of farming to them.

Liliane sighed as she positioned the milk jug, now used for water, next to her son's Ricard glass, and noticed a yellow tidemark beneath its rim. Yes, she too had lost the will to keep up her former standards since Albert had landed on the rocks by the river Florentin. She remembered the early days when he'd smack her rump appreciatively at simply being back indoors and away from the rigours of his trade. She'd grown to love him and he'd been a good father, never once suspecting her terrible wartime secret.

However, Albert had never made Belette the subject of a *donation entre nous*, meaning that after his death, Samson had two thirds the value of the farm. His whims soon became her command and obey she must because she alone stood in the way of his full inheritance.

The bed linen stayed unwashed, and cooking

utensils harboured the dried strata of past meals, and the mirror that hung near the window in her bedroom stayed turned the other way.

Liliane moved over to the dresser, reached up to the second shelf and switched on the ancient wireless – a gift from Sturmbahnführer Fritz Brandt in the days before Albert Bonneau's proposal to her. She'd soon scraped away the 'München 1943' label glued underneath and lied to everyone that it had once been her mother's, but the black *rosenkrantz* he'd also given her had never left her neck and would remain with her even in the grave.

Strains of some religious work for Vendredi Saint filtered from the wireless' dingy mesh into the room and as she bent closer to listen over the racket of yet more bells, she smiled to herself. The soprano was beginning *'O quam tristis et afflicta'* from Pergolesi's *Stabat Mater* – her favourite classical work – because to her, the sufferings of this 'sad and sore distressed' mother, were not so different from her own. In fact, even though more than a millennium divided them, they had one thing in common: they were both women of tears.

She sang along in a wobbly voice as she returned to the stove, lifted the lid off the stew and ladled another layer of pinkish fat into a separate bowl. This would be firm enough to spread by morning, and she must see to it that enough rye bread was brought from the damp cupboard under the sink and left as normal in the old metal bin on the dresser. Liliane crossed herself as the half hourly bells ceased. She knew she was committing a cardinal sin by deliberately choosing mouldy rye bread for her son's lunches, but she had no choice,

58

given what she knew. She also knew that the Holy mother Mary would understand her motives.

Having replaced the cooking pot's lid, she was about to remove her apron when the noise of an unfamiliar car engine outside sent her over to the one window, the half-closed shutters of which afforded her a view of the track up to the *fermette* Hibou. But that wasn't all. Here was the same brown estate car that had turned up at the beginning of the month, but this time two unfamiliar youngsters sat behind the adults, while on the roof perched a large old table, its legs up-ended in the air, like a sickly cow on its back.

With a fresh shiver she recalled September 1980, when Samson's costly herd which had depleted most of his father's savings, succumbed to disease. The stricken animals had lain unburied in the misty morning pasture until the digger arrived from Monjuste. The corpses, both large and very small had quickly turned yolk-yellow, and the smell of rotting flesh meant that Belette's shutters were closed tight for the rest of the week. Nor could any water be drawn from the well, and even the local *jardins* adjoining Hibou's track had remained unvisited.

Since then, whatever the season, whatever the weather, not a morning had passed without that same sickly odour reaching her nose, or the condensation from the fields seeming to rise and coalesce into lumbering half-dead beasts which evaporated into the daylight.

She'd once made the mistake of calling Samson from his bed across the landing to show him this eerie phenomenon, but he'd hit her across her nose, calling her *une Imbécile,* then hidden himself once more under his stale blankets.

Liliane peered closer at the English family with her nose pressed against the window's murky glass. Their GB sticker was too big, too obvious for these parts. Someone should tell them. And why not a French make of car? Samson would be sure to ask. The two children stared out at her as if unsure whether or not to smile, so she gave a little wave. Was the little fair-haired boy crying? She couldn't tell. Without glasses, her eyesight was limited to things that were close and very close. The widow glanced back at the clock above the stove. Everyone knew the *Anglais* would be arriving at eight o'clock on the evening of April 6th but here they were, almost a week early. Keen, obviously.

She sighed to herself as their exhaust faded into the darkening afternoon.

Quels pauvres.

How could she just stand by and watch them fall into the trap of her son's hatred? She had her conscience to think about. They would have to know that there were some folk who detested the English with their disease-ridden meat, their affluence driving up property prices too high for the French themselves, and who might make life difficult for them. And top of the list was her son, Samson.

Having crossed herself again and exchanged her Menthe-smelling slippers for her mother's slip-on shoes, Liliane Bonneau left the farmhouse, scuttled over the Rue des Martyrs and began following the smell of Volvo exhaust up towards the derelict *fermette.*

CHAPTER EIGHT

After a few moments of letting Bonneau sweat, Natalie dropped the Suzuki's stabiliser into the abattoir yard's dried earth and dismounted, wincing in pain as her bruised left ankle took her weight. Bastard. The green transporter was the one that had just shoved her down into that stony gulley, and now its driver was heading towards her: the man who terrorised his poor old mother yet who was nevertheless first into church every Friday and Sunday for Mass.

She took a deep breath. Although this was only her fourth assignment since January, she wasn't going to let the oaf's height and bulk, nor the fearsome expression on his face, deflect her from her purpose. Instead, she removed her helmet, extracted the pack of radishes from her black leather suit pocket and, having torn it open, popped one in her mouth. It was surprisingly cold, its flavour a shock but then, still chewing, she undid her pony tail and shook her blonde hair free.

It was important he didn't have things all his own way. So eye contact wasn't now an option. Nor polite preliminaries. Certainly not after his behaviour on the road and her sore ankle. She took a deep breath.

'Are you Monsieur Samson Bonneau, of Belette Farm, St Sauveur?'

She took his silence to be a yes.

'You could have killed me back there. Was that the idea?'

Again, silence. Just an angry swipe at a fly that had landed on his nose.

'I'd like to take a look at your calves,' she pointed at the truck, his pungent sweat reaching her nostrils. 'I believe you've brought fifty two calves for slaughter who've been reared illegally, contravening recent EU directives...'

'I know you,' he scowled, his neck by now blood-red. 'Whore.'

She steadied herself inwardly before speaking again.

'I represent the League of St Francis and you're obliged to let me see your livestock and any relevant documents concerning their provenance and nutrition since birth.'

'That blasphemer Metz has put you up to this. What's your reward, eh? I can imagine.'

'I'm not listening to that crap.' She avoided his eyes by producing her impressive-looking ID, which he ignored, then a notepad and ballpoint, which he didn't. A huge half-gloved hand reached over to snatch them away, but she was too quick, and, having sidestepped away from him, strode across the yard to the truck. Her aching ankle was nothing to the hurt in her heart as she drew closer and smelt the calves' terror. Some were probably dying right now, with no chance of any reprieve.

She'd spoken to Berthe Vervins on her phone just before reaching Aujac and warned her that if her brother-in-law were to slaughter Bonneau's latest stock for human consumption he'd be done for. But she'd not expected this. The barrier

62

down. The truck trapped. She was careful not to have her vulnerable back to him as she lifted a corner of the green tarpaulin and gasped.

'For Christ sake,' she pleaded. 'Help me get at least some of them out.'

'I've told you once, fuck off.'

She ran over to the abattoir's closed door and yelled for Monsieur Rufin. Bonneau had swiftly re-padlocked the truck's cover and was now driving behind her, slowly, menacingly circling the yard. It would only take one twist of his wheel. A little more acceleration...

A trail of yellow dung dripped in its wake on to the earth.

To her relief, the abattoir door slid open, but the stench from within left her standing. She covered her nose, realising that Hell was right here in Aujac, not in some cooked-up afterlife.

'Monsieur Rufin! Quick!' she yelled.

A stout man appeared from the nearby office, and saw Bonneau attempting to drive through the barrier.

'Stop, you fool!' The slaughterer bellowed after him. 'Stop!'

Bonneau ignored him as the Daf's bonnet nudged the pole. Suddenly Rufin dug in his over-all pocket and produced a small handgun. The essential tool of his trade if things went wrong. Like now.

Rufin ducked under the barrier and pointed the gun barrel at the truck's windscreen. The effect was immediate. Brake pads sighed against those ten giant wheels and the truck ground to a stand-still.

'Leave your cab and walk in front of me. That way.' Rufin waved his gun in the direction of the abattoir. Natalie watched as Bonneau obeyed and, once inside the cavernous interior was shoved on to a chair away from the door while the shorter man stood over him, gun still poised.

'One move sir, and you too will be just another piece of meat.'

He then shouted for one of his employees to stay with Natalie. To her, the youth he summoned looked too young to be working at all, never mind in a place like this, and the moment he was outside, offered Natalie a cigarette. She declined, but he lit up anyway, and she noticed his hands were shaking. His overall spattered with brown blood.

'I smell trouble,' he said, driving his smoke upwards into the darkening sky. 'Bonneau won't be pushed around. You'll see.'

'You know him, then?' she asked, as nonchalantly as possible.

'Yeah. Used to go over to his place with me mate whenever the calf scouring got bad...'

'Was that often?'

The boy threw her a suspicious glance, his mouth firming up.

'More to the point, what are you doing here?'

'Just passing through.' She looked over to the truck where all was ominously quiet under the tarpaulin. Inside her head was different, where questions churned around like her clothes in a washing machine. Should she trust this boy? Would he be willing to help her? 'Look,' she began, avoiding eye contact. 'What's your name?'

'Luc.'

'OK Luc. We need to get those calves out quickly. Please.'

To her surprise, the lad duly dropped his dimp, crushed it under his bloodied boot, and together they jogged over to the Daf.

'Damned padlocks,' he muttered, trying to work one open from his own set of keys. Then he stopped. Glanced towards the hangar where the whites of Bonneau's eyes stared out from the gloom. 'Look, I can't do this. No way, mate. Me job here took me ages to get and there's nothing else around here. You sort it.'

She kicked a wheel in frustration. She knew now that something terrible had happened within the transporter. But what to do next? The farmer was less than five metres away, and Rufin already had his hands full.

'Most of them are dead anyhow,' the lad shrugged. 'What's the point?'

Instead of replying, she produced her knife and, while the lad looked on, prised open the blade and began to slit open up the tarpaulin as if it were silk – enough to show her the worst of what lay underneath.

One calf lay barely alive on top of three others. Natalie saw that elsewhere ears had come adrift, eyes gouged out, and skinny legs that had never walked, stuck out like kindling wood. All weakened from too-early weaning, illegal narrow crates and lack of anything solid to eat, let alone any iron or minerals. Her camera was too risky right now. It could get damaged. She'd have to find the right moment...

She heard Bonneau shout, then other raised voices from inside the abattoir. The crash of something hitting the concrete floor. Then Bonneau defending himself against an increasingly harsh Rufin.

'As God's my witness, I rear my stock to the letter of the law,' he hollered, 'and, may I remind you, *monsieur*, I have rights too. There is such a thing as defamation, and that creature out there, that *biche*... God help her, is all I can say.'

Natalie shivered as Rufin doggedly repeated his agenda. As pet food meat was still a lucrative part of his trade, he'd pay Bonneau twenty euros for each calf carcass. He was lucky to be getting even that, he added. She bit her thumb skin hard and was about to move even closer to the door but the angry sounds from within changed her mind. After all, she'd damaged Bonneau's truck and implicated Rufin for previously trading with him. There'd be too many questions, and besides, she had her job to think about. None of her students or colleagues knew what she did in her spare time and so far, the cases she'd dealt with had protected her anonymity. This was different.

Damn.

She had to get away and think things through. Get some food and drink inside her for a start. It would take half an hour to get to Loupin where at least there was a bar.

Her watch showed six thirty. Still no photos for Paul. She glanced back once more at Bonneau's lorry as she reached her bike and crammed her helmet on to her head. Too risky to take any close-ups now. He was already wound up, and seeing her with a camera might just drive him over the edge.

Instead of starting the Suzuki's noisy engine there, she gripped the handlebars and jogged alongside the machine, until she was under the barrier and on to the tarmac leading down to Aujac.

Her left ankle ached even more and her head felt as if it had been used as a punchball. But none of this mattered as much as her own self-loathing, for she was a coward. Some of those poor calves could have been saved if she'd only been more assertive and had bodily tried to get them out. But Bonneau was more than tricky. She could smell it on him. See it in his eyes. He was more than dangerous too: he was evil.

She pulled in by some defunct village shop to phone Paul from her mobile. It had miraculously survived the fall and, as she dialled the number, she worked out an excuse for not having any photos. He seemed stressed. His first question more like a bark.

'Mission accomplished?'

'Yes. Rufin's keeping his stock for the vet to see.'

'Excellent. Any pix?'

'Sorry. Could have blown the whole thing. I took notes, though.'

'Remember our objectives? A picture paints a thousand words?'

She frowned. How could she forget?

'OK. Will do.' She said, nevertheless.

'Good. Speak soon.'

Natalie looked around as she pocketed her

mobile. The silence of this seemingly dead village was unreal. Instead of being a peaceful antidote to the past hour's events, the atmosphere made them bloom even more horrifyingly in her mind and, with the light failing she felt far too alone.

Before setting off she located the area map from her saddle bag then realised her fuel was low. Just enough left to get her to Loupin, but not via the *péage*. She'd have to shortcut through St Arnac but, having flattened the map on her saddle, she saw with dismay that particular road was represented by a thin spidery line.

As she re-started the Suzuki's engine, that hideous vision of that one still-living calf returned like stomach bile. How its huge eyes had fixed on her almost accusingly. Its nostrils stuffed with dried blood. Then another equally unappetising train of thought took over. Supposing the angry, vengeful Bonneau were to come powering through Aujac to finish her off? Her heart pumped in her chest as she turned left from the main street. She'd been right about this road. No white line down the middle, just a high rocky bank on her nearside and on the other, after she'd crossed the N20 and passed beneath the thundering *péage*, a dim view of the Florentin down below. How different this landscape was from the pretty hills and lakes of Gascony, she thought. Here was bleak, seemingly unpopulated, with a distinct air of menace in every limestone outcrop, which in parts almost formed a tunnel over her head. There was neither any place to pass nor room for oncoming vehicles and she prayed hard that none would appear. This certainly wasn't somewhere to break down or run out of fuel and, with mounting anxiety she checked the gauge every few seconds.

There was also the matter of her ankle. She'd only been riding for a quarter of an hour and already fresh pain was kicking in. She gritted her teeth and hugged the stony edge of tarmac until, following a 1 in 8 gradient downhill, the barely readable sign for St Sauveur and Loupin came into sight.

Merci, Dieu.

She slowed up as she approached the cross-roads in front of her but any relief was short-lived because in that deep stillness of dusk came the distant rumble of a large-engined vehicle. A feeling deep in her bones told her it was *him,* having left the *péage.* So why hadn't she hung around in Aujac? Given him the chance to shove of?

There was nowhere for her to hide. All the earlier rocks and boulders were gone, replaced by scrubby weeds and an openness leaving her in full view.

As the oncoming engine noise grew more distinct she decided to brazen it out, let him see she was there, that she wasn't afraid. While she waited, she remembered something her Dad had said when he'd sent her that knife: she'd always had more balls than all of Quebec's ice hockey team put together.

That decided her, and within seconds the Daf radiator set between badly adjusted headlights swung into view. The empty vehicle lurched from side to side, well over the speed limit and almost out of control; its damaged tarpaulin flapping out like a ragged wing.

She drew back to let the thing pass, but what the hell was going on? Bonneau was suddenly jamming on his brakes.

Merde!

Before he blocked off her access to the Loupin road opposite, she had to think fast. Forgetting her aches and pains, forgetting everything except a fleeting vision of her absent parents' faces, she roared over the crossroads, missing his truck by centimetres. By then, he'd travelled too far along to swerve round and follow her. Besides any three-four-or even ten-point turning was impossible there, and that fact alone enabled her to escape.

Still shaking with fear, Natalie noticed a vast colourful poster depicting the local viticulture, when what she really wanted to see was that Loupin was only eight kilometres away.

Thankfully there was no one in the Café de la Paix that she recognised. On the odd occasions she'd been in here with Metz, he'd always found a table tucked away in one of its darkened corners and they'd let the busy world move round them. Right now, she needed to sort out her next move: to take shots of the rest of Bonneau's suffering creatures. And, as the lorry had been empty, she knew that meant Belette Farm.

Having forced down a slice of pizza and a bottle of Stella Artois, she worked out a plan. What was to stop her sneaking into his calf shed? Nothing. Not even Paul's warning. He was desk-bound. She was in the field. End of story.

One more thing.

She accessed the Café's Minitel. Second best

invention after the wheel. Good. All the region's abattoirs were listed in alphabetical order. Béartville, Ermonfort, Mainsert, Percues...

Despite the din, she left a voicemail with Paul's office suggesting he call them first thing tomorrow and forewarn them that Bonneau might be seeking to offload any remaining stock. Failing that, there was always Spain and Italy. Longer journeys, but there they weren't so fussy and he'd doubtless come away with plenty of cash in hand.

She then dug out her silver Fujifilm camera which had also mercifully survived her fall. The film inside barely used. Hadn't her shots of the Cracow horses resulted in a prosecution a month ago? Yes. And in half an hour, she'd be doing the same again.

According to that revealing chat with Madame Bonneau, her son was a creature of habit. By now he'd have eaten and would be resting by the telly. 'He likes naked women, you see,' she'd added surreptitiously under her breath, clearly meaning porn.

Natalie stood up, collected her gloves and helmet, and struggled through the heaving bar to the door. Once outside, two passing lads wolf-whistled at her. She was thirty for God's sake, not eighteen. Besides, the opposite sex was the last thing on her mind now. She was thinking of what else Bonneau's old mother had told her about the strangely missing relatives and her husband's horrible death.

How by now, Belette must be full of some pretty unhappy ghosts.

As she walked towards her bike, it was as if the

71

bitter late March air had infiltrated her leather armour and gnawed not only at her whole body, but also her very soul.

CHAPTER NINE

Liliane Bonneau rested her weight against the stove as she stirred the rabbit stew yet again. Her leg muscles had given out halfway up the rutted track to Hibou and she'd been forced to return to Belette at a snail's pace for fear of Samson catching her hobnobbing with the *Anglais*. She felt a failure. She'd let them down and hoped that later, if she had a chance to explain, they'd understand.

The 7.15 p.m. bells brought not comfort but anxiety in her old breast. Where *was* her son? What was he up to? And then, like a summer's lightning bolt, came the realisation that maybe, just *maybe* her mouldy rye bread was doing the trick. Perhaps he'd eaten every crumb of it and been taken ill. Perhaps St Anthony's Fire was beginning to kindle inside him after all, and the thought of him afflicted by St Vitus' Dance aroused not the slightest shred of sympathy.

She rapidly crossed herself for these unmotherly thoughts, and had just resolved to go to Confession on Sunday morning and tell Père Julien exactly what she was doing when she heard that all-too familiar engine noise approach the farm.

Holy Mary mother of God...

She knew something was wrong by the way the

truck entered the front yard, its headlights destroying the dusk beyond the room's still-open shutters. Then came the brakes, sounding like a calf's squeal, next the slam of his cab door followed by thudding boots on the stone flags.

She kept her place by the stove where she felt safest, because that sound brought back too much from her past... The *Werhmacht* strutting into Pech Merle's market square, then the knocking on doors along her street. Before she'd met Fritz. Before falling in love...

'Did you get a good price?' She averted her eyes, trying to keep the tremble from her voice. But he ignored her by pulling his late father's chair away from the table and crashing his weight down on to its old torn seat. 'It's rabbit tonight,' she went on, checking his every movement for signs, however small, of the desired Fire. 'Your favourite.'

'Where was it shot? You know I won't eat flesh that's had a hole in it.'

Liliane blushed. 'Ninon's ferret got it for me. Not a mark to be seen.' She knew the old widower who lived in number 10, Rue des Martyrs had been sweet on her for years, and why shouldn't Samson be reminded occasionally that she had an admirer?

'You're no better than that Musset tart.' He spat on to the back of his hand to dilute a smear of dirt. 'She'd open her legs for the devil, that one. Already has. Been busy at Aujac too, the bitch.'

Liliane froze at mention of the girl's name; his perception of her. Wondered what he meant. The ladle slipped from her hand into the stew.

'What are you staring at, you old crone?' His

black eyes suddenly on hers then on the nearly empty pastis bottle. 'And where's all the Ricard gone?'

'You've drunk it, son. Not me, I swear.'

Samson drained what was left into his glass and added water from the jug, instantly turning the yellow liquid a milky white. She saw the mixture pass down his throat then he slapped his empty glass down on to the table in irritation.

'Sweet Jesus, woman. You'll be telling me next my calves have been at it.'

She stayed silent, her mind slipping back almost sixty years ago to when the tall black-haired Fritz Brandt had purchased a bottle of Ricard from Pech Merle's one *épicerie,* and they'd hidden themselves away in her mother's attic to share the single glass stolen from the kitchen. She'd matched her lips to the prints his had already made on the glass as they'd taken turns to drink. And afterwards when the bottle was empty, they'd lain together, dizzy with desire.

Small wonder their son imbibed nothing else, she thought, watching his anger grow.

Samson shook his head from side to side – as he'd done since he was a baby; and confirmation surely, that things hadn't gone well at Aujac today.

The old proverb *Aujourd'hui roi, demain rien* came into her mind as she fished for the hot ladle amongst the slivers of moistened meat in the casserole then placed it on to the table where two unmatched plates waited. His plain white with an ochre chip on its rim; hers light blue, stained in its centre.

'Will you be off to Mass afterwards?' she patted

74

a mound of mashed swede into shape alongside the rabbit portion then set the meal in front of him.

'Of course. And you'd better be coming with me.'

'Why's that, son?'

He lifted his head and fixed her with his black eyes.

'The rye bread was mouldy today, mother. Are you trying to kill me or what?'

Her christening spoon fell from her hand and tinkled against the stone floor. She clasped her throat for the rabbit meat in her mouth had suddenly become rotting flesh; the swede gouged from the bowels of the dead. But she must ignore all this and think quickly of a diversion for he was waiting, his eyes now on her mother's shoes, still on her feet.

'The English are here,' she pointed to the window. 'They came early.'

He showed no reaction, instead got up and positioned himself behind her chair. Then he stood deliberately on her special spoon and flattened it.

Fear made her stop chewing.

'Forget them, woman. Answer me!'

'The bread was fresh yesterday. I swear. Maybe you took it too early this morning. Maybe your lorry cab's too hot...'

He didn't let her finish. A blow to the side of her head sent her toppling from her chair and she lay curled up on the cold stone floor making no sound. And because silence was defiance, a kick to her legs soon brought a sharp cry from her lips.

The sound of his boots faded and the farmhouse door slammed behind him. She lay for a moment refusing to cry. In her own limited way, with what age had left her, she had to be stronger than him. The one whose very blood was hers, who'd torn her badly as he'd arrived blue feet first into the world. The one whom God would surely punish. And as she hauled herself up by gripping the nearest table leg, she heard an unfamiliar car engine move into a lower gear past the farm and turn right up towards Hibou.

CHAPTER TEN

The hole in the roof had been Tom's first priority once the wooden table had been installed. Although the day had so far remained cloudless, he knew from his research into the region's climate that its spring weather could be unpredictable. So, with Flora's help and three old car cushions – one crocheted by his mother-in-law – he'd usefully blocked out the day's darkening sky.

Now, half an hour later, with his hair and eyes full of dust and dried bird droppings, he knew that at least his family would be protected overnight should any rain arrive. He was just about to go outside to brush himself off when his daughter tugged on his arm.

'Dad?' She whispered. 'I think I can hear someone coming.'

Immediately, all four Wardle-Smiths fell silent, even Kathy, who'd been fuming non-stop about the state of the *fermette,* from no glass in the rear lower windows, to no water, no nothing. And that was just the start. Tom listened and sure enough came the low snarl of an oncoming diesel engine drawing closer and closer...

'I'll take a look,' he said, nerves kicking in. Why, he didn't know. Maybe because they'd barely been in the place. Hadn't yet got their bearings. This could be anybody calling and, for a crazy moment, thought of the Simistons.

With the family standing behind him at the open front door, he was almost relieved to see some black Jeep and not their former neighbours' luxury Pilote reach the plateau at the top of the track and park next to the Volvo.

'Christ, I don't need this,' Kathy pulled Max and Flora back into *the fermette.* 'Look at the sight of me. Of you with all that muck in your hair. Look at the kids. Whoever it is, will think we're bloody gyppos.' Her voice ended on a shrill high as the Jeep's two occupants crossed the dusty weed-strewn area and walked towards Tom, holding the fort on the top step. A smartly dressed woman, in her early forties, he guessed, and a tall lean man, slightly younger, wearing the all-too familiar navy uniform of a *gendarme.*

Tom instinctively shrunk back, wondering what he might have done wrong. Speeding perhaps? OK, so he'd hit 120 kms an hour past Souillac, but that was to lose all those creeping Brit caravans. Other possibilities lurched through his mind and, if both newcomers hadn't been smiling at him, he'd have shut the door in their faces.

'*Bonjour,* Monsieur Wardle-Smith,' began the

man mounting the steps, removing his gloves and *képi* as he did so. His fingers compacted together as if they might make a salute instead. They felt cool, clean to the touch. Unlike his own. 'Major Râoul Belassis, Gandoux *gendarmerie*. And this is...' he stalled for a fraction of a second, 'my colleague, Pauline Keppel. Clerk to the town's Examining Magistrate.'

'Enchantée,' she kept up her smile as her hand met his. Firm, purposeful, with an elaborate ring on her wedding finger. Her surprisingly dark eyes were very focused yet full of the kind of warmth he'd glimpsed on the covers of Cosmo and Elle in Prestige People's reception area. Her musky perfume reached Tom's nose as the day's late sun reddened her smooth coiffed hair. 'We heard you were moving in today and,' she glanced at her companion for concurrence, 'we always try and make a point of visiting new settlers in our Commune just in case there's anything they need. Anything we can help with.' Her English was good. Each word clear and precise.

'That's right,' added the major. 'We've just called in on a German family in Villefort. However,' his sharp blue eyes scanned the *fermette,* alighting for a second on its broken chimney, the heaped-up tiles. 'They seemed to have everything organised already.'

'Unlike us, then,' snapped Kathy. Tom turned to see Max and Flora edging closer behind him.

'We're still waiting for our removals firm to arrive. There's been some anti-British beef demo outside Le Mans. But once they arrive, we'll be fine...'

'Oh, really?' Kathy again. 'Don't believe a word my husband says. Come and take a look.'

With a sinking heart, Tom gestured to the darkness beyond the door.

'She's right. It *is* pretty basic, but...'

'How about a cup of English tea?' the man interrupted, reaching out to the children who introduced themselves and shook his hand in turn. 'That would be very welcome.'

'You'll be lucky.' Kathy's voice again. 'There's nothing whatsoever here.'

'Let's try, eh?' Tom ushered both visitors in. 'You never know.'

'Nice kids,' observed Belassis, following the woman into the low-beamed main room, ducking as he did so. 'Have you contacted any local schools for them yet?'

Max grimaced.

'I'm afraid not,' Kathy spoke for him as she hunted in the picnic bags. 'We need water first...'

'And lights,' Max chipped in.

'And furniture,' added his sister, helping to disembowel the now cold Thermos, the last slice of Safeway's Madeira cake and Max's rejected baguette...

'Please don't trouble yourselves.' The clerk seemed to be taking care not to let anything touch her pristine hound's-tooth checked suit, and more than once raised an elegantly shod foot to check the level of black earth on its heel. 'We can imagine it. Maybe next time, *hein?*'

'Yes, maybe next time,' the major echoed her. 'And if we can speed anything up for you, please say. Again why we're here. Both of us have the ear

79

of those in high places. People who matter.' He withdrew several utilities leaflets from inside his jacket pocket and placed them on the old brown table – the sole item of furniture so far. 'Max mentioned the lack of lights,' he went on. 'So what did the previous owner use?'

'Open fires and oil lamps,' sneered Kathy. 'I must have been mad to agree to all this...'

'EDF will need at least a week's notice to install you, especially over Easter.' The major pointed at their blue and yellow brochure. 'But I did notice...'

'What?' Tom's stomach took a dive.

'The nearest cable appears to be in the Rue des Martyrs.'

'Meaning?' barked Kathy.

'You'll have to get a pole installed by your track.'

'OK. So we do that,' Tom countered. 'No big deal.'

Belassis coughed diplomatically.

'It'll need planning, *monsieur*. But, like I said, we can advise you on this. I have a good friend in the *Mairie*...'

'Thanks.'

A defeated kind of silence followed in which Kathy began slamming around in the semi-darkness. The Thermos hit the ground first, its insides ominously tinkling. Then a pocket-sized English–French dictionary whose splayed pages covered the words *enemy* to *entangle*. Next came Tupperware, then the cheese baguette, aimed at Tom.

The visitors backed away, clearly embarrassed as he picked grated cheddar from above his left ear.

'Look,' began the clerk eyeing him then Max. 'I have an excellent idea. Why don't you bring your little boy over to play with my son tomorrow afternoon?'

'What about me?' complained Flora, before anyone could answer.

'*Chérie,* you can come next time. Right now, I think Didier needs another young man to keep him company.' She shrugged her padded shoulders. 'All his friends have gone away on holiday. I, unfortunately, have to work...'

Flora retreated in a sulk, but Max gripped Tom's hand.

'Where do you live, then?' His boy asked.

'Aha,' she smiled first at him then her companion whose nostrils seemed permanently flared on the smell of damp and decay. 'In what *he* would call the lap of luxury. How it will soon be here for you, I'm sure.'

'I *don't* think so,' said Kathy picking up the Tupperware, replacing lids and wiping the filthy cartons against her already stained slacks.

'Anyway, there's a large pool for residents and their guests. Heated all year round...'

'A pool?' Max's eyes widened. Then came a frown. 'But I haven't got my cozzie.'

'Cozzie?'

'Swimming trunks,' explained Tom.

'You can wear my knickers,' sneered Flora. 'They'll suit you.'

'That's very inventive,' the woman smiled, 'but Didier has plenty of outgrown swimming trunks. You see, I'm a sentimentalist. I can't bear to throw anything away.'

'How old is he, then?' asked Max.

'Twelve. Almost thirteen.'

'Same as me,' said Flora proudly.

'He loves the water.'

'So do I.' Max grinned. Then, when he thought no one was looking, stuck out his tongue at his sister.

'Good. All settled, then. Oh, by the way,' she clicked open her snakeskin bag and withdrew a small gold-coloured card. 'I'll write my address on the back. It's the Quartier Louis Pasteur, Gandoux.'

'Do you have a cell phone number?' the major asked Tom as she wrote. 'Be useful for us to have it.'

'No probs,' he scribbled on a page of his filofax, tore it out then handed it over. 'By the way, how did you know we were here? I mean, that we arrived today. I'm impressed.'

'It's my job to make newcomers feel welcome. And safe. After all, contented individuals make a contented country, *n'est ce-pas?*'

'We do appreciate it, don't we, Kath?'

No answer.

'Mummy's not happy,' said Flora. 'We thought we'd be left more stuff. Looks like it's all been nicked, though.'

Both officials looked concerned.

'What was here when you first came to view?' asked the *gendarme*. 'Because presumably you didn't buy unseen like some foreigners do. From the internet or magazines.'

'God no,' Tom protested. 'There was a dresser, four chairs, shelving and a fridge. OK, not much but something at least. Good job we bought this table.'

'You've forgotten the wardrobe and bed.' Kathy again. 'And what about the sink and draining board?'

'We'll look into this of course. If Monsieur Metz wasn't away I'd be asking him a few questions. After all, you bought what you first saw.'

'Exactly.'

'Leave it with us.'

'Cheers.'

'Metz is an honourable man,' added the woman. 'Besides, he's far too successful to resort to thieving, because that's what this is.'

Tom led the way outside into the chilly darkening light. The bells had started up again and all but drowned the farewells and his final thanks for tomorrow afternoon.

He and Max waited together and waved as the Jeep made a dusty circle and disappeared down the track.

'Hey, you,' he jabbed him playfully on the arm. 'Who's a lucky boy, then?'

Max paused, fingers in both ears.

'I wish Flora was coming too.'

Tom let it go. Thoughts of having to arrange a new power cable and the rest took over. Plus the fact that Kathy was screaming again. No towels. No soap...

She'd had enough.

CHAPTER ELEVEN

'Welcome, *monsieur,*' Père Julien ushered Bonneau into the sparsely populated church which smelt of the permanently lit candles clustered under the Virgin's statue, and the cold wet rocks that formed the end wall behind the altar.

So far, no sign of Georges Ninon.

'Would you like me to hear your Confession after Mass?'

Why? What did he know? Could he mind read as well?

Bonneau felt sweat break out on his forehead.

'No. Not tonight. I've nothing to say.'

'Very well.' The priest, startled by this terse response, moved on to more compliant parishioners, murmuring his hopes for the English family. That his devout Christian flock would soon make them feel part of their community.

Left-wing con, thought Bonneau, crossing himself then swearing inwardly as he found the nearest pew. He lowered himself to his knees. It had been a disastrous day, particularly with that interfering whore and Rufin's derisory amount of euros feeling like feathers in his pocket. All the more reason, then, for getting God on his side, he thought, closing his eyes.

But, minutes later, instead of intoning the prayers with the rest of the congregation in time with the bells, he was mentally devising strategies to keep officials away from his farm and, most importantly how to ingratiate himself with the English family at Hibou. To draw them into his confidence, under the pretext of carrying out essential renovations. He needed their trust. Step number one. Step two, with Bernard Metz in mind, was already under way.

He stood up, hoping this time to spot Georges Ninon and sure enough, the old ferret breeder was stooped in prayer near the lectern.

'How's the dog minding going, old friend?' he asked, his hand on the old man's bony shoulder. Ninon looked up from his breviary, his eyes glazed by tears.

A dream come true.

'You've not seen Filou by any chance?' he asked.

'No. Why?'

'I put out her dinner at midday, and normally she'd have bitten my hand off. But,' he shook his head, 'there was no sign of her.'

'She'll be back. Pregnant bitches often take themselves off near to giving birth.'

'I hope you're right, or I'll be in trouble.'

Bonneau patted the man's arm. God had listened and given him some light after all.

'I'll keep a look-out for you, but I must go,' he grimaced as if in pain. 'It's the usual migraine. Time for bed, I fear. Light a candle for her, Georges, why not?'

'I will, thank you, Samson.'

'My pleasure.'

With a hand clamped to his forehead, he walked back up the aisle and out into a different darkness, but, instead of continuing along the Rue des Martyrs as far as Belette, he turned left past the hamlet's cultivated *jardins* and, taking care not to dislodge any noisy stones en route, followed the deeply potholed track towards the *fermette* Hibou.

Still no lights and no heating, that was obvious. All good news as far as he was concerned. No water either and until a *fosse septique* was in, God only knew what they were doing for *toilettes* and, sure as the farmers' saying *'Noël au balcon, Pâcques aux tisons'* had always proved true, this family would need him like a body needs blood. Bonneau smiled to himself, because, once their *fosse septique* was installed, there'd be new legislation for compulsory connection to a mains supply, costing double what they'd paid Metz for the place. Their ignorance of French law and his motives for helping them would be his trump cards in getting rid of them. He'd be doing his bit for *La Patrie*. The land of his fathers.

He recognised the *Anglais'* estate car and, beyond it, the dark shape of the *fermette* just distinguishable against the sky. Torchlight wavered from room to room and from somewhere within he heard yelling, then a woman's voice raised to a shriek. Her words, although unintelligible, said it all.

A bad start. But just what he wanted, wasn't it? And, for a change, no bells. He checked his luminous watch: 8.20 p.m. Too late to knock on their door, he decided, besides, he'd probably scare the family off in such darkness. Best to leave the socialising until tomorrow. A few hours wouldn't make much difference to his plan. As he turned round to go, he spotted a motorbike wending its way out of the hamlet until suddenly it disappeared from view.

CHAPTER TWELVE

Natalie was afraid her hastily consumed beer and pizza might instantly re-appear. Such were her nerves as she finally parked out of sight of Belette, where the Rue des Martyrs becomes nameless and the public *lavabo*'s dark water swills over the washing trough's edge.

She sniffed, then shivered as she took in her surroundings. A grim combination of a sour dairy odour and the distress of separated beasts rose into the cold night air. On those rare occasions she'd stopped over at Metz's house, she'd not noticed any of this. In those days, she'd owned a car, an elderly 2CV. Perhaps biking had heightened her sense of smell. Of danger.

Not a soul around. The whole hamlet seemed deserted and as she rounded the bend, keeping close to Belette's high front wall, woodsmoke from somewhere reminded her of her grandmother's cottage in Connemara.

Homesickness welled up in her and for a moment she faltered as if her soul, that precious inheritance which her mother, Maureen Boyd, believed in more than God himself, was trying to tell her something. Whatever the reason, she pulled up with a start. Someone was coming her way from the track opposite. A man, recognisably tall, built like a bus.

She waited, breath quickening as Bonneau's huge dark shape lolloped past her and into his front yard. She could hear him kick open the door and then slam it shut behind him.

Let's go.

But then she froze. In the lull of cattle noise she picked up two distinct sounds. The snatch of breath and the scrape of a boot against earth. He'd appeared, as if from nowhere and eyed her with contempt; his top lip curling up. His smell even more repulsive.

'Get off my property,' he growled, 'I've seen enough of you for one day, and if I get so much as a sniff of you round here again, you'll be dog food. Got it?'

With that he lunged forwards and, before she could defend herself, he delivered a mighty shove which sent her sprawling on to the hard rutted earth.

'You sod.' Natalie spat after him. 'You wait!'

The farmhouse door slammed a second time behind him as she picked herself up, heart thudding in anger and fear. She thought hard about her next move. The nearest *gendarmerie* was in Gandoux – not too far – but to involve the law at this stage might open up an even more tricky can of worms. The other option was little better, because to ask so soon for extra support from the League of St Francis would prove she'd disobeyed orders by going to the farm. Yet how else did Paul expect her to get photos?

She imagined her two friends in Greece probably having a candlelit meal together somewhere by an island beach. Was it Rhodes or Paphos they'd headed for? She couldn't remember. Whatever, they'd be looking into each other's eyes as balalaikas played in the background. Their wineglasses refilled, anticipation of bed growing with each mouthful. So why wonder about her, risking her life in some Godforsaken hole, shaken and humiliated yet again? The answer was, they wouldn't. Nor would any of her English students, out there somewhere, having fun.

Yet still she was determined to trespass. To prove to herself that Metz had left her something with which to rebuild her life. Those tragic creatures needed a witness. And who else was there but herself?

Five long minutes later, she'd managed to creep across the farm's front yard, courtesy of the deep shadows beneath the line of oaks, which, over the centuries, had grown to become the biggest trees in St Sauveur. Then, through into the rear yard where she skirted the reeking midden, all thoughts were submerged by the din of beasts, kept both inside and out.

She bent low along the farmhouse's back wall so as to be invisible from the upstairs windows until she spotted a dull strand of light beneath the barn door.

Voilà.

The rising moon now revealed ancient lengths of guttering adrift of the wall, and roof tiles in disarray. But those already dislodged lay treacherously underfoot and clattered whenever they were disturbed.

Damn.

She inadvertently stepped on one and nearly lost her balance. How the hell can anyone live here? she asked herself, recalling that time she'd met Madame Bonneau. How her clothes seemed to have been unchanged for months and any remaining teeth resembled tiny grey flints. Poor lady.

These observations brought her nearer to her target until a sudden thought made her straighten up, keep her back to the barn door, thinking dogs.

Calm down...

The last one had been poisoned and the culprit never found, so Metz had told her. Her ex, whose house stood less than a hundred metres away.

By now, Natalie was holding her nose, aware of her eyes beginning to water, and that was before she slid the door's main bolt back and recoiled in disgust at what lay beyond in that dimly lit interior.

She set the flash and pointed the lens at the heaving sea of 'white veal' that filled every centimetre of available slatted floor space. Living skin and bone stood crammed between narrow wooden-sided crates, necks chained tightly to both head-clamping bars. Like those huge bewildered eyes that had stared at her from Bonneau's truck, so this multitude of misery turned her way. Not so much pleading as resigned. And which was worse? she asked herself feeling her stomach turn over.

Click.

She felt more than ill.

Click, click.

Aware of a light being switched on upstairs. Someone looking out.

Click.

She didn't dare lose her concentration. There were just two shots left.

Click. Click.

Natalie then squinted up at the oblong of light. Unless Bonneau had suddenly shrunk in half and done his hair in a bun, it was the old girl. *Time to exit,* she told herself, pocketing the camera and re-bolting the door. *And quick.*

She was creeping back towards the front yard when suddenly she became aware of movement under the oaks. A mass of young Charolais heifers whose murmuring faded to an uncanny silence as she approached. Her instinct was to run, but the vision of these palely swaying beasts, their eyes all fixed upon hers, seemed to turn her legs to lead. She then realised that the only thing separating her from a wall of solid, grieving meat was a length of thin wire and God knows what they could do, being so upset...

The moment their baleful and insistent lowing for their young started up again, Natalie began to move.

Her Suzuki lurched away into the darkness and it wasn't until she'd reached the Loupin turning that she switched on the bike's headlights, her thoughts still dwelling on that vile farm. She had to get the film sent off, that was priority. Then decide whether or not to find a bed for the night.

Soon the welcome village of Loupin came into view. She parked once more outside the Café de

La Paix, where the local night-life was still in full swing and frost had already lightened the other vehicles' windscreens. Apart from anything else, she badly needed a drink.

With her breath like mini puffs of bonfire smoke in the cold air, she left a second answer-phone message for her boss saying that the film would now be on its way to him. She then extracted it from the camera, slipped it inside her leather jacket and opened the café door.

'Are there any *Tabacs* round here? I need to buy an envelope and stamps,' she asked a baseball-hatted lad stacking the cigarette shelves behind the till.

'One just up there. Should still be open.' He continued to cram boxes of Camels and Gauloises into their narrow berths without bothering to turn round.

'Thanks. I also need somewhere to stay. Do you have any rooms, by any chance?'

With all this racket, there wouldn't be much chance of sleep, but at least a bed was a bed and the idea that she could trek all the way back to her flat near Limoges now seemed like madness. Besides, the prospect of encountering a deranged Bonneau along the way had been the deciding factor.

'Reckon there's one left. Best ask my boss, though.'

She watched him disappear through a nearby doorway where a staircase ended. She held her breath until he returned with an unreadable expression on his surly face.

'Well?'

'How fussy are you?'

'I'm knackered if you must know.'

'OK. It's yours.' He opened a drawer below the counter and held out a large key in his grubby hand. 'Fifty euros up front. You return this tomorrow by midday and you'll get twenty back.'

The drink could wait.

She took the key, handed over the notes and stuffed the scribbled receipt in her pocket, feeling relief and apprehension in equal measure. She'd already noticed the nearby Bar Hotel's *Complet* sign, and being Easter, it would have been impossible to find anywhere else.

Having retrieved her Suzuki from behind the café, she wheeled it down the alleyway with a growing sense of isolation, adrift from her normal support systems. Even Paul Ormonde hadn't been in his office as promised, and just to hear his crisp, authoritative voice would have felt reassuring.

Past a heap of flattened cardboard boxes and defunct garden chairs, then a row of *poubelles* brimming with uncollected junk. It was hard not to make comparisons with her town, where there were refuse collections twice a week, and every day some litter picker would prod his way past her apartment. As a student she'd even done that job herself one summer holiday for pay equal to that of a new nurse.

Here was so different. It was as if Loupin, like St Sauveur, had been forgotten by the bureaucrats. Where paid employment was rare. She shivered, aware of her ankle playing up again and one anxiety after another piling up in her mind. Suppose Bonneau knew where she was? Suppose he now felt he'd nothing to lose? She found the *Tabac* and bought an envelope and stamp from the middle-aged woman serving there. As the till closed shut, Natalie leaned forwards to ask her a question.

'Does someone called Samson Bonneau ever come in here? Veal farmer from St Sauveur. Big, you know, like this?' She heaved up her shoulders and frowned. The woman behind the counter stared at her as if she'd escaped from some asylum.

'He does. Why?'

'Nothing really. Just curious.' She popped the roll of film in the envelope and licked down the flap.

'He plays the *Loto* and sometimes gets his old mother a box of chocolates,' the woman went on. 'Pity he never found a wife. He's a good sort.'

Natalie left the *Tabac* angry and frustrated. She wanted to run back and tell the stupid creature in the shop what *she'd* found out. That apart from anything else, he probably bought the chocolates for himself. But what was the point? It was enough that with luck Paul Ormonde would have the photos of Belette at the League's Headquarters to-morrow morning and would be organising their next move. Meanwhile, having found a nearby letterbox and posted the precious envelope, she felt at least something had been achieved. Now she just needed sleep. A sleep without nightmares of calf eyes and Bonneau's dark angry face closing in on hers...

This time Natalie double-padlocked her machine to an empty bicycle rack behind the café. Its lights and saddle were, after all, still covetable. Having prowled around the rear of the premises and glanced up at the two uncurtained rear windows, she re-entered the noisy warmth and ordered a vodka and lime.

It felt cool and numbing against her throat. She closed her eyes, unwilling to open them again for at least the next eight hours, listening to the chat, the banter and the bass throb of some ballad she couldn't identify.

Bliss.

Then a nudge against her arm. A tap-tap-tap on her helmet, safe in her lap. She opened her eyes and saw that same lad hovering close by.

'Seen you in here before, yes?'

Not now, please...

'With that sculptor guy. I used to do stuff for him, you know. Mix the plaster, pour the bronze, you name it...'

She sat upright, jogging the table. Her glass nearly toppled over.

'When was this?'

'Oh, last August. Still help out when I'm needed. Mind you, not heard so much from him since he finished the last of them gargoyle things. Now he's got some big commission for Albi cathedral, so I heard. Just wondered if you'd give me a mention when you next see him. Robert it is. Robert Farges. He'll remember me,' he winked at her. 'Money's always useful, as you know.'

'I'm afraid you must be mistaken. I've never heard of the man.'

The lad took a step back, his greasy head cocked to one side. Looking her up and down.

'Swear to God it was you. I'm good at faces, me. Always have been.'

Natalie gripped her helmet and pushed back her chair. She felt dizzy. Sick, almost. Whatever the bed upstairs was like, she needed it. Immediately.

'Anyway,' her companion persisted, 'he must be raking it in. He's just sold his mother's old place to some English lot. I knew he was planning to.'

'Nicolette?' she said without thinking, then slumped back in her chair realising her folly.

'See,' he gloated. *'You do* know.'

'I've heard of her, that's all.'

'Anyway, I said to him, what about the locals? People like me who can't afford nothing no more? And guess what he came out with? That his buyers were civilised. Unlike us lot. Charming, eh? What *I've* heard about England is they all do drugs and steal each other's wives...'

Natalie saw someone she presumed to be the manager summoning him back to work. Just the let-out she needed and within one minute she'd reached the top of the stairs and unlocked the door to room number 2.

The moon seemed to monopolise the whole window and there was nothing, not even a towel, with which to keep its daunting stare at bay. She decided to stay in her leathers rather than freeze to death as the only heater with a dodgy looking wire connection was pumping out a strange, cold smell.

At least the longed-for bed seemed usable, despite a green cord bolster pock-marked with fag burns instead of pillows and a badly stained 1970s patterned duvet cover.

She laid her phone and camera down on the rickety bedside table and was just about to switch off the heater and light and subside on to the mattress when, suddenly, there was a knock at the door.

What now? she wondered.

'Call for you, *mademoiselle*,' said a young woman's voice. 'Down in the bar.'

At least it wasn't that lad again.

Who the hell was phoning here? Who *knew* that she was here for a start?

She followed the waitress to a small office which led off at the foot of the stairs.

'Did whoever it is give a name?' she asked.

The girl shook her head, passed her the receiver and closed the door behind her.

'Hello? Who is it?' Natalie frowned. After a short pause came what at first seemed to be gobbledygook. A man's voice, definitely, but muffled and menacing.

'Fille .... faille .... faux ... femme...

Aïe! Semelle de blaude evanouie (ne glisse manne,)...

Bee y a l'ail-vore, bee y d'aide.

A la graille (ne dis ce beaune tout) Meque, maille brette.'

'Who *are* you?' she urged, but there was no reply. Just the dialling tone, nothing more.

She stared at the receiver, suddenly realising what the apparent nonsense meant. That despite the muffled voice, the words were all too clear: *'Fe fi fo fum, I smell the blood of an Englishman. Be he alive or be he dead, I'll grind his bones to make my bread.'*

97

Why did Bonneau's name come straight to mind? And, if it *was* him, how come he was into early sixteenth century stuff from the Château de Coucy near Amiens? Because that's what it was. She'd given a lecture on these very rhymes as part of her students' last phonetics module. The originals probably reached England with the Huguenots, after which, the sounds mutated to mean something else entirely. But why was she the recipient? Maybe it was all a mistake. The call meant for someone else. Somehow though, that wasn't convincing.

Natalie thought of room number 2, that dingy but nevertheless welcome bed, knowing she wouldn't sleep while that ditty's last line played over and over in her mind. Ten minutes later while she pulled the pungent duvet over her head and squeezed her eyes shut, Liliane Bonneau was struggling to reach Belette's distant lavatory for her last visit of the night, and, to blot out the day's events and to remind himself of tomorrow, her son had switched to a hardcore flick set on some Caribbean island.

CHAPTER THIRTEEN

The Wardle-Smith's wobbly table purchased for 600 euros from a brocante near Uzerche, hogged the small living area which on paper, during a rainy Sunday afternoon back in Guildford, had been designated the *séjour*. On it, altar-like, stood not any consecrated items for the Eucharist but an unopened bottle of Moët et Chandon and two plastic thermos cups.

However, there was precious little to celebrate because apart from having no corkscrew, Tom now realised that in impulsively buying Hibou he'd probably just made the biggest mistake of his thirty eight years. And Kathy, his wife for nearly fourteen of those, wasn't likely to let him forget it. He could see the newspaper headlines already: WIFE KILLS HUSBAND IN DEEPEST FRANCE.

'What the Hell have you done bringing us here?' she shouted, holding their daughter close to her. 'There's no water of any kind, no lights, no nothing. And it's freezing. We could all *die* in this place. D'you realise that? *Do* you?'

'I'm sorry Kath, but...' He was thinking of the officials' recent visit. How the brief fizz of optimism still lingered in his mind at least.

'*Sorry!* Is that all you can say?' She gripped twelve year old Flora's shoulders which were visibly shivering under her pink puffa jacket. 'You promised that at least there'd be basic stuff sorted by the time we arrived so we could cook a meal, use a toilet...'

Tom could hardly bear to make eye contact with his daughter, normally so bubbly and full of beans. She looked worse than her mother, obviously missing her friends, her cosy bedroom with its lacy curtains and soft toy family ranged along her bed.

'You're a horrible daddy,' she snivelled, not looking at him. 'How *could* you?'

'He could, alright. Selfish bastard.' Kathy

chipped in.

'Look, just think *why* we've come here,' he began, although each word seemed like a fish-bone in his throat. 'The schools for a start. The French have much higher standards, respect for teachers, no disrupted lessons. Then there's the food, the wine, sexy clothes, the brilliant shops...'

'What shops?'

'I promise you, in two months' time all this will have faded away.'

The IT consultant trained his inadequate torch on her face. She seemed ten years older. Her skin drawn taut over her cheekbones; her habitually groomed hair a tangle of plaster chippings and bits of cobweb; hands as mucky as if she wore grey gloves. 'You're a born liar,' she snapped. 'And just listen to those bells. Don't they *ever* stop? It was so quiet that other time when we came here.'

That other time, he thought. Wednesday the first of March. A bright early spring day, with the birds, mostly skylarks, congregated along the roof's ridge tile and white cattle in the fields below like an advert for best butter. In fact, the whole thing had been utterly seductive. Not least the clear blue sky and the bottle of Cahors red he and Kathy had finished off in some bar in Loupin...

He saw her drag Flora away into what might one day be a dining area, leaving him with a creeping nausea at the enormity of his error. Then, just as he was planning a mental list for the morning, which now included the possibility of a speedy exit back to Surrey and a grovelling session with his boss to get his job back, he heard Max sobbing.

Oh Jesus, no.

He rushed forwards, bumping his head against one of the ceiling's sagging beams. He couldn't bear to hear his lad upset. Not big brave Max who'd taken on his prep school's bullies for nicking his lunch. Who'd befriended another pupil teased for being partially deaf and living with his grandmother.

He groped his way towards the rear of the *fermette* that would eventually be their kitchen – through to a deeper darkness where cold was an understatement. It was as if in this one spot, the Ice Age had never melted and, despite his brushed wool shirt, jeans and leather jacket he felt that it wasn't only his internal organs freezing up.

Even the *carrelage* around the black leaking stove had been prised away from the wall leaving mould in its place. Tom wondered again about Metz as his son's sobs became sniffles. Could he be responsible? No. That particular assumption didn't make sense, because not only had Pauline Keppel dismissed the idea but the vendor himself had seemed genuinely pleased they'd be occupying the old place. Even listened patiently to his evening class French. So these depradations must have happened after their last visit to sign the papers. Probably some opportunist neighbour, Tom reasoned. He must speak to the vendor first thing in the morning, but right now, morning seemed as far away as Mars.

'Max?' he whispered. 'Where are you?' His flickering torch beam found nothing other than filthy corners and piles of old sacks. Then suddenly the light died altogether.

Damn.

He found a wall and followed this to where wet stones became smooth rock, and under his feet, instead of the old tiles, lay rubbly soil. Its dampness choked his nostrils.

He guessed this was the cave.

'Max?' Feeling a trickle of fear pass down his back. 'Answer me, for God's sake!'

He could hear his son's breathing and, as if osmotically, felt the heat from his body. He must only be a matter of inches away... Tom stretched both his hands into the blackness and, to his relief touched the top of Max's head. He was crouching, his chin almost on his knees.

'What's up, eh?'

But the lad made no move.

'Look, you can tell your dad.'

'It's really weird in there,' Max said.

'Don't be daft.' Tom tried to lift his son up, but two young fists beat him off.

'It's *true*. It's spooky.'

He sighed. 'Come on, big boy. You're tired and you've got a busy day tomorrow. We've got a bed made up, so how about some shut-eye?' What he didn't add was that the bed would be a car seat shared with his sister.

'Dad, I'm not stupid.'

'But you're knackered. We all are.' Nerves raised his voice. Then he recalled how withdrawn Max had been after that last service station stop. How he'd not eaten anything. Even cola bottle gum sweets. His favourite.

'What's really bugging you?' he asked. 'You've not been your usual self since we had our picnic.'

Max's forehead puckered into deep folds. The

same as when he'd been born.

'That giant who helped get my thumb out of the chain...'

'The giant?'

Max nodded.

'Where was this?'

'On that cross thing. You know. Where we had our picnic. My thumb was stuck and it hurt. He had black eyes and blood in his fingernails. He was weird.'

Tom's nausea returned with a vengeance. Visions of the Guildford Stalker occluded his thoughts. Some creep who most likely still lived with his mother, and who, for the past six months, had lain in wait for kids by their school bus stops. Not among suburban streets, if you please, but out among the foxgloves and the cow parsley. Surely the pervert hadn't legged it over here?

'Jesus Christ,' he murmured to himself.

'You tell us not to say stuff like that.' Max accused him.

'You're right, son. Sorry.' He suddenly wanted a fag more than anything else in the world. Kathy had made him give them up when he'd first brought home a copy of *Live France*. When Prozac still topped the weekend shopping list.

'Tell me, did this man do or say anything else to you?'

'No.' Max stood up. His curly head cocked, listening as Kathy and Flora came nearer. It was now her turn to cry. The noise heartrending. 'But I saw a dead dog in the bushes there. A big brown one.'

Tom swallowed. This was getting worse.

'Why didn't you tell us straight away?'

Max shrugged. His round blue eyes close to tears. 'I just want to go home.'

Tom noticed damp dark patches on his red shorts which hadn't dried. There wasn't time for any more questions, or for him to fetch another pair from the one suitcase because Flora and Kathy were too close. Kathy's mouth twisted in anger.

'Listen to her,' she barked at him. 'Your *daughter.*'

'What can I do now, for Christ's sake?'

'Mrs Hemming gives two hour detentions for saying that.' Max again, seeming to forget he wouldn't be seeing his Year 3 teacher again. He then imitated his sister's sobs.

'Baby!' Flora sniffed, before burying her face in Kathy's grubby fleece.

'Nutter!'

Normally Tom would have stepped in with a few choice words plus his own late mother's pet homily about the importance of brotherly and sisterly love, but despair was all he had left. He saw the moonlight seeping through a fresh hole in the roof had turned all their faces the colour of old brie. Kathy especially, looked grim as Hell.

'Look,' he faced her, 'if we can just get through till morning, try and get a few hours' kip...'

'No chance. There's that old farm opposite the end of our track. The place with all those cows. I'm going there, OK? Come on Flora, and Max, you hold my hand.'

To his annoyance, the lad took it gratefully, then just as quickly let go to buffet his way out of

Hibou ahead of his sister. Kathy followed them both without looking back.

'You can't go out in the dark. Hang on!' He yelled.

'Bring the torch, then.'

'It's kaput.'

Silence, save for the tread of three pairs of shoes on the stony path and the distant calling of cattle. He suddenly recalled Max's story about the *'giant'* and involuntarily pulled up his jacket collar as he ran to catch up with his family. However, his legs felt sluggish, his heart full of guilt as he tapped Kathy's arm.

'We don't know what we're getting into here. Let's think this through first, eh?'

'Find a hotel for us, then.'

'I've tried, remember? Everywhere's full.'

'So, what else do you recommend?'

She kept on walking, her chin stuck out as she always did to annoy him, until the hamlet's *jardins* came to an end and the Rue des Martyrs began.

'What's that noise?' asked Max tilting his head towards the farm.

'Baby cows,' said Flora.

'Calves,' corrected Kathy, peering to read the sign nailed to the boundary wall. 'Belette.' She frowned. 'I don't remember seeing this the last time we came.'

'What does Belette mean?' Max again.

'Weasel,' replied Tom whose evening class course in French at Denewood College had left him with an A★ at AS level. An achievement it was important to remember. Especially now.

'I'm cold and my new Nikes look gross,' wailed

105

Flora, lifting up a foot to pick off something dubious from underneath the sole of her trainers. 'Mu ... m...'

'And I've got tummy ache,' echoed Max, hanging back.

Just then, something inside Tom seemed to snap. They were his kids, too, and no way was Kathy taking them into some unfamiliar dark farmhouse. French newspapers had been full of the Nanterre shootings and the forthcoming trial of Kamel ben Salah who'd allegedly murdered two Dutch couples in their restored home in the Gers. He'd been their trusted factotum, and now... Tom shivered, enough to jar his teeth together. Now they'd paid the price of naivety. 'If anyone's going in there it's me,' he said. 'You three wait outside, OK?'

'Don't you tell me what to do!'

Suddenly, a stinging slap met his cheek.

Silence followed, except for the cattle and bells beginning yet another round. As Kathy re-grouped the kids and pushed past him, he sensed that during the past three hours the existing gulf between them, which this move to France was supposed to heal, had widened like the nearby Gorge de St Arnac itself. Every word they spoke, every look and now that slap eroded his ability not just to love her, but to even care.

Admit it. Two years ago he'd been seriously hitting the bottle instead of meeting work targets and had taken himself off to Oban for a weekend to get stoned – to forget about her obsessive cleaning, her control freakery. For the woman with everything – two normal kids, a part-time job she enjoyed and the comforts of a mock-tudor home on Berris Hill Road – was bending away from him like a willow in the wind. And here, now, the future seemed like that cave behind Hibou. A creepy void, swilling with fear and uncertainty, without even his *Private Eye* back issues to cheer him up.

'What's that pong?' asked Max as they entered Belette's front yard.

'Yoghurt, stupid.' Flora nudged him with her knee. Tom sniffed. It was more than that. The late picnic rose up in his stomach, and not just because Kathy was already at the farmhouse door searching for a bell.

Something else was wrong. The moonlight. Of course.

Tom glanced up at its oppressive brightness and then at the farm itself, oddly untouched by any of it. What the hell was going on? All around was illuminated well enough. Too well, in fact. The skeletons of old tractors and balers and other farm junk loomed in the half darkness. And then there was Kathy, knocking with all her might on the door. Half in, half out of the silver light. Her left side fusing with the gloom.

'For God's sake,' he snapped. 'There could be guns. And who knows what else...'

'Bog off, you,' she hissed as Tom tried to clamp his hand over hers.

'No. Listen.'

Too late.

Heavy footsteps. A phlegmy cough and then the drawing back of at least three bolts. The door opened on to a dimly lit room and in its far corner he spotted a flickering TV screen. Smelt the remains of some kind of stew.

107

Suddenly a figure emerged from behind the door and Tom heard Max's gasp of alarm but there was no time for him to react, for the huge man was smiling, displaying bad teeth, while those dark eyes flicked over the foursome on his doorstep, settling for the briefest moment on Max.

'*Messieurs, dames. Bienvenue.*'

Tom reluctantly took the man's big rough hand. It felt hot, slightly moist. The nails rimmed by dirt. 'Samson Bonneau. Farmer in St Sauveur since I could walk,' he boasted. Tom saw Max turn his head away, biting his lip.

'I'm Tom Wardle-Smith,' he began in his best French. 'And this is my wife Kathy, with Flora and Max. From Hibou, up there.' He pointed towards the track opposite.

'Ah. *Hibou.*' As if this was the first time Bonneau had heard the name. 'So *you* are the English who will live there?'

His ability to speak their language, albeit simply, caught Tom unawares. 'That's right,' he said.

'You are early. Everyone said April 6th.'

Everyone?

'Well, we're here now, and we need your help. Just for tonight,' Tom persevered. 'We've no water, no light...'

'All our furniture is still outside Le Mans,' complained Kathy. 'There's not even a bed to sleep on.'

Tom was also about to mention the totally stripped *fermette* when he heard more footsteps approaching in the semi-darkness.

'Samson?' An old woman's voice suddenly interrupted these introductions from halfway up

108

the stairs. *'Qui est là?'*

'Anglais,' he replied in a way that Tom found mildly unsettling. *'Ils sont arrivés.'*

A pair of old red shoes bearing thin ankles encased in wrinkly brown stockings came down the rest of the stairs bringing a tiny woman whose skin barely covered her fragility.

'I'm Liliane Bonneau,' their owner began in her own tongue. 'Samson's mother. I've been so looking forward to meeting you in person.' A nasty bruise had spread under her hairline and Tom noticed her few remaining teeth were the same as her son's. Discoloured, neglected. But not the eyes. They were a rheumy blue and, like a butterfly with a glut of flowers to consider, lingered on each of her visitors in turn. 'You poor souls. And look at the children, how they shiver. How frightened they seem, and you, *monsieur,'* she stared at Tom, a smile creeping along her mouth, 'are exactly Antoine St Exupéry's double.'

He wasn't sure if comparison with the balding wartime hero depicted on the old French banknotes was a compliment or not, but thanked her anyway.

'And who were your visitors?' she asked. 'I hope you don't mind my asking.'

Tom stalled. She obviously never missed a trick.

'Just two officials from Gandoux. Checking we were OK. They said they'd look into why all the furniture's missing, for a start.'

'Good,' said Liliane. 'That's something.'

Tom nodded, and Kathy was about to add her own special brand of optimism, when the farmer interrupted.

'*Maman,* please.' He stretched out an arm to keep her at bay. 'These good people haven't time to hear an old woman wittering on. Come,' he signalled to the family and led the way through the main room towards a door set in the kitchenette's end wall. Tom saw Kathy's reaction to the clutter and neglect, the dirty dishes congealed one on the other on the single wooden draining board and a chipped glass bowl full of suppurating fruit. 'Belette is an Aladdin's cave. Nothing is thrown away.'

So I see, thought Tom, bringing up the rear, suddenly aware of what was on the TV as he passed. The earlier garden scene had changed to that of a four-poster bed with a young couple entwined together on its silky sheets. So, that's what friendly Farmer Giles gets up to in the evenings, he thought to himself, seeing the old girl's resigned expression as she hobbled over to turn the set off.

'Excuse my son,' she mumbled, before disappearing back up the stairs. 'It's just the way he is.'

The store, as Bonneau called it was a repository of not only every item under the sun but of smells of death and decay, which seemed to seep upwards from its stone floor. This large damp room whose sloping beamed ceiling ended just above the ground at its furthest end, was lit by a single bare bulb enabling Tom to see his family cover their noses as their helpmeet rummaged through the piles of junk for whatever it was *he* was after.

There was every kind of wire and string, mattresses dotted with what looked like bloodstains, embedded in piles of yellowed bed linen and an assortment of old crockery with handles and spouts missing. He wondered if some of this might have been nicked from Hibou. After all, the place had been empty for long enough. Then he dismissed the idea. This Monsieur Bonneau surely wouldn't have stooped so low, or risked a visit from a passing *gendarme*.

He suddenly felt Max's cold little hand in his. His features strained as if he was holding something back.

'What's up, son?' he whispered. 'You OK?'

Max replied by sidling up to Kathy and sticking his free thumb in his mouth. He was playing Baby all over again, and who could blame him?

'*Voilà*. Your bed,' Bonneau interrupted, as he hefted the biggest mattress on to his shoulder, knocking the light bulb into a frenzy at the end of its flex. 'It did my uncle for forty years.'

'Thanks.' But when the thing passed by he saw torn holes in the filthy fabric where rusty springs poked through. He also registered Kathy's look of horror. He tapped her arm.

'Something's up with Max.'

'He's a ninny,' said Flora, picking up an old jug and sniffing it. 'A *baby* ninny.'

Max kicked her on the leg.

'Stop it!' screamed Kathy, turning to Tom. 'This is unreal.'

And so it was.

As they followed Bonneau through to the front yard, Tom noticed the old girl sitting on the top stair, her thin stockinged legs jutted out as if they belonged to some old-fashioned doll. Her eyes missing nothing. He wondered what kind of life she had in this dump. And how she'd got that bruise on her forehead. Meanwhile, the mattress that had been folded over against the farmhouse wall, began to slide downwards. Max let go of Tom's hand to perch on the bottom end of it.

'Wait please,' the farmer brushed past them, his black smile like a wound across his face, and when he re-emerged from the store he held up a grimy oil lamp and began rubbing its glass with his forearm. As he did so, a strange little song escaped his lips – more a growl than a tune – and Tom realized Madame Bonneau had disappeared from her stair. *'Si'l tonne en février, monte les tonneaux aux greniers. Noël au balcon, Pâcques aux tisons...'*

'What's he singing?' asked Max. 'I don't like it.'

'Just a little country song about the weather. Do you speak any French, young man?'

'No.'

'He'll soon learn.' Tom eyed the mattress, wondering who'd be playing Atlas, carting it up to Hibou. Wondering, also, how on earth it could accommodate all four of them.

Bonneau meanwhile unscrewed the lamp's base, refilled the canister inside and handed it over to him.

'Used to belong to my father,' he said. 'But you can keep it till EDF connect you.'

Tom could have mentioned the lack of a pole, but didn't. He just needed sleep.

'How long will this oil last?' said Kathy too angry to say thank you.

Bonneau shrugged.

'One night, two nights. Oh, and you must decide which power band you want.'

'Power band?'

'I know what he means. Come on. Let's go.' Tom made a move for the mattress, but Bonneau beat him to it, startling Max into getting up, then lifting the whole thing up on his head.

'Here, let me...' Tom protested.

'No. It's an honour, *monsieur.*' The farmer began walking towards the main gate as the bells began to peal yet again and the white herd dispersed away from the rear yard into the moonlight.

'When's *my* bed coming?' whined Flora.

'Tomorrow, with a bit of luck.'

'And our Easter eggs?'

'Of course.' The four enormous ones in a Waitrose bag had been accidentally loaded on with the furniture.

'Dad, I don't want him to come to our house,' whispered Max, finding Tom's hand again.

'Why not?'

'It's a secret.'

'What have we told you about secrets?'

'I don't care.' Once again, he let go of his hand and went over to his mother. Tom saw him trying it on with her. She stopped, and Bonneau turned round.

'What's the matter, *mon petit?*'

'Nothing.'

Flora tried to wrench Max's hand away.

'Ninny. Ninny.'

'Ouch!'

'That's enough you two, for Christ's sake!'

Bonneau turned round again.

'*Mesdames et messieurs,* let me tell you. I'm Catholic, and to me, our *Seigneur's* name is sacred.'

The bells had stopped. The silence oppressive. Bonneau's heavy footfall between the potholes the only sound.

'You believe in God, then?' Flora challenged.

'Flora…' Tom began, but Bonneau once more interrupted him.

'Of course, and God sees everything.'

'So he saw you in your lorry staring at me? And that horrible dead dog in the bushes?' Max suddenly challenged.

Tom saw Bonneau flinch for a moment, then resume his stride towards Hibou.

'He's over-tired,' Tom pulled the boy towards him, kept him close, glad that Kathy was too far ahead to hear. 'He'll be better tomorrow.'

'I won't.'

'God is good,' opined Bonneau, in an overly pious tone. 'God will provide.'

'Then why did I have to give my rabbit away, and my gerbils?' Flora again.

'We must all make sacrifices. It is the way to Heaven.'

Tom felt Max's first tighten in his hand. Saw his forehead crumple. This wasn't going well, but right now, despite everything, the farmer had to be kept sweet. They needed him like a duck needs water. Who else had offered them any practical help? How many *fosse septique* diggers had responded to his notice in Live France? None.

'Tell Monsieur Bonneau about your terrapins,' he urged his son.

'No.'

'And that you fancied Anna-Louise Packer,' quipped his sister, stopping to extract a small stone from inside her trainer.

'Shut up!'

Tom gave his son's hand a warning squeeze. That was enough.

Bonneau re-positioned the mattress over his head and in the moonlight, a dark map of sweat was visible under his armpit. The smell rancid, sour.

Five long minutes later the stony track became earth, muffling all footsteps. Kathy had pushed open the door to the *fermette* and now pointed to where the mattress could go. In the middle of the floor of the one main room. Bonneau let it slip from his shoulders, then straightened up.

'Thanks for your help.' Tom placed the lamp on the table and lit it, whereupon a thick fug filled the room. 'We're really grateful.'

'My pleasure, but if Monsieur Le Pen has his way, no one will be helping anyone. Least of all people like you.' The farmer licked his lips, casting his black eyes from one family member to the other as his mother had done.

'What d'you mean?'

'Foreigners. *Étrangers*. Just listen to that daughter of his. It's on the news day in, day out.'

But Tom hadn't kept up with the imminent French election. How could he? He'd been too busy trying for a decent pay-off from work. Too busy keeping Kathy on board. Yet hadn't Una Simiston smugly mentioned at the party how the FN were gaining ground in the south. And what about those Jewish graves vandalized near Cannes?

He felt Kathy's glare. His stomach tightening

again in anxiety. He looked up at the hole in the ceiling into that blackness under the roof, willing dawn to appear, to give them all a break. But the reality lay in his watch face. Another seven hours to go.

'I wish we could offer you a drink of some sort,' he said to Bonneau instead. 'That was heavy work.'

'My reward won't be in this life.' The farmer stood in the doorway, facing out towards his own farm. Then he tucked his shirt back into his dungarees and raised his hand in farewell. '*À demain*. Until tomorrow.'

'Tomorrow.'

'I hate him,' Max plonked himself down on the mattress once more. In the flickering gold light, its dubious history reasserted itself. A battlefield of life and death.

'He's OK.' Flora sat next to him. 'Just a lonely old man.'

'We can't upset him. He can at least help us make a start.' Tom heard his own voice, disembodied, as though it belonged to someone else.

'He's that giant I told you about.' Max insisted. 'The one who got my thumb out of the swing. I'm telling you, Dad, he's evil.'

'Evil?'

Max nodded. 'And I bet he killed that dog. I saw his fingernails.'

'Dog? You never said,' Flora accused. 'Where?'

'Leave it, eh?' Tom's turn to snap. He too recalled the farmer's nails, but there'd been no sign of blood. Just plain black dirt. 'We've enough to deal with at the moment.'

He looked at Kathy, digging in her bag for her pills. Her face taut, jaundiced in the lamp's flame. Her mouth a silent line. There was nothing he could say or do. It was all too late. He fetched the old car rug and spread it over the mattress. As he did so, this relic of Bank Holidays spent on the beach in Littlehampton and the like, triggered another pang of regret. Then, having escorted his kids into the darkness for a pee, told them to take off their trainers, and to get into bed.

'Where are you sleeping?' Max asked him.

'In the car. So no worries. OK?'

'OK.'

Tom kissed them both goodnight walked out to the Volvo. It still smelt of those three most important people in his life. The family he'd let down. He rarely prayed, having come from a long line of agnostics, but now he did, with eyes tight shut. He gave God the works. And just as his improvised offering ended, he saw Kathy run from Hibou, holding something small and luminous in her hand.

CHAPTER FOURTEEN

By a quarter to midnight Samson Bonneau had made two trips in all to Hibou with his John Deere tractor and its trailer full of junk for the *Anglais* and tools for a prompt start on the *fosse septique* in the morning. Step Two of his plan drawing ever closer.

Thanks to his efforts, the family now had five full

buckets of tap water, a thirty-year old Primus stove and a selection of old blankets which none of them had seemed keen to use. Ungrateful lot, he thought, dumping yet more tools near the opening to the land. When he'd first called to deliver an almost empty tin of Ricoré and a packet of the local almond biscuits whose sell-by date had long gone, the father had been fast asleep in the car, then woken up shouting, as if in the middle of a dream. As for the other Anglais, he'd presumed they were inside the *fermette* on his dead uncle's mattress: the angry wife, the boy who was already proving troublesome and the girl called Flora.

In fact, little did any of them know what lay in store.

Bonneau set the tractor into reverse for his final mission: collecting an aged cement mixer from the farm. He saw the Volvo door left open and the man gone. For a moment he felt tempted to step down from his cab to take a look inside. Why not? A pair of sunglasses might come in handy. Maybe he'd find a credit card receipt or some other useful item. But such lack of forethought has its consequences. Unlike himself, where nothing was ever left to chance. No, he decided, giving the throttle a good push and engaging first gear. Best to keep their trust. Smile at the kids. Be Mister Nice Guy – an expression he'd heard on TV. Just like easy meat and dead meat.

Yes, being Mr Nice Guy was his priority, given his agenda.

As he bumped down the track he reflected on things so far. On balance, a disaster. He'd have to

118

find a new abattoir within five days. After that the rest of his live meat would go the same way as his last lot. Too old. Not white enough. If he wasn't careful, he'd soon be the laughing stock of the Commune again. Like he'd been when Metz had turned down his offer on this place. Not only was his livelihood about to go very publicly downhill, but here he was with his French nose up the *rosbifs'* backsides. The tractor and trailer parked there for all to see, and no doubt his mother would be adding her embellishments wherever she next set foot outside Belette. His mother, who, according to Flamand the hunchback, had already been seen sneaking up to Hibou.

Before going into the farmhouse to give her the shock she deserved, Bonneau parked the vehicle and cast his torch around the rear yard where the heifers were still calling out to their young. Just as he was considering silencing the lot of them with a bullet apiece through the brain, the church bells pealed out their midnight chime. However, not the usual twelve as you'd expect. Oh no. This passing from day to day was designed to send even the sanest inhabitant mad. It was time for another complaint to the Bishop.

He threw back his head and roared his protest into the cold night air. The beasts murmured their surprise at this sudden din, and he was aware of an upstairs light coming on as one animal began to climb upon another, to press against their restraining wire. He stepped back and tripped over a raised cobblestone, his skull colliding with a metal down pipe against the wall. He heard the fence wire snap in two, and before he could stand

119

up again, saw those huge creamy bodies buffeting towards him. Closer and closer they came until, suddenly, as if he was no longer important, they veered towards the calf barn.

Above him, the oblong of window light disappeared as he struggled to his feet, watching as the beasts battered its double doors with their heads and heaved their flanks against the century-old wood until an ominous splintering sound rose above that of the bells. If he used his rifle to shock them into leaving, they might turn on him instead.

By now both doors had fallen inwards, releasing the pandemonium of squealing calves, their mothers on a wrecking spree. Powerless to intervene, he calculated that already fifty thousand euros' worth of damage had been done. A year's earnings down the pan. Never mind what he'd just shelled out five days ago.

Jesus help me.

He heard the back door open behind him and a frightened voice call out, 'Samson? Can't you see the bulls are loose now? Come in son. Before they kill us both.'

'I'll kill you first, you meddlesome old crow.'

But she was right. His most valuable beasts, normally kept in the big field, were already on the move.

He saw her mouth open to scream as his hands went for her throat; a black hole gurgling, then silent as she swayed under his grasp.

'You leave those Anglais alone, d'you hear me?' he threatened. Then followed it with a lie. 'Ninon saw you trotting up to their place. Just remember, mother, he doesn't fancy you enough not to spy

120

on you.'

Suddenly she surprised him with a kick in the groin, enough to knock him off balance and topple once more to the ground, clear of the door. The moon filled his eyes and panic his heart. He was blind but not deaf as the cobblestones juddered around him under the army of hooves. One clipped his head, another pressed for what seemed like an eternity on his chest, emptying his lungs, squashing out his breath.

He tried calling out but those damned bells were at it again.

Dong, dong, dong ... louder than ever it seemed, until the stars above him appeared to multiply in their millions, then vanish into blackness.

CHAPTER FIFTEEN

Liliane drew all three heavy bolts across the door to keep her son out, should he recover from his fall.

Her breathing no more than shallow gasps, her old heart pummelling against her ribs. She was his mother, God forgive her. She crossed herself four times and, for good measure, muttered the Paternoster over and over as she sat down near the telephone and dialled Docteur Craval's number in the Avenue des Chênes in Gandoux.

Because of her throat, it was almost too painful to speak, yet Madame Craval who answered, saying her husband was in Agen overnight, never once referred to it. She'd suggested Pia Bordes, his locum. Her number was to hand.

'Thank you, but my son's never got on with lady doctors...' Liliane knew that sounded foolish, but it was the truth. There'd be hell to pay afterwards. If there *was* an afterwards.

'In that case I suggest an ambulance.' The other woman rattled off a list of digits, but just as Liliane was about to ask her to repeat it, the doctor's wife ended the call.

Her frightened heart was now the only sound she could hear. Supposing Samson was dying? Dead even? She might fall under suspicion if bits of her mouldy rye bread were found in his system. Surely evidence of her intended crime? Without bothering to exchange her slippers for shoes, she reached the front door and hesitated for the briefest moment before setting off into the night.

She had no choice but to go and seek out the English to ask for their help, because in her heart she knew that despite Samson's opinions, they were decent people. After all, hadn't Bernard Metz been glad to sell to them? And he was as good a judge as anyone. Someone whose opinion she could rely on.

Short wheezy gasps accompanied her steps. A far cry from the old days, when she used to visit Metz's mother, Nicolette there, who had kept bees and goats. She, Liliane, had always been nimble, or so Fritz had often told her. Quite the opposite of his former girlfriend in Munich. Now she felt a hundred years old, weighed down by guilt and fear, and once the peal of bells had ended, she cocked her head like a nervous

122

chicken to listen for any signs of the herd, or worse, of Samson moving around. But there was nothing save the dying moon forging St Sauveur's church spire into a bright point piercing the sky. She saw the constellations in the same position as always. As if time had stood still for all those years, through the passing of wars and the ever-depleting family of Bonneaus who had, she knew, been called not to rest, but *un*rest. Their un-worldly legacy was palpable, and not for the first time did she glance over her shoulder sensing another presence hovering nearby.

She shivered, trying to increase the distance between her and Belette, her nervousness grow-ing with each step. This family should have a dog, she mused, quickening towards the low unlit dwelling in front of her. Metz's bitch Filou was expecting a litter any day now, but Georges Ninon was sure to be taking good care of her in his neighbour's absence. Yes, she thought to herself. A Fauve de Bretagne puppy would be just the job here. A loyal guard and *chien de chasse* all rolled into one. She then resolved to mention it to Ninon tomorrow, assuming of course the Good Lord would spare her that long.

Having halted by the brown estate car, she im-mediately noticed that its closed windows were all misted up. She peered in to see the father fast asleep in the driver's seat, the whites of his open eyes staring upwards like those of some wild horse.

'*Monsieur?*' She tapped on the glass. 'Help, please.'

'What the...?'

Those same eyes closed then blinked open in surprise as he reared up. Then came recognition.

'Madame Bonneau?'

'Yes. Samson's had an accident. His cows, they're *partout*...' Her French as slow and clear as she could make it while her arms did the opposite. Waving like some crazy windmill. To her relief, the Englishman seemed to understand. He fumbled for the handle, pushed the door open and got out. Handsome though he was, he looked terrible, she thought. Weary beyond belief, in fact, but, having heard her story he punched in 18 on his mobile phone and handed it to her.

After a short one-sided conversation the call to the emergency services ended and she turned to him.

'I'm sorry, you were fast asleep. But they'll be at Belette in six or seven minutes. I need to be back there in time.'

'Sure. No problem.'

Yet she saw him glance at the *fermette*, where no one else was stirring. Indecision was written all over his face.

'Look, I can't leave them,' he said finally.

Her heart sank.

'It'll only take a few seconds. Please, *monsieur*. I have to be there with my son.'

At that, he relented and during the brief journey she mentioned Filou's imminent puppies and hinted that a local registered builder might be better than her son for the renovation work at Hibou. Especially now, because God alone knew what had happened to him.

'Thanks, Madame Bonneau, but we'll get a dog

once we're sorted out, and your son's done us proud so far. Let's just hope he's alright.'

He pulled into the front yard and hauled up the handbrake.

'Besides, he might be able to help us with another little problem.'

'What problem?' She extricated herself from the passenger seat and the surrounding junk, feeling unsteady on her feet.

'My wife Kathy found a bone behind the kitchenette. In that cave place.'

'A bone?' Liliane sensed her innards turn to ice under her clothes. That strange damp hollow in the rock, used by Nicolette Metz to store honey and goats' cheese away from the summer's heat. She'd always had the distinct impression that there was something odd about those few square metres of ancient space. Primitive and secret. Somewhere she'd never liked to linger.

'Yes. But whether it's human or not, we can't tell.' His voice tailed off. 'And, if it is, where's the rest of the skeleton?'

'I wouldn't go getting upset, *monsieur*. Hibou goes back a long, long way and all sorts of creatures may have sheltered there after it was left to go to rack and ruin.'

'That's possible, I suppose.' Although he didn't sound very convinced.

Liliane edged closer. It was time for her to warn him. Something she should have done before now. She took a deep breath.

'My son's always had his eye on your place,' she whispered. 'Did he never tell you?'

'No.'

125

She saw a frown forming but she had to go on. It was important.

'Six hectares is very useful to any farmer. Especially round here with so much land taken up with vines. He could have expanded the business. More barns, more stock. Of course when Nicolette Metz died, he made her son a good offer. All he could afford.'

'And?'

She shook her head.

'Metz wasn't going to do him any favours. Samson had been complaining about his sculptures from the word go. Hibou was sold to you out of spite. For double what Samson was prepared to pay.'

His expression darkened. He looked at her.

'I see. Does he still want it?'

She nodded.

'I tried to tell you earlier, *monsieur,* but I'm sure you know how difficult it...'

Suddenly the white SAMU car approached, slewed into the yard and came to a halt. As its headlights faded, and the moon once more reclaimed the secret shadows of the high wall that abutted the hamlet's street, and the oaks beyond, she was convinced of someone – a man – standing near the entrance. Not only that, he was pointing quite distinctly towards the field behind Belette. Her old pulse quickened. She closed her eyes and opened them again, just to make sure.

'Samson? Is that you?' she whispered, feeling suddenly very cold. 'Are you alright?'

But her questions were foolish. How *could* it be him? This faceless half-illumined figure was tall

126

and lean. His clothes quite different from anything her son normally wore. So, who on earth could this apparition be? And why here, at Belette? She thought of Fritz, killed by firing squad in Pech Merle's village square. She even thought of Albert, but no. Neither man had been as tall as this. And then came a gasp of recognition.

Holy Mary save me...

Eric?

The one who'd never done any of those things the Examining Magistrate at the time of his disappearance had claimed. Who'd never strayed from Belette in a state of confusion, or met someone from his past. These had been convenient lies, but since the New Year, she had suspected that the missing man had in fact stayed much closer to home; grown to become like the oaks themselves. One day she would tell someone. But, why, after all these years, had he appeared like this? What else was he trying to tell her...?

'Madame?'

She spun round from the fast-fading apparition to face two youthful paramedics, one male, one female.

'You called us about your son,' said the girl.

'Yes... Yes, that's right.' Her hand trembled as she waved at the Englishman to go, but for some reason he stayed put in his car. Perhaps waiting to see if he could help, but when she looked more closely, he seemed deep in thought. 'Follow me,' she said to the ambulance crew. 'Samson's round the back. Please excuse the smell. I keep nagging him to clear the middens before we both die from their fumes.'

She scuttled ahead, illuminated by one of the torch's beams, then hesitated upon seeing the broken wire alongside the field.

'Be careful,' she warned the couple behind her. 'Two whole herds got loose. They could be anywhere.'

Soon she located the spot where Samson had fallen. Now both beams of light trained on the cobblestones; on the blood near the doorstep. But where on earth was *he?* She held her breath, scanning the yard's moonlit emptiness. The costly destruction. The broken calf pens and wooden ramps strewn everywhere.

'He's not here,' she rasped. 'You can see for yourselves. He's gone.'

CHAPTER SIXTEEN

At 7 a.m. there came another knock on the door.
'Yes?'

Natalie's eyelids seemed gummed together as she tried to open them.

'Phone again. For you.' A different voice this time. An older man. Rough. Local. She swung her still-leathered legs out of bed and, half-blind, groped her way to the door. She'd had a bad night after that first call. Was this about to make things worse?

She knew immediately something was wrong. The speaker's tone, although slightly lower than for that weird nursery rhyme, purveyed an equally chilling message in French with a slight regional accent.

'You love animals, *hein?* Well, I've got something for you. Better get your skates on, before it's too late...' Then the line grew faint and all she could make out were the words, 'Better try the service station...'

'Jesus Christ.'

You love animals ... try the service station?

No trace on the call. An automated *numéro caché* being the only response. Then she pushed her way into the bar where that same older man was sweeping the floor between the tables and chairs.

'Did that caller ask for me by name?' she asked him, suddenly thinking Metz playing mind games.

The man shrugged. Kept his head down.

'Don't remember. That phone's on the bloody go all the time.' And, as if to prove his point, it started ringing yet again. She ran back into the tiny office.

'Yes?' Her heart hitting her ribs.

'You still there then?' The same male voice. More threatening this time. 'I'd get a move on.'

'Who *are* you?'

Silence.

Time to go, but no time to wash, brush her hair or change her briefs. She was also owed thirty euros for the room, but that could wait, and within five minutes she'd wheeled her bike from its moorings and squealed away from the kerb.

The still-dark Rue Voltaire darkened further once the last street lamp had gone and her tired eyes strained to adjust to the loss of familiar landmarks. A wine bottling plant, a caravan dealership. A massive heap of old vine roots still heaped up by the roadside since she'd first come to the area.

But which service station? she wondered, now shivering at the crossroads, desperate for a pee. She knew there were two in the vicinity plus the usual *aire de repos* where foreign caravanners provided the region's users with easy pickings. At this juncture, part of her said, go and find out. The other, get back to university; see what was going on there. Bound to be something on offer, she mused as lights in the apartments opposite came on. Staff bike rallies to the hills, the odd party...

So, what was she still doing here, in this dive? She'd done her bit, hadn't she? Evidence of Bonneau's cruelty in full lurid colour was on its way to Clermont Ferrand, so what was to stop her simply heading back north?

You love animals, that's why...

As she rode towards the *péage*, another stray thought wormed its way into her befuddled brain. She could hear that horrible voice again, and in the cold sneaking light of day she realised with dread certainty whose it was. Samson Bonneau. Hadn't most farmers got computers for their farm's accounts? If so, he'd have Internet access for knowledge he didn't possess? *Voilà.*

'...*Une semelle de blande evanouie ne glisse manne...*'

The time had been 21.00 hrs. After her visit to Belette.

Damn.

She was *half* English, wasn't she? But surely that was too tenuous a connection. Anyway, that last word had been Englishman. She thought hard for a moment then, with an almost physical pain, realised why the veal farmer had made contact.

Metz had sold to an Englishman.

Frost everywhere. Worse than yesterday when she'd set out from Boisseuil, so she kept the throttle even, the gears low. She'd had one spill already, thanks to the farmer, and her ankle still protested when she bent it too quickly.

The *péage* at toll number 57 was eerily quiet. Its greyness snaking away between the high newly quarried banks of limestone. For a moment she wondered if this trip was such a good idea after all. She'd taken twenty minutes to get there. Twenty precious minutes when she could have been in St Sauveur, warning the family at Hibou about Bonneau.

Nevertheless, she parked the Suzuki alongside another bike and walked over to the nearest of the two occupied booths. Here a guy of around her age was busy sorting out his till. The slightly misted, tinted glass lent him a mystery which raw daylight would surely soon scupper.

He seemed typical of so many of her students she thought, with that preppy look of smooth brown hair and glasses. But there the similarity ended: the cable-stitched jumper zipped up to his chin was evidently homemade, and deeply uncool.

'Hi,' she began, as he looked up from his calculations. 'Where's the nearest service station?'

He shrugged his woollen shoulders.

'Florentin or Monjuste. Take your pick. Both

131

fifteen minutes either way.'

She picked up a ticket, waved her thanks and, within a few seconds, had skimmed past the toll booths, her wheels burning up the tarmac, heading for Toulouse, too loudly to hear the bespectacled cashier yell after her to watch out for black ice.

No livestock transporters here, but plenty of the usual Danone, Giraud and Norbert Dentressangle juggernauts lying nose to tail in the Monjuste lorry park. Plenty of commercial travellers too, judging by the BMWs and Lagunas carelessly strewn outside the *boutique*. She also noticed the neat ovals of new-laid turf and a total absence of litter, while quartz fragments set into the pristine white concrete sparkled in that cold bright morning light.

No sign of animals of any description, or any kind of shelter amongst the newly planted trees where they might be sleeping. No dogs on or off leads, no slatted transporters. Nothing. What you saw was what you got. Life-sized Legoland. Bald and bland. There wasn't any point in hanging around, she decided, especially after a surly employee had pointedly denied seeing any non-human in the vicinity. It was time to try the other one.

Rather than take the back roads to the Florentin services, she reached that same toll once again. This time the guy surreptitiously let her through without asking for the five euro charge. That was nice of him, and perhaps she'd ask him for a date. Perhaps underneath those homely clothes, there lurked a tiger. But there was no time to dwell further on this speculation as each second that passed added to her growing frustration.

The eponymous Florentin service station, named after the nearby river, was far more busy than Monjuste, and therefore it took her longer to scour the already full parking bays and keep an eye on the numerous people carriers and 4x4s entering and leaving the premises. Her still-helmeted head behaved as if she was spectating a tennis match, while the rest of her shivered in that bleak morning. She stamped her booted feet on the ground to restore some circulation to her toes. Leather was OK most of the time, but not in the dead cold like today. And not when her heart seemed to have slowed right up. Just one glimpse of what that mysterious caller had meant would make all the difference. Just to see something with four legs like he'd said...

But no. Dreams don't come true. She'd cottoned on to that fact very early on, aged eight, in fact, when her parents finally divorced and she'd been powerless to prevent it. In her book, to make a wish was unlucky. To pray, a total waste of breath. Always a sore point between her and Metz, even though he rarely went to Mass.

Unlike Monjuste, this facility seemed to have no boundaries on its southerly side, where storm-damaged forestry formed a dense screen behind a children's play area.

Natalie wheeled her machine down the slope towards it, away from the petrol pumps and the special yellow-striped bay set aside for air and water and the like. Each step made her normally generous mouth tighten in disappointment, for apart from a few tacky looking plastic playthings and a strange rusted cross-like structure, the place was deserted.

Suddenly, however, as she crossed the dusty play surface to investigate the edge of the woodland, something did catch her eye. A soft brown creature of some sort was hanging stiffly from the play sculpture's cross-bar, almost camouflaged by the rust.

Her empty stomach joined her heart in freefall as she edged closer to see that this wasn't some wild mammal or other having a long breather in between stunts, but a large dog – a Fauve de Bretagne – whose gunshot wound to the neck was clotted with dried dark blood, attracting early morning flies.

Jesus wept. She felt sick. Unsteady on her feet. This was a dog she recognised not just by its colouring and texture, but by the white patch on the near-side paw. Could this really be Filou, Metz's pregnant bitch? His devoted companion who'd sit for hours watching him at work? The dog she herself had played with, walked with?

She moved closer. There was no sign of the studded collar she remembered, nor any other means of identification. Just rings of yellow twine wound around its neck connecting it to the crossbar. But her trained eye could see this was indeed a bitch whose unborn puppies still lay inside her swollen body. From what she could tell, the animal had been dead for at least a day, but surely during that time, someone must've noticed her hanging there?

With acid rising in her throat, Natalie pushed her Suzuki back up the slope, sometimes slipping on the loose stones before finally reaching the fuel bay. She parked the bike by the *boutique*, where an army of decorators had taken over the shop and half the trading area lay under huge white sheets. The smell of gloss paint made her sneeze twice.

'A pregnant bitch?' A café worker repeated, as she handed a salesman his hermetically sealed sandwich. She then laughed. 'You're joking.'

'I'm not. Please fetch someone. And something to wrap it in,' Natalie added. She was fighting off hysteria, knowing that if she gave into it, no one would take her seriously. Particularly in this uptight bureaucratic country. However, five minutes later, having shown the employee her ID and explained why she was there, she was leading a small phalanx of red-suited personnel towards the crime scene, all the while unaware that every move she and her companions made was being closely monitored by the man hidden deep inside his nest of broken branches.

Natalie didn't like coincidences. Especially in the modern crime fiction that she often read. She preferred to suspend belief totally and utterly, not be manipulated by an author's shortcutting devices. The easy way out. Never mind *who*dunnit, she was more interested in *why?* Perhaps because her father had originally trained in psychology and that interest still lay in her genes. Perhaps because she knew that human beings possessed a limitless capacity for deception. But now, faced with *this* gross reality, any analytical skills had deserted her and she could only ask herself why, if this was indeed Metz's pet, what could have driven someone to shoot it?

She knew what her two absent friends would say. The two who by now were probably heading down to their villa's pool for a swim. 'The guy dumped you. He didn't give a toss. So why are you getting involved? He won't thank you...'

Because I have to...

Then another viewpoint, equally valid, snaked into her mind. From where, she didn't know. Metz had dumped her. Correct. Ergo, could this be seen as her revenge on him, six months on? Panic ripped through her as she watched two service station staff free the animal and bundle it up inside a decorator's sheet they'd brought along with them. The gaping wound smeared the white cotton a dull red as they carried the corpse back to a door marked *PRIVÉE* behind the *boutique*.

Still time to run. Or try for justice?

No competition.

'I'd better keep the twine,' she said, feeling more than sick. 'Just in case.'

One of the young men handed over the coarse yellow coil. Free of blood she noticed and thicker than the usual variety used by gardeners. This seemed more for agricultural purposes, and yet wasn't the typical orange or green colour she'd spotted on her travels. As she carefully placed it in her leather jacket pocket, she tried to work out its origins.

'No collar.' Someone interrupted her thoughts.

'I'm pretty sure this is Bernard Metz's dog. From St Sauveur,' she volunteered. 'And as you

136

can see, she was pregnant.' That last word made her throat close up. Her stomach churn over once again.

'Ugh. My God.'

'We should call the police.'

'It's not a *person*, Yves. They eat them in China, remember?'

'Excuse me, but dogs are *people*.'

'Get a life, eh?'

Natalie listened until this surreal conversation fizzled out, while the creature itself was laid inside a small bare room whose far corner was taken up by stacks of empty crates. Then once the staff had gone, she stared down at the lifeless bundle, saw how the stain had spread and how a black-padded paw had slipped free of the sheet and lay starkly defined against the tiled floor. Her instinct was to bend down and hide it, but just the thought of touching that cold stiff flesh made her recoil. Seeing Bonneau's veal calves had been bad enough.

Bonneau...

Now things were beginning to slot into place. Of *course*. Why hadn't she put two and two together before now? What was the matter with her? She shivered again and tried to get a grip. He'd protested long and hard about Metz's work. Especially a tau style cross at some service station play area. Hadn't he parked his truck over where the foundations were to go, to prevent any digging from starting, and moreover written those poison pen letters to the sculptor, enough to give anyone less stable more than a few sleepless nights? Now, in this cold little room with poor

137

dead Filou for company, the things Metz had said were all coming back.

This must be the work Bonneau hated so much. But enough to kill for?

She had to find the bullet. If she could match it to one of Bonneau's guns, she'd have him.

She pulled back the sheet, studied the wound in close up, then froze. The poor hound had already suffered enough without her digging around, making the wound worse. But what choice did she have? If Bonneau was to pay for this wickedness, finding the bullet was vital. She held her breath, gritted her teeth and pulled out her knife from her jacket pocket. With the blade drawn, she used its tip to probe beneath the fur, waiting for the expected sound of steel against lead, but there was none. She tried again just to make sure, but knew that whoever had killed Filou, had removed the evidence.

She hurried outside, closing the door behind her. In less than a minute she'd wiped the knife blade on some nearby grass and was exploring the base of Metz's 'cross' for any kind of plaque bearing its creator's name, when suddenly she noticed a large blob of semi-dried blood near her feet. Even though the sun wasn't giving off any warmth, it was nevertheless beginning to smell. She found a large dried sycamore leaf to clear away the mess and reveal the words, *LA CROIX DE ST ANTOINE. CRÉE PAR BERNARD METZ.* Exactly a year ago. Was that fact significant? she asked herself as she dug out her mobile from her back pocket. Maybe.

Natalie punched his number on her phone, only

to be met by an automated message. His number was no longer available. Why? she wondered. Had he moved from the area? Was he lying low for some reason? She'd have to find out. Again she tried, without success, and then remembered her brief meeting with Robert Farges at the Café de la Paix. If his information about the sculptor was correct, Metz could well be in Albi.

However, there wasn't time to phone the cathedral there because three more employees and a man in a grey suit advancing towards her. Buckets and cloths at the ready. She would have to do it later.

Apart from the problem of keeping them away from the site until she'd called the *gendarmerie,* she had to know if they'd seen anyone hanging around the play sculpture. Anyone looking suspicious.

'No, we haven't.' The guy she presumed to be the manager looked grim. 'And this little episode is the worst possible news for business here, especially with Monjuste opening only last week.'

Little episode? Is that all *you can say?*

She bit her lip to restrain her anger.

But, instead of faltering and giving in to this man's offensive appraisal of the crime, she held her ground and, for added effect, produced her League of St Francis ID. He barely glanced at it.

'There could be crucial evidence here,' she persevered. 'Can't your cleaning wait till I've called the police?'

The quartet looked at one another with those expressionless faces of the bored who spend their days clicking tills and stacking shelves. She knew all about that. The Spar in Wimbledon High Street to be precise. Almost her second home while at school studying for A Levels. Before France had pulled her back and changed her life for ever.

'OK. Ten minutes, no more. Then we get to work.'

'Thanks. It'll be sorted by then.' But that optimism now seemed misplaced, because once they'd gone, and she'd dialled Gandoux's *gendarmerie* number, an engaged tone met her ears.

Dammit.

For a moment she was tempted to go there herself. However, no way could she leave the site. She'd have to keep trying in the hope that someone was bound to answer soon.

Having also found the Albi cathedral line to be engaged, she made her way back up to the little store room, waiting for the sun to pierce through the thick blanket of white-grey sky. Smells of coffee and baking filtered through an air vent above her head, bringing on a sudden and intense hunger; the overpowering need to bite into something warm and comforting. Instead she found another radish in her pocket and munched on it, all the while watching to forestall any stray children tempted by the play area. She punched the Gandoux number again. Still no joy. It was useless. Never had she relied upon anyone else to get things done. Not her absent father, her busy mother. Nor even Metz...

If he'd changed his phone, he may not even be living in St Sauveur. Perhaps the Albi job had ended and his hankering for the coast, especially the port of Banyuls, where Aristide Maillol once had his studio, may have taken over. He may also have decided to leave Filou with someone on her home ground. However, all this conjecture was meaningless until she'd contacted Albi.

Having made her number untraceable, Natalie then dialled Belette farm to ask about Metz's whereabouts and to check if Bonneau was around.

'Yes?' A woman's croaky voice answered.

'Madame Bonneau?'

'Who are you? Have you found Samson yet?'

Found Samson...?

Time for some quick thinking, her first question now derailed. This was a gift, but a disturbing one nevertheless.

'What d'you mean?'

'He's disappeared. His herds are all over the place and I'm frightened if I step outside the door I'll be trampled just like he was.'

Natalie glanced round for any sighting of the boor, and despite a fresh fear leaching under her leathers, managed to sound normal.

'I'm sorry to hear this, Madame Bonneau. I simply wanted to speak to him about a new milk supplement we've developed at Duclerc. I'm Maya Peron, by the way. Sales representative for the Midi-Pyrenées.' She'd picked the biggest name in calf products including Vitacal and Bactrix. It was a risk to mention it but the old girl clearly had enough on her plate and was unlikely to check if her story was true. 'I'm in the Lot till Tuesday.'

'And I'm frightened.'

Join the club, Natalie nearly said once she'd got over her surprise. Then, to her huge relief, she saw a white *gendarmerie* van – plus blue light on the roof – snake its way through the crowded fuel

141

bay and stop in the car park.

'If it wasn't for those English people who've just moved into Hibou, I don't know what I'd do,' the farmer's mother continued. 'The man's very nice. I can tell.'

'Look, would you like to speak to the police?' she asked, jogging towards it. 'They're not far from me here.'

'No. No thank you.'

Her tone took Natalie aback.

'Or the vet? Another farmer, perhaps?'

She missed the click on the line as Liliane Bonneau ended the call and it was only as she reached the parking exit that she realised she was speaking to herself. So, unless his mother was lying, Bonneau wasn't there. But why that short sharp response to her perfectly logical question? Did he have a gun to her back? A hand around her throat? And then she realised that she'd not asked about Metz, or if Filou was pregnant.

Damn again.

She spotted a uniformed *gendarme* step out of the Citroën van, accompanied by the thud of a shutting door. She guessed he was in his late thirties, lean but fit, and, as he drew closer, Natalie wondered why he was heading her way when there were plenty of other people around. Could he see fear on her face? Did she look like the freak she felt?

Justice, remember? She told herself, standing her ground.

'A dog's been shot, down there,' she pointed towards the cross and both pairs of eyes followed her finger. 'She was strung up on that play sculpture. I've never seen anything so wicked. You've got to do something.'

'She? You mean a bitch?'

'Yes. Filou.' But why that slight hardening of his tone? Was he stressed? Too busy to deal with a mere dumb animal?

Then she noticed his eyes. The kind of blue you don't get in real life. They were in startling contrast to his eyebrows, and right now were fixed on her. Almost as if he recognised her.

'Where is she?'

'Follow me.'

She led the way past a small group of Portugese holidaymakers debating whether to stay or leave.

Better leave, she thought as he went inside the store room and came out holding the weighted red sheet between both hands.

'I'm convinced she belongs to Bernard Metz, the man that created the sculpture she was hung up on,' she added, as he hefted the so-far unexamined corpse into the boot and slammed the door shut. She could also have mentioned that she and Metz had been lovers, but not here. Not now. Maybe never. She wasn't stupid.

Despite the cold morning, the distinct sour-sweet death smell still lingered in the air, but closing her mouth to breathe through her nose only made it worse. 'I had a really odd call at seven this morning,' she began then relayed the whole story. 'But why me? And why wasn't whoever phoned me more specific?'

The officer didn't reply. His attention momentarily drawn to two Hell's Angels roaring away towards the *péage*. She raised her voice. 'I'd like

143

that call traced, if possible. I've an idea who it might be.'

'Who's that then?' Still keeping an eye out.

'Samson Bonneau, Belette Farm.'

'We'll need clearance.'

'OK, so please get it.'

'One step at a time. You can't go making rash accusations. We need hard evidence. Besides,' his laser-like eyes probed hers, 'there may be any number of people who might have had reason to commit this crime. I can assure you, nothing is ever as simple as it looks.'

Why did she feel queasy all over again? What was he getting at?

She nodded. Just then, that was all she could do.

'What breed of dog has this Metz got, then?' He suddenly changed the subject.

'Same as this. A Fauve de Bretagne.'

'Plenty of them round here. Specially with the Dutch who like to play at being farmers. My uncle's dog's the same. Like I said, they're *partout*.'

Natalie sighed. Although she couldn't risk handing this *flic* her connection with Metz on a plate, she'd not finished. She had to press her case. 'There's something else,' she went on, 'Samson Bonneau hates the sculptor for lots of reasons and now, according to his mother, he's vanished too.'

'I see.'

He was now tipping water from a plastic bottle over his hands and drying them on a grimy rag. She noticed their slenderness. The way they almost caressed each other. She felt her cheeks begin to burn. Anger approaching. Why wasn't he

144

asking about the when, the where? This was slapdash beyond belief, as if he'd been on duty all night. He certainly looked as if he could do with a shave. Perhaps this incident lacked the buzz factor, because so far, he'd not shown the slightest emotion. The reaction of what she considered a normal human being.

'I'd like you to take a look down there,' she indicated the play area. 'It looks like some blood's been dumped deliberately over Metz's plaque. I've already cleaned most of it away.'

'Leave everything to us, eh?' he suggested. 'Don't go getting involved. It could all backfire.'

'Backfire?' An odd word to use.

'I mean, confuse things. Now then,' he turned to her once again. 'What's *your* business here, by the way?'

'On holiday. I'm an English lecturer at Limoges University.'

'That your bike?' He pointed to the Suzuki, clearly unimpressed.

'Yes. So?'

'Your ID, please.'

She dug it out of her wallet and thrust it at him, not quite quick enough to retrieve her St Francis membership card or her knife which just then clattered to the ground. The *gendarme* got there first.

'Those are mine. Personal.' She reached forwards, but he angled the items away from her and, having glanced at her ID, began to read the other card out aloud.

'Natalie Bridget Musset, Number 8, Grade 2 Activator, League of St Francis. 24, Avenue Charles de Gaulle, Clermont Ferrand. I see.' He handed both back to her without saying a word. Yet she was sure his eyes had flickered on her name. Was it possible he knew about her past? St Sauveur was a small place and perhaps in some minds, maybe his, she was still connected to Metz. Maybe as a wronged woman, therefore a possible suspect? She thought of that wax model stuck with pins, in full view on her shelf. Evidence, surely, should anyone find it.

Then she realised she should have kept her mouth shut about Filou's markings.

His eyes were now focused on the knife. He deftly opened the blade with a clean trimmed fingernail and examined it more closely, turning its bone handle over and over as if to unnerve her. It was then, to her horror that she spotted a dark smear of blood along the blade's cutting edge.

'May I ask why you possess such a thing?' he asked without looking up.

'For my League work, OK?' she spoke too quickly aware that he wasn't missing a trick. 'In case I have to cut loose an animal that's been tied up. Phone my boss if you like.'

'I will. And in the meantime, I'd like to keep hold of this.'

'Why?'

'Security, *mademoiselle*.'

He tore a page from a blue-covered notepad. *Receipt of Goods*. Signed, dated. Illegible. Then he passed her the small lined sheet, holding it pincer-like at the corner, while she mentally prepared her defence.

'The reason there's some blood on my knife is because I wanted to find the bullet.'

'So you say.'

Her empty stomach contracted. She bit her lip again. Time to fight back, Natalie Musset, she told herself. To return the compliment. Show she wasn't a push-over.

'And who are *you?*' she challenged. 'Where's *your* identification?'

Half a smile. Perfect teeth. 'Major Râoul Belassis. Gandoux,' he said, opening his driver's door and getting in. 'Normally desk-bound but today too many of us are on holiday.'

I want to see your card, not hear your life story, she almost added, but managed to restrain herself.

'There we go.' He handed it over. The slightly blurred mug-shot showed how much weight he'd lost since it was taken. In fact, she decided, glancing up at his hollowed cheeks, his oddly waxen skin, he looked terminally ill.

The details confirmed he was indeed full-time with Gandoux. One of the Chiefs risen quickly through the ranks since starting there in May 2000. So, he could have known about her and Metz. She handed it back.

'What about my knife? I might need it.'

'You'll hear from us in due course.'

'Where are you taking the dog?'

'For examination of course.'

'Stuff you,' she muttered as the driver's door slammed shut. The van reversed before circling away out of sight. She then felt the twine in her pocket. At least she'd got something. She now had to find a bag to protect it. Having returned to the *boutique* and found a handy plastic *sac* by the pick-and-mix counter, she informed the impatient manager that the major had gone.

His cavalier attitude left her feeling bereft and angry. Even the sun beginning to warm her face, represented nothing less than total hopelessness. She stared at the play area, the fallen trees and what lay mysteriously beyond them. It was the kind of place she'd never let any kid of hers play in – not that kids would be on her agenda for a long while yet – but it was still deserted, as if any new arrivals to the service station's attractions had already sussed out its bad vibes.

However, that wasn't going to put her off, and if she had to do the police's job for them, then so be it. Her humiliating encounter with Belassis only strengthened her resolve, but as she made her way towards the blue train and the battered sports car perched on their rusty coiled springs, she suddenly noticed she wasn't on her own after all.

Someone was occupying the nearby phone box. A tall figure in working clothes who filled its limited space to capacity. A man, she was sure of that: his back turned towards her making it impossible to identify him. Whether he was using the phone or not, she couldn't tell, but this surprise discovery brought fresh fear. His body language clearly showed he didn't want to be approached so, still keeping him in her sights, she sneaked between two holly bushes beyond the toy car and immediately entered a world of moribund stillness where even the sun was invisible beyond the dense filigree of bare crowns. Every dry leaf, every stray twig crackled under her boots. It was impossible to avoid them, but each time her steps broke the silence, she held her breath.

There was little open ground now, just a narrow track resembling her broken Life Line, which an old palmist in Limoges had picked up on straight away. She'd have short relationships, the old crone had told her. Lapses of good health, and, worse, before she was thirty five, might well meet a violent death.

Afterwards, Natalie had run without paying from that musky top floor apartment, and the numbness that followed her forecast had lasted all week, spoiling her lectures, affecting her marking. Even now, a year later, that imagined final scenario was never far from her mind.

This track led into what once must have been attractive woodland and, before negotiating yet more fallen trees, she stopped to glance back at the play area. She could just about make out two service station staff members covering the cross in sheets of polythene, but more clear and more alarming was the empty phone box; the man inside it had gone.

Why did she think of Bonneau again? Would he really be hanging around here if he'd anything to hide? Yet why'd his mother's agitation now become hers – part of her already jittery nervous system? And what if he was to confront her here, in the middle of nowhere? She had no knife. No nothing.

Hunger fuelled her panic. Why not just get the hell out? Get her bike and go? It was still in the parking bay for all to see and, if that mysterious man *had* been Bonneau, he'd surely have noticed it. All the proof he needed that she was around.

Natalie froze, listening for every tiny sound. The

employees' fading voices, the brush of pigeons' wings against the larches' upper branches, and then came the overpowering sense that someone evil had in fact come to this very place. Someone who was still close by. And never mind an acute awareness of danger, she, Natalie, owed it to herself and the poor dog to get help and crank the slow wheels of French justice into motion. It was time to try Albi again.

CHAPTER SEVENTEEN

'Mummy's lost her pills,' Max bellowed outside the Volvo's misted-up door. 'She's just gone off on one. On her own.'

Tom woke from his second still-vivid nightmare of falling rocks, only to be faced with another. He cleared a patch of glass with his cuff to see the mess of tears that was his son's face. He fumbled for the driver's door handle and almost knocked Max over when he pushed it open.

'Where?'

'The field.'

'OK. Come with me.' He could have said the f word, or worse. Could have told his kid not to blub, but he didn't. He was too shattered.

Max's hand felt like ice against his; his sobs bringing white puffs of steam from his mouth. It was still bitterly cold, even at 9 a.m. and Tom removed his jacket to cover the lad's trembling shoulders.

'Where's Flora?' he asked.

'Asleep.'

A minor miracle at least. That car seat had not been a good idea: his legs suddenly felt eighty years old. The middle of his back worse than sore. And the fact that the apparently injured Bonneau had buggered off didn't help to improve his mood. Today was supposed to be the start of the Big Dig. The advent of their new life. Easter Saturday, 2002.

Dream on, he told himself bitterly as they both passed through the gateless gap into knee-high grass. And then tried to cheer himself up by recalling Hibou's first visitors.

'Who were those two who called last night?' quizzed Max as if reading his thoughts, parting the obstructing grass with his hands. 'Film stars?'

'Good Lord, no. The man's a major in the police. And the lady's an official in Gandoux.'

'What were they doing here?'

'You were around, son. You heard what they said. Just seeing if we were OK and needed any help. It's good to know someone's looking out for us. D'you know, that kind of thing would never happen back home.'

'*This* is home,' Max corrected him.

''Course it is. Silly me. Anyway, you looking forward to swimming?'

Max looked up, a broad smile across his face.

'Yeah. Cool. Is Didier a boff?'

'I don't know.' Tom resisted the urge to say that not all kids who liked school were boffs. Nevertheless, judging by what the clerk had said during the short walk back to the Jeep, Didier Keppel seemed to be something of a prodigy. But that wouldn't do Max any harm. Besides, who knew where a spot of networking might lead? Maybe his team leadership skills would pay off here after all.

He realised Max was slowing up. Holding back, studying a piece of dry cow dung.

'That's dirty,' he chided. 'Throw it away.'

'OK, but what about that bone Mum found? *That's* dirty.'

'In a different way, son. What you're playing with is animal waste, still full of bugs and germs...'

'Gross!' Max flung it into the air and watched it land further away. 'But it's weird how Mum really freaked out about it,' he said, sniffing each of his fingers in turn. 'None of us could sleep after that.'

Tom knew the 'us' wasn't intended to be hurtful, but it was. OK, so he'd managed a kip after helping the farmer's old mother and the strangers' visit. Big deal. He was bloody well going to need it.

'Where's the thing now?'

'Dunno,' Max shrugged.

'We mustn't lose it.'

'Why?' His lad looked up at him. 'Because it belongs to someone buried there?'

'Don't be daft.'

His bleary eyes cast around the brow of the so-called grazing land. Another sick joke. Everything had grown out of all recognition in the few weeks since their last visit, and now looked as if the wildest part of Borneo had been transplanted there. Plus, of course, its insect population.

Despite last summer's heat, every species of weed seemed to have flourished and the further on he and Max walked, ankle-height became knee-high with giant hogweed and the odd premature sunflower breaking into the sky.

'Look Dad.' Max pointed to the left where a trail of flattened vegetation seemed to be leading back to Hibou.

'Clever you,' Tom patted his head as they fought their way towards it. The rank smell thickened in his nostrils as they reached the easier terrain, and Tom realised that despite this newer disturbance, they must surely be on an existing animal track. Hadn't Bernard Metz told him and Kathy that his parents had once reared Limousins there after the war? That the Bonneaus had always tried to compete with them, and failed? But all that was a long time ago, and this was now, with not exactly another World War looming, but something pretty damned close in the Wardle-Smith family.

'Kathy!' he yelled, aware of an eerie, faraway echo.

'Mum!' bellowed Max. 'Where *are* you?'

'Don't worry,' Tom reassured him. 'She can't be far. So let's keep going. Six hectares isn't exactly the Serengeti.'

'I found that dead dog in a place like this,' Max suddenly piped up as the track that had first seemed so promising, now became part of the wild again. 'Did I tell you its neck had a hole in it?'

Tom started.

'You didn't tell me that.'

'I won't ever eat spag bol again, that's for sure.'

Tom gripped his hand. Pulled him up short.

'Man to man time, right?' He stared into the boy's big blue eyes. Max nodded, his curls, like

153

his face, in need of attention. 'We're all in this together: you, me, Mummy and Flora, OK?'

'OK.'

'So, we all help each other.'

'How d'you mean?'

'We don't go round making up stories. Especially nasty ones. D'you understand?'

Max's top lip quivered and Tom duly softened his tone.

'Mummy's not well, as you know,' he began. 'And we've not had the best start here. But things will get better. I promise. Meanwhile, we try and make life as pleasant as we can. Promise?'

But Max's face had changed colour. He turned away and, with surprising strength, tried to free himself.

'It's *true!*' he protested. 'And if you don't believe me, I'll tell everyone about the giant and what's in our cave as well...'

'What has Mrs Hemming written on every single school report of yours since you started at Oakdene? Go on.'

Max lowered his head.

'She said you had too much imagination. That sometimes you can't tell between what's real and what isn't.'

'No she didn't. She said that you're rubbish parents and I'd be better off with new ones.'

Tom looked at the bloated red face, that troublesome mouth, and something inside him snapped. He slapped his son's soft downy cheek, then watched his hand print darken.

'Ow! Daddy, don't!' Max took advantage of Tom's hesitation by head-butting his stomach before stumbling away into the thickest part of the field, where the sky disappeared from view and where nature's madness all too eagerly received him.

He felt sick, and it wasn't because of that knock to his stomach. Christ, he was losing it. Losing everything, if he was honest with himself. He heard the church bells invade the silence, designed, surely, to add to his growing guilt. Then, for the second time since arriving on French soil, he said a prayer.

Standing on tiptoe to scan the scene ahead, he was aware that while Max and Kathy had become part of this vegetative orgy, his daughter was still on her own at Hibou, probably waking up and panicking that no one was around. Needles in haystacks seemed a doddle compared to this.

He called out his wife and son's names. Loud at first, then louder, then listening to catch the slightest clue as to their whereabouts.

'I'm sorry I hit you, Max,' he yelled next. 'Come on, both of you, for God's sake.'

Bells again, drowning his voice, then all at once, the panting of breath – animal or human, he wasn't sure. He steadied himself for a possible dodgy encounter, then suddenly noticed the black-clad figure of a young woman fighting her way through the weeds towards him. A blue crash helmet under her arm. What was a biker doing here? he asked himself. And more to the point, what did she want?'

'Who the hell are you?' he barked, still tense, nervy.

155

'Charming, I'm sure.' Her English was accented, but was not it seemed, from this region.

'Sorry. I'm on edge, that's all.'

'Natalie Musset. Sorry too if I gave you a fright.' She set down the helmet in the grass and produced her ID. The photo showed a lively laughing face; an address south of Limoges which he and his family had driven through only yesterday morning. 'Are you Tom Wardle-Smith, by any chance?' she asked, her grey eyes squinting at him in the sunlight.

'I am. Why?'

'Your daughter said you might be out here, and I had to find you.'

'Flora?' he interrupted.

'Yes.'

'Is she alright?'

''Course she is. She's with your wife and son.'

'You're kidding. Where?'

She looked puzzled.

'Inside Hibou, of course.'

'Thank God for that. So,' as he surreptitiously studied the rest of her. 'Why did you need to find me?'

'There's no one else I can turn to.'

'What for?'

'I need your help. Madame Bonneau gave me your name. Said you were nice.'

'Better pay her something then,' he quipped, with no hint of a smile.

She ignored this and instead, bent down to wipe the remnants of damp weeds from her trousers. He noticed she was a real blonde with no dark roots visible. How her cheeks had pinkened when she straightened up and began her bizarre account of the day so far. He glanced towards Hibou for any signs of Kathy. This wasn't a good moment to be seen chatting to a good-looking young woman in black leathers. In fact, it could well prove the last straw.

'I've just found Metz's pregnant dog at the Florentin service station,' she said, finally. 'I know for definite it's her as Madame Bonneau's just told me she was expecting puppies.'

'Filou?' Recalling names was key at Prestige People. His speciality. 'So?'

'She's dead, *monsieur.* Someone's killed her.'

His mind flipped to rewind. The sculptor had made such a fuss of her when they'd come to view Hibou. What was she doing at a service station so far away?

'Are you sure?'

She nodded, her eyes filming over.

'I've tried to tell Georges Ninon who's been looking after her,' she went on, 'but he's nowhere to be seen. Madame Bonneau reckons he's lying low till Metz gets back, which is hardly surprising. And to cap it all, the police round here don't seem to give a toss.'

'Police?' He flinched inwardly at the word. 'Please explain.' This was supposed to be *Fosse Septique* day, not Get Involved With A Mad Stranger time, however stressed she seemed.

'Look, I'm begging you to come to the Florentin Services with me.'

'Why?'

'I'll tell you more on the way.'

'Tell me something now.'

157

'OK, because I need a witness. Another eye on where it happened. To see if there are any more clues as to who did it.'

The newcomer turned and began to walk back the way she'd come. 'It won't take long. Please.'

Damn.

The day was already slipping away, and without Bonneau, he'd soon have to start the bloody digging himself, as well as find a more permanent solution for the roof.

'You can see what I've got to get sorted here, and I don't know where Bonneau's got to. He's supposed to be making a start...'

The girl stopped in her tracks. Turned to face him almost accusingly.

'The farmer from Belette?'

'Yes. He's offered to lend us a hand. Seems to need the money, but Christ knows where he is now. I rang his old mother first thing and she hasn't a clue either. Maybe he's lost his memory after his herd went over him, gone walkabout somewhere. People sometimes do crazy things after an accident. Look,' he pointed towards the clobber piled up by the gateway. 'That's all his stuff.'

'I don't trust him, and you shouldn't either.'

Tom felt the force of her gaze.

'Why ever not? What d'you mean?'

'Sssh.'

They'd just reached Hibou. He noticed her earlier tension had returned and she seemed not to register Flora hanging round her motorbike, or Kathy and Max sulking in the *fermette's* shadowy interior.

Suddenly his companion gripped his arm.

'Just don't let him get involved with you here. You don't know the man like I do. His mother's a gibbering wreck down there. She's scared stiff of him.'

'Who's that?' Kathy stared out at them both from the open front door. 'Found yourself a bit of spare already?'

He winked at the biker in an attempt to make light of that crass taunt.

'I'm Natalie Musset,' said the young woman brightly. 'Pleased to meet you.'

But Kathy wasn't biting. Instead her mouth tightened to a dry pink hyphen while he explained where he was going and why.

'Please don't leave here till he gets back,' Natalie told her. 'Keep an eye on your kids. OK?'

'I don't need someone like you to tell me how to look after my children. The cheek of it.'

'You're right. I'm sorry.'

She then turned to him. 'Do you each have a mobile?'

'No. Only me.'

'Best to let your wife have it.'

'Excuse me?' she retorted.

'You might need one.'

Tom duly handed his over feeling more than a resentful twinge at being bossed about, especially in front of Kathy. Natalie handed over her number on the back of a fuel receipt, just in case anything should happen in their absence, but Kathy screwed it up into a ball, dropped it to the ground then reluctantly picked it up.

'Just get out.'

'I'm only trying to be practical.'

'Look, I don't know who you are or what you're after. I mean, for all I know this could be some kind of set-up. You could have an accomplice lurking somewhere. Christ, Tom, just get rid, will you?'

'I'm a lecturer, if you must know. Limoges University.'

'And I'm Queen Victoria.'

Tom felt queasy. The lack of breakfast didn't help. Not even a gulp of that Ricoré coffee Bonneau had left for them last night. And as for the family... He'd have to find a shop soon. A shop that sold Prozac or its closest equivalent.

'I'm scared,' said Flora, staring at the biker and then Bonneau's junk.

'What of?'

'Everything.'

She left the Suzuki and went indoors. He noticed her creased skirt, her dirty knees. Then Max stuck his head out into the daylight and blinked.

'I hate you!' he said.

Kathy glared at him, then Natalie.

'Don't bank on us being here when you get back, that's all. And as for that weird bone, I'm going to show it to the police once we've got a hire car sorted.'

'Hire car?'

'You heard. So I don't have to rely on you.'

'May I ask what bone?' Natalie interrupted.

Tom sighed. Weary wasn't the word for how he felt.

'It's nothing. She just found it last night, before going to bed. I mean, the place has been unin-

160

habited for years. It could easily belong to some tramp or other. Metz mentioned there'd been gypsies hanging around...'

'So, it's human, then?'

'Kathy seems to think so. I'm no biologist.'

'Let me take a look, eh?' And, before he could stop her, Natalie had mounted the four stone steps into Hibou's unlit interior. He watched her every move, her confidence highlighting how much of a failure he felt. How he was slowly losing the will to make everything come right. He saw her smile at Max, still flushed, still gripping Kathy's grubby fleece.

'Can you fetch it for me?'

'No, he can't. Anyway, what's it to you?' Kathy snapped. 'Isn't it enough you're seeing my husband?'

The girl stood her ground.

'Look, believe me, I don't do married men, and,' she glanced outside, catching Tom's eye, 'certainly not those old enough to be my ... my...'

Tom waited as she chose the rest of her words. What did it matter if she said grandfather? Get a life, he urged himself, aware of a blush creeping up his neck.

'...older brother,' she said finally, and his relief was so secret that he feigned offence.

'Great. Thanks.' Then he had an idea. 'Why don't we all go out together? And on the way we can call in on Madame Bonneau. See if there's any news of her son.'

Natalie frowned.

'I'm not sure about that.'

'Look at this dump. We've got to get started on

161

it. At least he's offered to help.' No way was he prepared to scaremonger about the farmer yet. He must steer as even a course as possible, otherwise there'd be no telling what any family fall-out might involve. Or who. 'Then when we've been to the services, we'll call into Gandoux.'

'For Mummy's pills,' Max reminded him pointedly.

'Yes. We'll find a proper *pharmacie,* then a supermarket. I made a list yesterday. Like the rest of you, I'm bloody starving. We'll eat like kings tonight. You'll see.'

'The bone,' Natalie persisted, as if he'd not spoken a word. 'Please, I need to see it.'

'I'll go,' volunteered Max before running off into the limestone cave beyond the kitchen. Seconds later, he returned, blinking into the light, pressing a hand over his nose.

'It doesn't half hum in there,' he complained, passing the thing over.

'Must be you,' sneered Flora.

'You wouldn't say that if you'd heard what I have.'

'What's that, then?' Natalie sniffed the yellowed specimen which to Tom looked more like a chicken's wish-bone than anything else. She then examined its every pore, every detail.

Max took a deep breath.

'I'm not making it up,' he said, 'but I keep hearing crying noises. Weird stuff. I tried to tell you before, Dad. You've got to believe me. Cross my heart and hope to die.'

'It's those computer games Granny keeps buying you.'

'Thanks for that,' Kathy barked, but Max was on a roll, his cheeks flushed with excitement. He threw Tom a challenging glance as his voice dropped, 'Dad doesn't like me talking about scary stuff. He told me to shut my gob. It's not fair...'

'None of it's fair,' Kathy was now leading both children towards the car. She gestured back at the *fermette*. 'What have we done to deserve all this? Do tell me.'

'I can't.' Nor could he say sorry, even though the merciless daylight showed up her unlipsticked mouth, her night-on-the tiles hair. When she used to set off for work back in Guildford, there wouldn't be a strand out of place; her make-up perfect and clothes always pressed, fresh on each day. But what good would apologies do now? The four of them were here, with good money in the bank to live on for the next thirty years if need be. There was probably some entirely rational explanation for the bone's presence. He had to give things a chance.

'And there's something else,' Natalie tapped the relic as if it was somehow significant. 'I've an uncle who studied dentistry. Used to love browsing through his anatomy books. I think your wife's right. This could be part of a human shoulder blade. It's tiny, mind.'

'Whatever it is, it's not good news.'

'Don't panic. Maybe some animal, even a bird, buried it.'

'Well, Hibou had been left empty for a while. Anyone could have got in.'

'There you go.'

'I'd still like to ask our vendor some questions

163

when he gets back,' Tom said out loud to himself, when in fact, that was the last thing he felt like doing. Bonneau's tools piled up nearby somehow symbolised that rosy future he'd boasted of to the Simistons, to his work colleagues and everyone else in that now faraway life. Was even this about to slip away?

It was bad enough believing what Liliane had revealed about her son's designs on the place, but worse, the implication that he, Tom Wardle-Smith and his family were about to live in the company of a decomposed corpse. A corpse which some-one not so far away might be anxious to recover.

The stranger checked her watch and, having handed the bone back to Max with a reminder he take great care of it, she made her way over to her Suzuki.

'Madame Bonneau first,' he said. 'I'll keep it short, mind.'

'Thanks. But can I check something out, too?'

'Sure.'

'You *said* we were going shopping,' whined Flora.

'What he says and what he does are two dif-ferent things, child. You better believe it.'

He saw the blonde biker watch Kathy and the children climb into the Volvo.

'I love your kids,' she turned to him, fastening her crash helmet. 'Especially Max. He's a proper little character, isn't he?'

'I could lose them all if this goes pear-shaped and, as you've just witnessed,' he glanced at the car where Kathy's pinched face peered out from behind the nearside window, 'my wife's already planning to leave.'

Apart from the Suzuki bike and his Volvo, nothing else was parked outside numbers 10 and 12, Rue des Martyrs. Both patently empty and, with their plain grey stone fronts, they seemed not unlike those memorials visible in the cemetery further along the road. Houses of the dead, Tom thought to himself, and shivered, despite the sun on his face.

He focused on number 12, the sculptor's home, where all four shutters were closed tight, while assorted plants that hadn't survived the winter filled a range of pots under the front lower window. There was no evidence of his craft in the front garden, or on any wall to relieve the bland yet immaculate rendering. Surely, he wondered, an artist needs all the publicity he or she can get? Even in this quiet place. He then recalled how, less than a month ago, over a glass of *anis* at Hibou with a large brown dog sniffing his crotch under the kitchen table, he'd seemed distracted. As if his mind was on other more exciting things than land registry information and the possible whereabouts of old wells. It had struck Tom at the time and, not without a small frisson of jealousy, that, unlike him, the older man had seemed full of plans and projects he couldn't wait to begin.

Not a soul about, and when he opened his window the only sounds to reach his ears seemed to come from Belette. He was aware of Kathy silently fuming beside him and his rear view mirror showed Max and Flora's heads together as

165

they dozed with their mouths open. So peaceful, so cute, that he couldn't bear to look at them any longer. Instead, he restarted the engine and kept it running as Natalie first of all tried the man's front door, banging the knocker down, ringing the bell, then that of his workshop at the side. She seemed extra wound up for some reason, and gestured for him to make his way to the farm without her, where he spotted Liliane Bonneau and an elderly man standing in the front yard deep in conversation.

His weatherbeaten face turned at the Volvo's approach. Unkempt, unshaven, he eyed Tom with suspicion. Or was it fear?

Tom pulled up the hand brake.

The kids woke up and immediately began to argue over Flora's last bubblegum and why couldn't they have a drink?

'Everyone stay put, OK? We'll be sorting you out soon.' He got out and walked over to Natalie, now busy leaning her bike against the stone wall near the tractor. Her movements sharp, decisive, and it was easy to imagine her out on the open road. One of those pests who weave in and out and think they own the bloody tarmac. The kind he liked to blast with his horn just to show who was really boss.

'Metz still isn't around. His car's not there. Nothing.' She interrupted his thoughts. 'Try and keep the old folks occupied while I sneak round the back, and please don't breathe a word about me finding Filou dead at the services.' Before he could ask why, she'd crept into the shade under the oak trees, her dark gear well enough camouflaged against their shadowy gloom. He joined the

166

elderly couple and waited for a chance to re-introduce himself to Liliane Bonneau. As he drew closer, he realised the previous night seemed to have dealt her more than one blow. Her skinny neck was striated by deep purple lines. Her sore-looking eyes half-closed as if keeping them open was too much of an effort. It was obvious that constant tears and lack of sleep had worn her out. Something they all had in common.

The old man, too, looked rough. His eyes bloodshot, as if he'd been crying.

'Has your son been home yet?' Tom ventured to Madame Bonneau. 'Is there any news?'

'No. And I'm having to pay for help to get the herd together. Most of the calves who could walk are loose as well, mind. It was terrible, *monsieur*. I can't begin to tell you...'

He nodded in sympathy, when what he really wanted to do was to put his arm round her and give her the kind of hug she'd probably never had. Then he noticed the biker signalling him to keep her talking. Why? he wondered. What on earth was she up *to* and what hadn't she told him? Maybe he should just leave her there. Drive away from whatever problems she'd got. Christ knew he'd enough of his own, not three yards away.

'I've been in the church since yesterday, but I'd best be going,' growled the old man. 'Père Julien told me to leave a message at Bernard's lodgings in Albi first thing this morning. Said it was best if I was honest about Filou being missing.' He sniffed loudly. 'But my friend's due back from Albi at four, and he'll want some answers. God knows, I kept her safe, Liliane. I always have, like

167

she was my own.' He wiped a moist nostril against his sleeve and the sunlight turned the snail trail of mucus into a shining thread.

So, *that's* where Metz has been, thought Tom as Ninon walked past, head low, leaving the unmistakable smell of urine in his wake. Just then Natalie appeared from the rear yard and followed Ninon, then tapped his shoulder. Her whispered questions seemed urgent and his replies seemed distracted. In the end, he merely shook his bald head at her and, having muttered something about a troublesome phone call, shuffled out of the gate without saying another word. Tom now knew why Natalie had warned him not to mention her recent find. The poor man was a wreck.

She returned to her machine looking pensive. Tom tried to block her from view, but was too late. Liliane's weary eyes were now fully open, peering round him, monitoring her every move.

'Why's *she* here again?' Not unkind, just curious.

'Again?'

'Yesterday it was her taking pictures. I saw her with my own eyes. Then this morning...'

'What pictures?'

'Samson's veal calves. He'd tried to get her off the premises earlier. Nothing I could do to help when she fell over, mind. I hope she's alright. I know better than to interfere, you see. That's my lot here.' She fixed on Natalie again. 'She's not going off to make more trouble, is she?'

'Look,' Tom placed a reassuring hand on her arm, choosing his words carefully. 'I don't know about any pictures, but I'm telling you, she's on your side. A friend of ours, too,' he lied. 'So please don't worry. By the way, if your son does show up, please tell him I'll be starting the job myself this afternoon. There's no pressure. I just hope he's not been hurt.'

'I'm praying every minute, if you must know, and, as God's my witness...'

A recurrence of the church bells drowned the rest and, as Tom followed the intriguing young stranger with his cargo of complaining kids and still silent wife out into the Rue des Martyrs, what little optimism he'd had seemed to be evaporating like the morning mist itself.

CHAPTER EIGHTEEN

'That's where the dog was.' Max pointed towards a thick bed of humus nestling between a circle of withered shrubs. Less than six paces in from the play area. 'Now do you believe me?'

'Yes. I'm sorry, son.'

'Apology accepted.'

The lad bounded away to re-join his sister, his feet lost in a swell of dust. Tom squatted down on his haunches to examine the ground. It didn't take long for him to detect dark red stains on some of the leaves, while a faint coppery smell still remained. He drew back, sniffing. His hungry stomach in turmoil.

'Looks pretty stale to me,' he said to Natalie, standing close by.

'So Filou was left here a while before being strung up. Whatever. It's disgusting.'

'I know Max is making light of what he saw, but it must be affecting him.'

'Kids are resilient. He'll be alright. Better he saw it than Flora.'

'You think so?' He looked up at her, impressed by her observation.

'Sure. She's the fragile one.'

'We're all fragile,' he said, aware of Kathy's gaze on his every move. Thinking that right at this very moment in Berris Hill Road, the Puri family would be moving in.

Twenty minutes later, with Flora and Max ensconced once more on the play area's toys and arguing as to why the main attraction was now concealed under polythene, Natalie led Tom further into the stricken wood, keeping the kind of distance between them both that even Kathy couldn't quibble with. She wanted to make sure that there were no other grisly finds, and no one dodgy hanging around. She'd told him about the guy in the phone box, how he'd suddenly vanished. How she couldn't go looking on her own. He'd hesitated. Glanced back at Kathy. She'd not said a word all the way there, and merely sneered when he'd offered to buy her some flowers and chocolates from the *boutique*. This was a losing battle alright, and he had to admit, it was something of a release to leave her behind. He found a stray branch and snapped it in half.

'How come you'd been to Belette yesterday?' he tested her once they were out of the kids' earshot.

'And why take shots of Bonneau's veal calves there?'

'OK, I'll be straight with you. I went to get proof that he's rearing them illegally.'

'Is he?'

'Yes. Big time. And I was hoping to leave today, until all this happened.'

Tom fell silent, their footsteps in unison as a sneaking unease began to grow in his mind. Questions he didn't feel he could ask, and answers he didn't wish to hear right now. Without looking round at him, she tossed her hair off her face, and he noticed how softly it hung, covering her black leather shoulders.

'Did you know that Bonneau's uncle Eric mysteriously disappeared?' Natalie said suddenly.

'Should I? Who told you that?'

She stalled as if he'd caught her on the hop.

'Liliane Bonneau. Last night. His body's never been found.'

Why did the air suddenly seem to cool? The wood seem to close around him?

'When's this supposed to have happened, then?'

'Back in the early eighties. Not a hide nor hair of him since.'

Hide nor hair...

Just those three words were enough to send an unwelcome tremor under Tom's stale clothes as she continued. 'And that's not including his father and grandparents. I tell you, it's one weird place. She even suspects her own son. Would you believe it?' The biker went on. 'It's unreal. Anyway, as for old Ninon, I suggested he try taking a shower.'

'Seriously?'

'No. I told him to get Metz to phone me asap.'

'And he agreed?'

'If a shake of his old head means yes, then he will. As you could see, he's pretty cut up. He also said he'd had a weird phone call about an hour ago. Some anonymous caller gloating that he'd soon be in trouble.' She glanced back towards the play area. 'I wonder if it was that man I saw in the phone booth earlier. And, if it was, I'll bet you odds on it was Bonneau.'

'Did Ninon speak to anyone in Albi?'

She nodded.

'Yes. He had better luck than me. Apparently, the woman who answered his call, said Metz had vacated his room at 6.30 a.m.' She pulled back the sleeve of her jacket to reveal a man's diving watch and looked up, frowning. 'It doesn't take three hours to get home from there. Even if it is Easter Saturday when everyone's out and about.'

'Maybe he's had to call in somewhere. See some official or other. After all, Ninon said he wasn't due back till four o'clock.'

'Not if his precious dog's gone missing. Not him.'

How could she could speak with such authority about someone she'd never met? Tom wondered as she too, armed herself with a stick to probe the undergrowth. Perhaps Liliane Bonneau had already mentioned the sculptor to her. That was the most likely explanation.

'God help them both when they find out what's happened,' she said, pulling a dried leaf from her hair. 'It's not going to be me breaking the news. I can't.'

As if to break the eerie silence that followed, Natalie then told him more about her own displaced background, her life as an English lecturer at Limoges University and her plans to be an investigative journalist specialising in animal welfare if ever she tired of the teaching. As she spoke, Tom's envy for her ideals, her freedom – yes, her freedom – seemed to grow. What had *he* got? he asked himself, brushing stray branches from his face. A wife hooked on a happiness drug, two kids whose murderous yelling now filled the air. A wreck of a house in the middle of bloody nowhere with a stray human bone hanging around, and, to cap it all, a seriously empty stomach.

'You know when I went round the back of Belette just now?' she interrupted his gloom.

He nodded.

'It's had it. You should have seen the mess. Jesus. The calf crates are all wrecked, the barn looks like it's been in a war. And as for the stock that's left... Do you know,' she slowed up and looked at him, 'I don't think Liliane Bonneau had any say at all in what went on there. She's just had to go along with everything he did. She's terrified of him, poor woman. Anyway, my HQ are getting vets organised. Some of the calves were just lying there in the back yard, unable to move. It was terrible.' She turned to face him, her eyes moist, yet unflinching. 'You don't eat veal, do you?'

'No, never.'

'I wouldn't even be speaking to you if you did.'

He could have said that breaded escalopes were Kathy's favourite whenever they'd gone out for a

173

meal, but now wasn't the time for that particular confession. Instead, he saw the morning slipping away as her black-clad figure dodged nature's debris and the kids' hubbub subsided.

'No one's been down here,' he said.

She looked defeated.

'So now what?'

'Follow me. I think we're missing the obvious.'

They retraced their steps to the play area where Max and Flora were sharing the toy train amicably enough, and Kathy now out of the Volvo, leant against its side in the sun; her face a blank mask in the brightness.

Tom looked away. Part of him wanted to reach her, another part was pulling him further and further away. He scoured the wood's edge once more and took ten steps in where he found a gap between two leaning larches, which revealed strategically placed snapped-off branches – their inner wood still raw, alive – supporting a mesh of brushwood and undergrowth.

'No storm did this,' he said to Natalie while taking a closer look. 'This is a hideout of some sort. Been made deliberately.'

'Kids most likely. I used to make things like this.'

'Pretty big kids then. Look.'

He felt his pulse quicken as he stared at the ground, because compacted humus inside the makeshift shelter bore traces of footprints. At least size 11. 'Don't tread on them,' he warned. 'They look quite fresh to me and may be important. But who'd want to hang around in this dismal place?'

'Someone we've got to find.'

That did it. His heart seemed to skip a beat.

174

'I need to see my kids.'

'They're fine. Can't you hear them?'

'You don't understand.'

'No, I don't.'

Tom turned on his heels and powered his way back to the play area. Where everything seemed normal. Kathy was still turned to the sun, and Max and Flora were now riding a springy toy apiece. This time next year he thought, they'd both be too big for them...

'You see,' Natalie's voice made him jump. 'They're in a world of their own.'

'Sorry. Didn't mean to snap at you.'

'It's OK. I understand. But I think we should tell the police about this shelter too. You never know.'

'Kathy's got my phone.' No way was he going to approach her. Not while a thin, plotting kind of smile lay on her lips.

'I'll do it,' she said, then, having dialled took a deep breath. 'It's Natalie Musset calling from the Florentin services. I spoke to a Major Belassis here earlier. Is he available?'

She frowned and slightly turned away from Tom. 'I don't believe this. OK, OK. So it's Easter...'

She glanced at Tom. Determination in her eyes. 'Don't you worry, I'll be chasing this up on Tuesday...What do you mean, no guarantee of anyone being available...?'

Tom pointed to the hideout to remind her.

'By the way,' she added, 'there's something else here. Blood and footprints. Big ones, right near the play area...' She pressed her ear to the phone listening hard. 'Four o'clock? Is that the earliest you can do? Give me a break...'

175

She then jammed the phone back into her pocket, looking fed up. 'Apparently there's been some pile-up near Villefort.' She turned to him. 'Look, I'll hang around till then. OK?'

'You can't. I won't let you.'

'I'm not your family,' her eyes began to glaze over, and just then he was tempted to say he wished she *was* family. That she might just be the one to save him from drowning...

'This Belassis. How did he come across to you?' he ventured, chucking the branch he had picked up further into the wood.

'Why?'

'He turned up at Hibou yesterday. After work, I presume. Him and a woman called Keppel. Clerk to the Examining magistrate in Gandoux. Very smart, wanting to be helpful.'

'My word, you were honoured.'

'You're not impressed?'

'What were they selling? Only joking.'

'Just wanted to see if we were alright. If we needed anything urgently. Said they could pull strings if necessary.'

'Great. Could do with them here. Mind you, I have to be honest the major did surprise me earlier on. Just didn't seem to care. As if he was dealing with some minor incident, not a butchered dog.'

'I'd say he's not the overreacting type. We had a guy like that at work. Ice Box we called him, but he did the business...'

'You could be right. But why would he...?' Here she stopped. Her lips clamped together.

'Why would he what?' Tom persisted, waiting as she gathered her thoughts.

176

'Take my hunting knife away with him?'

For a moment, that hidden place was far too quiet. Too full of unwanted possibilities. So, she'd had a knife. Who was to say she'd not got another? He made a move. Away from her.

'For God's sake,' she sighed. 'My dad sent it to me last Christmas when he knew I'd joined the League. My boss insists we each have one, but that's obviously not enough for Major B. He was playing mind games with me. Pathetic, really, except that it hurt.'

She followed him away from the shelter and again a frisson of unease made him quicken. Was she too close? Too familiar? This young woman he'd only met an hour ago.

'Did he try anything like that on with you?' she asked, and Tom sensed a ploy to divert his attention away from her.

'No. Not at all. Anyway, the Keppel woman's offered to have Max over to play with her kid this afternoon, which I thought was a nice idea. Help him settle and all that.'

'Where does she live?'

'Quartier Louis Pasteur. All modern, she said. No expense spared.'

'It is posh there, I've heard. So she's on a good whack then?'

'Must be.'

'Any husband?'

'She wore a big wedding ring.'

'OK.'

'Anyway, it's a start.'

'So's this.' She reached deep into her trouser pocket and pulled out a semi-opaque plastic bag, full of something yellow. 'The twine used on Filou.' Then her eyes fixed on his. 'Please don't tell a soul, promise?'

'Sure.' But he didn't sound certain; it wasn't only the twine's colour and texture that made him uneasy. Then, out of the blue, she answered his unspoken question.

'I had to take it, didn't I? Probably all the real evidence of that crime that's left.' She stuffed the bag and its contents back in her pocket. 'Trouble is, I've not seen this type at all. Whether it's from another country, I'm not sure. But what I do know is that Liliane Bonneau didn't want me to make contact with anyone about her son's 'accident.' Maybe she's protecting that evil bastard. Maybe *he's* behind everything that's happened.'

Her theory about the farmer caught Tom on the hop. How could she be so sure? OK, so Bonneau was a porn-lover, a rough diamond and probably one of many farmers not abiding by the book. So what? No big deal. Agriculture, like everything else was riddled with scandal and malpractice. But did all this add up to make him a dog-killer, as she was suggesting? And could Madame Bonneau be part of it all?

To his mind, no.

Yet in truth, he felt all at sea. About this young woman and equally, the farmer. His own impressions of the man who'd shown so much interest in his family – generosity, even, in his own limited way – simply didn't tie up with her imagined scenario. Then he remembered Max's account of the way Bonneau had released his thumb from the cross. The way his son had been so inhibited at

Belette. But what had Mrs Hemming emphasised yet again at last term's parents' evening, when he'd gone there on his own because Kathy had suffered muscle spasms after taking her last dose of pills?

'Max still has far too much imagination for his own good,' the teacher had said sternly. 'One day, believe me, Mr Wardle-Smith, it'll get him into a lot of trouble.'

Strong words indeed. Nevertheless, he resolved that he must at some point in the near future, take his son in hand. Have a heart to heart to find out what was really going on in that head of his. For now, though, there were other more pressing matters.

'Best get back,' he said, glimpsing Kathy coming towards them. 'Got quite a bit to do in Gandoux.'

'I don't know how to thank you,' his companion smiled again. A smile that seemed to highlight all his pain. His failure.

'It's not thanks I want,' he muttered to himself as he felt his wife's already hard stare hardening further. 'It's a lifebelt.'

'For God's sake, get the kids and let's go.' Kathy ignored Natalie completely. 'There's me feeling like death warmed up and all you can do is go swanning off into *that* place.' She waved a white hand in the direction of the wood. 'With her.'

'You're the boss.'

'Like Hell I am.'

Flora, meanwhile, was hitting Max with a length of broken branch; chasing him around the toys. Tom charged towards them, Natalie and

179

Kathy following.

'Cut it out you two!' he yelled, gaining on his daughter. 'Supposing you fall over? Supposing you need a hospital?'

Max turned to him, panting.

'Go on,' he goaded, undoubtedly for Natalie's benefit, 'why not thump *her* like you did me?'

Kathy took his hand. 'I should get the police on to your father for what he did to you earlier.'

'Yeah, look,' Max embellished, now the centre of attention. 'See my cheek. It still hurts.'

'I don't know what's got into you lately,' she said to Tom.

'Everything.'

Tom saw Natalie's gaze resting on him. She wasn't judging him, he decided. It was more a look of pity in her eyes and, seeing it, brought the sting of tears to his own.

'I want to go home,' wailed Flora.

'Me too,' said Max. 'Why can't we just drive off that way?' he pointed towards the *péage* going north. 'Please.'

'Haven't you forgotten something?' Tom reminded him.

'What?'

'Remember our visitors last night? What the nice lady said?'

Max shook his head. 'I don't want to play with anyone. I've changed my mind.'

'And you look a mess,' piped up his sister.

'Shut up.'

'Look, son, it'll be fun. She said you could borrow anything of Didier's that you wanted...'

He saw Max mouthing the boy's name over and

over as if preparing himself for the encounter, while Flora's sulk showed no sign of waning.

'Hey, you guys,' Tom mustered all the Prestige People-speak he could. He'd always suspected it might come in handy one day. But never here. Not now. 'Once we've cleaned you both up a bit in the *boutique*'s toilets, we're going to Gandoux to grab burgers, fries and whatever milkshake you like. And once Mummy's got her pills, she'll take you shopping. Your every wish will be her command.'

'Thanks,' she said grimly as Flora's eyes widened in disbelief.

'I mean it.'

'Yippee!' His eldest jumped up and down. Always a mark of her excitement. Max however, still looked stern. He asked if Natalie would be coming with them into town.

She shook her head.

'You have fun with your dad. I need to see Madame Bonneau again.'

'Why?'

'She may know more than she's letting on. And, anyway, if your mum and dad are agreeable, she can show that bone to the police. Be better coming from her than any of us. She's an old French resident who'll be taken seriously.'

'Who's to say she won't lose it?'

''Course she won't. I'll be with her. But I'll have to collect it from Hibou, if that's alright with you.'

Suddenly Max dug in his shorts pocket.

'No, you don't,' he said. 'I've kept it safe, like you said.'

'Creep.' Flora pulled a face.

'Good lad.' Natalie took it, at the same time

giving them both an appreciative smile. Then she turned to Tom, lowering her voice. That smile suddenly all gone. 'There's something else I've not told you.'

More secrets. She was full of them.

She took a deep breath. Crammed her crash helmet down on her head without looking at him and said, 'In case you're wondering how I know things about the Bonneaus, about Filou, and the rest...'

'I was. Especially how you knew she was Metz's dog in the first place.'

She still didn't look at him. Her voice steady but low enough in case stray ears might be listening.

'The sculptor and I were an item, OK? Over and done with. last September. Before he sold Hibou. Before all this...'

Then, without further ado, she jogged towards her bike and pushed it away from him up the slope.

CHAPTER NINETEEN

The dog's blood left in the bushes was more than a careless mistake, Bonneau mused to himself from his hiding place once all the fuss had died down. He should have brought a supply of water to wash away all traces and swore loudly to himself for his forgetfulness. The whole thing was getting out of hand. Especially since Musset and the *Anglais* were on the case, getting far too involved.

182

At least he'd witnessed all that. At least he knew what he was up against. He'd expected her to scream and run from the play area, not cause all this. It was a good job he'd returned here to check on things, and all the more reason for Step Two of his plan to follow sooner rather than later.

He stood up, pulling twigs from his hair, wondering where the cop had taken the dog and knowing from past experience that nothing, despite Metz's inevitable protests to people in high places – those who'd paid taxpayers' money for his trash – would be done. A bitch was a bitch. Worth little when alive. Less when dead.

His groin still ached from his mother's kick, while his head, made worse by a cold night out of doors, continued to disgorge black blood from above his left ear whenever he bent down.

Until he was in more open country there was nothing he could do except clamp one of his fingerless gloved hands over the wound.

He picked his way through the wicker-work of dead trees to the far edge of the woodland feeling as if death was lurking too close by, but if this was the price to pay for teaching the sculptor the lesson he deserved, then so be it. But things weren't finished yet. Not by a long chalk. It was this sense of righting wrongs, of clearing away the debris that had accumulated over the past few years, that spurred him on. However, he must regain control. That was his priority.

Suddenly the Florentin river came into view.

He soon found a shallow pool half-covered by mulched leaves, but clear enough in parts to enable him to wash his fingers again and, with a thin twig, to prise away the dark sediment from under his nails.

With his breathing still shallow, his lungs complaining, Bonneau continued down towards the river, while uppermost in his mind was that blonde meddler who might have spotted him in that phone booth. His troubles seemed to be piled higher than a plate of mussels at a seafood restaurant. And where would it end? He dared not think.

He stumbled down the grassy slope, which levelled out by the wide accessible river, unlike the more westerly stretch embedded in that perilous Gorge de St Arnac where his father had tumbled on to the rocks like any other piece of household rubbish.

He checked his watch: 12.23 p.m. Time to be back at Belette and the sooner the better. It had been risky enough having phoned Metz's house from the booth in view of everyone at the services. From now on he must be extra careful.

His head began to throb again as he lurched along the *randonée*, used by walkers, gypsies and pedlars, bypassing Loupin and over the river by means of a rattling wooden bridge. He suddenly felt trapped. Way out of his depth, like the foreign *foux* who came each summer to bathe their white bodies in 'his' river and who occasionally have the decency to drown. He'd go into Church to ask God's advice on what to do next. Then give his mother the punishment she deserved. But first, he must locate his van and make as speedy an exit as possible.

He parked the Transit at Belette and stumbled

along the Rue des Martyrs to the church of St Sauveur. The cemetery was deserted as he made his way round to the church's back door. The sun full in his eyes, the silence never before so unnerving.

The Ninon family sepulchre was first in the row behind those cheaper graves, all heaped up with plastic flowers, small resin models of young men skiing, in cars, on motorbikes. According to the framed messages stuck to the marble, they'd all died doing what they loved best. Yet in this unsettling land of the dead, their grainy black and white photographs told quite a different story. He'd known them all. How unemployment and drink had brought them here; in pieces. Unrecognisable even to their relatives.

Next, the FAMILLE FLAMAND-CORDES tomb and then the Bonneaus', which never failed to slow him up and bring a certain disorder to his mind. Its dark grey lettering contrasted with the bright oxide-streaked marble. There were three drawers still unoccupied, designated SAMSON ALBERT, née 1945–, LILIANE VICTORINE (NÉE LAMOTTE) née 1924–, and lastly ERIC OLIVIER, née 1919–. Little did anyone know where this miserable relative really lay...

He was just about to move on towards the church when the magnified sound of its bells once again reached his ears; each crash of iron on iron sending shock waves into his brain. Just when he needed to be on top of things.

Merde.

Alize Flamand was refilling a plastic water bottle near the cemetery entrance. He crossed

185

himself for his unholy thought: if only he had his rifle to finish off the nosy hunchback.

All at once his gaze fell to the foot of the Bonneau family tomb. He gulped, stepped back as if stunned, for there, where dead foliage lay strewn over a heap of hardcore destined for new pathways, lay Metz's bitch. Her dry tongue uncurling from her mouth. He looked again, frowning. Something was different. Her stomach had been slit open, her womb was empty. Its contents gone. He didn't stop to stare any further. Old Flamand was still busy with her flowers but could catch sight of him at any moment. Who the Hell had done this? Here, in the bloody public *cimitière* and right by the family resting place? And then the thought occurred to him that maybe, Metz himself had had the last laugh. But how was that possible? He'd witnessed the corpse being driven from the services by a *gendarme*.

The bells stopped and, fearful of attracting the old girl's attention, Bonneau slunk away, all thought of prayer abandoned. He manoeuvred his bulk between the huge limestone boulders that lay at the base of Le Fer à Cheval. However, instead of feeling protected by either this massive limestone shield or his faith, the veal farmer sensed only dark shadows looming. Shadows of treachery and death.

CHAPTER TWENTY

Mademoiselle Musset had stayed on Belette's front doorstep just long enough to realise that Liliane had nothing to add to the case of the poor dead dog, and to request that Madame Bonneau take the little bone to the police as soon as she could.

'Of course I will,' she'd replied. 'This afternoon, in fact. I have to collect some form or other from the *Mairie* for my son. So it won't be out of my way.'

'That's brilliant. Thank you, *madame.*'

The young woman then ended her brief visit by springing a rather odd question on her, which, in all honesty, couldn't be answered. Had Bernard Metz been seeing another woman after her? And if so, whom?

'I don't think so,' she'd replied. 'At least, I never saw anyone near his house. He seemed to be even busier that autumn. Away a lot of the time, as I remember. And as for now,' she'd shrugged her shoulders, 'I really can't say.'

Mademoiselle Musset had seemed so pre-occupied, she'd left without even saying goodbye. Strange such a question had seemed so important to her, Liliane had thought. Until Fritz came to mind.

She'd just wrapped the little specimen in an old woollen scarf and secreted it away inside her

187

basket when her son's all-too familiar tread across the front yard reached her ears. Where on earth had he been since the stampede? What had he been up to? And why had his van suddenly appeared, never mind the *gendarmerie* one that had scooted in and out of St Sauveur like a dose of salts earlier that morning?

She straightened, listening for the moment when he'd surely come inside the farmhouse, but no. Gratefully, she touched her rosary and muttered *deo gratias* several times, for there he was, visible from the rear landing window, loping away, apparently uninjured, towards the big field that sloped gently down to the pond. She breathed another sigh of relief, because most of the stock had scattered over the thirty hectares and, with no dog and no other help to herd them together, he'd be kept occupied for a good while yet.

Her thoughts then turned to Georges Ninon. He'd looked nearer ninety than eighty, sick with worry that Filou might have run off somewhere and become lost. If only he knew. But Mademoiselle Musset had been right. How could she tell him about her fate? She couldn't. It would break his heart. And, thinking of blood, where had all that near the back step come from? Maybe Samson had suffered an injury to his hand. Maybe his head. Please God, no. She'd once read about the effects of brain damage at the doctor's surgery. How would she cope with a possible personality change, when it had taken her all of fifty-five years to adjust to how he was?

Her free hand trembled on the banister's newel post as she made her way downstairs, all the while wondering if he might be implicated in these recent events. He'd known Mademoiselle Musset was one of the hated League of St Francis, and judged Metz to be the devil incarnate. All the more reason to keep herself safe, observe as much as she could of his behaviour and to think hard what she should do about Samson's blood-stained trousers she'd found hidden in the store yesterday morning.

Liliane drew breath on the bottom step, feeling trapped in a net of fear and suspicion. Just to hear the girl's motorbike roar away from the farm towards Hibou reminded her how different her plight was now from that summer spent on Fritz's motorbike all those years ago. She'd loved its noise, its smell. The soft air caressing her skin. The way he'd turn to look at her with those big dark eyes...

Merde.

There was also the matter of the mouldy rye bread. Supposing Samson should find the evidence of her wicked ways? She'd lain awake all night worrying about this possibility, and decided she should get rid altogether.

Meanwhile, there was the bone. Could it possibly be Eric's? It seemed far too small to belong to a full-grown man. But she was no expert and, given that no clue as to his whereabouts had so far appeared, anything was possible.

She should have suggested this to the girl. It was a sin to, if not lie, then withhold her doubts. Simply touching her rosary was too easy and God would surely now punish her?

She went into the kitchenette, pausing as she

189

always did by her late husband's old armchair. Suddenly, she realised something was missing. Albert's pipe and hat. Where on earth could they be? She searched everywhere, moving the heavy armchair this way and that, to no avail. Her anger over this apparent loss drove her with greater fervour towards the cupboard under the window where she hid the rye bread.

Its door, which Eric had knocked up from old floorboards, was jammed, and for yet another anxious moment she wondered if Samson had already guessed about the rye bread and secured it fast, but no. With one last tug on the little wooden handle, it opened and she withdrew the nearest packet. How deceptive are appearances, she thought as she unwrapped the moist, grainy loaf then sniffed it, wrinkling her nose. The first slice seemed normal, as did the rest. The ergot well concealed. It would only have taken weeks at the most, but as she'd already reasoned, that would be far too quick, far too easy.

First a furtive glance to check her son was still safely out of the way, then having emptied the shelf of the other fermenting packages, she placed them in her shopping basket alongside the bone to dispose of later in one of the many public *poubelles* in Gandoux. Her next port of call. The bus would be at the stop outside Belette in forty minutes. There was no time to waste. She rested her worn-out knees on the edge of the little window seat which faced out over the front yard, and prayed to the Holy Mother to forgive her sins.

'Eighteen dead, ten to be shot. The rest for dog

190

food. It's over.' Bonneau stood in the shaft of light from the kitchenette's one window, which highlighted his crimson-clotted head wound, his grim mouth. Liliane kept her distance, setting the table as silently as possible. He'd returned just as she was about to leave. Now the bus was on its way north without her. The bone and rye bread lay vulnerably in her basket by the door. Her outdoor shoes on her feet.

'We'll manage somehow, son. It's not the end of the world,' she said. But it was. Her throat still felt sore from his latest attack. Her plans for the day ruined.

'Don't give me that rubbish.' His black eyes scanned the stove then the table. 'And where's my meal?'

'It's nearly ready. Cold today, I'm afraid, son.'

'What d'you mean, cold, you lazy old nothing? I need something hot after what I've just been through.'

'And what's that?' she asked as she brought over a baguette and began slicing it into four long chunks. 'Have you been up to no good?'

'Why do you ask?'

'Because those blue trousers of yours that I found in the store yesterday, won't come clean you know. They should have had a long soak in salt.'

He stared at her. That look again. The slight narrowing of those hateful eyes, his big body that had once come from hers was coming closer, closer.

'And so should you, you interfering witch. How about the pond, eh? No one'll ever find you in there.'

She gasped, snatched up her basket just in time and headed for the stairs, losing one of her shoes on the way. Twelve steps lay between herself and the relative safety of her bedroom.

One... Two... Three...

'And what's that nosy *Kraut* bitch been saying to you?' he bellowed after her. 'What kind of muck has she been spreading about me?'

The *Kraut* word stung like a dart.

'Nothing. I swear it. Anyway, she's not German. That's just her bike's number plate...'

Four... Five... Six...

'She just called in to ask if I'd seen the *Anglais*, that's all.'

'Liar,' he wheezed from the bottom of the stairs. 'Like you've always been. Even Uncle Eric detested you, remember? Always trying to make him what he wasn't. Telling all the widows around here that he wanted a wife. And the rest.'

A pause. Making her mind's pain worse.

'And where were you about to disappear to with those shoes on, eh?' He threw the abandoned one at her. It hit her bottom hard. 'Up to some more mischief?'

Now, she could say it.

'Your van went missing from the farm the day your father died. Don't think I didn't notice. Just like at five o'clock this morning. And what have you done with his pipe and hat, eh? Troubling your rotten conscience, were they?'

The death sentence was now closer than ever.

Seven... Eight... Nine...

A sudden tug on the hem of her dress made her pull away. Then he was swearing again. There

192

wasn't time to dwell on that cruel taunt about Eric. She'd loved him almost as much as her own Albert, and had only wanted to see him happy...

Ten... Eleven... Twelve... The basket felt heavier by the second.

'Mercy, Jesus. Mercy...'

'He won't help you. And I bet that Musset bitch doesn't know it was you who kicked me in the nuts. Made me fall under the cows.'

Her own door. At last. She was just too quick for him and managed to slam it shut and turn the big rusty key in its lock before his bulk shoved against the thick-slatted oak. Once, twice, then a groan of frustration left his throat.

She could have opened her window under the eaves and called for help, but silence had always been her best ally. It confused him. Denied him the punch ball he needed. Like treading air, she supposed.

'I'll count to twenty, and then, God help you, Mother, I'll shut that lying mouth of yours for ever.'

Liliane looked out between the drab curtains and half-open shutters to the quiet street beyond the yard, her pulse like that of a trapped rabbit. He'd nothing to lose, had he? It wouldn't matter what he did to her, and this realisation sent a violent shiver through her whole body, together with the fact that there wasn't a soul around to help. It was only when she noticed Hibou's roof at the top of the opposite hill that she knew what she must do.

She discarded the one shoe on her left foot and found a different, older pair. Then, having

193

struggled to tie the laces, stealthily pulled both upper and lower sheets from her bed and knotted them as tightly as she could together. If only her fingers hadn't been shaking so much. If only she felt stronger.

The bells again. Half past twelve, and still he was outside her door, breathing as loudly as might a dragon while she tied the first sheet's corner to the shutter's inner handle. She barely weighed more than one of his calves, and now she was grateful she'd never been a glutton.

'What are you up to in there?' her son growled, as she tucked her rosary safely down the front of her black dress. The one she'd worn almost every day since Albert was found dead. Making each day a day of mourning.

The first kick vibrated the door. The second caused a fissure of orange wood to appear in the middle panel. This was accompanied by a blood-curdling yell, enabling her to part the shutters and wait, poised for his next onslaught before making her move.

But nothing came. Instead, she heard whimpering and cursing in turn, growing fainter and fainter. Had he finally given up and was going downstairs? As if in answer and, to her huge relief, she heard the back door slam so hard it shook the whole farmhouse, bringing a shower of dead flies down from the beam.

Silence, in which she returned the sheets to the bed, smoothed down the cover and willed her breathing to calm down. Then, having closed the shutters, she picked up the basket and placed her ear to the door. Still no sound, so she ventured on to the landing and crept towards the rear window, all the while keeping a watchful eye on the stairs.

Vite! she urged herself, once she was outside the front door, remembering how she and the black-haired Fritz used to race each other in the Forêt du Diable. Now she imagined him alongside her once more, breathing encouragement as she crossed the road and began to climb, hidden from view by the *jardins'* overgrown boundary.

She should hate Fritz Brandt for what they'd produced between them. But how could she? He'd been the only man before Albert to ever think anything of her. To show her that a life did exist outside her strict Catholic home, and that love with the 'enemy' was possible. She'd even learnt German, along with many in her town. Not like them, for self-advancement in a future German state, but to prove to him that apart from useful hands in the kitchen, she possessed a mind as well. She'd learnt about the Danish philosopher, Kierkegaard, of Goethe and the paintings of Fritz's favourite artist, Caspar David Friedrich, whose depictions of small solitary figures set amongst nature's vastness had represented to her then as now, how despite the church's comforts, we really are alone. And right now, as the bells ceased and she struggled towards Hibou with Samson's threats still in her ears, she did truly feel more alone than ever.

All at once she spotted his familiar tractor looming large at the top of the plateau. Then his shovel and other paraphernalia for work on the family's *fosse septique*. The excuse for him to be

195

there, legitimately part of their lives. She must remember to tell them about the new laws on mains before they hand over any money. Apart from anything else, it was despicable he was pulling the wool over their eyes about this unnecessary expense.

She threw the mouldy rye bread as far as she could into the overgrown jungle at the top end of the *jardins*. Next, aware of her rapid heart beat, she looked for the brown car. For the girl, even, because her bike was there, and her crash helmet. *Merde* twice over. Where on earth could she hide from her son? Out in that overgrown pasture or in the *fermette* itself? Just another look at those enormous tractor tyres and imagining them crushing her like an ant was enough to make her hobble towards the dilapidated building.

Within a few minutes, having chosen the low, empty window nearest the wall of rock as her point of entry, she and her basket slipped from the light into a dank darkness. She felt a spongy sensation under her worn shoes and moisture seeping between their soles and the uppers that chilled her skin. This was damper than she recalled from the old days, and not so much cold as an icy evil that pervaded every part of her. She must find somewhere else to hide, or she, too, would be joining the ever-growing army of the dead.

She groped her way through to the kitchenette and the main room, where daylight delivered a shock. She stared at the bareness of it all. The decrepitude. Compared to this, Belette was Versailles and this comparison brought a deep shame for what she'd allowed her son to do. For when Nicolette Metz had died, he'd begun to help himself to the *fermette's* contents. Bit by bit at first, then, once the sale to the *Anglais* had gone through, all the furniture and fittings found their way deep inside his Store.

The sculptor had blamed gypsies, presumably never suspecting that the successful farmer living close by in the same hamlet could have stooped so low. Like thieves at *les ventes du charité*. Nor did he ever learn that his mother's carved oak *bateau* bed had fetched sixty thousand francs at an auction near St Antonin Noble Val. Far enough away not to arouse any suspicion, except that a few days later, she, Liliane had found the bill of sale and the crumpled catalogue in Samson's trouser pocket.

But what could she have said or done about it? No, she told herself. One whisper out of turn and *her* bones, too, would be lying undiscovered somewhere. Just like Eric's. She saw her dead brother-in-law's old stained mattress, a dingy car rug, two pairs of children's shoes and a colouring book showing a half-finished picture of four lambs trotting into Noah's Ark. A tear formed in her eye as she turned the pages to the frontispiece where she read,

To Darling Max. Have fun. Mummy XXX

Poor people. They couldn't have known how much Samson had wanted Hibou. They didn't know to what lengths he might go to drive them away.

Her tear became two, then more, blurring her vision as she made her way back towards the cave, and whatever else its pungent darkness might reveal.

197

CHAPTER TWENTY-ONE

The mediaeval town of Gandoux perches high on the Colline des Chrétiens, and is surrounded as far as the eye can see by hectare upon hectare of still-brown vineyards which have thrived there since Roman times. Like so many other expanding towns, the administrative centre of the St Arnac department, twinned with Caladra in southern Spain, is a mix of old and new, with four recently built apartment blocks for upwardly mobile professionals positioned in such a way that they seem to stand guard over the Quartier Louis Pasteur's nest of narrow crowded streets. The 1987 storm, which had destroyed many of its ancient rooftops, left the Église de St Marc's spire tilting perilously over the dwellings below.

Now fully restored, complete with stone gargoyles hewn by Bernard Metz's chisels in a much less abstract style then his usual work, this church, a potent symbol of earthly failings and promised redemption, dominates the skyline. These grimacing infant faces still distract passersby and have caused more than one traffic accident since their installation, while students of sculpture come from far and wide to pay homage to the local man's craft, wondering whose portraits, if any, they represent. For his part, he remains reticent as to their meaning, thus fuelling all manner of interpretations. They are angels in torment;

devils returned to the fold; innocents burdened by Original Sin, and so on.

However, on this particular Saturday morning, Tom was far too busy trying to find a parking slot to notice them. He wondered how Natalie was getting on. Natalie, whose life seemed to resemble the layers of an onion. He also tried to imagine what kind of a man Metz really was, and what had attracted her to him in the first place. How had it ended? She'd not said.

Meanwhile, the events of the past few hours had left him with an inability to separate the concrete from the imagined, truth from lies, and, as he finally spotted a space near the Hôtel de Ville, a moment of madness gripped him. Hell, why not do a runner? Ditch Kathy and the kids in the newly opened McDonald's opposite, and fly as free as those greedy seagulls amassing near the town's market stalls. What was to stop him?

Something was. A biker whom he'd only just met. A thirty-year-old he barely knew.

'There's a *Pharmacie,*' Max called out, bring him back to cold reality. 'And it's open.'

Tom saw the boy's nose pressed up against the window glass. He turned to Kathy.

'You'll either need an old prescription,' he said, 'or our E111.'

'Don't you tell me what I need,' she snapped back at him. 'Damned nerve. I want Dettol, Jif, a gallon of bleach and four cans of insect spray. One for each of us. And that's just for starters.' Her hand was already wrenching the car door handle as he waited for a Berlingo to manoeuvre out of the neighbouring space and, before he could suggest a rendezvous for later, she was outside, urging Max and Flora to follow her. However, their son was plainly full of surprises.

'I'm going with Dad, remember?' he resisted her hand. 'Natalie said.'

'Natalie, Natalie,' taunted Flora. 'She's too old for you. Baby.'

'Anyway, *I'll* be swimming. Not you.'

She stuck out her tongue and Max reciprocated.

'Make sure you're back here in two hours,' Kathy shouted to Tom. 'And keep a close eye on Max – if you're not too busy eyeing someone else up and down, that is.'

'Mu–um.' Max protested before Tom could. 'I *can* swim you know.'

Tom pulled the Volvo's handbrake up with more than a sense of despair. She wasn't going to let up on that one, he could tell. Something she'd never accused him of in their old life. Yet there'd been women a-plenty at Prestige People. All ages, all skirt lengths. She knew that. Had even socialised with some of them, no problem. Eight hundred miles had certainly changed things in every department. For the worse.

Soon the Hôtel de Ville would be closed. Also the bank, and most likely the *gendarmerie*. He pulled the E111 insurance booklet out of his wallet and handed it face down to Flora; the happy family featured on its front cover being too much for him to stomach.

'You promised we could go *proper* shopping,' she whined through his window, passing it to her mother. 'You said we could have what we liked.

200

Not just cleaning stuff...'

'I meant it. Look. Take this.' His fingers struggled to extract a wad of euro notes for her, but too late, the twosome had already gone. He saw them waiting at the cobbled kerbside of the Rue St Marc, backs turned towards him for the traffic lights to change in their favour; their shadows merging with those of the crowds on the other side.

'Hey, can I have some of them?' Max eyed the notes being slotted back into the wallet as Tom climbed out of the car.

'Treat you later. OK?'

'Look, there's a McDonald's. I'm starving.' He pointed over the busy road where the all-too familiar logo dominated its neighbours.

'Join the club.'

Suddenly an ear-blasting dose of Berlioz from somewhere preceded a crackly announcement about some forthcoming fair or other. Public brainwashing, Tom thought when he'd calmed down enough to spot its source. An overhead tannoy attached to a nearby streetlamp. No one else had reacted. Just him, it seemed. He felt as though the plate tectonics of his world had shifted too far apart, leaving a chasm swilling with nerves and apprehension.

'Let's go,' he said to Max, who'd stopped by a rotating poster display of forthcoming regional attractions. Alongside a mug shot of Nicolas Grazès, the local Front National candidate, lay an enlarged engraving of a Charolais bull advertising a Bull Fair in Loupin on Easter Monday.

Was this the event that had just been so noisily promoted? If so, it might be worth a visit.

'Dad, why's that bull's willy so big?' Max's podgy finger rested on the creature's penis, which almost reached the ground. Tom smiled to himself. A first since yesterday morning. It felt strange, almost indecent, given what had happened so far.

'Tell you one day, son, but for now, just listen to me.'

'I am.'

'I know you've already met the lady, Madame Keppel, but when we're in there with her,' he indicated the double doors at the top of the flight of marble steps, 'don't interrupt me, and if you're asked anything, no fibbing.' He took Max's hot hand, squeezed it affectionately and, within one minute they were inside a cavernous tiled foyer and heading towards a sign marked Reception.

'Can we go to that Bull Fair, Dad?' Max looked up expectantly. 'It'll be cool.'

'I don't see why not. We'll ask the others later.' In fact, something like that would make a welcome change. A chance to get out of Hibou and meet some more locals. The downside was he'd probably have to give Max some kind of sex education. He was just about to say sorry to him again for his earlier loss of control, when he spotted three other people converging on that same office. He lengthened his stride and got there first. No way was he going to wait in any queue. Not with his agenda.

Felix Laurent's clerk was apparently still on the phone but, true to her word of yesterday, she agreed to see him. He and Max made their way up to the second floor. Pauline Keppel, dressed in the same hound's-tooth check jacket as yesterday, seemed genuinely pleased to usher them into her high-ceilinged domain, where the hum from two computers on her desk was the only sound in that oasis of soothing calm. A row of certificates bearing her name and credentials hung from the nearest wall. Tom noticed their dates spanned the last five years; that all proclaimed excellence. He also noticed that same musky perfume she'd worn on Friday evening, lingering in the air.

She wasted no time in seating them both in front of her and, having thanked her once more for her solicitous Friday night visit, Tom then relayed events so far.

When he'd finished his account with Max thankfully silent throughout, the clerk twirled her gold pen between her fingers. The pen matched the tiny crucifix lodged in the hollow below her throat. Her neat stud earrings. Her elaborate ring on the wedding finger.

'So, who are you implying phoned Mademoiselle Musset about the dog?' she asked, fixing her liquid basalt eyes on his. The effect of this made him pause. He'd been used to blue for so long. There was something about her. Definitely. He'd felt the same at Hibou. A kind of magnetism...

'Samson Bonneau, I suppose. I don't know.'

'There is *le corbeau*, of course.'

'What's a crow got to do with this?'

Keppel leaned forwards. A hint of cleavage between her suit lapels.

'Much of this region is a primitive backwater, *monsieur*, and St Sauveur is no exception. A place

203

of sluggishness, inertia, where envy breeds like the plague. Several instances of poison pen letters, untraceable phone calls, minor vandalism and thieving have been reported to us from there during the past few years. I'm thinking particularly about the loss of your furniture. And, as for this other matter...'

Here she paused.

'Yes?'

'I will certainly pass on your concern to our friends in the *gendarmerie* and Major Belassis, of course, but please, let me emphasise that this kind of thing is not uncommon. However,' she half-smiled, 'I've been told the police will be at the Florentin Services at four today.'

Word spreads fast, he thought.

'Incidentally,' she watched Max all the while, 'we only have Mademoiselle Musset's word for all this. Why isn't she here herself?' A dark furrow bisected her forehead as she waited for his answer.

'She's waiting there for the police,' he replied, as the clerk's pen finally moved across a sheet of official headed paper leaving a trail of blue loops in its wake. 'Can't risk missing them.'

'I'd be interested to know of her relationship with Bernard Metz,' said the woman suddenly, sending shock waves through his system.

'Relationship?' he feigned ignorance. 'What d'you mean by that?'

'Exactly what I said.'

Her eyebrows rose.

Where the hell was this leading? He had to think quickly, yet at the same time, be careful.

'That's news to me.'

She kept her pen poiscd in mid-air, whether deliberately for effect, he wasn't sure. 'Monsieur, she was once very close to our sculptor friend. More than very close, I'd say.'

Clearly warming to her task, her writing was growing apace. She looked up. A half smile on her lips.

Tom saw Max fidgeting with his T-shirt. Screwing up its front into a tight knot.

'He's due back from Albi this afternoon and, if I may say so, with regard to this whole incident, methinks the lady doth protest too much. After all, he ended the relationship. It must have affected her.'

Tom tried to keep his surprise to himself. Wondering why the man had done that.

'Natalie may have finished with him,' he countered.

Despite the heated room, he felt cold. Unsure what to think any more.

'I hardly think so, *monsieur*. Consider it. A man in such great demand. Doing very well with any number of important commissions. Handsome too, in a typical Causses kind of a way. You know, when jealousy's involved, anything's possible.'

Tom shook his head, yet hadn't he felt a certain unease in that undergrowth by the play area? The need to keep his distance from the stranger?

'I'm only surmising, *monsieur*,' the clerk went on. 'And Major Belassis has just confirmed that the knife she was carrying did have bloodstains on it and will shortly be undergoing tests.'

'Tests? This is absurd.'

'And I'd urge you to suggest to her that she

doesn't stray far. She may well be needed for questioning...'

Tom saw plain stupidity written all over the official's unmade-up face. But stupidity implies an innocence, he reasoned, and there was nothing innocent about this woman's innuendos.

'This is ridiculous!' he banged his fist on the edge of her desk. 'Mademoiselle Musset loves animals. She wouldn't hurt a fly.' He glanced across at Max, who must have surreptitiously helped himself to a ballpoint pen from the clerk's desk and had drawn a pair of black lips in that cleft of skin between thumb and index finger. The effect, when it moved, was grotesque.

'She *fancies* you, Dad,' Max said simply, avoiding his eyes. 'I'm not dumb.'

Tom felt the blood leave his face. That pale green room now resembling a swaying sea with his feet unable to feel the bottom. He gripped the arms of his chair and tried to stand. Loneliness now too gentle a word for how he felt.

'And another thing,' added Max, pointing at the paper on the official's desk, obviously secure in the presence of a third non-parent party, 'my teacher says big writing's childish. She makes us do it again, if we don't get ten words to a line.'

Exasperated, Tom drew in a deep breath, but he saw a tight little smile stretch across the woman's mouth.

'We never stop being children, Max,' she looked up at him with a benign expression. 'That's the trouble, don't you agree?'

Her desk phone began to ring and she snatched up the receiver with a practised hand, almost as if she'd been expecting the call. Her dark eyes rested on her expensive-looking watch.

'Keppel here.'

Tom strained to listen to a man's voice which, to him, even a desk away, sounded like muffled bursts of gunfire. The woman frowned, then without speaking, replaced the receiver and dialled another number. Amongst her rapid French, he detected the words *'incident'* and *'péage'* followed by *'quel dommage.'*

'What's going on?' he asked. He could tell from her face that it was somehow related to him. 'Something's happened, hasn't it?' He thought of Natalie, then of Flora and Kathy. In that order. He couldn't help it. In fact, if he was honest with himself, he couldn't help anything. She gestured for him to wait. Finally she finished her call and stood up to join him round his side of her desk.

'Go and look out of the window,' she said to Max. 'There's a good boy.'

He obeyed and Tom saw his filthy socks gathered round his ankles; his matted curls after a night on that bed. He'd not let Kathy stick his head under the *toilettes* tap at the *boutique*.

'Two things.' She kept her voice low. 'Bernard Metz has been involved in a traffic accident, and secondly,' staring over at his son, 'it's bad.'

He gulped and not just at hearing Metz's name. Max was peering through the window's slatted blinds. He looked so small, so vulnerable that Tom wanted to grab him and hold him safe for ever. Then he remembered something Natalie had said.

'Was it at Villefort?' he asked, noting her sudden look of puzzlement.

'No. Not there.'

She twisted her pen cap back into place, her eyes now on his. 'I'll certainly pass on what you've told me to Monsieur Laurent,' she said. 'In the meantime, for your family's sake, be careful.'

'What's that supposed to mean?'

'Trust no one. Oh, and by the way, if you have time, do go and take a proper look at the church. Monsieur Metz has certainly helped put it on the map. I just hope he'll pull through.'

'What about the swimming?' asked Max. 'I got washed specially.'

'Another time, *hein?* I'm sure my Didier will be disappointed too.'

With that, she gathered up the single sheet of paper, now covered with her jottings, slotted it into a black briefcase by her chair then called Max away from his post.

Tom didn't remember leaving her office. Nor hoisting a sulking Max on to his shoulders to cross the road and ask for directions to the town's main *gendarmerie*. However, what he did later recall was an unease that had seeped into every corner of his mind.

The bells from St Marc's church tolled more solemnly than those of St Sauveur, matching his mood as he steered his nine-year-old up along the main shopping street towards a grey single-storey building from whose roof hung a faded Tricolor. He wanted to call Natalie, but Kathy still had his mobile and where were any public phones when you needed them, for God's sake?

No sign of her either, or Flora, but at least en

route he and Max had both devoured a Big Mac and a carton of fries apiece. The food felt solid, comforting in his stomach, and he could easily have eaten another portion.

Max's lips were still reddened by the burger's relish as they walked up a wheelchair ramp leading to a side door marked *Entrée Publique*, where a notice stating *Samedi – Fermé à 1400 hrs* hung protected by black wire mesh. Twenty minutes to spare. Tom looked around the razor-wired compound at the rear for any sign of the white Citroën van that Natalie had seen. But there was nothing to suggest that this was the home of the Commune's principal police force.

He wiped his son's mouth with one of Flora's old Pooh Bear handkerchiefs, then reminded him again not to speak out of turn. No good telling the lad off for his last performance, he told himself, because Max was the kind of boy who'd be worse next time round, just to see how far he could go. Especially now their rudderless boat was already miles out to sea.

They made their way towards a glass-screened reception desk, behind which lurked a uniformed *gendarme*, whose angular cheekbones reflected the computer screen's green glow. Tom registered two family photographs showing a striking young black woman holding a dark-skinned baby, then a nursery shot with that same child lying on a rug.

After the formalities had been conducted through a slatted gap in the glass, Tom realised the thin, strained-looking guy with the widow's peak, was none other than Major Belassis. Just as yesterday, his English was far superior to his own

209

evening school French. All the more reason, then, to get the thank yous and other formalities out of the way and try for some answers. And he mustn't use Natalie's Christian name, he told himself. Keep it businesslike.

'Mademoiselle Musset says you removed Bernard Metz's dog from the Florentin services at 8 a.m. this morning,' he began. 'Is there any news yet as to who might have shot her?'

'*Monsieur,*' the major fixed his ice-blue eyes on him. 'I appreciate your interest, but such matters are, at the moment, confidential.'

'Madame Keppel assured me she'd be examined on Monday.' A lie, but so what?

The man's expression changed. His features tightened, those arctic eyes imperceptibly hardened.

'You mean *Mademoiselle* Keppel?'

Tom nodded, puzzling to himself why, if she was single, she'd worn that elaborate wedding ring. On Friday evening as well. She'd also got a kid.

'Why speak to her?'

'Mademoiselle Musset was getting nowhere when she phoned here. We found a possible hide-out and distinct footprints at the service station. Someone needed to know.'

'We have already agreed to meet up there with your friend later today. I don't understand her agitation...'

'She's agitated because you've kept her knife.'

'Ah.' The *gendarme* transferred his gaze to his screen. A forefinger tapped out thirteen letters. Tom counted. Took a guess: Natalie Musset... 'We have a job to do, *monsieur.*' He suddenly turned to look at him. 'You, as a new resident in our country, would expect nothing less.'

Tom felt wrong-footed, uncomfortable. But he wasn't quite ready to leave just yet.

'Is it true that Metz has been in an accident on the *péage?*' he asked, watching for the slightest reaction. A pause. The man swallowed. His Adam's apple slipping up and down his throat.

'How did you know?'

'So, it *is* true.'

Belassis's gaze returned to his screen. He pressed a few keys and immediately his cheeks' colour changed from green to blue. The effect was oddly unsettling.

'Is he still alive?' Tom pressed.

'We're waiting for news.'

'Where's he now?'

'I can't say.'

'Was anyone else was involved?'

Another gesture, meaning go away. Or was it *allez, étranger?*

Tom bristled. Sod this for a lark. He let go of Max's hand and pressed himself closer to the glass slats. Bonneau and the baler twine in Natalie's pocket could wait.

'Look, it's been implied that Mademoiselle Musset may have a problem with him.'

'Who has implied it?'

'Guess.'

'I don't like your tone, *monsieur.*'

'Tone rhymes with bone,' piped up Max, clearly bored by the whole encounter. 'And I found a one in our cave...'

Tom nudged him to be quiet. That had been for

211

Liliane Bonneau to mention. Not them. But too late. The major fixed on him again as he placed a lean hand over the pc's mouse.

'What kind of bone?'

'Human. Our friend Natalie thinks it's part of a shoulder. Whatever, it's pretty small.'

Tom cursed his son for having said her name. He'd seen how the *gendarme's* eyes had flickered with recognition.

'*Natalie* Musset?' he quizzed.

Max nodded again. 'But it was my mum who found it,' he said. 'Kind of sticking up out of the ground, she reckoned.'

Two arched eyebrows rose towards that peak of dark hair, and Tom couldn't help thinking of a rhesus monkey he'd seen once in Cologne zoo.

'Where's this cave exactly? I don't recall seeing one yesterday.'

'Beyond the kitchen,' Tom explained tetchily. The day was disappearing. 'It goes deep into the Fer à Cheval rock. We're planning to turn it into a cool room.'

'When exactly was this specimen found?'

'Last night.'

'Nine thirty seven,' said Max impressively.

'And where is it now?'

Tom and his son exchanged a glance. The boy let him speak first.

'We gave it to our neighbour, Liliane Bonneau, to bring to you. She's French, lived in the hamlet for ages. Thought she might carry more weight. After all, you and Mademoiselle Keppel are among the few people I've met here who can speak English...'

212

'I wouldn't do any renovations for the time being,' the man added distractedly. 'At least, not until we've taken a proper look.'

'You'll hear the crying, then,' Max informed him. Tom bit his lip. Kept his cool.

'What crying?' Had the major suddenly paled, or was it the overhead strip light's sudden brightening?

Tom pressed a hand on his son's shoulder signalling that enough was enough, and fixed the *gendarme* with one of his 'let's cut the crap' stares, used to such good effect at work.

'Look, as you could see from yesterday, we're up to our eyeballs in problems...'

'That's why we're here, *monsieur*. Why we called in on you.' The major stopped fiddling with the computer's mouse, pulled a square of paper off its block and scribbled some words then a phone number on it. He passed it through the slats, face downwards. 'Now,' he gave Max a strange smile, 'if you don't mind, I have much work to catch up with.'

Tom took his son's hand and just as they reached the door, he read what the man had written.

Major Râoul Belassis. Tel: 05 88 43 12 76. Trust me.

'That's the first time you've mentioned any crying.' Tom paused to tie up his shoelaces outside the *gendarmerie*.

'Flora's heard it too. It's scary. Like a baby...'

Tom let it go. Instead, he wanted to go back inside and say what was really on his mind. Natalie had been let down and it wasn't just because of the language issue. It was being a foreigner in an-

213

other's country, where you could, with varying degrees of subtlety, be kept in your place. He'd not thought of that when he'd slavered over the blue-sky *Maison À Vendre* pictures on the net and in *Live France,* but now an overpowering sense of exclusion burned at his very core. He had to see the sharp-suit again in the Hôtel de Ville, to try and twist her arm about Metz. If what she'd said was true, this was getting too close to home. First there was the dog, now Natalie's ex...

As he and Max were re-tracing their steps up towards the Hôtel de Ville, the nine-year-old suddenly pulled on his hand.

'Hey, Dad. Look up there. On that church.'

Although a bloody church was the last thing on his mind, Tom humoured him by turning his gaze upward on the nearest gargoyle which seemed newer than the rest, its stone slightly lighter, jutting out against the sky. He saw the open, functional mouth. The large round eyes, almost inviting him to enter its world...

'Very nice,' he said. It was one o'clock, and there was still the bank and Right Move to chase up.

'Dad, look,' Max yanked his jacket sleeve, pointing a chubby finger at the sculptures. 'They're all babies.'

'Don't be daft, son.'

'They *are*...'

'You mean angels?'

'Funny looking angels then.'

Tom stared again at their rounded foreheads, the fleshy features and formalised quiffs of sprouting hair above each ear and realised that maybe Max could be right. There were certainly no wings nor any other holy trappings visible, and each seemed subtly different from its neighbour.

'Who *are* they?'

'I've no idea.'

'Can't we see the rest of them?'

'Look, I've got to chivvy up the removals firm. Do you want your own bed tonight or don't you?'

'I'm not fussed.' Max still pointed resolutely at the gargoyles. 'Please...' And before Tom could restrain him he was inside the church's porch, pushing open the vestry's double wooden doors into the building's dark, cold nave.

Tom sniffed. That perfume again. The same as in Hibou yesterday and the Hôtel de Ville. He knew he wasn't alone. He spun round to see Pauline Keppel gesturing towards a Merc parked by the kerb, its raised badge on the bonnet sparkling in the sun.

'Come, Monsieur Wardle-Smith. We'll have the swimming after all. I couldn't bear to see the disappointment on Max's little face.'

'But I thought...'

She rested a hand on his arm. The lightest of gestures.

'I do apologise for my haste back there in the office. I tend to be impulsive, you see. Blame the pressure of my job, if you like. Some days I'm too busy even to breathe. You see, my previous boss took a lot off my shoulders, but Monsieur Laurent is different. Laid back, as you say in England. Who gets called for questioning by him is largely down to me.'

'Really?'

'Oh yes. So I have to get things right.'

'Of course.'

Tom immediately thought about Natalie. Maybe he should warn her of what he'd heard. Maybe not...

'By the way, *monsieur,* as you seemed so concerned about the Metz accident, let me reassure you, the police are fully operational and will keep me fully informed. And we will pray. Meanwhile, my son is waiting. He, too, would have been disappointed not to have a companion for the afternoon.'

'Are you quite sure about this?'

'Of course I'm sure.' She checked her watch. 'But I can't stay parked out there for long.'

Tom peered into the nave's gloom ahead and filled his weary lungs.

'Max? Come back at once!' The echo of his voice combined with Max's tread, filling the whole dismal place, and an old man at prayer nearby looked up at him with a disgruntled expression on his face.

'Ssh,' he urged. 'Or God can't hear me.'

'Tough,' Tom muttered, striding past him over the chequered stone floor towards the altar. 'Max?' he called out. 'For Christ's sake, get back here.'

'This is a house of prayer not a school playground,' came a voice of such restrained hostility that Tom stopped in his tracks. 'And I'd therefore ask you to show some respect.'

A priest stepped out from one of the side chapels, a flickering candle in his hand. Tom saw how it shook. How his mouth, too, seemed to tremble at each corner.

'I'm sorry,' he began, aware of a knot forming in his stomach, because Max was still nowhere to be seen. 'My boy's just run off.'

'So I see.'

'He wanted to look at those other gargoyles. You know what kids are...'

'You should have restrained him.'

The remark surprised him.

'Why?' he said.

'Are you *Anglais?*'

'Yes.'

'One day you'll find out. But for now, please respect our church.'

Tom stared after the man's straight back, his fit muscled body as he returned to what he now realised was the Lady chapel, and knelt down by its marble altar.

All at once, Max appeared out of the darkness, the whites of his eyes startlingly luminous. Normally Tom would have clipped him round the ear, but not with Pauline Keppel waiting, silhouetted against the sunlit street outside.

'You're going to see Didier after all,' Tom hissed, escorting him back over the huge black and white tiles. 'So, no more antics. Promise?'

'I promise.'

CHAPTER TWENTY-TWO

It was music that Tom heard first. Faint subtle sounds reminding him of his public school. Bach's 'St Matthew's Passion,' he guessed, which the Head always pumped around the corridors on the last day of the spring term. This particular work had always unsettled him. Like those Flemish crucifixions of which the Louvre and National Gallery had more than their fair share. Turning you into a sinful voyeur. Sinful because you were kept at arm's length, powerless to intervene. All you could do was stare agog at the points of piercing where drying blood leaks from the thorn, the spear. Wonder at how mere brushes and oil paint can render flesh so real...

He also wondered where the Bach was coming from. Her silver car, of course. As immaculate as herself.

'I'm convent educated,' the clerk explained with a winning smile as her pristine garage doors closed without a sound. 'I've never shaken it off. Not that I'd want to, you understand. Bach was a genius, don't you think? And to me, music like that is the closest we'll ever get to Heaven.'

'Where's the pool?' Max suddenly interrupted, letting go of Tom's hand. He'd not stopped goggling at this luxurious otherworldly enclave since getting out of the Volvo, embarrassingly out of place amongst the other sleek models occupying

218

the residents' parking bays. A new Range Rover with *Bébé à bord* in its rear window. A metallic blue Boxster. Two Passats with Swiss plates.

'*Attends*,' she removed her sunglasses and slotted them into a slim gold case. He noticed her gold ring still in place. Wondered whether he should now address her as *mademoiselle...* 'You'll never guess how close it is.'

In fact, despite the four high-soaring apartments arranged in a spacious square beyond the garage's courtyard, he picked up the whiff of chlorine.

'Amazing place,' he said, mentally comparing it to Hibou and its overgrown environs. Here there wasn't even the smallest weed and he did wonder if the strategically placed potted palms were real.

'It's useful for work, that's the main thing,' she gestured to the rear wall of the honey-coloured Hôtel de Ville, just visible beyond the lock-ups. 'I usually walk there in the summer.'

'Speaking of work,' he ventured, 'can I ask if there's any more news of Metz or his dog?'

'*Monsieur*,' a hand rested for a second on his jacket sleeve and another smile followed. 'We are here solely for pleasure. So, how about making a start?'

She led the way round the nearest block and Tom shielded his eyes against the building's extra whiteness as tarmac became tiles; textured slabs of red and green stretching away to a sliver of the most startling blue he'd ever seen. Apart from the Virgin's robes in his school's chapel stained glass window. Was this real? he asked himself, as Max rushed forwards, tripping momentarily then

219

righting himself without a murmur on his way to the water.

'Hold on, son,' he called after him. 'Be careful.'

'See how excited he is.' Keppel acknowledged two women drinking coffee at a nearby table. They smiled indulgently after him, then resumed their conversation.

When the trio reached the poolside, she stopped to rumple Max's curls.

'If you can wait just a few moments, I'll go and fetch Didier and some towels and trunks. OK?'

Max nodded and the moment she left he began pulling off his filthy trainers. Black dirt fell from inside each one on to the tiles and Tom immediately bent down and dispersed it by hand.

'Thanks,' he called after her, puzzled by trunks plural. Was he expected to change out here and swim with them, too? The natural thing to do as a father, of course. However, he was experiencing enough vulnerability without exposing his pale body to all and sundry. Especially such a confident and, he suspected, controlling woman.

His questions were soon answered by the splat-splat of unseen bare feet on the tiles. He spun round and blinked. Behind a skinny red-haired lad in black shorts came someone he hardly recognised. Her gold swimsuit matching her watch, ring and crucifix, luminous in the sunlight. Her skin...Well, her skin...

'Didier,' she began. 'This is Max Wardle-Smith and his father. They arrived from England yesterday.'

'Yesterday? Wow.'

Max nodded and the boy dutifully held out his

hand. His stance shy, his smile uncertain. The freckles covering his nose made him look younger than twelve. Yet there was also a certain maturity about him. A knowingness.

Prestige People again, and how to spot a winner or a loser. An anarchist or a brown-nose. Tom mused to himself how long it would be before he lost that ability altogether.

'Dad, it's brilliant here,' beamed Max, snatching a pair of trunks and a fluffy white towel out of Didier's hands. 'Can you swim?' he asked him. But his mother answered first.

'He's Gandoux's junior champion. But he'll never tell you that himself.'

'*Maman...*' the boy protested, then held the towel while Max changed. Two youngsters clearly getting on instantly. However, Tom's relief at this and the fact there were no trunks for him soon turned to anxiety. Kathy's command about keeping an eye out, was ringing in his ears. Where was the shallow end, if indeed there was one? OK, Max could swim two widths, but he always needed to be able to feel his toes touch the bottom. Problem was, he mustn't embarrass him about this.

'How deep's the pool?' he asked instead, as Keppel took a hand in each of hers and headed for the steps.

'*Da-ad,*' Max hollered, aggrieved. 'I *can* swim you know. Three lengths. Deep end and all.'

Tom noticed he was shivering.

'It's all level, *monsieur,*' she said. 'You'll see. When Max stands up in the water, his chin will be clear of it.'

Pride gripped him as he watched his boy bravely

221

follow his new companions into the blue. The couple now leaving their table began to clap and Tom joined in despite himself. His watch said 3.20 p.m. Plenty of time for his boy to have the fun he deserved. And Flora, he hoped, was enjoying herself, whatever she was doing. And then, he resolved to treat them all to the Bull Fair on Monday.

Perhaps now, things were looking up, albeit in little ways...

Keppel was lithe, graceful; there was no denying that. As if she used a gym, kept to a good diet. He'd heard about the Atkins diet from Kathy and she'd planned to start it before Christmas. Not that she needed to. She'd lost two stone in weight already since the French idea had germinated.

Kathy...

He wondered if she and Flora were buying new clothes, treating themselves to what they wanted, and if Natalie would spring any more surprises. Surprises that might bring more turmoil into their lives.

He watched the happy scene in front of him and, for the first time since the ferry crossing, a sense of calm descended.

In that rarefied world where only the intermittent calls from one swimmer to another broke the silence, time passed as if someone up there had speeded up the clock.

4.35 p.m.

Kathy had said four o'clock.

Tom, who'd been sitting on the pool's edge dangling his white feet in the warm, soothing water, sprang up.

'Hey, Max!' he shouted. 'Time to go, old son.'

Max turned round. He was piggybacking on Didier's freckled shoulders while the clerk was completing yet another length of the butterfly. His face said it all. Five minutes later, he was dressed once more in his dirty clothes, his hair just like when Tom had first seen him an hour old. Darker, stuck to his head. His skin too, bore a pink glow and seemed to shine. But his eyes were blinking back tears.

'You can come again,' said their hostess, giving her own hair a rub before tying the towel in a knot around her midriff. 'Flora, too. And don't forget, *monsieur,* when it comes to choosing schools for both of them, don't hesitate to contact me. I do know the best ones...'

'Thanks. I will.' He patted Didier on the shoulder. The rounded bone hard under his palm. 'And thanks to you, as well.'

'It's OK. Max is great.' They shared a playful punch before separating.

'When our house is ready, you have to come over to us,' Max said.

'Absolutely,' said Tom, aware of seconds slipping by. Keppel consulted her watch. An expensive one, he guessed. And waterproof.

'If you'd excuse me,' she said, smiling wet lips. 'I too need to get organised for tonight. *À bientôt, tous les deux,* and see you again soon.' She strode away, hips swaying under the towel, as if she owned the place.

'Bye,' said Max, then imitated, *'À bientôt.'*

'Come on, son.'

'Didier said I could call him Sandy, because of his hair.'

'And what's your nickname?'

'He's working on it.'

They ran back to the courtyard where the Volvo was parked and while Tom unlocked it, Max peered in through the Boxster's side window.

'Hey, that's such a cool car. Is everyone rich here?'

'Yep. Looks like it. Jump in now. We're late.'

He glanced left as he reversed out of the Visitor space for apartment 3 and saw Didier Keppel standing where they'd left him. A small figure getting smaller, yet with an unmistakable expression on his face.

Was it because he hadn't wanted them to leave? Or was it more than that? The one word that came to Tom's mind was 'fear.'

CHAPTER TWENTY-THREE

As soon as the old girl who'd been tending the grave had hobbled away, Natalie straightened up from her hiding place behind the Ninon family tomb. This beige-rendered block with interment dates going back to the mid-nineteenth century had given her perfect cover until the pair of wrought-iron gates had clanged shut.

When she'd arrived at Belette earlier, Liliane had mentioned seeing a white *gendarmerie* van head towards the cemetery. She'd also managed to

224

record the first two digits of its local number plate. Metz once said that in all his years of living in this quiet spot, he'd never seen any police vehicle go past his house. So, true or not, this was quite an event. Yet when she reached the graveyard on foot and made a quick survey of the scene, nothing seemed to be amiss. There'd not been a soul around until the old woman had arrived.

Her bad ankle still ached and her stomach hadn't yet recovered from seeing Filou that morning. It was still too vivid, too awful, and just as she edged out from the tomb, her mobile began to ring its Blur tune. The last thing she wanted to be heard in a place where even the tinkle of water cans by the gates was audible. Instinctively, she ducked down again.

'Yes?' Still looking for any signs of a police visit. Still careful not to make herself too obvious. The nearest dwellings on St Sauveur's main street weren't that far away and, for all she knew, someone else might even be visiting the cemetery but, like her, be hidden by the various memorials.

'It's me. Kathy Wardle-Smith. I'm wondering if you've seen Tom and Max anywhere.' Her strained voice magnified by a bad line. Natalie steadied herself against the nearest gravestone, tilting her head away from the sun. His wife knew damned well she'd made her own way back to St Sauveur, so why think he was with her now? Was she that suspicious or just not thinking straight? That's what Natalie preferred to believe.

'I'm sorry. I haven't. When were you last together?'

'Two and a half hours ago. They went into the

Hôtel de Ville and then...' her voice raised a notch, her words quickening. 'He was supposed to go to the bank and after that...'

'The *gendarmerie*,' she reminded her. 'So why not try there? Or, he's probably taken Max for something to eat and lost track of the time.'

'No, no, Pauline Keppel had invited Max for a swim with her son.'

Natalie had forgotten that. The dead dog had taken over her mind.

'Maybe they're having too much fun.' Then realised that wasn't a very tactful thing to say. 'Have you her private number?'

'You don't understand.' The Englishwoman's tone hardened. 'He's always punctual. That's his thing. In all our years together, he's never let me down in that respect.'

Natalie felt as if a great big fence had suddenly been dropped between them. How could she have known any of this? They'd been married for almost half her own life, for God's sake. Yet here was a man for whom she'd felt an instant attraction and had more than once, albeit guiltily, imagined sharing his bed. But if she was serious about him, then this was just round one and she'd better toughen up.

'Look,' she began, 'give him another thirty minutes. Gandoux's a crush on Saturdays. They've probably finished swimming and got caught up in the crowds.'

'I wouldn't be phoning you if I wasn't worried sick. Who else can I ask in this Godforsaken place?'

Natalie thought of her Suzuki deliberately left

at Hibou. She ought to feel flattered, but didn't. This woman was not to be comforted.

'Where are you now?'

'At McDonald's.'

'Wait there. I need to go to the service station first, but I'll be with you as soon as I can.'

The caller's reply was drowned by the church bells beginning their three o'clock peal. Prolonged and ear-blasting. Natalie ended the call and covered her ears as she made her move. She was just about to creep behind the northernmost row of tombs when she stopped dead. Her pulse leaping in her neck, her wrists, everywhere.

Here stood the half empty Bonneau sepulchre in all its glory. But that wasn't all. Not by any means.

'Filou? My God...'

She stared at the dead hound, flopped on a nearby lump of gravel, as fresh tears began to blur her vision and, it seemed, her reasoning as to who had brought her here and why.

OK, so she'd seen Major Belassis take her from that store room and drive away. Perhaps someone else had seen him. Waylaid him even. Someone with a grudge against Bonneau. It all seemed so implausible, but if that was true, then the whole picture was changing in a way she couldn't grasp. At least, not yet.

She eyed the corpse again. It was far too conspicuous, stuck out here like that. 'Obscene' was a better word. There were two choices. Take her somehow into Gandoux or hide her away from possible predators. Then another stray thought sprouted in her mind. If someone should appear right now, she could well be incriminated. Given her connection to both the sculptor and to the farmer...

Panic.

She glanced up at the church spire – one of the tallest in the region – and its oddly shaped bell tower resembling some giant man-trap.

'Please God. Tell me what to do.'

And he did. The only solution. She took a deep breath and, trying not to heave, slipped on her leather gloves and took hold of each of Filou's front paws.

'Come on, old girl,' she said, pulling the creature off the mound and over the gravelly path to an overgrown spot behind the nearest tomb. At least with gloves on, her bare fingers were spared the feel of soft brown fur or claws scraping her skin.

It was only then, with the corpse angled away from her, that she noticed the bitch's stomach. Nausea swamped her. She leant against the sepulchre trying not to be sick. Trying not to faint... Then, when she felt she could string enough words together, she called the *gendarmerie* in Gandoux.

'Major Belassis, please. Natalie Musset speaking.'

'Is it important?'

'Very.'

'I'll connect you.'

He took at least a minute to answer and when he did, his voice was accompanied by a growing din.

'Yes?'

'I need to know if you actually delivered Filou's

body to the *gendarmerie?*'

'Of course. Why?'

She hesitated. Something holding her back.

'Look, can you get here as soon as possible, please?'

'Where's "here"?'

'The cemetery at St Sauveur.'

A short silence followed. The background noise growing.

'Filou can't be with you. She's next to me, by the Bonneau tomb, for God's sake. Cut open. Her puppies gone...'

'I don't understand, *mademoiselle.*'

'Nor do I.'

'We have her safe in our laboratory.'

'Where's that?'

'I'm afraid that's confidential, but perhaps there's an identical dog in St Sauveur. I've already told you the Fauve de Bretagne's the most common breed...'

'No way. It's her, I'm telling you. The way her hair's parted above her tail, and the four dark spots on her gum...'

Damn. Despite her earlier resolution, she'd said too much. Given him a chance.

She was right

'So, you knew her well, then?'

She took a deep breath. Composed herself. 'Look, Major Belassis, could you possibly let me have the registration number of that Citroën van you drove this morning?'

'What are you implying, *mademoiselle?* Why exactly do you need to know?'

His voice more like the sharp edge of an iceberg

than anything human. Cutting into her resolve.

'Nothing really... It's just that...'

'Four o'clock, then. As arranged.'

Damn. Come on, girl.

'Madame Bonneau says she saw a *gendarmerie* van heading for the cemetery at eight thirty this morning. Nine Seven were the first two numbers on its plate.'

'How old is this woman?'

'In her eighties. What's that got to do with it?'

'Her eyesight may not be what it was.'

'Major, she was adamant.'

Any response was lost amongst an even greater hubbub. The *gendarmerie* sounding more like the Champs Elysées on a Friday night.

Don't give up ... keep up the pressure...

'Did you stop for fuel? Anything like that? Someone with a similar looking van must have taken Filou from yours. But why place her here?' She was shouting now. 'You ought to check it out, Major. This is getting weird. And I bet you, whoever did this, rang me this morning. Sicko.'

'You've had a shock, *mademoiselle*,' his tone more mellow now. 'I think you need to get away from there, have a coffee, meet a friend...'

'How can I? You don't understand.'

'I can assure you I do. Now, if there's nothing else...'

She thought of her absent knife, then Tom's wife. She should come first...

'There is. Has Mr Wardle-Smith called in to see you yet?'

'Yes. With his son.'

'His wife's worried sick. She needs to know

where he and Max are.'

'I'll ring her.'

Just as Natalie wondered how he'd got the Englishwoman's number, the major ended the call.

She returned the phone to her pocket, forced to admit that Liliane may well have been mistaken about the van. Also angry with herself for not having noticed the major's number plate for herself. The League's training emphasised acute observation for later record-keeping. That's why she'd memorised all Bonneau's number plates. Then she remembered the twine. More evidence that could well point to her. However, if she hid it somewhere safe, she could always find it later if need be.

She buried the plastic bag and its contents near Filou's body, whispered goodbye and dodged her way to the cemetery's entrance at the end of the main street. Georges Ninon's house seemed empty, and she wondered if he was still seeking solace in the church. If Liliane Bonneau had told him the truth about his charge.

Meanwhile, Bernard Metz's house and adjoining workshop seemed no different from that morning. As blankly still as if he'd never lived and worked there, nor she ever walked past the varnished door inlaid with dusty wrought-iron work and up the stairs to his bed. Or stroked that once affectionate hound who'd liked to lie by the gate. Feeling a mixture of loathing and cowardice, she quickened her pace to pass it, wondering once more why his phone number was unavailable.

Belette, however, was another matter. Here was now a hive of activity, with the noise of men and cattle in distress rising from the land behind the

231

farm. Three 4x4 vehicles and an unmarked covered truck stood parked in the front yard. No time to linger at the scene, however. Anyone might spot her, especially him. Her photos must have done the trick. The promised vets had arrived. And who knew where this could lead? What other aspects of the man's murky life would be uncovered?

Natalie silently thanked God that her machine and crash helmet were still where she'd left them at Hibou. So, too, was the farmer's tractor, looming large against the sky. She pushed the blue helmet down over her hair then just as she was about to mount the Suzuki, she noticed with a start, Liliane Bonneau's familiar figure standing in the *fermette*'s open doorway, as if driven there by some peril from inside. She was visibly trembling. Her face too fearful to even acknowledge Natalie as a friend, while her fingers clenched and unclenched on her basket.

'What on *earth* are you doing here?' Natalie challenged her. 'I thought you were going to town.'

'Samson was in one of his rages. I couldn't. I had nowhere else to go.'

Bastard, she thought, tempted to go and challenge him.

'Your neck looks bad. Did he do that?'

Liliane tried to cover it with her hands.

'I had a lucky escape, thank the Lord.'

Minutes were ticking away. Natalie took a deep breath. The poor old girl would have to know sometime. Better coming from her than some

232

gloating gossip.

'I'm sorry to have to tell you this, *madame,*' she began, 'but I've just found Metz's dog dumped in the cemetery. On your family tomb.'

Liliane whitened. Her dry lips parted in disbelief. She gripped the nearest doorpost.

'That can't be true.'

Still that little old head shook in denial and when she saw tears cloud over those weary eyes, Natalie stroked her thin trembling arm. 'I'm only trying to get to the bottom of all this. You must tell me everything you know. Please understand. Did you see who was driving that *gendarmerie* van?'

'No. It went by so fast. As God's up there looking down on us, I'm telling the truth. But when I next meet Alize Flamand, I'll ask her. She's the eyes and ears of St Sauveur, that one.'

'Where does she live?'

'Number 30, Rue des Martyrs.'

An idea for her next port of call.

'I think I saw vets at Belette,' she said. 'Did you know they were there?'

'No, but if I had, I'd have told them to give him the final jab.'

Natalie blinked. So, she hated him, too. And for all she knew her son could be lurking around Hibou somewhere. Hiding in the overgrown pasture, or even in the dwelling itself. Maybe that's why the old woman seemed so afraid. Then Kathy's plea returned to haunt her and for a brief moment she felt frustration that Liliane Bonneau was stopping her from simply riding away.

'Have you still got that bone?'

'Yes,' Liliane held out the basket, pulled back

233

her old scarf, then crossed herself. 'And more from that cave behind the kitchen.' Her free hand dipped into the basket to emerge as a closed fist.

Natalie wished she'd not left her bike here after all. Especially as those knobbly fingers were now uncurling to reveal four yellowed pieces of vertebrae followed by a blade-shaped specimen pocked by small holes, like the original portion of scapula. She stared as one by one the old woman's finds appeared. Now six in all. Different in shape but not colour and tone. Surely from the same skeleton?

'I'm convinced there's more to come, mind you,' Liliane mumbled. 'But I couldn't stop in that awful place a moment longer.'

'I'm not surprised.' Natalie replied, secretly wondering what Tom and his family would do if they found out, and equally, what Bernard Metz had been playing at, if indeed he'd known anything about them.

'Madame Bonneau,' she announced, suddenly patting the Suzuki's pillion seat. 'I'm supposed to be meeting the police at the Florentin services at four o'clock. I think you should come with me and show them the bones. We'll get Major Belassis to visit the cemetery too, then we'll go to Gandoux to help Mrs Wardle-Smith find her husband and son.'

Liliane studied the motorbike for a moment, then shook her head.

'Thank you, but I'm too old. Too far gone.'

'Rubbish.' Natalie stepped forwards and took the woman's other hand. It felt cold, like everything else, despite the sun. 'Have you a coat of

234

any sort?'

Another shake of that bird-like head.

'Then take this.' She removed her black leather jacket and held it behind Liliane's thin shoulders for her to slip her arms into its sleeves. 'And put your basket on here,' she attached its handle under one of the pannier's buckles then checked that the collection of bones inside it weren't likely to fall out. 'Now, up you get, *madame,* and no fiddling in my pockets.'

'I wouldn't dream of doing that, but what if Samson sees me?'

'Just keep your head down till I say so.'

The old woman's agility took Natalie by surprise. Had she been a biker in her youth? she wondered, setting the Suzuki into gear and hitting the throttle. Anything was possible, and that was why, as the wheels bumped along down the track, she was more vigilant than she'd ever been in her life.

CHAPTER TWENTY-FOUR

Samson Bonneau felt as if his wounded head was about to explode. Not just because of the bloody bells again, or the fact that his mother had given him the slip while he'd gone into the calf barn, but because he couldn't ask anyone, especially the cops why Metz's dead bitch had been placed near his family tomb. To cap all these anxieties, vets had arrived. Three of them from God knew where, poncing about on his land, creating yet

235

more havoc. Finally decimating his livelihood.

They'd waved papers at him authorising immediate intervention in his affairs, then added insult to injury by ordering him indoors, out of the way. Now, through the *séjour*'s front window, he could see Rufin's covered truck rumble its way round to the rear yard. The takeover was complete.

'Sod you all,' he muttered, and in the silence after the bells, a series of muffled shots reached his ears. He winced at each one which represented ruin and more ruin. Better to use the ammo on that meddling girl and the *Anglais* who were wrecking his life, he thought, watching one small carcass after another being lifted into the truck. The last of his stock.

A weary sigh left his lips. Wasn't it just a week ago that he'd collected a decent cheque from the abattoir? Hadn't he kept a good table all these years and paid outright for his then new Daf transporter? That was all down to his skill. His love. What he'd worked all his life to achieve. Perfect seven-day-old meat. And now, all that was over with not enough savings in the bank to rebuild the barn, re-stock his herd or make any kind of loan a viable proposition. The bank manager had told him as much when he'd phoned just moments ago. That damned nonentity, who thought he ruled the bloody world.

Bonneau blinked back hot stinging tears as the truck's rear door was finally closed, and he offered up not a prayer for himself, but a curse on the *Anglais* who'd been a bad omen from day one, and all those others who'd delivered him into Hell.

'Amen,' he ended, then looked up as the stamp

of boots on stone drew nearer. These vets were strangers, their dialect northern, maybe Picardie. Whatever, they brought the smell of death into the room. It was in their hair, on their breath and under their fingernails. He could tell.

The tallest of the men then laid two pieces of paper separated by a carbon sheet on the kitchen table.

'Sign here please, *monsieur*,' he pointed to the top sheet, which Bonneau recognised as an invoice. The total fee for their work, in heavy black ink, read 3,000 euros. Just to see it made him feel dizzy. 'You have twelve calves, two cows and a bull surviving...'

Only one bull...

'I want to see Rufin.'

'*We're* taking them, not him. We need to run further tests.'

'You've no bloody right! I've built up my stock, treated them as if they were my own kids...'

One of the others laughed out loud, his open mouth inviting a fist. Bonneau restrained himself, suddenly wondering where his own mother was. The rat who'd left the sinking ship.

'The bottom line is, *monsieur*, you've been producing veal unfit for human consumption in an environment of gross neglect.' The man stared at him, secure in the knowledge of a good salary, a fat pension to follow. 'And look at it this way, the value of what's left of your herd can be set against your defence costs.'

'Defence costs?' Bonneau felt the blood drain from his cheeks. Then, for one brief and terrible moment, their faces seemed to blurr and re-form as those of his male forebears: Jean, Albert and Eric, who all in their own ways had smoothed his path to eventual ownership of Belette. Now, their mocking smiles lingered too long, forcing him to slump down on the nearest available chair.

'You've violated very specific rules and regulations,' the northerner went on. 'And it's only fair to warn you that when we've left here, we'll be recommending prosecution.'

Bonneau gripped the table edge and swallowed a mouthful of bile.

'Rufin and the others were happy to take my stock and pay me,' he growled. 'So why not finger them as well?'

The three men looked at each other as if to say, who'll tell him? Finally the one who'd introduced himself as Patrick Uhlmann came closer.

'You've lied to all the abattoirs here. Your paperwork made no mention of your dependence upon antibiotics or growth retardants. I could go on all day...' He checked his watch then pointed to the invoice. 'But we're waiting for you to sign.'

'What?'

'This.' His finger stabbed the dotted line near the bottom edge.

'It was that girl, wasn't it? The blonde one. Bernard Metz's tart. They stitched all this up, and I bet you anything, he was behind it because I went public about his sculpture at the Florentin Services. It was sacrilegious. A disgrace. But you don't want to hear things like that, do you?' He knew he was saying too much, being careless, but in the heat of the moment, he didn't give a fig. As far as he was concerned, that part of his life was over.

'Like I've said, *monsieur,*' said the vet, 'just sign the paper, or we're into another hour of fees.'

Bonneau snatched the proferred pen and scored his name through to the wax tablecloth underneath.

'Parasites,' he muttered as the sheet was gathered up and the three men made their way to the door. 'No wonder this country's on its bloody knees, choked up with bureaucracy and pen-pushers like yourselves, when it's the likes of me who put bread on people's tables.'

'*Monsieur,*' Uhlmann turned to him, 'if it was merely bread, then we wouldn't be here. Oh, and by the way, just to let you know, we'll need to take some samples of your pasture.'

'The calves never went out of doors.'

'But your cows did. And your bulls.'

'Where will you be digging? I'll want compensation.'

'Better you dream for the moon, my friend.'

With that, the door closed behind them and, one by one, the vehicles left the front yard. First, Rufin's truck then the muddied off-roaders. Bonneau stared at the dust left in their wake. Dust and ashes, he thought. Then, with a stab of panic, bones.

Bonneau collected the one remaining spade from the store; the others were up at Hibou and there was no time to collect them now. This one would have to do. As he closed the door behind him, he wondered where his mother had gone. Who she'd been yapping to. The bus from Gandoux and Loupin was due in half an hour. Perhaps she'd be on that. He hoped so, because apart from his stomach needing a good meal, she had to be put in her place for going off like that. New door locks even crossed his mind, with him having sole charge of the keys. Failing that, there was always his cellar.

Trust her to have noticed the absent van the morning his father died and again yesterday. What else had the secretive old crow seen? And where was she now? Her bedroom was empty and that basket gone too. Her left shoe abandoned by the window.

He scoured the land that had been in the family for generations. It had never seemed so empty. The silence never before so threatening. The throb in his head increased as he strode over to the secondary midden in the nearest field. Like the one in the rear yard this had risen and spread to such a degree that he was no longer sure where the exact target area lay. The recent stampede had also moved the bulk of it in different directions. The ground, too, was harder, trampled upon, crisscrossed by others' trespassing footprints, unlike that time twenty two years ago, when the sodden chalk soil had instantly covered his working boots.

Then, during his uncle's swift inhumation, there'd been just enough rainy light at the day's end to enable him to work at speed. In fact, while the body was still warm. Once more, speed was of the essence in case his mother should return and see what he was doing. And what if those vets should notice where he'd disturbed the ground? But then, what if this was the very spot they chose to dig? He hadn't a bloody prayer. Best get himself to church tomorrow and make sure that Père Julien lay the biggest communion wafer on his tongue, and allowed him the longest draught of wine from the chalice. Yes, all things considered, that was priority.

Suddenly, like the Death's Head moths that regularly flitted across his sleepless eyes at night, the troubling thought occurred to him that way back on April 1st 1980, his mother might well have witnessed something. She'd been around after all, upstairs and changing the beds. He'd have to interrogate her. Force the truth out of her somehow before she started blabbing.

As the spade now began to shift the solid clods of manure, these intentions raced through his mind, bringing a rush of sweat to his skin as he worked. As he dug deeper without success, the ugly word *blackmail* – yes, his mother was more than capable of it – loomed up like one of those towering waves he'd once seen as a kid on holiday in the Landes. The one time he'd been away from Belette. To him then, that Atlantic storm had represented everything that was evil, uncertain, reducing its spectators to mere specks of life. Fragile. Expendable.

He heard the local bus come and go with no sound of his mother's return. Neither was the burial ground yielding what he wanted. There was nothing other than stones, the odd tangle of rusted wire. He stood back to survey the scene. Maybe the past twenty two years had distorted his memory. Maybe the spot he was looking for had been further away after all. He needed time to think. To clear his head and, as he returned to the store, he resolved to come out later and resume the search.

'*Maman?*' he called out, once inside. 'Where the hell are you? Have you seen the bloody time?'

No reply.

He sniffed, because an all-too familiar smell met his nose. Nothing to do with the room's contents nor the saturated stone walls, he was certain. This was Ashes of Violets, his mother's favourite scent. He sniffed again. Could this originate from the same gift set Albert had bought her just before his unfortunate fall off the bridge? That lilac-coloured box containing two wrapped soaps, four bath salts and a tin of talc? The answer was yes. And never mind the soap which she rarely used, it was the talc which he, Samson, had seen her pat over herself that very morning.

Was she there after all? Or, was he going mad?

'Maman?'

No answer.

He straightened, looked through into the kitchenette and beyond. Gripped by indecision, he then thought about the newly dug hole hurriedly covered over. If she'd sneaked back, she may well have spotted him. What should he say? That he'd been shifting the manure? Making a new vegetable patch?

Merde.

He kicked a pile of junk with the toe of his boot. Maybe he should have made the hole under the midden bigger and lain in it himself, because right now, his punishment for past and present sins was going to be that he still lived. Still drew breath.

His mother was nowhere to be found and, to take his mind off her absence and the afternoon's events, he decided to take the tractor and trailer and re-visit Hibou to make a start on the *fosse septique*. Forget the concrete mixer. Digging simply to make a useless hole might enable him to think afresh where Eric was lying. It would also keep him in with the *Anglais*. Still very much part of his plan.

He lumbered along to the site for the hole, aware of how many roof tiles had fallen since Metz had put it up for sale. How its rooms would soon be stuffed to the beams with expensive furniture which, like Nicolette's goods, would one day fetch a tidy sum for him. There'd be televisions, computers ... he could see it all now. Just like the items emblazoned in the glossy *Carrefour* brochures which blocked up his postbox every Christmas and Easter. Promoting a life where food came wrapped in plastic. Where nothing was grown, nothing dug for. Everything so easy...

The *Anglais* were no different. He could tell. No wonder the woman was going off her head.

The afternoon became dusk, and even though it wasn't yet April, Bonneau's exposed skin had darkened in the sun. The exercise had done little for his memory. He was still no clearer as to where exactly his dead uncle might be. His arms ached and his calf muscles spasmed as he rested from his labours at the edge of what would be the *Anglais'* *fosse septique*. But where were they? Why no sign of their car? And another anxiety was the prospect of Bernard Metz's arrival, his search for his bitch.

243

Best to be on home ground for that, he decided. Best to be locked in with the shutters closed.

He returned his two spades to the trailer and was just about to slurp a mouthful of stale Orangina from the bottle in his cab when he heard the noise of an unfamiliar car stopping and starting in the street below. Then came the wail of burning tyres and a diesel engine drawing closer. He hesitated, looking around for the best place to hide, but his boots could only take him the few paces to his tractor. It was as if the land itself was holding him fast, but as soon as he saw who was driving the silver Mercedes C-Class, bringing it to a swift, purposeful halt, all reason left him.

Who the hell is this?

He peered through his grimy cab glass at the woman in a well-cut business suit who emerged and set the car's alarm with a flick of her gloved hand. She then removed her wrap-around sunglasses, slipped them into her breast pocket, and scoured her surroundings.

What was someone like this doing here? he asked himself. Perhaps she knew the *Anglais,* and if so, why hold back and not introduce himself? Because something about her made him nervous. Something he couldn't quite fathom. He crossed himself three times and steadied his bulk against the wheel arch – the closest thing to a woman's body he was ever likely to feel for a long time. Was this some official or other looking for him to serve notice about his veal calves? Had the vets acted *that* quickly? Anything was possible.

She mounted the steps to Hibou's front door and, after a few token knocks, opened it and

244

disappeared inside. He wanted to follow, but if she were to suddenly reappear, he'd be done for. The only option was to try his luck round the back and, sure enough, the smaller unglazed window revealed her shadowy figure and a torch beam probing along the rock's edge.

Why was she kneeling down scrabbling at the ground like that with her rear in the air? he asked himself. What could she possibly be after? He watched as she continued her search, creating small heaps of turned soil then flattening them until all at once, her beam fell on several small light-coloured objects, just then too far away for him to identify.

Surely they were just bits of rock or the odd fungus that thrived in those damp conditions? If so, was she some biologist or other, doing research into limestone? He shook his head. She hardly looked the part, judging by the odd science programme he'd seen on TV.

Having blown the dirt off each of the specimens in turn, she dropped them as if in disgust. As if they weren't what she'd been looking for. Then she stood up, letting the torch beam rest for an instant on the window's gap. He ducked down just as she turned his way, then crossed himself again as the soft thud of a door closing and the click of high heels on the steps reached his ears. Next, the two-tone disabling of the car alarm, her door slamming and the first gear's thrum as she sped away.

Bonneau shivered and not just because he was now in shadow. He sensed trouble beckoning. The law's iron finger soon to be pointing his way.

So would penury. Frantic thoughts fast-forwarded to his next possible move because Metz would soon be back and, with the bitch still lying near his family tomb would soon know where to come looking.

His legs still ached as he emptied his bladder into the earth then climbed up into his tractor cab to settle himself on its hard iron seat. The little key turned sweetly in the ignition. Something going right at least. No sign of that luxury saloon in the Rue des Martyrs, or of Metz's people carrier. Another small mercy. He parked his workhorse in Belette's back yard and began chaining it to what remained of the broken barn. As his fingers untwisted the iron rings, he recalled his first encounter with the young *Anglais*. That softness. How easily he'd extricated him, as if he'd *meant* to be there with God looking on. And the *poule* with her cheeks stuffed full of baguette. He smiled to himself.

Yes, it was time to make a move. Time to set Hibou firmly in his sights. He could feel it in his bones. It wouldn't take much. The *Anglais* had money. Lots of it. Metz had let that one slip. So, all things were possible and, as he clicked the heavy padlock shut began itemising his strategy. First on his list was Natalie Musset. Then the rest would sweetly follow...

CHAPTER TWENTY-FIVE

'Didier wants to be my *copain*,' declared Max as Tom slipped the Volvo into the only parking slot he could find, behind a row of shops. His son's excitement still bubbling, his face glowing.

'That's brilliant,' Tom squeezed his hand affectionately, but once out in the sunlit street, this glimmer of optimism soon gave way to worry. Where the hell were Kathy and Flora?

He and Max had just reached the end of the cul-de-sac that opened out on to the Avenue des Sapins when suddenly he heard a motorbike's roar. Within five seconds, right in front of his eyes stood a familiar Suzuki with not one, but two people on board – young and old. The young with pinkened cheeks and a Cher T-shirt sitting in front of none other than Liliane Bonneau wearing a black leather jacket, looking equally at ease on her perch. Her normally neat grey hair like a wild spray of Old Man's Beard around her head.

'Hey, Natalie!' Max yelled out, beating him to it. 'We're here!'

She looked round and slowed up. However, instead of a smile of recognition, her eyes fell on Tom while her lips mouthed the words, 'Where on earth have you been?'

'Your wife called me,' she began. 'Sounded pretty frantic. Said you were never late. That you were

247

the most punctual man on this planet.'

'So, I'm OK at something, then.'

Her smile didn't last long.

'There's too much to tell you, and they're waiting.' She indicated the main street behind them where Kathy and Flora with a pile of shopping bags at their feet, could be seen leaning against McDonald's window looking fed up. He had to go.

'Ditto,' he replied, making sure Max couldn't hear. 'So, where can we talk?'

'Why not Hibou? I'm taking the old girl back there, if you don't mind. She's not safe at Belette. Look at her neck, for a start.'

He did, and saw the bruising on her old skin had darkened further. Just like his own thoughts since visiting the Hôtel de Ville and the *gendarmerie*.

'Who's to say she'd be safe with us?'

Natalie looked puzzled. She began to whisper all her news, then squinted up at him. 'Why are you looking at me like that?'

'I'm not.'

'You are. I'm not an idiot.'

'He always looks weird,' Max added. 'Take no notice.'

'Did you have fun?' she asked him as if to defuse the sudden tension.

He nodded, then spotted his sister and mother, and tried to run, before Tom restrained him.

'It's weird about Metz,' he said, trying to hold on to Max. 'Have you heard anything?'

She paled instantly.

'No. What?'

'Look, I don't know how to say this but...'

'Go on.'

Tom took a deep breath, wishing he was somewhere else.

'He's probably dead. Judging by the major's tone of voice. On the *péage* somewhere.'

'Oh Jesus.' Her hands left the handlebars to cover her mouth. 'Who told you?'

'Look, better shift. Catch up later.' Now wasn't the time for further explanations or dredging up her past. She looked choked enough as it was. Perhaps now was the time to let her go. To explain that he had a family to see to. That if he didn't make it up to Kathy, the whole French venture would be on the skids. However, it seemed there was something else she had to say. She leant closer, lowering her voice. Her hair briefly touching his cheek. It smelt of grass and fresh air.

When she'd finished, his gut felt numb. He turned to Liliane.

'Is this true, about the bones?'

The old girl nodded. The strangers' faces around them ugly, threatening. Tom held Max's hand more tightly. A yelp of protest.

'Quite a graveyard there, it seems,' she said.

'Where are they now?' he asked.

Liliane indicated the basket still secured to the pannier.

'And guess what,' Natalie went on. 'No one turned up at the services as promised, and because we hung around there living in hope, we found the *gendarmerie* here was already closed.'

'Surprise, surprise.'

'You said it.' She then whispered in his ear about what she'd found in the St Sauveur cemetery and before he could react, turned on the

249

bike's ignition and revved the throttle. 'See you back at the ranch,' she shouted over the noise. 'And you, Max. You watch out for everyone, eh?'

'Hang on a minute.' Tom tried to run after her, to no avail. He could only watch with growing foreboding as she and her passenger proceeded to a mini roundabout and sped off in the opposite direction to the Hôtel de Ville.

'Right,' Tom tried to sound positive, in control, for his son's benefit. 'Foot soldiers advance. One ... two ... three...'

Max turned to face him his still-damp hair clinging to his head.

'Why did you want Natalie to hang on? You do like her, don't you?'

''Course I do.'

'So?'

'It's nothing.'

How could he explain his growing lack of trust. The sense that, just as with Bonneau – a man she so despised – she, too, had cast her agenda like a lead bait into their lives.

'What are you thinking, Dad?'

'Just how good it was to see you enjoying yourself this afternoon.'

'You stupid man! You're a stupid, stupid man!' Kathy's fists pummelled his upper body, her face a mass of red blotches. 'And that's what I told that major when he called just now.'

'Nice one. Thanks. Why not go on the radio?'

'At least he seemed to care that we were panicking.'

'Words are easy. Did he actually show up and

take you on a guided tour to find us?'

'Don't be so facetious.'

Flora, too, began raining blows on his back, as she yelled, until he realised a small crowd of curious onlookers had gathered to watch.

'You're a horrible Dad and I want to go home!'

'OK, so I'm a horrible Dad. Least that's sorted.' He looked at the shopping bags which all bore the Champion supermarket logo. All filled with cleaning stuff and toilet rolls, not even any food. 'Why's your mother not bought you any clothes? Things you like?'

Kathy hit him again. This time it hurt.

'What else did you expect with us having to go back to that heap?'

'*Anglais*,' someone muttered, then added something uncomplimentary about British beef.

Once Tom had ducked away to stuff the shopping bags into the boot and opened the Volvo's doors, the little gathering drifted away.

Now the barrage against him continued in private and there was nothing he could say or do to reassure them. He couldn't even reassure himself and, as he pulled into a garage for petrol and a chance to phone Right Move about the missing furniture, he thought of what he'd be doing now in Berris Hill Road. Him and the kids watching the local teams' rugby match, or a film matinée at the new cinema complex. Even just chewing the cud in the Sailor's Arms with Mike Carr, who'd started work at Prestige People the same day as himself...

Work...

Since leaving the UK, he'd not thought once about his pale ash desk, his comfortable swivel chair and the waxy yucca plant thriving in the corner of the office. The jokey emails, the tea and coffee that Rose trundled round twice a day. But now an ache of longing gnawed at his gut as he filled the petrol tank and walked over to the cashier's booth to pay. Did he really want the furniture to arrive? Did he really want to go on with all this and become embroiled with possible murder?

He returned his Visa card to his wallet and slapped its two leather halves together, aware of nothing but misery staring out at him from the car. Then he thought of Natalie and old Madame Bonneau. Two problems he could do without. He looked up and saw St Marc's spire and its gargoyles like so many black boils against the sky, now representing something less than holy and comforting. He'd never been one to dodge tricky situations at work – yes, work again – or in family matters. Hadn't he been the only one in his team to stand up to the boss when things got too tough? To sort out Flora's music teacher who was pressurising her into playing the oboe when she preferred the clarinet? Exactly. And he mustn't forget these achievements, for right now they were the very glue holding him together.

When he returned to the car, he asked Kathy for the mobile. She stuck it out of the window to connect with his ribs.

'Ouch!'

'I've bought my own now,' she announced. 'Because I've had it up to here. I'm going back home. I can stay with my mother. It's all arranged. I'll be flying from Brive tomorrow morning.'

Tom gulped.

'Brive? You can't.'

'I bloody can. And,' she glanced round at Max and Flora, 'I'm taking the kids with me.'

He looked into the open window, his ribs hurting. Max and Flora's faces were turned away.

'You can have that slapper all to yourself.'

'She was good enough for you to phone.'

Below the belt, he knew. But what the heck?

'You bastard. I was desperate.'

'I don't want to live with Mrs Whiskers,' muttered Max. 'I've just made a friend here.'

'And what about you?' Tom asked his daughter. She gazed up at him, her cheeks damp with tears.

'Remember last year when Max fell and broke his little finger in the play park when you two were shopping?'

''Course I do.'

'Well, I was the only one there when it happened, and I tried to make him better till you got back.'

'I know you did. You were amazing.'

'He said he was glad he'd got a big sister and that he didn't want me ever to leave him...'

'Liar,' Max protested, blushing a deep crimson.

'You did! So I'll stay if Max is,' she sniffed and wiped her eyes with the back of her hand.

'Oh well,' Kathy broke in, her tone cold as ice, 'now we all know where we stand. Thanks, you two.'

Tom fought his own tears as he punched Right Move's number. This was crunch time and in three weeks, bones or no bones, the place could be turned around. The home he'd dreamt of, night after night, while Kathy had slumbered next to him.

'What are you doing?' she snapped.

'We're a family. We're in this together, and come hell or high water, we'll make this work.' He didn't hear what she said in reply because news was coming through from Guildford that, barring accidents, all the furniture would be arriving at St Sauveur at six o'clock that very day.

'About time!' he gave a thumbs-up sign. 'Hey kids, you'll have your own beds, your Easter eggs, all your gear...'

'And my computer?' asked Flora.

'Yep. Mind you, we'll need to get the electrics sorted first. Could even get a generator if we have to.'

He got into the driver's seat. The car still smelt of chlorine.

'Don't let him fool you,' hissed Kathy, applying orange lipstick to her mouth. 'There's still an earth floor there. Hardly any water left and nothing to cook with. So, let's get real, shall we?'

Tom felt as if his own personal balloon was shrinking fast. Negativity and more negativity was always her forte. How could he ever forget? Prick ... prick ... prick...

'We'll have EDF round on Tuesday and then we'll sort out about getting mains water in.'

'So no *fosse?*' Max quizzed, relief in his voice. 'No Giant either?'

'That's right.'

'Yes!'

Kathy began to get out of the car. Her face set hard as granite.

'I'm withdrawing my savings. All the money my

father left me. I'm entitled. In fact, I'm going to the bank this minute.'

'They're all closed,' said Max checking his watch.

'A hole in the wall then. Doesn't matter.'

'If you get out now, that's the last you see of us.' Tom's severity surprised even himself. As though this ultimatum had come from someone else. 'So, make up your mind.'

'Mu-um,' wailed Flora. 'Dad's right. Please, let's give this a chance.'

Tom saw her rummage in Kathy's bag which lay on the back seat between her and Max. 'Have another pill,' she said, producing a slim pastel green box labelled DOUCELUX and passing it over. 'Here we go.'

Kathy waved it away.

'I don't need stuff like that any more, thank you. My mind's clearer than it's ever been, OK?'

'With both his children's faces pressed up against the same window glass, Tom watched her cross the road and disappear up an alleyway between the shops opposite. It was clear she wanted out. Plain and simple. So what could he say? Things had gone too far. The tide had already reached his throat. That he was already drowning was an understatement.

Half an hour later, she returned to the car, tense and tight-lipped. Not even the kids quizzed her as she looked at them all then, having slumped back in the seat beside him, closed her eyes. Tom reached over and touched her knee. She didn't move. Then he took her hand and squeezed it.

255

'Did you do it?'

'No, I couldn't.'

Relief washed over him. They were both now in with a chance.

'Look, Kath, let's count our blessings. We've got each other, two healthy kids, plenty of capital behind us – more than we'd ever have had in Surrey...'

'I'm not living in a house full of old bones.'

'You won't have to. I'll come into Gandoux again on Tuesday to find a builder who'll lay a concrete floor in the cave. Then we'll do the roof, put new windows in...' All thoughts of Metz and the dead dog were superceded by clear visions of what Hibou could be. A luxury three-bedroomed farmhouse with more land than all the Berris Hill Road plots put together. That would rub the Simistons noses in it should they ever come to call. But what about Natalie? Had the encounter between them been nothing more than that? An encounter? A glimpse of what might have been?

'And you get rid of that biker,' Kathy said, as if she'd been reading his thoughts.

'OK. When we get back.'

Max pulled a face while Flora looked bemused.

Nevertheless, as Tom restarted the engine and drove away from the garage, he sensed a collective calm settle over his family. The first for days. However, just as he was about to join the road back towards St Sauveur, the lad leaned forwards and touched his shoulder with a clenched fist.

'Dad?'

'Yep?'

'Look.' He opened up his hand to reveal a roll

of film. Kodak. 200 ASA.

'Where did you find that?'

'Sandy gave it to me when we were changing. Told me to get it developed. That's all.'

'Why?'

'Dunno. That's all he said.'

'Who's Sandy?' asked Flora.

'MYOB, OK?'

'The lad he met today, I expect,' said Kathy flatly.

Tom glanced at the film again, then focused on the road ahead. Odd that, he thought. Maybe there was funny stuff on it. Maybe the Keppel kid didn't have the money to get it developed himself, although that seemed unlikely, judging by where he lived. Either way, it seemed an odd thing to do.

'We'll have to hand it back there on Tuesday,' he said. 'When we go and find out about schools and builders.'

'Your dad's right,' said Kathy, taking it from him and putting it into her bag.

Tom threw her a glance – part disbelief, part gratitude. At last. Round One to him in the blue corner. But any relief was short-lived as fierce headlights invaded his rearview mirror, heralding a *gendarmerie* van doing easily over a ton; its flashing blue roof light and eerie wail brought back memories of that winter night in 1994 when his parents had perished on their way home over the Hog's Back. He'd been following behind them with Kathy and the kids after a meal at The Pilgrim in Farnham. Never again would he take a wet bend too fast.

Never again did he want to see anybody die.

257

'It's a wonder they don't crash, driving like that,' remarked Kathy obviously thinking the same as him.

He made a mental note of the local number plate, also thinking about Metz. Was *that* where the van was heading? Certainly not north-east to Villefort but south, towards the *péage*. An irrational thought took hold of him and he felt he just had to follow it, find out if it really did have something to do with Metz's accident.

Max, still peeved, pressed his nose to the window glass. 'Why aren't we going home? That sign back there said St Sauveur to the right.'

'Just checking something out, son. Won't take long.'

'Look,' Kathy turned to him. 'What if that furniture van turns up and we're not there? Can't we get *something* sorted for once?'

'And I'm starving,' Flora whined. 'We only had milkshakes for lunch.'

'*I* had a quarter-pounder,' boasted her brother as they sped away from the Fer à Cheval and its tiny symbiotic hamlet – a mere speck against its grandeur – towards the *péage* going south.

Fifteen minutes later, the Volvo was hitting 90 mph on the *autoroute*'s outside lane, towards Cahors. Of the *gendarmerie* van there was now no sign, but at least he knew this was the road it had taken. Then, without much warning, came a narrowing of the tarmac and yellow Highway notices declaring that this extension to the Toulouse route would be finished in 2005.

'Damn!' Tom checked his watch. There'd been

258

no sign of any accident so far. Angry and tired, he turned off for Cahors, on the route Nationale. Having negotiated ten kilometres of hairpin bends marked by black cut-out figures representing the travelling dead, and crossed the foaming River Lot, he joined the motorway to Montauban.

Kathy looked grim. He knew exactly what was going through her mind. However, he had no choice. At the first ticket stop, he pulled over to the side where the driver of a service truck was lighting a cigarette, blowing the smoke out of his window.

'I heard there's been a pile-up near here,' Tom began in his best French.

'Only the one.'

'One what?'

'Other vehicle. The stiff didn't stand a chance, mind. We'll all need an armoured car the way things are going. Specially on these roads...'

'Where did it happen?'

'By the St Jory exit. Probably all cleaned up by now.'

'Any idea who it was?'

'You one of those that likes to watch accidents?'

'For God's sake.'

'Some artist or other driving a green people carrier. Death traps at the back, they are...'

Tom didn't wait to thank him. Detaching himself from the growing tension within his car, he snatched a ticket then floored the throttle to make up for lost, precious time.

A huge smooth water tower, a row of dark poplars and a two-tone graphic image of the region's

259

bounty straddled the hard shoulder. But what lay cordoned off on the far side seemed just then far more appropriate. A bloody mess.

As the Volvo crawled along in first gear, boxed in by other travellers' curiosity, he could see over the central reservation of trimmed shrubs that, although the ambulances had gone, a number of official looking vehicles still surrounded the wreckage. He recognised the same *gendarmerie* van and its two occupants from Gandoux.

'People who gawp at accidents are sick,' said Kathy all of a sudden. 'Anyhow, it's nearly five o'clock.'

'We won't be late. I'm telling you.'

'God knows what we're doing here. I should have got out while I could.'

'I want to wee,' added Max.

'And me.' Flora unwrapped a bubblegum and pushed it into her mouth.

Tom barely heard them, because if this was the crash that had killed the sculptor, he, for one, wouldn't be late for anything ever again. No one could have survived what appeared to be a massive driver's side impact. The gaping hole revealed the interior's barbecue-like debris. The only green colour remaining lay near what had been the roof. Had the sculptor been burnt alive? And where was the other vehicle? Had it been driven off in a panic, or did it deliberately leave the scene? Judging by the damage, it must have been something pretty substantial.

He frowned. Despite all the other setbacks, this whole Metz thing gnawed at his mind and it wasn't just because of what Keppel had implied

260

about Natalie: He could feel it for himself. Then he remembered the knife she'd mentioned. How, apparently, it was bloodstained. The yellow twine she'd shown him only that morning. Her begging him not to tell anyone. Yet why ask him to go with her to the Florentin services in the first place? Surely that was the last thing a guilty person would have done?

No, the whole notion that she could be involved was preposterous. Grotesque, even. And as for this latest development, her bike had seemed perfect, not a scratch on it, but surely that wouldn't have been big enough anyway – it would have done far more damage to her than to Metz... Unless she'd got hold of something else, something bigger...

The major's card was still in his pocket. *Trust me.* He slowed up even more only to cause aggressive honking from the people carrier behind him. Now, the crash scene was slipping away from view. Frustration became anger as he dialled the major's number, without any great hopes of a response. However, to his surprise, a woman answered.

'Yes?'

'I need to speak to Major Belassis.'

'His office closed at two o'clock.'

'I'd like to thank him personally for phoning my wife. That's all. It was very kind of him.'

'Wait. I'll put you through.'

He heard a brief murmured exchange, before recognising the man's voice above the noise of some engine. This time he sounded different. Wary even, but Tom ignored it and took a deep breath. Sod saying thank you. This was far more important.

'What kind of vehicle crashed into Metz's Galaxy?' he asked.

'Where are you?'

'Gandoux,' he lied. 'Why?'

'Don't go interfering, *monsieur*. Crimes would be solved far more quickly if well-meaning members of the public left the job to us professionals.'

'So, you *do* admit there have been crimes?'

'We have our procedures. *You* have your family.'

Not the first who'd mentioned his family. He glanced over at Kathy, who was now studying a local map. The kids were still grumbling in the back.

'Was it something with a bit of weight behind it?' He persevered, nearly adding that it certainly looked that way. Then stopped himself. Damn. He was getting careless.

'Whatever the vehicle was, it didn't stop. That's all we know. And this is what our spokesman will be telling the media in an hour's time.'

'Surely there were witnesses? Other road users? It's a busy Saturday after all, not outer Mongolia.'

'No one's come forward so far. I'm afraid this was a tragic occurrence which is becoming more and more frequent on our roads. Drink and drugs are causing havoc. There's also the possibility of an insurance scam. That, too, is on the increase.'

'Sorry I don't buy any of that. Not with what's happened to his dog.'

'*Monsieur*,' the *gendarme's* tone hardened. 'I have an important meeting to attend, so if you wouldn't mind...'

'Why didn't anyone turn up to the Florentin services this afternoon as agreed?'

'Please tell Mademoiselle Musset that we are forced to prioritise. Her request was finally not considered urgent enough. May I remind you, *monsieur,* that here in France, unlike our neighbours over *La Manche,* we treat Easter with great devotion. This is something to consider if you're settling here. I did touch on it when we first met. We have a strong faith. The Catholic faith. If you don't believe me, see what happens in the elections.'

With great difficulty, Tom restrained himself from sounding off about religion. He tried another tack. It was time to mention the farmer.

'Has anyone spoken to Monsieur Bonneau, yet?'

'It's not Monsieur Bonneau we're interested in.'

Tom felt a sudden chill embrace his heart.

'Who then?'

'I really must go. My meeting's about to start.'

The major ended the call. Tom felt ill. He knew damned well whom the major had meant. Natalie. He'd taken her knife, hadn't he?

'Damn it.'

'Bad words, Dad.' Max was still wriggling ominously in his seat. 'And I told you, I need to wee.'

'You'll have to wait, son. Won't be long.'

Kathy scowled.

'If they wet themselves, don't forget I've got no washing machine, no clothes line...'

'There's the public *lavabo*. You saw the local women using it last time we were down here. Chatting away, having a laugh.'

'You must be joking.'

A surly silence reigned in the car as they left the *péage* then re-joined it amidst all the traffic head-

263

ing north. Daylight, too, was ending, and the array of too-early headlamps made his head ache, forcing his eyes into being more shut than open. To him, after what he'd just witnessed, every bull-barred or heavy vehicle that passed on its way at speed was not only a possible killer, but was connected to someone he could have loved.

'Tell you what, kids,' he said suddenly, forcing a smile. 'Let's play a game.'

'Yeah!' they chorused.

'Don't you think the priority should be getting back for our furniture?' Kathy's stare was alarming. The whites of her eyes reflecting red tail lights.

'Agreed, but we can still watch out for anything that looks like it's had a bad knock, OK?'

'What'll we get?'

'A tenner a go,' dared Max excitedly.

'Fine.'

'You're kidding?' Flora's bubblegum billowed out between her lips, then subsided into a web of yellow strands around her mouth.

'I'm not. This is serious.'

'Cool. We'll be rich at this rate.'

He kept up his speed. Natalie and Liliane would be waiting, worrying, as if there'd not been enough of that for one day. It was now ten past five. Still fifty minutes to go before his desk would be installed and more importantly, the wine rack, its contents and a corkscrew.

'Now I really *do* know you're barking,' Kathy muttered, folding up the map and stuffing it into the door's pouch. 'We're supposed to be getting the dump ready so we're not having to live like bloody cavemen. Using the kids to play detect-

264

ives is crazy. Anyway,' she added, turning her head to the left, 'that's where it happened, and now look. Not a sausage.'

He looked, then blinked. She was right.

'Got their skates on then,' said Tom drily, overtaking a sluggish Rapido caravan, thinking how the French thirty-five hour week might have something to do with it. Then how Belassis wanted him off the line.

That was more to the point.

Nearing Cahors, traffic predictably lost speed, nudging bumper to bumper, while the surrounding hills dotted by the typical Quercy farms and their long sloping roofs passed by in slow motion. He kept to the lorry lane because anything in a hurry would be trying to overtake, with front and passenger side fully visible. At least, while some residual daylight remained.

He sensed a creeping tension that was nothing to do with full bladders or the lack of time, and he switched on the radio for one of *Musique & Infos'* many brief bulletins, whose words he recognised all too clearly.

'Well-known sculptor Bernard Metz, from St Sauveur in the Department of the Lot, has died following an accident on the A10 between Cahors and Montaubon. The Department's police chief has declared they are not looking for any other vehicle. The artist's drinking habits were well known, and although full tests have still to be carried out, cause of death is likely to be an excess of alcohol in the blood...'

'Rubbish.' Tom switched stations and turned to Kathy as Sylvie Vartan began to sing about the sea.

'Remember when we went to see him about the sale? He drank Cola while we each had a Ricard.'

'Dad,' Max suddenly pushed him from behind. 'Look!'

'What?'

'Something's coming up alongside.' Both kids were now kneeling to face the rear window, their chins resting on the back of the seat.

Tom cursed the Volvo's blind spot, which had let him down more than once before.

'I can't see it.'

'A kind of jeep thing. It's huge and it's black. Like that one last night.'

'Get down,' snapped Kathy. 'We don't want whoever it is inside getting a look at you.'

'They can't see us. Their glass is all dark,' said Max.

'You're so dumb sometimes,' Flora laughed. ''Course they can.'

Tom angled his rear view mirror to see a bulky black 4x4 cruising past in the middle lane. Not only was its chrome bull bar buckled in against the radiator, but even in the poor light it was obvious that the door and wheel arch had been in a fight. Something about the vehicle was vaguely familiar. He momentarily lost control. Had to brake hard behind the Fiat in front.

'Any green bits?' he breathed. 'For God's sake, everyone, keep your eyes peeled.'

'There's something near the front wheel,' Kathy said suddenly. 'I'm sure of it.'

'She's right.' Flora said, almost sitting in Max's lap.

'OK, OK. Now try to get the make and the

266

number plate. Hurry.'

'Got it.'

'Write it down, then.'

'No pen.'

'Memorise it.'

'I already have,' said Kathy, calmly repeating it. 'Remember all those patient files I had to organise?'

How could he ever forget?

Tom stepped on the gas and pulled out to follow, but another vehicle, some red Picasso with three canoes on top, beat him to it by swerving out from behind. His fist hit the horn, to no avail. The black jeep was moving away.

'Get back into the inside lane,' urged Kathy, 'then nip in behind it.'

'Good thinking.'

However, a white van with no lights pulled over. A van not previously noticed.

'Da ... ad!'

'Hold tight.' But his brakes felt spongy, the distance between them shrinking too quickly. He thought of another mess on the road. 'Jesus, that was close.' A centimetre at most. He glanced at Kathy, her lips moving on unspoken words. Her eyes on her wing mirror.

'I don't want to die here,' she announced.

'You won't. None of us will.'

'In half an hour I'll have my own bed,' Flora tapped his shoulder. 'And my own duvet.'

'Me too,' added Max, and as the van became part of the dusk, so too did the north/south traffic thin. Tom found himself thinking of that spot where Metz had perished. The ghostly water tower looming up towards the sky, that black fringe of trees edging the land beyond.

His mobile rang. He snatched it from Kathy as she was about to answer and listened with a freshly churning stomach as Natalie began to speak.

'Tom? Where the hell are you?'

'Why? What's the matter?'

'I've just had a call.'

'Who from?'

'God knows. Some man or other. Sounded like the one who called me this morning at the Café.'

'Not Belassis, then?'

'No. Definitely not.'

'And?'

'I'm ... I'm wanted for questioning.' Her voice began to tremble.

'God. Keep going.' But he knew already what was coming.

'For Metz's murder. And Filou's. Tom, I can't believe he's really dead.'

'This is crazy. Did you hear the news on the radio just now?'

'No. Why?'

'They're saying Metz was probably drunk and no one else is thought to be involved.'

Silence.

'Natalie?'

'He never drank. Said it would impair his coord-ination. Tom, something's wrong. We're also being watched. I'm sure of it.'

'Try and hang on, for God's sake.'

'Please hurry.'

'I am.'

'By the way, remember what I told you about

Filou? How I'd moved her? Well, Liliane and I called in on this old girl, Alize Flamand, in the Rue des Martyrs to find out if she knew anything.'

'And?'

'She confirmed Liliane's story about seeing a *gendarmerie* van speeding towards the church this morning. She also spotted the driver. Said he was dark-haired, in his late thirties. If she'd not been on the telephone at the time, she'd have followed it. But the really weird thing is...'

'Yes?'

All he could see was a landscape bare of any trees or homesteads, spread towards the horizon.

'When I sneaked to the cemetery just now to see if Filou was still there, she'd gone.'

CHAPTER TWENTY-SIX

The day had turned into an even colder night and, under a clear starry sky with its ascending moon, a frost already glazed the Suzuki's curves. Natalie watched the massive Right Move truck grind to a halt outside Hibou, and four men of assorted ages leap down from its cab to release the rear ramp. They seemed fed up, in a hurry, letting the first few items of furniture fall to the ground before hefting them to the front door. A rattan bucket chair, then two velvet bean bags. Things she'd never dream of buying but which no doubt had come from a spacious, comfortable home. Part of Tom's life she'd never shared.

269

Maybe never would. Why the hell had she told him about the knife? The twine? That weird call? Couldn't she keep anything to herself?

'Sod it,' said the tallest man, then, throwing her a furtive glance, 'This the Turdle-Twits' place?'

'Wardle-Smiths, if you don't mind. And please be careful with their stuff. They'll go ape if they see what's going on.'

Four burly guys to one, she thought, waiting for the inevitable tongue-lashing.

'We'll need the final payment tonight,' the same man muttered instead. 'So no vanishing acts. Got it?'

Why not? she thought, thinking only of her own predicament. That caller hadn't specified *when* she'd be questioned. Could be next week or within the hour. But could she risk it? Was it better to be here or out on the open road? Then she thought of her League boss, Paul Ormonde. He never gave out his home number to anyone, but might just be in his office. She had to tell him she was being stitched up. That this was serious.

'Yes?'

It wasn't him, but a woman she'd not heard before. Someone in a hurry.

'Natalie Musset here. Grade 2 investigator. Limoges...'

'Is it crucial? We've got trouble over in Sarlat. Need to clear the line.'

Charming.

She heard Liliane Bonneau call out in surprise from inside the *fermette* where her son's oil lamp was now casting everything in a flickering light from its flame. She'd felt bad enough about leaving her on her own for that half hour while she'd checked out the cemetery again.

'I'm being accused of mutilating a dog, *and* of murder. OK?' The words seemed to come from someone else.

'Can someone call you back later? I can't promise when.'

'Tell Paul, please. Here's my mobile number.'

'I expect he's got it.'

'Well, here it is again.' She relayed the numbers as a cream leather three piece suite was humped into the room behind her and hit the earth floor in a succession of thuds.

'Like I said, I can't promise anything.'

'Nor can I.' She ended the call in silent fury. She'd risked her life more than once for the League, and what did she get when she needed them? Zilch.

Damn it...

Suddenly, headlights appeared over the top of the track and Natalie sprinted to the side of the *fermette* out of their beam, just in case whoever it was might see her. Then she realised it was the family Volvo trying to edge past the removals truck. When it stopped, Max scrambled out first to pee, followed by Flora. They giggled their way past her into the dark field, narrowly missing the *fosse septique's* partially dug hole. Moments later, Kathy's voice rose above the hubbub.

'What in hell's name is Bonneau's mother doing in our bed? Could somebody please explain.'

Natalie left her hiding place and pushed her way into Hibou, between the clutter of too many

271

bulging bin-liners and an enormous blue soft-toy panda. Avoiding Tom was priority. She knew what he'd be thinking.

'Leave it to me,' she said, seeing Liliane's startled face.

'And you're here as well?' the other woman glared, getting her oar in first. 'I'll give you both one minute to get out and leave us alone. Look at this mess. *Look* at it! You wouldn't keep a dog – at least a *British* dog – in these conditions. You'd be prosecuted.'

Natalie shivered, thinking of Filou's absence from the cemetery. Her owner dead. That incongruous hint of perfume lingering in the *fermette*'s cave area. Nothing made sense.

'We can help,' she offered without thinking, because every inch of that ancient place was being jam-packed with goods far too large for its mean spaces. 'God knows you need it.'

'We don't. So just go.'

'OK, OK.' She held out a hand to the old girl. 'We know when we're not wanted.'

'I'm not going back to my son!' came the cry. 'Not the way he is at the moment.'

'Quite right, too,' came a voice from the doorway. 'No one's going anywhere. Least of all tonight.' Tom propped up the bookcase he'd been carrying against the nearest wall. Then he straightened. 'We need to talk, all of us. Once this lot's safely in and paid for.'

Natalie saw him turn to one of the men – a skinhead with bruised lips – bearing two uplighters and asked how long the rest of the job would take. Tom certainly wasn't looking at her.

She should have got out while she could. She'd have been on the *péage* for Limoges by now.

''Nother hour at least, sir. We wasn't expecting nothing like this.' The man glanced around. 'I'd always go for new-build, meself. Can't be arsed doin' up some dump. No way. Hey missus, got any beers? We're bloody parched, aren't we lads?'

'No beer, no water, no gas, no nothing. So don't even ask.' Kathy perched on the chair's arm next to Flora. 'And by the way, while we're at it, please say you've got some room on that lorry of yours for a return trip.'

'That bad, eh?' The guy grinned inappropriately.

Natalie saw Kathy's bottom lip tremble and Tom turn pale. This was getting worse. However, she had to speak to him.

'About this talk you mentioned,' she ventured, only to have him stare at her as if she was a complete stranger. 'Shall we get it over with?'

'In the car. In five minutes.' Then he addressed Liliane.

'Basically it's this. No disrespect to you, *madame*, but we won't be needing a *fosse septique* here after all. Your son should have told us about the new mains regulations right from the start. We could have had a lot of unnecessary expense.'

'I'm sorry, *monsieur*. But what could I have said to him or you? If you must know,' she lowered her eyes, 'I've spent most of my life wishing he'd come from someone else's body.'

Flora tittered at Tom's rough and ready translation, and Max promptly clamped a hand over her mouth.

'That's not funny, stupid. *I* don't want him here either.'

'Right,' said Tom, once the men were out of earshot, '*madame,* where are those bones?'

'Here. With me.' She patted her side then peeled back the car rug to reveal her basket.

'That's disgusting,' muttered Kathy, who'd somehow managed to change the kids' clothes and was now escorting both to the one accessible armchair jammed tight against its partners. 'At least we won't have to use *that* stinking bed again.'

'We need to take great care of them,' Tom went on, trying to stay focused. 'I suggest that until they can be examined properly, we find a hiding place. That way, no one will feel under constant pressure to keep them safe. God knows there's enough to deal with at the moment. Any objections?'

Silence followed, in which a luxury king-sized bed was brought in, propped up on its end and the old mattress taken out. Natalie glanced at it, noting its two slight hollows, and wondered which was Tom's.

'Suggestions, then?'

'The fridge,' said Max. 'Who'd think of looking there?'

'Clever you,' Natalie took Liliane's basket over to the upright Zanussi which contained the hopeful looking bottle of Moët et Chandon. She hid the bones in one of the opaque salad drawers. '*Voilà.*'

'No you don't!' screeched Kathy. 'That's even more disgusting. For Christ's sake, woman, that fridge isn't even yours!'

'Mum. It's *my* idea,' Max glared at her. 'Stop picking on Natalie.'

Natalie caught Tom's eye as she shut the Zanussi's door. She knew he was trying to stay detached, while at the same time she sensed the end of whatever there might have been between them. She'd only known him a few hours, but already they'd seemed to be mentally connected. It had been the same with Bernard Metz. An instant, intuitive kind of bonding. Or so she'd thought at the time. The sex had come later after she'd posed for the last of those maquettes, while flames from his wood burner cast their naked bodies in its honeyed glow. That smell of brown wax and thinners intensifying in the heat as she'd ridden him to a climax then watched him sleep; his clever hands uncurled from her body to rest so still on the old rug, as if they belonged to the dead...

And now they did.

She barely heard Tom as he went over to Kathy.

'By the way, where's that film you took from Max?'

She dug in her bag and handed it over.

'Why do you want it?'

'Like I said, it needs to go back. Just so we don't forget.' He put it in his jeans' pocket.

'Hey up,' interrupted the man with the sweatiest underarms. 'Just a reminder, sir, that if you're thinking of leaving here, you settle up first, eh?' His body blocked the only way out. Tom produced a scrap of torn paper headed Invoice from his back pocket, then scribbled out a cheque.

'Where's our money, too?' Max piped up. 'We spotted that black jeep just now. You said *we* could have a tenner each.'

'What black jeep?' asked Natalie, reality now

275

kicking in. She was no longer back in that warm studio but by Hibou's front door, where the evening chill had reached her skin under her leathers. As if to add to her sense of desolation, the church bells in the Rue des Martyrs clanged out the half hour. The chime seemed longer than usual. Maybe its mechanism, too, was going crazy. Meanwhile, Max perched himself behind Flora on the back of the armchair so he, too, could be heard and seen. Especially by Natalie.

'When we were out just now, Dad took us to this mega accident...' he began.

'Accident? Where?'

'Not now, son, if you don't mind. Natalie and I must talk.'

'Why can't you go and get some grub instead? Our Easter eggs all got smashed up.'

'I will, later, alright? First things first.'

Natalie saw Max's face crumple in disappointment.

'There we go,' broke in Kathy. 'He puts that slapper in front of us, in front of me, yet again, and only an hour after saying he was going to get rid of her.'

Natalie bit her lip. She was not going to react. Instead she watched Liliane Bonneau unpack a box of *Le Creuset* saucepans and stack them up, one inside the other. The old woman glanced up at her as she did so. A look of tenderness in her eyes. She knew all about harassment too.

Meanwhile, Kathy busied herself making sure all their handles were facing the front. Size order, too, seemed important as she re-arranged Liliane's careful pile seemingly oblivious to the old girl's curious gaze. Then, having neatly folded all the newspaper sheets and squashed them into the tea chest, she gasped aloud at her black-stained hands.

'Ugh. Look at these! And nowhere to wash them either,'

'*Madame,* please let me do that,' Liliane offered. 'I'm used to such things.'

But Kathy turned on her. Prodded her arm before letting rip with her Sixth-form French.

'You mean filth, ordure, and the rest. I'm not surprised. Just look at that hole you live in. And who's to say you're not bringing some vile infection with you here?'

Liliane looked mortified. Stopped unwrapping a set of expensive bone-handled cutlery and looked at Natalie as if to say, what do I do? But the truth was, there was nothing Natalie could do for anybody, let alone herself, and, as Kathy resumed her tirade against Tom, Hibou and the poor defenceless old girl, Natalie crept from the *fermette* into the night.

She hoped with every bone in her body that Tom had noticed her leave. But that was hardly likely given what was going on in there, and a hollow sense of loss enveloped her as she zipped her jacket up to her chin. She was about to pull on her gloves, when she sensed someone behind her.

'How about that talk, then?' His voice made her spin round.

'Jesus!'

She must have been too deep in thought to have heard him. His shoulders were hunched; his whole demeanour one of defeat. She wanted to pull him towards her. To hold him tight. But that would never happen now. Not in a million years...

She simply said, 'I'm sorry.'

'If only you'd been straight with me in the first place.'

'You'd never have gone near me. Right?'

'I didn't mean that. But you've seen for yourself how precarious things are. Kathy's still harping on about jumping ship...'

'But she's been unpacking. Fussing about the fridge...'

'Doesn't mean a thing. She'd do that anyway. Even if there was a two-minute warning...'

'And I'm about to have my life ruined all because I fell in love.'

He still didn't look at her, but she saw more than tiredness in his eyes.

'What exactly did your caller say?'

'That I had the motive and the time not only to wipe Bernard Metz off this planet, but to kill Filou. That the blood on my knife matches hers...'

Her voice gave out.

'His words?'

'Exactly. And like I said to you, no way was it Belassis. Even though he'd hinted at things this morning at the services and lifted my knife. Someone *else* has got it in for me. But who?'

'It's cold. Let's sit in the car.' Tom unlocked her door and could still smell the faintest hint of chlorine. 'At least we can hear ourselves speak. As you can see, my wife's in top gear...'

She barely heard what he said.

'You don't believe me, do you? I used that knife to see if I could prise the bullet from her neck, but it wasn't there. You think I'm making all this up to get your sympathy. But who the hell's got my phone number? Who knew where I spent last night?'

'Look,' he finally turned to face her. 'You need to get away from here.'

'Is that what you want?'

He didn't respond. Instead, a grey tension seemed to alter his whole face.

'Someone out there also knows what I do at the university, and where I live in Boisseuil. Scary or what? I tried to call the Examining Magistrate's office, to see if anyone there knew anything, but too late, of course.'

'OK. I've accused you of being less than honest. Now, *I* need to come clean.'

'You? How come?' She sensed a knot of alarm lodge in her hungry stomach.

'Max and I saw his clerk today, as you know. Before the swimming session.'

'Keppel?'

'Correct.'

'And?'

'She implied...' he stalled, lowering his head, 'that you might have been driven to revenge because Metz...'

'Metz *what?*' she challenged, feeling anything but assertive inside. 'Finished with me? Is that what you're trying to say?'

'Exactly.'

'Cow.'

'Look, we could go and see her. Together. Clear the air and give you a chance to explain...'

'It's not her I need to see. She's just a pen

279

pusher. Collates material from the police and passes it on...'

'Not what she told me. Seems to have far more clout than that.'

'Well, she had to show off to you, didn't she? No, I need to get myself a lawyer. Now.'

'What's crazy about all this is, whoever killed Metz must have had a pretty substantial vehicle. I saw the damage for myself.'

'Not my bike, then?' Her sarcasm surprised even herself.

'For Christ's sake, Natalie...'

Yet why wasn't his protest quite convincing?

'I'd say someone with a hefty 4x4,' he went on.

'That's me out of the frame, then.'

'We saw one near the crash scene. Going north like the clappers. Quite bashed up on the driver's side...'

'Look, don't bother trying to dig yourself out of your hole, Tom, it's no good. I know what you really think.'

She pulled at the door handle but he restrained her. His hand on hers. Cool, calming, and it would have been the easiest thing to leave hers there. However, she withdrew it and baled out, sprinting towards her bike.

'Come back, for God's sake.'

'Get lost, you.'

She forced her helmet down on her hair and ran with the bike to the top of the track. Then, with a flying leap, she landed in the saddle; stones spinning and dried earth spewing from beneath her wheels.

Daylight had died with the sun's disappearance behind the Fer à Cheval, binding the small farms and their land as one. Blurring the bare plane trees and the endless rows of vines in a dull purple light and worst of all, filling her eyes with tears.

CHAPTER TWENTY-SEVEN

There was no placating Kathy, whose fury was now in full flow, and Tom didn't even try. She'd turned on Liliane, accusing her of deliberately putting her son off helping them, of trying to turn Max and Flora against her, while all she was trying to do was keep the family's precious possessions from being ruined by the *fermette's* foul black earth. No, he was too busy thinking about Natalie's parting shot, *Get lost, you...* And realising with a hollow ache that he'd probably just lost *her*.

She'd appeared in his life like that candle he'd seen in St Marc's church that afternoon. A fragile light, jostled by no logical forces, but by his own thankless mind. What if he never saw her again? What if she were to have an accident on her bike on some lonely road somewhere? Would he care? Move Heaven and earth to reach her, willing her to survive against all the odds for himself and the kids?

How can I be sure...? Those words from an old Dusty Springfield tape of his came to mind, summing up his confusion, preventing him from getting into the car to try to find her.

As he watched Kathy slop yet more of Bonneau's precious water into her washing up bowl, he realised now there was nothing he could do to forestall a disaster. It was that bad. Like the final downward run on the Water Shute ride, always the first attraction for them at Littlehampton's summer fair. Strapped in close to one another, the collective trepidation, the cries of humans and seagulls mingling and the gut-churning inevitability of hitting the water fast had held them together. Unlike now, six months later, when the very idea of togetherness felt like a joke.

Suddenly, as if matching his mood, the light from Bonneau's oil lamp seemed to dwindle causing the once-lively shadows it had created to merge with the room's natural gloom.

'Dammit.'

He went to check the level inside the filthy glass casing and realised that soon, without a top-up of oil, they'd be in total darkness.

'Can't you go and get us some more, then?' Kathy snapped at Liliane. 'Do something useful?'

Before she could reply, Tom was heading for the door, but the old woman came out from her relative place of safety and gripped his arm. 'Don't even think of it.'

'Why ever not?'

'Do you want to risk making your family fatherless?'

'Who'd notice the difference?' Kathy snapped, groping around inside one of the full shopping bags.

'*Madame,* what are you saying?'

'I know that lamp. It'll last till you go to bed.

Stay here for now, I have bad feelings. In here.'
She patted her chest.

A defeated lull descended upon Hibou, during
which, the last of the goods and chattels were
brought in and Tom resumed his shifting of
various bookshelves and his former study's desk
while there was still some glow remaining. He
also tried to shift Liliane's warning from his mind.

'I'm so fed up,' sighed Flora, abandoning Max's
colouring book and picking up the blue panda
instead. 'I can't see to do anything.'

'Nor can I.' Kathy vehemently squirted something into the bowl and all at once a sickly floral
smell filled the crowded room, making Flora
sneeze. 'I've given up on the furniture. Now I'm
just trying to get at least one clean work surface
sorted. Not that there's anything to prepare on it.
Joke, eh?' She turned to Tom, looking murderous. 'I'm telling you, if–'

'Hold on,' he interrupted, suddenly back in the
beautifully fitted kitchen in Berris Hill Road with
an evening meal on the go in the fan-assisted oven.
'Do you remember that last September weekend
we spent by the sea? The kids were sitting on that
wall by the beach, and we went into that funny
little kiosk thing–'

'You should never have insisted on leaving
them there like that. Never. Anything could have
happened–'

'We were fine, Mum,' said Flora. 'Even though
that dog did come up and eat all our crisps...'

Kathy let her latest cleaning cloth flop into the
water, and scowled at it.

'You could have caught rabies. Any kind of infection, you silly girl. But hey, why should him over there care about anything as trivial as a life-threatening disease?'

'But we *didn't*, did we? I mean, catch anything for anyone to worry about. We're still here.'

Flora vacated the cream leather armchair and moved away into the darkness beyond the kitchen. After which, came sounds of whispered voices. Hers and Max's.

'For how long, I ask myself?' Kathy shouted after her. 'And here's me doing my level best to keep everyone safe and sound... Oh, damn it! damn everything!'

With that she kicked the bowl so hard that its contents slopped over the sides and into the soil. 'Now look what you've made me do.'

But Tom wasn't there. Couldn't see her rage, her hate. He'd drawn himself back to Sussex to that mellow afternoon with Max and Flora silhouetted against the blur of sky and sea; their laughter rising above that of other weekenders strolling by. With Kathy's hand in his, they'd both stood by a small weather-beaten shack sandwiched between two more prosperous-looking enterprises, where an enlarged Tarot card filled its one window. An image that had caught his attention earlier in the day.

Le Pendu.

He'd scrutinised this man hanging upside down, engraved and tinted to an unnerving degree of realism. Even down to the hairs in his eyebrows and that strange expression on his face, not of fear but resignation...

284

Now he was back in the hell that was Hibou, with a small but hopeful strip of sticking plaster at the ready.

'Remember what that gypsy woman inside told us when we'd asked about it?' he began. 'How we'd been *meant* to see it. How the hanged man represented transition, the change of life's forces. Regeneration, improvement. Hell, Kathy, that's all I kept thinking about when I first saw the advert about this place. Can't you see?'

She kicked the bowl again – a hollow sound this time – then stumbled towards him, holding it. That spray smell suffocating now, clogging up his throat as Liliane quietly took herself outside.

'And what did she say about the other side of the card, eh?' Kathy sneered. 'Go on, seeing as you seem to have a photographic memory.'

But just then the reverse hadn't seemed relevant. After all, he'd endured another grim week at work, with the hefty mortgage and life insurance due to go out of the bank the next day, plus car tax at the end of the following week. All so pointless, so defeating, it seemed.

'OK, I'll spell it out.' She fixed that glare on him again. 'Lack of sacrifice. Unwillingness to make the necessary effort. Failure to give of oneself and obsession with the ego. But the best one was false prophecy. I should have listened to her. Kept listening to her, not *you.*'

She stomped away still clutching the bowl, then suddenly turned to fling it at his unprotected ribs.

'Jesus.'

The pain was bad enough but it also seemed to sharpen the memory of all those years spent trying his best. Giving everyone security in the widest sense. Her the knowledge he'd always be there for her, beside her, and the leeway to keep the house like a chapel of rest. Where the kids' presence was continually tidied away and school friends stopped coming over to play. Word had apparently got round that Mrs Wardle-Smith was a bit odd because they'd had to remove their footwear outside by the front door and wash their hands before eating a snack or even playing with anything.

And the kids, he'd always been there for them. Taught them how to swim, taken them to dance classes and football practise, tried to teach them how to behave to get on in life. But none of that seemed to matter now. It was all slipping away. And it was all Kathy's fault. If only she would *try*. If she would just snap out of her constant pessimism and try to see how good it could be here. But she wouldn't. She wouldn't do it for him and she wouldn't do it for the children. He felt his anger boiling under his skin and clenched his fist by his side, intending, for a split second, to march after her and make her see sense. But then he saw Flora and Max watching in bewilderment from the cave entrance and all the fury seeped out of him, leaving him exhausted.

He turned round and walked out to the car, where, despite now having the furniture, he knew he'd be spending another night.

CHAPTER TWENTY-EIGHT

Natalie finished her Espresso and thanked the girl at the nearest table for the life-saving cigarette she'd given her. With the thirty euros' refund from last night's room she bought five large pizza slices, six bars of nougat and eight brioches. Quite why, she wasn't sure.

She left the Café de la Paix and, for a moment, stood on the brightly lit pavement outside, checking she'd not been followed by whoever had been lurking outside Hibou. It would be so easy to leg it. She could be two hundred kilometres up the A10 by now, with London as her destination. Big, anonymous London with any number of EFL teaching vacancies plus some studio flat in a grungy area. No way would she have camped out at her mother's. Too easy to guess what she might say. That is, if she was in at all to answer the door.

But would she miss her students? Her friends? The university lifestyle? Staff seminars, away-days in some grand hotel or other? No. But she'd miss Tom and his kids, whatever he'd said. Which was why, instead of aiming for the *autoroute,* she turned her machine right for St Sauveur. Was that selfish? She asked herself, passing the dark, seemingly unoccupied Belette Farm. Probably. Was it to save her own skin? Hardly. She could well be a sitting duck there. Was it because loneliness had lived in her heart for too long?

That despite her League work, her busy life, there was no one to share it with? Yes, absolutely.

She was in Metz's hamlet now, and it was still impossible to imagine him dead. She shook her head as if to clear him from her mind, then switched off her lights to avoid any chance of Bonneau's warped gaze. Dismounting, she pushed the Suzuki up to Hibou. All at once, a rustling sound made her stop. Was it that same someone she'd heard earlier, or a creature hiding in the *jardins'* hedgerow? Hard to tell, but instinctively she reached for her precious knife only to realise it wasn't there.

'*Keep walking,*' she told herself. '*Not long now,*' and then looked back to see a shadowy human form hurrying away, almost one with the unruly hawthorn. Her mind raced with each step. Who the hell was that? Someone keeping tabs on her? She'd certainly not been followed from Loupin and if it was Bonneau, he didn't seem injured in any way. Perhaps it was someone who was curious about the English family, or even an opportunist thief waiting for his chance. Whatever, that figure had definitely been male. Definitely suspicious. Where had she read that most burglaries occur just after the victim has moved house? That was probably it. Best to warn the Wardle-Smiths then.

She heard shouting and yelling from the *fermette*, now obscured by the Right Move truck. Things still bad, she guessed, having to push her bike harder along the last, steepest part. It was slowing her up but there was no point in remounting now, for she was almost there. Her own breath sounding more like Liliane's. Shallow, rasping. Fear had

had that effect. Then she became aware of another figure standing at the plateau's edge, facing her way, slapping his arms across his body as if to keep warm. Was he looking at her or at something else?

Tom.

'Christ. You...' he dropped his arms and came towards her.

'I couldn't go. I'm sorry.'

'No more sorries, OK?' He took her gloved hand, squeezed it. Stared so hard into her eyes that her next words came out too fast.

'I've brought some food. Not much, but something you and the kids might like...'

'Thanks. You shouldn't have, though. We'd have managed till tomorrow.' He then gestured towards the *fermette*. 'Listen, it's getting worse. I think she's finally lost it.'

'You mean Kathy?'

He nodded.

'Madame Bonneau's been a brick but Kathy's just hit out at her with the frying pan. God knows what would have happened if I'd not been there.'

'Are the kids alright?'

'So so. They don't really grasp what's going on.'

'Is there anything I can do? Have a word with her, maybe? Calm her down...'

'I wouldn't.' He waited as she parked the bike by the side wall and carried the food bags in, past the men now chucking empty tea chests into their truck singing, 'You'll never walk alone.' Clearly glad to be getting out.

'Tom, wait.' She called out. 'There's something I forgot to tell you.'

'What?' Hunger seemed to drive him on, away

289

from her.

'I swear someone was following me a moment ago.'

He halted, looked around. She guessed what he might be thinking. Her fault. Nothing but trouble. Nevertheless, he checked with the four men, still singing with half an hour left to go. No, they said. They'd not noticed anyone else hanging about.

'It's me, isn't it?' Her voice sounded like a little kid's as he relieved her of both the café's bags.

'Look, please let me pay you for all this.'

'I'd rather it was eaten.'

'A deal. Then we go and see if your stalker's still around.'

In the semi-darkness, Natalie saw Liliane finish her pizza first, then suffer the indignity of finding her remaining teeth embedded fast in the nougat bar. Flora tried to help by using the sharp end of a purple crayon until Kathy, who'd left all of her snack untouched, screamed that if she continued doing such a monstrous thing, she'd fall victim to some dreadful illness.

She was wiping down the bookshelves with a cloth scrounged from the removals men and the place stank of bleach. Her hair clung in limp strands to her neck. Her face a study in misery.

Max meanwhile had taken his booty and had gone to hide behind a louvred wardrobe, presumably for fear someone might try to steal it. Tom chewed mechanically, as if his mind was far away.

Natalie watched each in turn, regretting now that that she'd not hit the road while she'd had the chance. By being a suspect in Metz's death, she was putting them all at risk. She couldn't hang around. No way.

She breathed goodbye, glad that her crash helmet was at least something to cling on to as she slipped outside seemingly unnoticed.

Night again. The temperature had fallen still further to suit her mood. They'd all survive, she knew. Even Kathy. Even Liliane. But what awaited *her?* That solitude she dreaded even more than death itself. So, why not simply find a convenient tree to collide with? A wall, or ravine even? Deeper than the one Bonneau had pushed her into. So deep there'd be no return...

'Get in,' said a voice from behind her. Tom was so close she could hear his heart. Her own flipped over.

'I can't. This is final.'

'I may be a lousy husband and father, but I do keep my promises. We're going to try and find who might have been tailing you.' He carefully removed her crash helmet from her hands, placed it on her bike's saddle, then opened the Volvo's passenger door.

'What about your family?'

'I told them we're going to get some oil and drinking water. Be twenty minutes at the most.' No way would he mention Liliane's words of warning. She was probably all shaken up anyway.

'I could have brought some with me. Didn't think. Sorry.'

'Don't say sorry. OK? We can last till tomorrow.'

A tapping sound came from outside the car, making Natalie jump. Someone was standing there.

291

'Off somewhere nice, then?' The oldest of the men bent down to address Tom's window, his breath rebounding, blurring his features.

Tom responded by setting his headlights on full beam, then revving up and engaging first gear.

'Hey up, sir!' the man banged his palm against the glass. 'You got big trouble back there. You know that?'

Tom let the window down a few inches. The man was right. Another rumpus was in full swing.

'Sure I know,' he muttered through gritted teeth. 'But it's none of your bloody business. I've paid you to move our stuff, not for marriage guidance...'

'Your *wife*'s paid me an' all,' he said. 'Going back to Blighty with us, soon as we're packed up. Her and the girl. Thought I ought to tell you.'

He checked his watch.

'Flora?' Natalie said out loud, and began to bale out. 'She can't.' She looked at Tom who rested his head on his hands, sounding the horn as he did so.

But they could.

Kathy, Flora and the huge blue panda plus two Champion bags came to the door. They must have thought that noise was the signal to go. Tom leapt from his seat and ran towards his daughter.

'You said you were Max's big sister,' he held her tight. 'That you'd always be there...' His words faded as she turned her face away to hide her tears.

'Don't you dare try and blackmail her, Tom,' said Kathy advancing. 'She saw how you almost turned on me back in there and she's had enough, and once we're back at my mother's I'll arrange for our things to be sent on.'

He stared at her hard, unyielding face. 'You're mad. What about Max? About me?'

Kathy threw Natalie a glance which said it all. Mainly hate. Flora disengaged herself and walked towards the truck.

'We ready?' That same removals man called out. 'Jump aboard, then.'

'I don't know how you can do this,' Natalie said, looking out for Max. 'You've only given it two days here...'

'Two days of hell's enough for anyone, I'd have thought.'

'Flora?' Tom tried to follow his daughter, but Kathy pushed him aside. 'Please...'

Too late. Both were being helped up into the seats behind the cab. The twelve-year-old gripping the panda, still not making eye contact with either Tom or Natalie. Next, the other three men joined the driver and the engine growled into life, pumping white exhaust out into the night.

'You wait,' Tom wiped his brimming eyes with his jacket sleeve. 'You bloody wait.'

Natalie spotted Max and Liliane holding hands in the *fermette*'s dark doorway. He wore his sister's pink puffa jacket over his grimy white shorts. His free hand clutched a whole piece of pizza and, as the truck pulled away, he crammed it into his mouth as if to stop himself from crying.

Pain is not always visible, audible even, thought Natalie. In Tom's case it seemed to fill and over-flow that diesel-smelling void in which they now found themselves. To reach up into the sky and stop even the stars from glittering.

'I want a drink,' Max said, having choked down his last mouthful of pizza. 'You said we were going to get some.'

'Look, I meant me and Natalie.'

'That's not fair.'

She exchanged a glance with Tom. His eyes moist. His pallor shocking in the moonlight. What was there to say? What *could* she say?

'Madame Bonneau,' he began. 'I wouldn't normally ask, but could you please stop here with Max while we go to Loupin. We'll be as quick as we can.'

For a moment she looked doubtful, then took Max's hand.

'You go carefully, mind. Saturday night in Loupin is not the place to be.'

'No!' shouted Max, struggling in her grasp. His face red with the effort. 'I want to go with you two. Please!'

'We'll be there and back before you can say abracadabra fifty times...'

But Max had pulled himself free of Liliane and was hurtling towards the car.

Tom turned to her.

'What do we do now?'

'He needs to be with us. Especially after what's just happened. You did ask.'

He hauled up the handbrake, leaning behind her to help his son open the rear door. The closeness of his body, his leather jacket's smell, different to hers, made her catch her breath.

'What if the Giant comes looking for his

mother? What if he's got an axe?' Max babbled as he clambered gratefully on to the back seat. 'I saw one in his store last night.'

Tom switched on the ignition. Didn't bother with his seatbelt.

'Let's just get going, shall we?'

'Thanks, Dad,' breathed the little lad. He shivered, then clapped his chubby hands together for warmth. Not surprising, thought Natalie, as Tom revved the engine once more. Flora's pink puffa jacket was only made of nylon. Probably grabbed by mistake in the dark back there. She held out her hand to him between the seats and he took it, not letting her go.

All at once, Natalie noticed Liliane gesticulating from the top step.

'What's she saying?'

'Listen.'

'I'm so glad you came back here, *mademoiselle*. Please take care of them both.'

CHAPTER TWENTY-NINE

Still no sign of his mother for the Day of Reckoning, or any chance of a meal. In Belette's kitchenette, with both inner and outer shutters tightly closed, Samson Bonneau squatted down by the small fridge, which held just half a portion of hard Brie and an almost empty jar of brown onions. The kind she'd used in his rye bread sandwiches. Now all that – his picnics on the road, the routine of making a good living – seemed a century away.

His injured head began to ache again; his groin, too, and his right foot from when he'd kicked his mother's bedroom door. He muttered to God to sort it all out before tomorrow, as he went to fetch a beer hidden in the store. Why? Because tomorrow was going to be a very important day indeed. The start of his Step Two plan.

Just then, he heard the sound of a familiar car engine coming down from Hibou and the phone in the hallway start to ring, pulling him up short. If it was about his calves, he was ready for a fight. If it was his mother, she'd have to eat humble pie. And that would just be the entrée...

'Bonneau?' asked a man's voice once he'd picked up the receiver. 'I see you're on your own, *hein?* Good.'

He tried to place the voice but couldn't. He looked around. Anybody with a mobile could be in the next room.

'What if I am?'

'It's important we're private.'

'Why? What's going on?'

'We need you, you need us.'

'I don't get it. Who the hell are you?' His stomach rumbled, partly in hunger, partly fear.

'Never mind that. If you want to be a very rich man, listen to me. Are you interested? Do I go on?'

Bonneau glanced down at the vet's invoice on the hall table. Proof of his recent downfall.

'I might be.'

'You *ought* to be, *monsieur.*'

'Why?'

'I'll be brief. Time is short. Very short.'

'For what?' He wondered where all this was going, sensing tomorrow's plans crumbling to dust.

'It's common knowledge that you not only killed but mutilated your neighbour's pet bitch. Boot prints of yours were found near both sites. Perfect matches, *mon ami.*'

Pure panic now. Put the phone down, he told himself, seeing his hand shaking on the receiver.

'I never took its pups, if that's what you mean. I don't do stuff like that.'

'I'm afraid that's not received opinion, *monsieur.* And then there's the late Bernard Metz himself. Nasty. Very nasty...'

Samson Bonneau sensed more than a shiver pass through his body.

'You mean, he's dead?'

'Yes, and let's face it,' the voice went on, in almost breathless excitement, 'you're in deep water, and that's before we even start on the question of your dead relatives. Not something to be shared with a wider audience, *hein? By* the way, who exactly *was* your father?'

'Albert Antoine Bonneau. Why?'

A sly little chuckle followed.

'*Non, non, monsieur.* Your *real* father.'

Real father?

'Listen. You're a true *Boche* bastard. Ask your *maman.* She'll tell you all about her wartime days in Pech Merle...'

Bonneau felt faint. Spittle dangled from his open mouth and fell on to his hand. Any protest at this blasphemy locked in his throat as the caller continued.

'Sturmbahnführer Fritz Brandt, he was. Fancied your mother on the rebound. Easy enough to check, my friend. Just like I did. Now, where was I? Ah yes. We have a job for you.'

'A job?' Barely a whisper.

'You won't refuse, will you? Whatever your faults, *monsieur*. You're not a stupid man.'

Blackmail.

Bile seemed to leach from his gut. His bowels began to churn as the swift instructions followed. Yes, he had a cell phone, a loaded rifle in good working order. Yes, a Transit van with half a tank of diesel. Just confirming, the man said. We have to get this right.

Strange, thought Bonneau. How come he knew all that?

Loupin's not too far, the caller went on. And best to move now. The target's well on its way. He had fifteen minutes to get there. Fifteen minutes in which to turn his life around. At least that's how it was put. And by Tuesday morning, thirty thousand euros – ten times the amount he'd lost to those vets – would be sitting in his bank account.

CHAPTER THIRTY

'What did the old girl mean about me taking care of you?' asked Natalie once the Volvo reached the bottom of the track and Hibou was out of sight.

'She's had the stuffing knocked out of her,

that's all. She's on edge, like the rest of us.'

'Mum said she was an old witch,' said Max from the corner of the back seat. 'And pulled her hair.'

'That's what I mean.' Tom wiped the inside of the windscreen with his hand. 'Maybe now we can just take one day at a time. Try to stay positive. That's the main thing.'

'Will Mum and Flora come back soon?'

Natalie glanced in the rear view mirror and saw Max's face on the verge of tears. She then looked at Tom. It wasn't her place to hazard a guess. Besides, she would definitely have said no.

''Course they will. I expect they're asking the driver to turn round right now.'

That seemed to satisfy him and he slumped back with his thumb jammed comfortingly into his mouth.

The roads out of St Sauveur were empty, whitened by frost, as the Volvo left the hamlet and its huge rocky landmark behind. To Natalie, it seemed that without the reassurance of light from any street lights or any dwellings they passed, another age had descended. Mediaeval, primitive even, where the forces of darkness seems to hold all the cards. Where apprehension swells unchecked in the mind. Not even the man who sat next to her, or his son, unusually subdued on the back seat could put her at ease. Even Loupin's distant pinpricks of light seemed too far away.

'I don't think that lorry will be turning round,' Max suddenly mumbled around his thumb. 'That's a lie. I heard what Mum said. "I'm never setting foot in this hole again."'

Natalie believed him.

'Look, son,' Tom half turned round. 'This kind of thing happens all the time. I mean, how many kids at your school had family problems? Look at Simon. And Marcus. And how about Toby...'

Natalie knew this wasn't the right approach. But then nothing was right at the moment. How could it be?

'But they weren't over here,' Max replied.

'I know. But I'm not going to keep being beaten up about it. Mummy had plenty of time to make up her mind about moving to France. And Flora.'

Natalie watched the village drawing nearer. A faint glow above the rooftops. Red lights from the local wood yard's lorries setting off on their journeys. Silver trucks pulling into the creamery. That same yoghurty smell as at Belette, creeping into the car.

Suddenly Max brightened. Removed his wet thumb from his mouth and leaned forwards to tap his father on his shoulder.

'You know that film Sandy gave me? You still got it?'

'Yes. Why?'

'Can't we get it developed. Just to see what it is?'

'Not now, son. We're getting drinks, then some oil from somewhere, though God knows where. That's our priority. Anyway, we'll be giving the thing back to him on Tuesday. Better all round, eh?'

Max sighed. The wind gone out of his sails.

'What film?' Natalie's interest was aroused. There'd been mention of it earlier but she'd not taken much notice. Other things had been on her mind.

'Didier, or rather, Sandy as Max calls him, gave him one today.'

'Do you mean Keppel's son?'

'Yep. Maybe he's a bit hard up. Hoping to see my lad again with the prints all ready and paid for.'

Tom's premise didn't make sense. The Keppels were comfortably off. Had to be, living where they did. OK, perhaps his mother was stingy like hers had been. Perhaps he wasn't allowed out much. Whatever, Max was right. It was definitely worth a go, especially as they were already in Loupin with that late-opening *Tabac* close by.

'I think we should take a look,' she said. 'I'll pay for it. And I'll get Max some sweets.'

'Cool,' he said.

'What are your favourites?'

'Cola bottles. The sugary ones.'

'No probs.'

'He's guzzled all that nougat and pizza,' said Tom.

She wanted to say that it wasn't every day your mother and sister walked out of your life, like her parents had done. A few extra sweets was the least she could provide.

'You win,' Tom gave her the briefest glance. 'I'm a beaten man.'

Max now pressed up against their seats, his eyes agog with curiosity. However, as they passed the Café de La Paix with its enticingly lit front window, the strained silence snapped like a winter branch.

'Dad, can't I have a Coke, *now?*' he whined.

'I'm parched as anything!'

Natalie suppressed a smile. He creased her up sometimes, with his funny ways.

'Not yet, son. In a moment.' Then, once he'd found a parking space by the crowded gravelly kerb some way down from the *Tabac* she'd used yesterday, he switched off the engine.

'Right,' he said. 'Everybody out.'

At this, Max snuggled deeper into the corner of the back seat. 'Do I have to?' he complained, making an exaggerated shivering noise. 'I've just got warm.' He looked up at Natalie who was already holding his door open. 'Can't *you* get me a drink and those sweets? *Please...*'

'What now?' she asked Tom.

'God knows. This is exactly why I wanted to leave him at Hibou.'

He peered into the car. She sensed his patience was about to snap.

'No way was I staying with the giant's mum,' retorted Max.

'She's a dear old lady,' said Natalie. 'And a friend.'

'I don't care.' The boy retreated further against the upholstery, bringing his legs up to his chin.

'Look, son,' Tom's tone signifying a climb-down. 'We're all cold and tired. If you want things your way, you stay put. You don't move. Understood?'

'Yes. Thanks, Dad.' He gave them both a cheeky thumbs up sign, but this did nothing to allay Natalie's anxiety.

Tom didn't alarm the Volvo, but locked it manually instead. Now his son's nose was pressed up against the window as if he was counting the minutes of their absence already, looking so adorable in pink; so cuddly.

'He should really be with us,' urged Natalie. 'Like Liliane said, we don't know who's out there.'

'Look. Let's just get on with it, eh? Before he changes his mind again.' He passed her the film and led the way along the gravel into the shop as traffic appeared as if from nowhere, and sped off into the night.

'We close in ten minutes,' announced the middle-aged woman as she dragged a rack of curling postcards into the *Tabac*. Its wheels grated on the tiles as she did so. She stopped to frown at the film Natalie was holding out to her.

'Can't do these now. Sorry,' she said. 'Why not wait till the morning? You'll still be around, surely?'

Natalie felt like saying their plans were none of her business, but instead willed a big smile to appear.

'We'd just be very grateful. Thank you.'

The woman glanced at her watch embedded in her fat arm.

'Be a rush, mind. I'll have to ask my son...'

Natalie handed over the cartridge case then bought a late edition of *L'Expresse*, two bottles of Coke and an Evian water, together with a packet of cola bottles. She pulled out a fifty euro banknote from her wallet behind the Les Angles skiing holiday photo, and kept her smile going. '*Voilà, madame*. Here's some extra for the favour.'

'No, let me...' Tom's wallet was already out and open.

'Hey, remember? This is my idea.'

303

The shopkeeper eyed her intently, or was it suspiciously, as she took Natalie's money and handed over the goods in a white plastic bag.

'You were the one who asked about Monsieur Bonneau and bought an envelope and stamps from here yesterday,' she said.

Natalie nodded, passed the bag to Tom, while the woman limped in slow-motion to the rear of the shop.

Seconds later, a stocky man in his late twenties, whom Natalie guessed was her son, duly appeared through that beaded curtain, wearing a plastic apron over his jeans and bringing the smell of cooking with him. His sharp blue eyes alighted on the money, the roll of film, then finally her and Tom. He untied his apron and relieved the woman of the film.

'Follow me, please. I work through here, but she's got me doing the dinner tonight. Me? I ask you.'

Next, he pulled a brown folding door across to reveal a purpose-built dark room, hung with an array of dramatic black and white prints featuring close-ups of oolite and concretionary limestones; gaping caverns guarded by phallic stalagmites. The stuff of which St Sauveur and its environs was made.

The combination of roast boar meat and acetate grew stronger as he unscrewed the top of the cartridge. Natalie felt sweat gathering under her armpits. The place was stuffy, unhealthy, but Tom seemed too engrossed in the prints to notice.

'All my own work,' the other man boasted, then pointed to a silver Kodak machine adorned by a column of red and green lights. 'And this is where I do the boring stuff. For *Maman*. Evenings only, mind. Not my main job, thank goodness.'

He opened a side drawer in the machine, inserted the film then closed it. Immediately a humming noise filled the room.

'200 ASA, eh? Indoor shots then,' he said to himself, garlic on his breath. 'Did you use flash?'

'No.'

'Friends and family, is it?'

'Yes, that's right.'

Natalie had been caught on the hop, and now prayed Tom wouldn't opt for honesty as Bernard Metz had tended to do. If they were out for a meal and his steak was too *bien cuit*, he'd send it back. His fees never more than for hours worked and cost of materials. His milometer untampered with when he'd part-exchanged his old Éspace for a new one. He'd probably have been called 'Honest Joe' in England. At least, so she'd thought at the time.

'How quick can you be?' Tom interrupted her reverie. 'We're running pretty late.'

'Fifteen minutes at most.' The man peered at what seemed to be a computerised dial below the drawer. He looked up at her, downy hair high-lighted on his top lip. 'Would you like an *apéro* while you wait?'

Natalie glanced behind her. The woman was hovering near the magazines. Listening, no doubt. 'No thanks. Really.'

'Did I hear *Maman* say you came in yesterday?'

'That's right.'

'Where are you from?'

'Nideheim. Near Strasbourg,' she lied again, risking Tom's stare. Then realised with a jolt that if he'd seen how easily she'd done that, how could he believe anything she said?

'So what are you doing in this one-horse hole?'

She wasn't sure why she hesitated, but the pause felt uncomfortable. OK, she was asking a favour. Didn't mean he had to know her life story.

'Visiting my friend over the weekend. He lives here.' Tom saved the day.

'Right.' From a pile of papers on a nearby shelf, the guy picked up a small clipboard to which a ballpoint was attached by a length of string. He passed it to her. 'I'll need a name and contact number. Just for the record.'

'Why? I'm not leaving the area for two weeks.'

'It's Kodak. Not me.'

Reluctantly, she obliged, then handed him back the clipboard.

'Nice name, Pascale,' he commented. 'Where are you parked?'

'Near the Café de la Paix.' She lied again. One never knew...

'Now there's a place. Raided last week. Right den of iniquity it is. Did you hear about that *noir* trying to send emails from there?'

'No.' She stared at his hands around the clipboard. Plump like his mother's, with pinkened fingertips. When he'd taken that money from her, she'd felt their clammy heat against her skin...

'Got a right duffing over. Someone thought he was a terrorist touching base in In Salah somewhere. Big mistake letting them all in, I'm telling you.'

She could sense Tom's disquiet at this blatantly racist view. And his impatience. He kept looking at his watch, then the door. Again, this was all her fault.

Come on. Come on... She willed the machine to deliver. Skimmed *L'Expresse* for any news of Metz or Filou, but there was nothing.

'And I'll tell you something else,' the other man went on. 'That bar is where everyone who is anyone in the criminal fraternity hangs out. It's *known.*' He tapped the side of his nose. 'Say no more.'

'You stayed there last night, didn't you?' Tom said, presumably to make conversation. His restlessness growing by the second.

'Thanks.'

'Need some fresh air, if that's OK with you,' he said suddenly, brushing the heavy plastic bag against her leg. 'Can I get lamp oil from anywhere here?' Natalie tensed up. Surely he wouldn't leave her there on her own?

'Nothing doing in Loupin, but Gandoux's not far...' shouted the man after him. Beads of perspiration twinkling his incipient moustache. He seemed genuinely edgy. Why, she couldn't guess.

She watched Tom pull back the folding door and disappear into the shop. Five minutes later the machine's hum stopped. Its green light glowing insistently.

'Here we go. Right on the dot.' The amateur photographer opened the machine's lid and tutted. 'Hey, you've only got five here. The rest are duds.' His tongs delivered these first, followed by the rest. Suddenly he seemed to freeze, letting the last one slip free to fall on to his trainer. Despite the gloomy light of the little room, she could see how he'd blanched. How his lips had tightened.

She snatched up the stray print and turned it round to make sense of the poorly lit, slightly blurred image. But why had the man now picked up a cordless phone and beginning to dial? Where the hell were the other prints? The negatives even? Nowhere. It was time to exit. She had no choice.

With that one print stuffed into her pocket, she charged back into the shop towards its front door, knocking a display of paperbacks to the floor. She noticed Tom in the DIY corner poring over a magazine, clearly having given up any idea of getting oil from anywhere.

'Come on, let's get out,' she shouted to him while the younger man followed, demanding to know where the film had really come from, threatening to call the police.

Once in the street, with Tom protesting behind her, she glanced round to see two silhouetted figures in the *Tabac*'s doorway. Why had he kept those negatives and prints? What were they to him? Because she now realised his reaction hadn't simply been one of alarm, but of recognition. And, while forty kilometres away at the Aire des Aigles, South of Souillac, Kathy and Flora were sharing a small bottle of Orangina inside the Right Move truck, Natalie spotted the Volvo. Its rear passenger door hanging open.

CHAPTER THIRTY-ONE

The only heated pool in the Quartier Louis Pasteur had turned the colour of midnight despite the dusky aura of the windless, sunless sky. Its surface unbroken save for a cinnamon coloured head and pink limbs thrashing out one length after another.

Didier Keppel liked to imagine he was swimming La Manche, or even the Atlantic, while his mother busied herself in their sumptuous ground floor apartment, or at work in the Hôtel de Ville.

Here, there's no need for any permanent life guard or protective fencing – due to become law in 2004 – as the residents of the four white apartment blocks that surrounded it keep more than a close eye on its swimmers, its jokers and the ball players who, in the summer months, practically live out on the expanse of Art Deco tiles.

Then the clusters of wrought-iron tables and luxurious sun-loungers are crowded with people at ease with each other, relaxing after weeks of travelling or maintaining businesses from home. People with time to spare and dreams to dream...

However, tonight, Pauline Keppel was in a hurry. She'd called out to her son repeatedly and told him to come inside and have his supper before her short but urgent trip into town. Damn the boy, she thought. In a world of his own as usual. Ignoring her.

She checked his meal – a shop-bought lasagne – the mozzarella topping of which was already bubbling brown in the oven, increasing her hunger; tempting her to lift out a little corner with the tip her knife and, without spoiling her lipstick, drop it into her mouth.

'Didier!'

At last.

A small hand raised in reply. A dripping figure heaving himself from the water, then snatching up his towel and running towards the apartment's rear entrance. She watched with a mixture of annoyance and admiration. For her young man, once a premature baby, was already turning into a fine specimen with firm muscles underlying what at first seemed a slender form. Yes, he was coming along very nicely indeed. His brain too, which loved nothing better than to complete *Le Monde* crosswords within the hour or gobble up Maigret novels, often announcing an even more credible villain at the end than the author himself. He also had an interest in art, which she'd tried to nurture by visits to museums and galleries, especially the Ingres in Montauban.

So, she mustn't be too hard on him. He was her future, after all. Where Christophe Keppel, his father could never be. A man whose coronary had felled him while fighting for Bobigny's FN seat in the last Presidential elections. Was it five long years ago that she'd given up on Paris? Five springs and winters lived in an area so diametrically opposed to big city life? It was hardly possible.

Her mind raced on as she checked the contents of her briefcase once more. But then, hadn't she

310

always been resourceful? Committed to her work, her beliefs? And wasn't the very fact that she lived in the most sought-after development in the whole of Gandoux testimony to her survival skills?

Absolutely. But since that recent phone call from Loupin, all that was under threat and her survival skills were key.

'*Maman*, where are you going?' The swimmer stood at the kitchen door draped in his Asterix towel, dripping water on to the terracotta tiles. The skin on his hands puckered white. His hazel eyes glazed over like some creature who's never known dry land.

She tried to conceal her irritation at his question.

'My usual meeting, why?'

The boy looked puzzled.

'But you went last Saturday. I thought they were once a month?'

'Something's cropped up, *mon petit*. One of my friends is leaving, so we're having a little farewell get-together.'

'Will you be back at the usual time?'

'Yes. But you've got my number, just in case. And don't forget, there's Lola if you've any problems.' That reminder about the concierge seemed to satisfy him. He sniffed around the oven.

'I'm starving.'

'Good. So am I. Switch it off when you're ready and don't play your music too loudly.'

'Change the record, *hein?* Anyway, what's wrong? Why are you so ratty?'

'It's nothing. By the way,' she added hurriedly. 'Don't go near the waste disposal. It's switched on at the moment.'

311

'I can't hear it.'

'That's why I'm warning you. See that green light going on and off?'

'OK.'

She walked towards the *salon* and the front door, where her pale blue NAF NAF duffle coat and low-heeled shoes lay waiting. Items she never normally wore in Gandoux. En route, she made a quick diversion into her bedroom to check there was nothing visible to arouse his curiosity, should he once again decide to pull the cotton wool from the door's keyhole.

'When's Max coming over again?' he called out from his own room across the corridor. She paused while secreting a man's dark green tie inside one of her many shoe boxes.

'Any time he likes. Great kid, eh?' She turned the gold key twice. Decided to leave his spy-hole unblocked.

'Yeah. His dad's not bad, either.'

'He's trying his best, considering.'

'You got their number? I could call Max. Ask him round again.'

'Look, son, I'm late already...'

'Please, *Maman*...'

She opened her briefcase again, located her filofax and wrote her own version of the number the Englishman had given during his visit to her office.

'Have a good time,' he said, studying the torn-off page with a little frown.

'I'll try.'

'By the way, who's leaving?'

'That's the surprise.'

With that, and cursing his curiosity, she closed the front door behind her. A heavy oak affair inlaid with oblongs of opaque glass. Impenetrable, designed for security. As was the CCTV recording her blurred image on to the concierge's screen.

'*Bonsoir, madame,*' the concierge nodded at her from inside her booth.

'*Bonsoir,* Lola. How are all your *petits-fils?*'

'Getting bigger every day, thank you.'

'That's good.' Pauline smiled at her, wondering if she'd need gloves. Circulation had always been her weak point, and already her skin, especially her fingertips, sensed frost in the air. After a day of sun, the night would be colder still. It wouldn't do for her to get a chill. Least of all now.

All at once, her phone rang in her coat pocket. The second time in half an hour. She waited until she was well away from the building before answering. The one downside of apartment living was that Lola Couzon was the nosiest creature in the whole of France. But as the clerk listened to her caller, a smile crept along her mouth.

'You couldn't wait to tell me, I know,' she said.

'A little gratitude might help.'

'I'll soon be there to show it in person. Even better, don't you agree?'

She then ended the call before he could reply. She'd never liked dogs for that same reason: they clung, they demanded, expected too much. Just like him.

As her shoes click-clicked across the courtyard towards the exit, she noted how many neighbouring lights were switched on. Imagined what lay beyond the voile drapes, the fancy blinds. TV-

313

meals being prepared, sex perhaps. Lives proceeding in an orderly manner, unlike those at Hibou. Unlike hers now, if she was truthful.

She'd felt nothing but disbelief at how the wife there had let her husband make all the decisions. Whatever criticism might be levelled at herself, Pauline Agathe Keppel, a hard-working widow and mother of one, she'd never have let that happen. Never.

Stars winked their presence high above the black vineyards. To the right of her lay the Plough, unmistakable in its simplicity. Then Orion, the hunter, wielding his sword. Such symbols of power created by men, for men, she thought, disabling the car's alarm. However, she knew in her heart – that unique repository of energy and renewal – that real power lay more subtly in the mind. Moreover, the mind of a visionary woman.

That same early frost had already settled on the mopeds and bicycles parked in the Quartier Louis Pasteur's narrow curving street beyond the Maison François Mauriac's social housing unit. Not that she'd read any of this particular author's work. Fiction in any form had never appealed to her. It was facts and knowledge that counted, not a writer's fevered imaginings. That's why she'd not lasted long at her Paris convent, before marriage and motherhood.

She pulled up her coat's hood, keeping her face obscured from any prying eyes. The ambience in this little backwater had always unsettled her, and even though there was no CCTV to monitor her associates' comings and goings, nevertheless the street harboured too many people with too many idle tongues ready to talk. This would be the last time she'd ever be walking up this circuitous route that led ultimately to St Marc's church. Recent events had seen to that.

Pauline Keppel glanced at the black Cherokee parked between less conspicuous vehicles near the town's main shopping street. To say it had taken a knock was an understatement and it was the height of stupidity to have parked it so publicly. She would have words with her arrogant colleague. Strong words.

And that carelessness wasn't the only irritant. Before leaving the office that day, she'd made some notes in her Filofax, recalling the *Anglais* brat's implied criticism about her large, generous handwriting. He wouldn't be half so cocky if he could read what was on the page now. Or see what lay in her heart. She checked her reflection in the windows that were still unshuttered, adding the bonus of glimpsing into the lives beyond.

She pressed the discreet entry phone's button, at the same time aware of her loyalty ring glowing under the security light. She doubted the *Anglais* or his kid had noticed it. Too wrapped up in the mess they were in for a start.

'*Hurry up,*' she muttered to herself, tapping her purple varnished nails impatiently on the black front door. Despite the risks of nosy neighbours, how much more convenient was this venue than the Palladian style Château du Lac set in the middle of Gandoux's public park, home to the left-wing Jewish mayor and his cronies' endless meetings, which had encroached more and more upon their space in the days when their numbers had needed it.

'*Oui?*' a man's voice crackled from the entry phone's perforations.

'Your Queen.'

In the good old days, when her special friends had numbered six or seven, she was always last to arrive. All part of her strategy. Now was different. Yes, very different.

A tall figure with a full head of blue-black hair and dressed in the casual clothes of leather jacket and jeans, opened the door and without a word or a glance led her along the black and white tiled passageway, past several locked doorways, to a small room at the very end. Its space was filled by an oval table and three chairs in a rustic style, while a single lit candle in a beaten pewter holder stood in the table's centre, giving off the scent of something disconcertingly akin to baby oil.

The man stayed in close attendance as she sat down in the chair nearest the door. She could hear him breathing, faster now. Waiting his chance...

'I don't like men standing over me, Râoul, you know that. And by the way,' she glanced up at his cold blue stare, 'get that Jeep of yours repaired, urgently. Why leave it exposed like that?'

'Too busy.'

He stared down at his hands. A sign for her to be wary. It helped of course, to be Parisian born and bred. Her French necessarily quite different to that rough tongue of the Lot. So, peasant that he was, he slunk to his seat next to her. She crossed her trousered legs and slipped her coat from her shoulders, aware of his eyes on her every move. His gaunt face reflected with added intensity in the table's glossy surface.

'That's why I'm here.' She kept her voice business-like for good reason. 'I speak, you please listen.'

'Where's the gratitude you promised me?'

She ignored this petty put-down and came straight to the point.

'We're in trouble, *hein?* A serious complication to our initial plan. And all because of a single photograph...'

Belassis began to press down the cuticles of each finger in turn, then systematically bent each of his knuckles until he heard the required *crack*. She winced, this being the one sound she couldn't bear. The breaking of bones. His way of dealing with stress. She went on.

'So, Alain's confirmed that everything on the five prints he's just developed can be traced back to here?'

An extra sharp *crack* from the major's wedding ring finger was his reply.

'Time you got rid of that memorial room then. Give it a make-over and quick.'

'That's for me to decide.' His tone hard as the winter ice on Gandoux's one public lake. 'When I'm ready.'

'Don't say I didn't warn you.'

Her companion muttered something unintelligible and left his seat to pace the length of the dining room. His cadaverous features had paled to an even more chalky whiteness, contrasting with his hair.

'Musset keeping one of those prints is more

than bad news,' she said. 'She's bound to start digging if and when she gets the chance. That's what she does for that League of St Francis outfit. Makes trouble. And she's good at it, don't forget. Did the bitch recognise him?'

The major shook his head, causing a slick of dark hair to fall across his forehead.

'I know how to keep her quiet. She was also his lover, remember...'

That last word still stung. Especially coming from him. Was the man *so* insensitive? So cruel? She let her palms hover over the candle flame, making it tilt and sway, grow dark at its edges.

'She's already been quizzing about Bonneau, so you said.'

He cast his eyes up to the ceiling and swore repeatedly to himself. Words she knew he'd never have used in his previous existence.

'All is in hand,' he said finally.

'How, exactly?'

'Patience, Pauline, *hein?*'

'Where are the other four prints and negatives?'

'Under lock and key.'

'Whose?'

'Alain's.'

'And the rest of the film?'

'Blank.'

'Do you trust him?'

'With my life.'

'You would say that, wouldn't you? But he must destroy them immediately. Understood?' She made a move to reach her mobile, but he got to his first and in just a few words, passed on the command.

'So,' she continued when his brief call ended, 'can we assume that either Musset or the *Anglais* were given this film by someone determined to undermine what we stand for? To destroy us? Someone who either attended or somehow witnessed our meeting at the end of January?'

'Impossible. There was only you, me and Metz. All loyal. All committed. And as for the *rosbif*, he wasn't around then. So, it must have been her. But she'll be interrogated, trust me.'

The major, who'd not taken his eyes off her, suddenly sat down on the nearest chair and attempted to place his hand on hers. However, she withdrew it and noted the small grimace spoil his mouth. He must learn to wait his turn, she told herself, ready with the next question.

'Surely Alain could tell what make of camera was used?'

'He's not a professional photographer, for God's sake. But it must have been small enough for no one here to notice. The film was for indoor use, that's all we know. The print quality's poor, but not poor enough.'

'So, which of us owns such a discreet camera? I have to ask.'

Two hands rose. The major's quicker than hers.

She sighed. Minutes ticking by.

'And the photographer sat opposite that wall with the blinds?'

'Yes, but we moved around more than usual that evening, remember?' said Belassis. 'We had the Stenckel kid to deal with plus Grazès's CV under discussion. You certainly kept us busy.' He now eyed her without mercy. 'However, I'm almost

319

sure that while Metz was doing his usual party trick, it was you who faced him.'

Silence. Only the candle made any noise, a soft spluttering. Its heat making no difference to the room's sudden chill. To the palpable air of fear.

She pursed her lips and stood up as if to leave, just as a mobile trilled, making her flinch. Stopping her in her tracks. The man pulled his from his suit's top pocket and listened hard. Then, without having spoken, ended the call. His turn to exert control.

'Now, in answer to your question, my action plan. Part One is completed and Part Two's already on schedule.' It was impossible to ignore his strange expression. If looks could kill, she thought... And, judging by the early morning news on the radio, they already had. The Jewish mayor of Gandoux hadn't arrived home from work yesterday. But now was not the time to mention it.

'You mentioned Bonneau?' She reminded him of his recent call.

He nodded.

'Lined up for us already, as you know.' He allowed himself a brief, mean smile. 'And nothing like a missing only son to focus Papa's mind on money.'

'This peasant,' she began. 'Are we sure he knows nothing about us?'

'Quite sure. And there's nothing like an eviscerated dog on the family tomb to encourage him to want to play ball.'

'So why couldn't *he* have collected that bloody dog from the cemetery today? My car will need a second, maybe even a third valeting. And as for my mac...'

'Too many trippers keeping us busy,' he explained. 'Just give me the bill.'

'No time,' she said. 'It took me long enough to dig up all that stuff about his past.'

'I was impressed.'

You should be...

'I don't have a Sorbonne history degree for nothing. You know how I love research.' She also knew how his education hadn't gone beyond the Bac. That it had been his other, less public skills that had impressed Gandoux's *gendarmerie* when he'd first joined them.

'I also know he's working for those *Anglais* at Hibou. They trust him. He's broke now his farm's down the pan, so I made him an offer he couldn't refuse. Pity he won't be around to enjoy it. Whether he finds that print on Musset or not.'

She shuddered inwardly at this fresh glimpse of how efficient this latest recruit had become. Not only that, he was as cunning as a wolf with an empty stomach. Perhaps she'd relied on him too much. Or rather, *used* him. She'd have to monitor this particular loose cannon, especially over the next forty-eight hours.

Just then, her inferior leaned towards her. His reflection in the polished table top now as elongated as that mysterious skull in Holbein's *The Ambassadors*.

'But why not the *petite Anglaise* as well?' he asked. 'Two birds with one stone, surely? Even more effective in keeping out the rest of the invaders, I'd have thought.'

'She left with *Maman* just before our crisis.'

'How did you know that?'

'It's my job. Besides, this means two less English *marginaux* in our country, which is good news. Anyway, I guessed the woman was cracking up on Friday.'

'So did I,' said the major pointedly.

She let this petty point-scoring go. Let him think he's top dog for as long as it suits, she told herself, aware of yet more precious minutes ticking by.

'We can still win against those who think they can sink their diseased roots into our precious soil. We've already given the Germans a fright, and the local *beurs*...'

Belassis suddenly sprang from his seat and stood facing the one shuttered window. His body as dark and lean as those cypresses in the vineyards. Still touchy whenever she used that derogatory word.

'But I've decided that from now on, we'll officially re-group on All Souls' Day. However, it won't be here, so make sure I know if your contact details change.'

'So, it's just you on Monday, then?'

'I know the Bactrix Sales Director. I'll be a familiar sight.'

'Surely you'll be too bloody public?'

His frown did him no favours. Made him seem more vulpine than ever.

'The more public the better on this occasion, surely? Besides, for your Warrior Queen it's the best place of all.'

'Not what we've usually gone for. What's wrong with our station locker system again? With anonymity guaranteed?'

'This is not our usual mission. For a start, there'll be Musset. Double trouble with that one, I'm telling you. I need to be there. I'll be trusted.'

'And the pay-out?' he persisted. 'When do I get my share?'

'11.30 a.m. Tuesday morning at the Ibis, Blagnac Aeroport. It's busy and usefully placed. I suggest you use your existing Swiss bank accounts.' She leant forwards, spat on her fingers and swiftly extinguished the candle flame. The lingering smell soon smothered her own distinctive perfume.

'It's a shame Nicolas Grazès won't be joining us until November,' she added. 'But, hopefully by then he'll have won Gandoux by a landslide and be even more of an asset to us.'

'I'm not sure about the Metz business,' he began unexpectedly as if mention of that other good-looking man had triggered his habitual jealousy. 'It could bring us more unwanted attention. As if we haven't enough.'

'What choice did I have?' she countered. 'No one should have treated me the way our so-called "friend" did. It was humiliating in the extreme.'

'There must have been another method. Again, less public.'

Her stomach tightened.

'There wasn't. Besides,' she shot him a forced but winning smile, 'you did it all for me.'

He looked back at her in way she found odd.

'Well, *didn't* you? And I like the way you've put the wind up Musset.'

'Look, Pauline, I can't work miracles. There has to be hard forensic evidence to nail her. I can only stop her from sleeping at night, OK?' He

323

removed his brown leather jacket, slipped it over the back of his chair and wiped the sweat from his forehead with his shirt cuff. He seemed distracted. Definitely not his usual self at all.

'Wrong. Even though you've made out Metz was drunk and it was a hit and run that got him,' she said, 'you'll keep Musset in custody after Monday midday while I make sure she's first in the queue for Felix Laurent to interrogate. After that, she'll conveniently disappear. It'll look like a suicide. Any objections?'

The major started on his knuckles again. *Crack ... crack...*

'And the English boy?'

She tapped her still-unopened briefcase and sighed.

'Simplicity itself.'

CHAPTER THIRTY-TWO

Suddenly a cry, followed by the slam of car doors. One, two three, four... Tom had sprinted past her to the car, where he stood as if frozen, accompanied by a few local inhabitants drawn there by the noise. A glance told her the Volvo was empty.

'It's Max. Jesus Christ. He's gone.'

'Try the boot.' Was all she could say. She'd seen too many crime films, too many thrillers.

'I can't.'

Natalie took the car keys from him and unlocked it but, save for a foot pump and a battered First Aid box, there was nothing.

She was about to ask the few onlookers if they'd seen anything, when Tom gripped her by the arm. Blame time was looming and she steeled herself for it, her eyes raking up and down the street where the Café de la Paix seemed to be doing a good trade.

'You had to get that bloody film developed, didn't you?' he hissed at her. Pale, tearful. 'Now see what's happened. And if we draw attention to the fact that we left a nine-year-old kid on his own, then God knows...' He buried his tousled head in his hands and the curious natives, now realising they weren't going to be involved, started to edge away.

She had to ignore this censure. Try to think.

Hadn't there been a high-profile case in Cahors two months ago where a German toddler had gone missing after being left in a buggy outside a *boucherie?* And something similar involving a baby in this very Commune two years ago? A wine shop seemed to ring a bell. But Max was neither a baby nor a toddler, and their visit to Loupin hadn't been planned. She watched the small crowd disappear into the night. Maybe there was a connection if only she could grasp it. Maybe...

She drew closer to Tom to comfort him as best she could, but he pulled away. That small spark between them all burned out.

'What if he just took himself off into that bar down there?'

'Impossible. He couldn't have.'

She turned to him. 'OK, but are you *sure* you

locked the car up in the first place?'

The speed of his reply caught her by surprise.

''Course I did. You saw me. Couldn't alarm it, though, could I? Not with someone sitting inside. Oh God, what's going on? What's Kathy going to say? And Flora? It's nine o'clock already.'

Natalie could just imagine. She glanced down the street towards the Café de la Paix's lighted window.

'Let me suss that place out, then I'll phone your removals firm. You got their number?'

'Only the UK office.'

Even with the hour's time difference, they'd probably be closed. She saw him slump against the car as if those four words were all he had left. The next bit was all going to be down to her and, strangely empowered, she ran towards the amber glow cast by the café's bright interior. People inside looked happy, enjoying themselves. She'd been there herself, not even an hour ago.

'You've not noticed a brown Volvo parked further up the street, have you?' She asked the brunette working the till. A cigarette stub hanging off her bottom lip.

'Why?'

'A little lad's gone missing from it.'

'No. Not seen nothing.'

'He's English with blond curly hair,' Natalie persevered. 'He was wearing his sister's pink puffa jacket and white shorts.'

The other girl shook her head and killed her dimp in a filthy saucer. 'Or, have you heard anything odd going on outside?'

'How old is he?'

'Nine.'

'All kids in here, mind. What with all this racket, I wouldn't hear if the bloody world was ending.'

'It already has.' Natalie muttered to herself, turning to the darkened hordes playing pool or crowded round the Café's many tables. She remembered what that man in the *Tabac* had said about its reputation, and looked around for any dodgy looking characters, even Bonneau. Yet hadn't she'd once read a media article in her university magazine about Hitchcock's penchant for innocent-looking guilties and guilty-looking innocents? In that case, everyone present tonight should be under suspicion.

She tried to corral her faculties, but with Max on the loose somewhere, and that photo still in her pocket, it was impossible. As she headed back to the Volvo, to her dismay, Tom emerged from a side street empty-handed.

'Any joy?' he asked, the moment he caught sight of her.

She shook her head.

'It's so bloody cold,' he shivered himself. 'He's only got that nylon thing on over his T-shirt.'

What could she say? Hell's River Lethe was beckoning and with every passing second, its bottomless silent water, was rising as swiftly as a midnight tide.

'I've got to call the police. I've no choice.' Tom paced up and down. Each step echoing the thud of her heart.

'You can't. I'm a suspect, remember?'

'Me, me, me...'

'How dare you! I risked everything coming

327

back to Hibou–'

'I'm sorry, I'm sorry. Look,' he turned to her, 'we won't reveal your name, OK?'

'What if I have to show my ID?'

'Cross that bridge, eh?'

'I can't. I'm sorry, I have to get back.' Suddenly his arms were around her. Fear, anger and something else just as powerful, locking her in. Not letting her go.

A white Laguna from Gandoux's *gendarmerie,* took fifteen minutes to arrive. No Belassis as anticipated, but two men with enough grey hair under their *képis* to suggest they were near retirement. The driver clean-shaven, his companion with a trimmed moustache. They wouldn't be wanting any challenges, she thought, watching them routinely fingerprint the locks, leaving a white smear round each one. Praying they wouldn't focus on her. There was no evidence of vehicle interference, they said. The lad may well have grown impatient of waiting and slipped out of the unlocked car himself.

'I told you already, he was with *us*. And what's more, my car was left locked,' Tom said grimly. He wasn't looking at her. The lie they'd agreed upon to keep accusations of negligence at bay, now seemed a flimsy one.

'Not alarmed, then?'

'In a busy street like this? Come on.'

Natalie knew they weren't impressed. She too was puzzled. Did someone else have a key or some other means of entry?

They climbed inside the Laguna, accompanied

by more than a whiff of McDonald's. Tom sat next to her in the back seat, separated by an arm rest.

The driver's moustachioed partner produced a file marked 'Statements.'

'We'll need one from each of you,' he said, unclipping it. Natalie and Tom exchanged a glance. She already had false details if need be, but when the moment came to sign her name, her resolve wavered. She was already in trouble. Maybe this would bring everything into the open. Give her a chance to clear her name. She took a deep breath but still her hand trembled. *Natalie B Musset. 30/3/02*

There.

She could feel Tom's tension like static against her. But there was no reaction at all from the *gendarme*. What was going on? Was she wanted for questioning or wasn't she?

She felt drained of everything as Tom also signed.

They also had to show their passports and she, her ID. Again, their was no visible reaction to these from the man.

'So, you claim your son ran off while you were walking to that café down there?' quizzed the driver, his dialect hard to understand. 'Why go there with a kid on a busy Saturday night?'

She was ready for that one.

'To meet a friend from my university. We arranged it ages ago.'

Tom stepped in.

'Kids aren't allowed in her flat,' he explained, and that seemed to do the trick. This pair were hardly thorough. Why not follow that one up with a request for an address? Her first assumptions were surely being proved right.

'Just find him,' begged Natalie. At this point, the driver's partner stepped in.

'First things first. Now then, *monsieur*. You say your son skipped off down the Rue Viollet le Duc. Why would he do a thing like that?'

It seemed an eternity before Tom answered. But she had to keep quiet.

'He's impulsive. Curious. Lots of kids are–'

'I see.' Tucking the Statement file inside his jacket.

The driver glanced round at her.

'Are you married, *monsieur?*'

Tom fielded that too.

'Yes, but my wife's unwell. This'll only make her worse. For God's sake, please don't tell her.'

'But we'll need *this* young lady's particulars.'

Natalie tensed. Said a quick, silent prayer.

'Like I told you, she's a family friend, that's all.' Tom's face now flushed with resentment. His hands working his hair. 'How dare you imply anything else. More to the point, why aren't we getting a move on with a search? Anything could be happening. Max is my boy, remember? It's dark, it's cold, and he can't speak the language.'

Both men looked at each other and was she imagining it or did a subtle collusion lie just beneath the surface?

'These are our mobile numbers, OK?' said Natalie. 'Please ring us if you find anything at all, however small.'

Once Tom had provided his, she rattled hers off

and began opening her door. She signalled for Tom to do the same. Then came the ominous click of the locks.

'*We'll* say when you can go.'

'For God's sake, please let us out.' Her voice sounded thin and useless. 'You've asked all your questions.'

'Not quite.'

'What d'you mean?' She was aware of Tom beginning to sob into his hands. Apart from those poor calves, the most gut-wrenching sound she'd ever heard.

'How long have you, er ... been Mr Wardle-Smith's *friend?*'

'Why?'

'We want to hear it from you.'

'I met him yesterday, if you must know. I was lost.'

A discreet snigger as the door lock unclicked.

'He doesn't take long, then?'

'Just help us, eh?' She got out and stared in at both men. Eye to eye, unflinching. 'Or, we'll be making big trouble. Starting with the British Embassy in Paris, where my father happens to work.' Her lie seemed to do the trick and, after an exchange of uneasy grunts, the driver set the car into gear. Suddenly there was a buzz from a two-way radio. The cop in the passenger seat unclipped it from his belt.

'Belassis? Placard here.'

Natalie listened.

'Right. We're in Loupin, ready to go.' He turned to the driver. 'Best be shifting. You know how he is.'

331

The saloon slid away and disappeared up the Rue Voltaire.

'Bastards,' she said, looking after them. 'Still, you didn't lose your rag, which is what they wanted.'

'I'm bushed, though,' Tom held her hand as if it was all he had left. 'Some father.'

'Don't beat yourself up. Max will be fine. He's a big, bright boy.' How easily those words came. How hollow they sounded. She must try harder. Take the lead.

He glanced at her. 'By the way, who was it that promised to visit the services today?'

'Belassis. That major at Gandoux with the weird eyes.'

'I don't get him.'

'Nor me.'

'Describe this Max of yours,' said the thin blonde woman who'd just unlocked her Mégane, parked in front of a hairdressers. An aroma of ammonia and hairspray hung around her as she leant over to slot the ignition key into place. Ready for a night out, thought Natalie, without a trace of envy. She saw Tom's eyes fill up again as he recounted the past ten terrible minutes.

'That's odd,' the stranger said, when he'd finished.

'Why?' He took Natalie's hand and squeezed it. In optimism or desperation? she wondered. Surely both.

'About half an hour ago the old girl sent me out to the post box near the florists. She reckoned that way her salon invoices would be ready for the first collection tomorrow.'

'Sunday?'

For a moment she faltered, then smiled.

'Stupid me. 'Course, it's Easter Day. Still,' she threw a backward glance towards the shop, 'she forgot that as well.'

'Never mind. And?'

'There was this white van. Clapped out old thing, too. Parked behind some British Volvo.'

'Go on.' His grip tightened on Natalie's hand, then he let go.

'Well, I checked out its plate. A 1997 model, and the dealership sticker said "Barrows of Kingston." Wherever that is.'

'Was anyone in it?'

'To be honest, I didn't look. Why should I? I don't take much notice of foreign cars but Grazès will. And his supporters. You'll see.'

Natalie's fists tightened inside her jacket pockets, still home to her mobile, spare briefs, and the half-eaten pack of radishes. Souvenirs of Boisseuil, which now seemed to exist on another planet.

'Please go on,' she prompted, dreading what might come next, unsure whether to believe her or not. Not *wanting* to, if she was honest.

'Well, I'd just posted the stuff and was on my way back here – I don't like leaving *Maman* on her own, you see.' She lowered her voice to barely a whisper. 'Not with a till full of money. And I heard this scuffling sound and a man's voice. Then a weird cry, like some eagle's prey. We often get that round here.'

Tom steadied himself against a nearby litter in. He'd turned a sickly yellow.

'Anyway I looked back and saw the same van burning up this street as if the devil was after it. You should have seen the smoke. Some old engine. Jesus! At first I thought it was someone who'd had a shot or a skinful – quite a bit of that round here, too – but then back it comes, heading the other way.'

'What kind, exactly? There are vans and vans–'

'Big, you know.' She drew a shape in the air.

'Going towards St Sauveur?' Tom's voice was barely audible.

'Could have been.' She shrugged.

Natalie's breathing was forced, shallow in that deep cold night, while the moon seemed more than ever to fill the whole sky, tingeing Loupin's featureless frosted streets in a bitter, eerie light. Nothing mattered now except to find Max and support the man she now knew she could never leave.

However, the Rue Voltaire was now deserted save for a few randomly parked bikes and runabouts, and she wondered how the police were getting on.

Just then that photo's image seeped into her mind. The man's square jaw, the dark brows, were certainly familiar to her. But why that strange gloating look in his eyes? And what exactly was he doing? If that was a sample of the film's contents, what were the other prints like?

She dared herself to examine the print again and, having extracted it from her pocket, used the moonlight to convince herself that no way could the man standing there be Metz. He' loved kids for a start. Even sponsored a young Somalian boy's schooling for five years. His photo had been prominently displayed in his studio. She'd seen the maquettes he'd created for those gargoyles, before the fifth and last had been installed. There was a tenderness in each mark he'd made with his delicate steel modelling tools. Every touch a testimony to his love of the innocent, the helpless...

'That crazy man we saw in the *Tabac*,' she began, switching her gaze from the photograph to Tom's face. 'He's kept four of the prints and their negs.'

'Why would he do that?'

'He thought they were mine. I'm sure he was calling the cops when we left. Thank God I gave a false name. I could be done for possessing stuff like that. Look at this.'

She bit back tears while showing him the sole remaining print. But his glance at it was too fleeting. His mind elsewhere. On Max, of course. And then, she realised with a jolt, his little boy hadn't even had his drink or his sweets...

'Please, look at this again,' realising that to name the man could spell the end of everything.

'OK. So it's some guy with a blonde kid...'

'It's a little girl...'

She tried to keep calm despite her mind fragmenting, but somehow, in the murky depths of her consciousness, she knew there had to be a connection between everything that had happened so far.

'For Christ's sake, Tom. I know there's Max to worry about–'

'Too bloody right.'

Moments later, she tucked the photo deep down inside her bra, then changed her mind about keeping it.

'Tom, you take it. It's obviously important, so don't let it out of your sight, OK? Just in case.'

He in turn stuffed it none too carefully in his jacket pocket.

'Didier somehow had to get that film to you. Why?'

He shrugged. 'All I know is Max had to keep it secret.'

'There we go then.'

'What if we'd not met the lad? That's what I'm thinking.'

'Me too. We need to find him. That film may not even have been his.'

Tom's hands left the wheel in a gesture of despair. The car veered sharply to the left.

'For heaven's sake. Haven't we enough to think about?'

And in that split second she could see her life as she'd known it, slipping into the abyss...

Tom fixed his eyes on the street ahead. Numb to everything it seemed, but his car's empty back seat as they circled the roundabout and went back the way they'd come. Down the Rue Voltaire.

Finally, as they left Loupin, she gripped his arm. 'That white van the woman mentioned. A *clapped-out* white van. It's his...'

'Whose?'

'Bonneau's.'

'Oh, come on.'

But fear hit her empty stomach and, as the car sped south, she recalled passing Belette's crowded front yard that very afternoon; the mess, the lingering stench of the midden...

'Why in hell's name didn't I think of it before?' she said, thinking how such an inconspicuous vehicle was ideal for carrying all kinds of loads. Loads she dared not think of. 'It's a Transit. On its last legs. He kept it round the back.'

'Thanks for telling me.'

'I'm doing my best, OK?'

'I know you are.' But his glance showed only pain and more pain.

The Volvo then swerved round into the Rue des Martyrs, and seconds later crawled past the farm's front wall.

'Slow up even more,' she said, craning her head out of the now open window. 'I'm sure it'll be around somewhere.' And sure enough, beyond the gap into the rear yard, there it stood.

Tom left the engine running as he got out. Then he stared down at her with an expression in his eyes she'd not seen before.

'You know Max had a thing about him from day one. And I never bloody listened...' His voice faded as he came round to her side and offered his hand. It felt as cold as a stranger's but he was trying his best. 'Strength in numbers, Miss Musset.'

However, she held back, suddenly feeling a traitor, a deserter. She'd been there, done this little trip before. Instead she glanced up at Hibou, where all was silent. Should Tom phone Kathy yet? she wondered. She didn't know. So far, there'd been no room for anything because the power of this particular vortex was increasing, trapping them together. Clinging to instinct and

337

gut feelings because that's all there seemed to be. And just then, her gut feeling was no longer fear, but terror.

'Do you think Kathy ought to know anything?' she ventured, without bargaining for his reaction. A pure white rage, stiffening the whole of his face.

'No! This is for me to deal with.'

Natalie left her seat and joined him. Those few words were all she needed.

'And me,' she whispered, missing her knife more than ever. 'So, I go in first.'

'Look, our friend's got a rifle and God knows what else. Keep out of sight. We want this as low-key as far as possible. For Max.' He stared at the van and edged closer, then nudged her. 'I'd say that looks pretty wrecked, wouldn't you?'

'Too right.'

'Stay behind me and tap my back if you see or hear anything. Are you ready?'

'I am.'

They crept past Belette's front door and through to the rear yard. The whole farm was completely unlit and the house and remaining outbuildings stood black as gravestones against their surroundings. There wasn't even a candle's flickering, or any sound at all. Just the middens' smell and the faint residue of sour milk hanging in the stillness.

'Here goes.'

Tom made straight for the van. A Ford Transit, with rust round the sills and a bent aerial. Its bonnet still warm, and all the doors locked. He pressed his ear to its side then whispered, 'Max? It's Dad. Answer me...'

Not a sound.

He tried again and again and she watched him, her heart breaking.

'Over here.' He then led her towards the ragged line of oaks where together they both stepped over the trampled wire and into darkness. 'We wait.'

'What for?'

'I know Bonneau's in there, so just keep an eye on that store of his. See that one window? Don't let it out of your sight. He might be taking a peep.'

Suddenly, without warning, the bells at the end of the street began their ten o'clock chime and, like the one she'd heard earlier, they lasted much longer.

'Loud enough,' Tom muttered.

'Handy if you don't want to be heard.'

And, as if on cue, the farm's back door began to open. Inch by inch, revealing an even deeper gloom beyond.

'Not a sound now. Leave this to me,' he urged, before a tall burly figure emerged with both arms holding a rifle at eye-level. Their eye level. The top of its black-holed barrel highlighted by the moon. 'Jesus Christ.'

'Ah, Monsieur Wardle-Smith and Mademoiselle Musset,' the veal farmer fawned as if in mock surprise.

She felt the blood drain from her face.

'Bienvenue.'

'We've come to ask if you've seen my son, that's all,' said Tom in a strangely even voice. 'You don't need to point that thing at us. Please, put it down.'

Bonneau snorted, now moving the weapon from side to side in a deadly rhythm. She edged forwards, but felt Tom's grip tighten on her arm.

339

'He'll pick us off, can't you see?' he whispered. 'Stay put.'

But there was one order she had to disobey. The law of silence. 'Odd how one minute you were happy to help out at Hibou, and now this,' she challenged the hulk. 'What's changed your mind?'

'You and the *Anglais* coming on to my property like vagrants. I do have a front door,' he waved the rifle again, and she heard the ominous click of his finger on the stock. 'That is what most polite visitors would use, eh?'

The farmer was coming closer. She, therefore, had nothing to lose.

'Where's Max? That's all we want to know.'

'Why ask me?'

She steeled herself. Took a deep breath. The League's stats might help.

'Seventy-four per cent of people arrested for cruelty to animals have also been found to have abused a human being. You, *monsieur*, apart from treating your poor calves the way you did, can happily strangle and mutilate a defenceless dog so...'

'You lying little tart...'

He took a step nearer. Then another. Quicker than she realised. Too quick for her to move.

'Natalie!' Tom yelled. 'Watch out!'

The warning was too late, eddying around and around in her mind, until her head seemed to cave in. She felt mush and fear. Before the second blow sent her sprawling to the ground.

CHAPTER THIRTY-THREE

He'd survived a serious screw-up. Just. His mystery caller had suddenly called again and said there were to be *two* catches, not just the one. Ten per cent more money, too, and both were to be kept in the Bouche de l'Ésprit, ready for collection at 10 a.m. tomorrow morning. He'd added that his mobile must be switched on at all times for further instructions. Easier said than done, thought the farmer. But luckily his second quarry had come up to him saving him the trouble of searching her out. Breathe again, Samson, he told himself. But not for long. No time for the usual Ayes and Paternosters to help him on his way. He must get out. Hit the road before anyone came to check up on him. He'd seen the *Anglais* off with the rifle but, by now, he'd probably called the police.

The *génisse* – the heifer – was beginning to stir. Calling her that felt right. What he was used to. He laid down his rifle on the cobblestones and dragged her by her boots towards his van. A second-hand Ford Transit, bought just before his father's 'accident'. Bump, bump, bump... Why on earth the tight-fisted old fool had never had the cobbles replaced by smooth concrete like everyone else he didn't know.

This one wasn't going to be quiet, either, so he tied a piece of oily chamois leather around her mouth and pulled some yellow twine from his

341

pockets for her hands and feet. Once she was tied up safely out of sight inside the van, he went over to what remained of the barn.

No need for a torch. The veal calf lay exactly where he'd hidden it, and even in the dark, its big eyes challenged him. The way they'd done at the play area while he'd freed it from Metz's blasphemy. So why use a blindfold? Why spoil things for himself? He pondered for a moment, then decided to ignore the very specific command. Surely he was allowed *some* pleasure?

'I'm thirsty. I want my mum and dad,' the calf murmured through his gag – a length of bandage which had given many years' service wrapped around Uncle Eric's umbilical hernia.

'Shut up.' He re-tied it taking care not to bruise or damage the pale skin underneath in any way. His way of doing things since he'd taken over the farm.

He picked up the calf, then sniffed. It had wet itself. Its shorts were soaking, making his own clothes wet and pungent. It wriggled, too, but one minute later, was keeping the *génisse* company in the back of the van.

It squealed. Sounded like 'Where are we going?'

'My special place, *hein?* Now then,' he soon located a rag inside the driver's door pocket, and wound it round on top of the bandage. 'An extra something to keep you quiet.'

The rag did the trick and he patted the calf's head approvingly. Little did it know that a million euros was resting upon it. More money than he'd ever spent buying a whole herd. His cut would be cash of course, to keep the tax parasites off his back. As it was, the state stole too much off decent law-abiding citizens like himself, to keep their hopeless cases in drugs and cigarettes. Their pockets full of his money.

He felt dizzy. His own head throbbing again, bursting with recurring fury at how that stranger had begun the call with the news of his real father, the Kraut, if he could be believed. And his mother who'd opened her skinny legs for him. Then, as if that hadn't been enough, the implication he was a serial murderer. Not something to be shared with a wider audience, was it? the caller had taunted before moving on to his proposition. The real reason for his call.

All lies, Bonneau told himself as he heaved his bulk into the cab. All damned lies trying to make *him* the fall-guy for everything. But right now, there was work to do. For whom he had no idea and couldn't even guess. His whole life had revolved around the farm, and even if he was half German, he was still a simple God-fearing soul. And surely God would preserve him?

He drove out of the yard in first gear as quietly as the old diesel engine would allow until suddenly, without warning, he could go no further. The impact with whatever lay in front almost toppled him from his seat while the rifle on the seat beside him clattered to the floor.

It was the brown Volvo. He saw a mobile phone clamped to the *Anglais'* ear. Just as he thought. The *salaud* was calling the police.

Bonneau reversed, then rammed the Volvo's side afresh. Then again and this time, as anticipated, its back end slewed round giving him

343

just enough room to push past into the road. There was no one else around as he booted the throttle to top speed, momentarily distracted by his cargo rolling around in the back. Why the hell hadn't he secured them to the sides in the first place? He thought back to his own calves' fine unblemished skin. Milky white, threaded by the most delicate blue veins. Wasn't that what he'd striven for all these years, for good reward? And the thought then occurred to him that if this particular one was cut and scratched some way, then money might be deducted, or worse...

But what difference would a few marks make to the heifer? None whatsoever.

Headlights now appeared in his rearview mirror, moving in closer behind him. The diagonal strip across the vehicle's radiator told him it was the Volvo again, not police.

Despite its proximity, he let out a grunt of relief, because where he was going, it wouldn't be able to follow. This was *his* country, and the agreed destination with the unknown caller was as familiar to him as the farm itself. A boyhood haunt, deep in the bowels of the Causse de Framat where the only sound is of weeping rocks. A place of perpetual night.

Next morning, Easter Sunday and the Lord's special Day of Rest, the gale woke him with a start, stirring all the region's church bells into excessive chimes, reminding him that normally he'd be in St Sauveur's front pew awaiting the first mouthful of wine and that melt-in-the-mouth hand-made wafer.

Meanwhile, this blast roared into the cave's entrance and the cavern beyond, which was host to an impressive army of stalagmites and stalactites; some twisted like those fancy loaves the hamlet's long-dead *boulanger* used to make, some sharp as the Ibex horn. Twice they'd stabbed him in the back, forcing him to bend low as he'd hauled both beasts to the darkest, least accessible part of the cave. The fear of discovery making him take risks where he should be taking every care.

The *Tramontane* drowned his captives' murmurings while he wedged them close together to take up the least amount of room. The same as he'd done with his calves. So, in a way, he thought, surveying his handiwork, his expertise wasn't being wasted. This was his specialism, after all. Then he noticed the female's oily mask had begun to slip. Time to regain control. A further brief phone call had told him to search her for one particular item. A normal-sized colour print. But why so important? He had no idea. He was just obeying orders like he had from the word go, and to that end, had already quizzed her without success. That stupid mouth had stayed shut. Now was time to try another method. A body search. The kind he'd seen on TV crime dramas.

He re-adjusted her gag then rolled her away from the calf and, when the gap between them was wide enough for his purpose, he emptied all her pockets, cursing his Kraut father for giving him such bulky fingers. Then, having removed his glove, he slipped his palm under her jacket to fondle each of her breasts in turn. But she was too noisy.

He stopped, and backed away, sensing something was wrong, then blinked at the pool of darkness where he'd positioned the calf. He blinked again in disbelief, and shuffled on his knees towards the spot, only to find it empty with just the churned-up ground remaining. He cursed then crossed himself. For Christ's sake, it couldn't have gone far. Not here. And how had it managed to move without him seeing it?

It was all the *génisse's* fault. Her lying there like that, teasing him. He kicked her, thinking of the promised reward slipping away like autumn daylight. If the calf was lost, what then? His orders had been clear and precise. Now look at the mess he was in. Supposing he got another call. A progress check?

He was right.

Merde...

The phone ringing from his pocket echoed like those damned bells from St Sauveur. Drilling into his brain. He stared wide-eyed towards the cave entrance, wary, rigid with panic as he placed the phone by his ear.

'Yes?'

'Is all well, *monsieur?*' That same voice. Barely polite.

'All's well.'

'And that photograph?'

'Not on her. I've checked.'

'Check again, or we may have to deduct from your payment.'

The call ended. Bonneau stared at the fading signal. *Fini...* Then the idea occurred to him that with no phone, there'd be no more calls. No more pressure.

He pulled his Nokia out of his donkey jacket pocket, and tossed it as far away as he could into the cave. Seconds later came the single comforting sound of water.

Plop...

His watch glowed green in the gloom: 6.30 a.m. An hour left to search for the missing calf, but first he had to move the *génisse* into the open where he could keep an eye on her. Once he'd found the calf, he'd bring her back. Easy. He picked up his rifle and hid it under a pile of rags behind the van's front seats, then returned to the task of pulling off her boots – not only to lighten his load but also to send out a signal to her: that he was in control.

He crammed them deep down into a secret crevice leading down to the subterranean river Florentin, where as a solitary boy he'd amused himself for hours. The big dark farmer's son who'd never been noticed by any village girl, yet who had a special way with cows.

Even without her boots, she seemed heavier, less pliant than yesterday, and it took longer than planned to drag her to the cave's mouth. Once outside in the murky light, with the sky still dark over the distant Pyrenées, he paused, trying to keep the wind from his lungs. To be spotted by anyone would be the end for him. Therefore, using the van to shift her was too risky. There was nothing else white on this limestone pavement. Just a subtle range of greys, from blue to ochre. So, best the vehicle stayed hidden, far enough away from the cave entrance.

He scoured his surroundings, for a moment disorienated by the wind's buffeting current and the dull blur of one rock mass with another. Unsure which direction to take to look for the calf.

'Help me, *Seigneur*,' he prayed, as the St Sauveur bells chimed seven and, for the second time that day, he crossed himself. All thoughts for a redemptive Communion with Père Julien devoured by this *Tramontane*, which tore at his hair and stung his ears. It was as if all the demons from now and hereafter had amassed forces to batter his mind. And what about the dead Bonneaus, and even that diseased herd culled twenty-two years ago? Were they, too, ganging up on him, seeking revenge?

He looked at the creature lying face down at his feet. Funny how it was her who'd pulled the plug on his business. Who'd bleated on about those calves in his truck at Aujac – and now look. At his mercy, just like them. God really does move in mysterious ways, he thought, bracing himself for the last arm-aching haul. Its feet felt cold in his semi-gloved hands, the black leather skin tearing against stray sharp stones. With the gale now behind him, it wouldn't take long. Nearly there, in fact. Then he would catch the calf. That was priority.

'Natalie! I'm he … re!'

He suddenly dropped the *génisse's* bare feet and turned into the blast. Someone had called out its name. Someone who must have seen them both. Was it the *Anglais*, or even his calf? he wondered, realising with dismay that his rifle was in the van. But when he squinted in the direction he guessed

348

that sound had come from, there were only rocks and more rocks cushioned by flattened clumps of dry brown scrub.

Stalling for a moment, unsure what to do next, he heard that cry again. Definitely the calf. The big one, carrying his future on his curly forehead. He gave the prone figure lying by his feet another kick, ensuring she wouldn't be moving any time soon, then he lumbered away towards his unseen tormentor accompanied by the sound of St Sauveur's distant bells and the smell of smoke rising from the west. Too early for forest fires, he thought, unless someone had set up camp not too far away. He glanced back at the motionless black-clad body as he picked his way across the pitted pavement, shaped by years of the freezing and thawing of chemical rain. Soon birds of prey would come to begin feeding. Soon, there'd be nothing left, not even bones, for this, his other world, some thousand metres above sea level, had no pity for the hunted. He'd have to get her back in the cave soon. Did he want the payoff or not? And was the lack of any photograph going to muck things up?

7.15 a.m. He felt his bowels loosen.

'You, kid!' he yelled at the sky, feeling the wind swell up his lungs. 'I'll get you wherever you are. I know every centimetre of this place, so watch out.'

He stumbled southwards, into the gale, muttering the rosary as if he was in the church below. Then he prayed hard for God to deliver him his prize before his time was up.

Having drunk his fill from a nearby rock's ice-cold

trickle of water, and taken a squat over a handy clump of fennel, Bonneau turned east, where, on a clear day, the sun rises over the Garonne's blue-green horizon. Now great rain-heavy clouds were blowing in, affecting the already poor light, turning that spring morning into premature evening.

God obviously wasn't listening or else He had other things on His mind, so he addressed Our Lady. He reminded her how a small boy would need a warm hearth and some filling food. But how would he find those here, in such a place, and how could she, in all her goodness, deny him?

As if in answer, the first rain hit his forehead, then his nose and unshaven cheeks, not in any kind of baptism or absolution, but an assault of steel needles against his skin. Was this a warning, perhaps? That like others before him, trapped at such altitude, the living, however holy, don't stay living for long.

He hurled his weight from one hollowed slab to the next. Sometimes the toes of his boots caught in the holes, and he'd lunge forwards like some sickly bullock, battering his knees, grazing those fingertips protruding from his gloves. Hating the foreign rogue calf and begging to punish his soft flesh in his hands.

West now, for a change, with the wind seeming to slice off the left side of his head. While the rain now become a diagonal downpour forcing him to crouch down between two boulders and lower his wet head out of harm's way.

Just then, he had the strongest sense he wasn't alone, for above the *Tramontane's* roar came sounds of stones being dislodged, of someone

behind him. He swung round to see
else's and blue. An open mouth and arms
a blue felt stone on bone. His skull. Then
upr?s filled with the shifting bodies of his
a his herd, the haunting eyes of his dying
Ch?s he staggered a few paces and fell.
ca?e him, more eyes, but this time, rapacious,
?nk-coloured, filled by a huge black pupils,
dra?ing closer and closer, embedded in a sea of
br?wn feathers torn upwards in the wind. Then
sharp gold beaks, opened ready for attack. Two,
three, four at least, taking turns with his hair, his
cheek, his ear. Whatever he couldn't protect.

The pick, pick, pick of skin from bone brought
such a deep, stinging pain, and so much thick,
metallic blood to clog his nose, his mouth, his
screaming lungs, he willed death to come, to spare
him. And, as the feeding frenzy passed from the
easy targets to the clothes on his back and what lay
beneath, he slipped into a deep, numbing blackness.

CHAPTER THIRTY-FOUR

The Volvo's rocking motion suddenly woke Tom
?om his dreamless sleep, and for a moment he
?ught he was back with his family on the cross
?nnel ferry, expecting to see the grey-green
? of water below. His children leaning over the
?ail, silent with excitement. He rubbed his
?ked around, his disillusionment complete.

He didn't even recognise anything from when he'd followed Bonneau's van as fast could go. For a start, here was daylight with the gale tearing through the surrounding lines this was no normal forest, for just beyond passenger window lay a massive wall of limestone rock, split by dark gaps resembling so many wild smiles and which, as far as he could tell, reched up out of sight.

He glanced back at the empty rear seat were only yesterday afternoon Max and Flora had been kneeling together watching the traffic. The emptiness now almost unbearable. He pushed open the car door only to have it slammed back hard against his arm. After three desperate attempts, he finally made it outside, struggling to stand straight, never mind keep his jeans dry.

Where was he? Where had the farmer gone? There didn't seem to be any obvious route through the forest that he could see, except that several small red and yellow markers had been nailed to some of the tree trunks.

So, there must be something to follow.

Then he spotted a battered white sign bowling its way across the brown humus floor. He bent down, caught it, and turned it over. Tried to make sense of the crude map and barely legible words.

FORÊT DOMINIALE DE FRAMAT
  Vous etes ici.
  PAS DES FEUX
  PAS DE GRIMPER
  PAS DES DÉCHETS

Don't breathe either, he thought. Not that he could.

All at once, above the trees' protesting groans, he heard his mobile ring from inside his jacket pocket. He dived back into the car, thinking Flora, Natalie, Kathy. The miracle of some familiar voice...

But not this time, and he knew it immediately. The pause was too long. The breathing that followed too obvious.

'Yes?'

'Monsieur Wardle-Smith?'

'Who are you?'

'Please give me your mother-in-law's name...'

There was something familiar about the deliberate, insistent tone of the caller's English. The slight local accent.

'Why, for God's sake? I'm holed up in the middle of God-knows-where. My kid's missing and...'

'Precisely,' interrupted the voice. 'That name, before we can proceed.'

Tom's tongue suddenly felt dry, but worse, his memory seemed to have crashed. Hardly surprising after the night he'd had.

Come on. Think...

Naylor?... Taylor?... Beggar man, thief...

'I'm waiting.'

Then he remembered: Mrs Whiskers...

'Hare. Marjorie Hare, that's it.'

'Correct. Now, *monsieur,* listen carefully. Where's that colour print your friend took from the *Tabac* in Loupin last night?'

353

'I've got it. Why?' Then he listened without breathing as yet another hell unfolded.

A million euros? Jesus Christ...

Tom saw the pine trunks bending and righting themselves in some kind of weird choreography. Clumps of fir tossed in the air. One landed with a thud on the car roof.

'I don't understand...'

'I think you do, *monsieur*. No cash and photo, no Max and Natalie...'

'You bastard!' Just to hear him use their names in such a familiar way made his stomach heave.

'So Bonneau did take my son as well, right?'

'Naturally. And remember,' the voice went on, 'keep the law out of this, or else...'

'Or else what?'

'You lose everything.'

Had Max been in that van all along? Been just a few inches away from him?

Jesus.

His whole body felt like plasticine. Thank God he was sitting down.

'Who exactly gets the money and photo?'

'You will know. And let me emphasise that once the money has changed hands, both our friends will be returned to you unharmed in any way.'

Our friends? Better he'd referred to them as scum.

The call ended. Tom tried to think.

Definitely not a woman... But who?

He closed his eyes. Nature's roaring turmoil filled his every cell, every pore. That multitude of swaying trees nothing more than grim metronomes, marking out the seconds until the moment when he would be seeing both Max and Natalie again. Just twenty-nine hours away.

After his sixth attempt to reach Natalie by phone to warn her against contacting the police, Tom paused in his upward climb, all too aware of the drop below into that typical wild boar territory where his car still lay. Those colourful red and yellow markers had soon vanished. Probably stolen for souvenirs, he guessed. The rain too, added to his misery. And the birds. Hardly the sort his kids used to tempt with coconut halves and monkey nuts near the kitchen window of the house in Berris Hill Road.

His only kids. Where in the world were they?

He glanced up to see a pair of eagles silhouetted against the sky, looping and circling in the wild south-westerly wind, letting the current keep them buoyed up until ready to strike. At what? he asked himself, transfixed. There must be something, or someone up there, beyond his field of vision. And however repellent this thought was, it kept him clambering up the last tortuous stretch towards the Causse de Framat's rocky plateau at the top.

Surely no adult, let alone a child, could have survived the night in the open without food and shelter?

He swore at himself as sharp reedy tufts sprouting from between the limestone segments tore at his palms. 'Why not *say* Max and Natalie?' Because unless some small hope existed for their safe return, that would have been too much to bear.

But hope there was. He had to believe it, but

355

delivered in the form of that recent phone call.

At least if that was the sick deal, they'd be alive, protected somewhere. Their ordeal finite.

Perhaps he should wait, sit it out, rather than jeopardise things. Christ, he was confused. Unsure what to do for the best, trying to connect one happening with another the way his kids used to press their building bricks together, attempting to make some kind of shape. In his case, that photograph represented a pretty big block. Then there was Natalie herself, her reaction to it was almost as if she knew something but wasn't letting on. Yes, he thought, shaking surplus raindrops out of his hair. That was it. But who wanted the thing so badly? Enough to do this...

Within seconds, the print was in his hand, now scored across by a white crease line and dog-eared on the top right corner. As for the image itself, he could barely look, except to ask what the hell the man was doing and what might have happened next?

Vomit suddenly shot up his throat with no-where to go but on to his shoes and the hems of his jeans. There was nothing he could do except save the photo from the wind's grasp and keep moving, as the top of the climb was now less than six paces away.

He could ring Pauline Keppel. She wasn't the police, and he might find out how her boy had come to have the film in the first place. Then he realised that although *she* had his number, hers on the little gold card she'd given him on Friday night, showed only work details on the front and her home address on the reverse.

Damn.

Drops of water slid down his neck as he continued upwards, his mind churning round and round until, like the *Wheel of Fortune* he'd watched as a kid, the needle stopped on MONEY.

How to get hold of it in time. How to get it to that particular place, where he'd planned to take the kids anyway. How no amount would be too much to pay...

If he shut his eyes, then opened them again after ten seconds, he'd realise that since Friday afternoon he'd been sucked into some alternative reality. A nightmare without end, and somewhere beyond him out of reach lay his son and the young woman whom he still didn't fully know. Maybe never would.

Who had phoned him? Known his number? He guessed what Kathy would say. Could hear her now, loud and clear even in this wind. Hadn't that high-minded slapper destroyed the farmer's livelihood? And wouldn't a fast buck for him be tempting? Couldn't he, her feckless husband, see *she* was to blame? Couldn't he?

That last imagined question of hers stung far worse than anything the rain was unleashing, so much so that he slowed up, forced to admit that perhaps her logic wasn't as off-beam as he'd like to think.

But it still didn't explain why he'd also taken Max. Supposing someone else was pulling the strings with quite a different agenda...

His limbs somehow found a swifter rhythm. He was determined to reach the top of the climb as

357

quickly as possible and face whatever was awaiting him there. But his powers of reasoning were in disarray as more possibilities became equally feasible. In a nutshell, he was going mad. The deadline was five minutes closer.

He made a decision. Instead of crawling back to Hibou and lying low until Monday, he was going to stick it out up here and seek help.

He withdrew his mobile from his jeans, checked it was still charged up enough, and punched the numbers 1 and 7 for Emergency Medical Treatment. Not the police.

'Where are you?' asked a woman once he'd given her the facts and a false name: that of his old primary school headmaster. She seemed a long way away and her French too rapid which only heightened his sense of isolation. 'We can't help unless we know your exact location.'

'Exact location? Christ, give me a break.' He'd only seen the one sign. Its map a splodge of grey.

'Monsieur Thomas, please try.'

'I'm climbing up the Causse de Framat. From the north, I guess. Above the forest.' His mouth tasted foul. His tongue sluggish.

'The Causse is huge, *monsieur*... The biggest natural barrier in the Midi-Pyrénées...'

'Haven't you heard of helicopters?' he interrupted the geography lesson. 'I'm telling you, there are three lives in danger here. For goodness' sake.'

'Does that include you?'

'Yes.'

'We'll try for Search and Rescue. Meanwhile,

can you make a flare?'

'In this weather?'

'OK. Anything white or red to wave if you hear us in the vicinity?'

'I'll find something.'

'Be careful, *monsieur*. Don't take any unnecessary risks. Keep warm and take fluids if you can. All will be well. You have to believe that.'

'Thanks,' he said and meant it. Yet couldn't help wondering if they gave everyone that spiel, just to keep the suicide stats down.

Having left her with his mobile number and feeling marginally relieved, he then tried to contact Enquiries for a British Consulate number – any one in France would do, it didn't matter – but, no sooner had he punched what he thought were the correct digits for Enquiries than message read *Incorrect. Try again.* How could he? Where was his brain? It was as if he'd forgotten everything.

A further mighty gust of wind seemed to bear the rain away as swiftly as it had arrived. His hair was sodden, his clothes damp, but worse, the stones he needed as footholds were still treacherously wet.

He slipped back a few feet, cursed, then recouped his position, only to see some vast brown-winged creature swoop low over his head, making an eerie repetitive call before flapping away into the sky.

His throat was raw from continued panting. His head spun from the unaccustomed exertion of climbing; in Berris Hill Road, Sunday mornings were low-key, with a pre-lunch drink at The Green Man being the main activity. Now look at him. No horror fiction he'd ever read as a teen-ager matched this. Nor any worst-case scenario which that boss always dreamt up for Training Days. This was something else.

When he reached the edge of the plateau, the gale almost felled him.

Was it possible that Bonneau, too, had got this far? If so, how had he managed it? OK, he was built like a bus, but he wasn't that fit. And surely the track between the rocks was far too narrow for anything with four wheels, never mind a large van. Unless the savage had local knowledge or willing helpers.

So far, he'd seen no trace of any human foot-prints or vehicle. It was a mystery. Unlike the scene he'd witnessed at Belette, where he'd been forced to stand and watch while Bonneau had shoved Natalie into the van, his rifle keeping him at bay. And once those bells had stopped, there'd been the heavy breathing, the sudden grunt as he'd charged at him. After the Transit's ramming, the farmer had taken the advantage. No wonder the damaged Volvo lost touch with Bonneau's van and had to be left in the rough beneath the rocks. Tom had baled out, tried to follow on foot, snatching a few moments' sleep where he could, driven by the knowledge that Max may have been in that van all along. Just inches away from his first inspection...

For some reason he thought of the Berris Hill Road garden again, and the kiddies' corner he'd constructed near the kitchen window two years ago today.

Two years. Was it really that long ago, with Max seven, and Flora ten? Different children then, playing on the three-seater swing bought for the third child he and Kathy would now never have. There was a trampoline and climbing frame too, all top of the range from the local garden centre.

Now all that was for the Puris to enjoy, while Flora would probably never sleep properly again and as for Max... He hollered out that name he'd chosen specially as it meant 'greatest', emptying his lungs in the process, to no avail. This was a primordial kingdom. Harsher than anything he'd discovered in mainland Greece or inland Spain during the annual self-catering holiday they used to take. Hostile, unforgiving; greedy for death.

Despite his legs feeling like old timbers after the ascent, he picked his way over the vast eroded limestone pavement, imagining that each raised lump of rock, each blowing shrub he saw might be human. Might be Max or Natalie.

Why then did he suddenly think of Kathy and how their life had begun together? So far away now and, like that departing bird, threatening to vanish altogether. Perhaps because the wind was butting his head, delivering guilt with each blow. Reminding him, but giving no promises for the future...

It was at a John Lewis sale on Oxford Street, back in January 1989 that he'd first met her. He'd left work early to chase up an Elvis Costello album in their record department and then buy his mother a birthday present. Having landed in Ladies' Nightwear, deliberating between a lilac silk

nightdress and pink winceyette pyjamas, a petite
fair-haired stranger wearing a blazer, jeans and
kitten heels had suddenly stopped to advise him.

'Is she dark, or like me?' she'd asked, with no
trace of shyness.

'Like you.'

'OK, try the lilac.'

'Thanks, I wasn't sure.'

'Girlfriend?'

'No. My mum, actually.'

The smile had widened. Her eyes had shone. In
fact, the more he sneaked little looks at her, the
more he decided she bore an uncanny resem-
blance to the woman the gift was for. Dorothy
Wardle-Smith. Ex-Windmill girl, lover of Latin
American dance music. Nevertheless, always the
mother he could never please. Who many years
later had died listening to her favourite band on
the car radio...

His parents' inheritance plus his savings had
been transferred into a separate account from
Kathy's in the Banque du Midi. He'd insisted from
the word go that his money be earmarked to pay
for all Hibou's renovations and the family's health
insurance, while Kathy's inheritance from her late
father, was for emergencies only.

Now they'd got one and he needed her help
but, at the same time, he didn't want to alarm
her. And then he realised it was Easter.

He pulled out his phone. What else could he
do? No one was answering, so he left a simple
message for her. Then a wall of noise met his
ears. Could this be the ferry? he wondered,
checking his watch yet again and winding it on

one hour. Again, a possibility.

Someone was on the line.

'Kathy, that you? Flora?...'

'Dad?' came a muffled voice. His daughter.

'Thank God. You OK?'

'Yes. Sssh. She's listening.'

'Do you know if she's called the bank yet, about her share of the money?'

'I don't think so. Why?'

'Tell her not to touch any of it. That's all.'

'But why?'

'Just *tell* her, for Christ's sake. Flora?'

But she'd gone. Leaving him with a ton of grief growing heavier by the second. Yet, as he stuffed his phone away and stared at the strange desolate landscape around him, he felt as if this ferocious bombardment wasn't only propelling him towards what seemed like a row of broken teeth against the sky, but also drawing him inch by inch away from deep gangrenous wounds he could never heal.

CHAPTER THIRTY-FIVE

From somewhere, the sound of a dog's bark was carried upwards on the wind, followed by the half-hourly bells, jittery, discordant, and when they'd stopped, Liliane Bonneau panicked at what to do next. Neither Monsieur Tom, nor Max and Mademoiselle Musset had come back last night after going in to Loupin to fetch the oil and water. Perhaps they'd stayed somewhere on the spur of the moment, and then the thought occurred to her that maybe, after all, he'd decided to follow his wife and daughter back to England. Whatever had happened, she felt lonely, bereft and fearful. Should she stay and wait for them to return or escape to wherever she could while she had the chance? Before Samson should reappear? She wasn't sure.

Then, like a burst of sunshine from behind a dark cloud, she recalled that brief call she'd taken before leaving Belette for Hibou yesterday afternoon. Someone she'd met two years ago, who, despite losing everything, had stayed in touch with her. And she with him.

She sat curled up in one of the cream leather armchairs, warmed back to life by an abandoned duvet. Still undecided as to what to do. Turmoil in her stomach and in her head. At least she'd kept the Suzuki's keys safe and wheeled the bike into the *appentis* where Nicolette Metz has been supposedly murdered by a gypsy all those years ago. The accused had died in prison, still pleading his innocence. But, despite her own misgivings about the case, nothing more was ever said about it.

What an end to both lives, she thought, suddenly shivering, despite the duvet. But would hers be any better? Burdened as she was with too many secrets, hounded for her son's wicked ways.

She considered the options. If she left the *fermette,* where could she go? Not to Belette, that was for sure, because in St Sauveur itself, there was no one she could trust as much as the Englishman and the blonde girl from Limoges.

But there was still her friend.

While the *Tramontane* – or Devil's Wife as she called it – beat her fists against the already damaged roof and the rattling front door, she knew she must get out. In the meantime, she had to keep those bones from the cave safe against her body until they reached the right hands. His hands.

She knew Mademoiselle Musset would be impressed and, for some reason, their meeting by that *boulangerie* van suddenly came to mind again. However, perhaps because a good sleep had restored her faculties, she now recalled how she'd tried to warn her that there might be more to the sculptor than met the eye. That he moved in strange company. But why would the girl listen to some old crone like her? She was in love, wasn't she? Yes, she'd admitted that much to her, as if she'd been her grandmother, not a relative stranger. And now Metz was dead in an horrific accident, his dog killed and left on her family's tomb.

It was then that Liliane made up her mind.

She uncurled herself from the chair and, as if by magic, spotted a black coat slung across a chest freezer. A man's coat, she could tell, because of its buttons. Apart from protecting her on her next journey, it would at least help make her anonymous. Most women who lived as she did, on the land, made do with their men's outer garments. Especially at busy times of the year when to go shopping was a luxury few could dream of. However, this looked too new, so she bent down to rub a clump of chalky soil on to its sleeves and hoped Monsieur Wardle-Smith wouldn't mind.

That was better.

Before putting it on, she noticed the label

inside the collar: *St Michael.*

Mon Dieu.

She blinked twice. Was this really *his?* Had the Archangel and noble leader of all the celestial armies come to the world and left it there as sign for her? Whatever. Just to see his name gave her courage. She might just be a single earthly combatant for her next mission, but at least he'd be on her back.

She then sniffed inside its collar, something she'd done with Albert's clothes ever since he'd died, but unlike those smells of soap and sweat which had now entirely gone, these were still strong, as if the Englishman had worn it recently and would soon be back to reclaim it. She thought of him and the little boy, just as Samson had once been, and the most profound sorrow at maybe not seeing them again, accompanied her as she made her way outside to begin her first battle – with the Devil's Wife and the onset of rain.

She had stumbled her way down the hill and found Belette's back door was unlocked. She stepped back from it, her heart beating too fast. Had Samson been in too much of a hurry to bother locking it? Whatever the reason, this was most unlike him; he was normally so fanatical about checking and rechecking the locks. Gone were the days when you could leave such a place unsecured. Albert had rarely bothered until a set of his mother's Sèvres plates went missing off the wall and six full feed bags from the store.

Its function before Samson's forays into bric-à-brac.

'Samson?' she called out. 'It's Maman.'

No reply. Just the wind ripping off more roof tiles, snaking in under the door once she'd closed it behind her. She reclaimed her purse containing just enough for her fare, and found a headscarf. His bed was empty, unslept in. The van too, had gone. Something was wrong. Very wrong, and the best thing she could do now was to get out and reach her destination as soon as possible. She blew a kiss at Albert's armchair, still missing his pipe and hat, then with a heavy heart, let herself out and locked the door behind her.

'Where are you trying to get to, *madame?*' The caravanette's driver shouted in bad French through his window, having stopped ahead of her before the crossroads outside St Sauveur. At first she thought he might be German, then with a tinge of disappointment, spotted an NL sticker on the back.

'Gandoux. By nine if possible.'

He consulted with his wife sitting alongside him, and to Liliane's huge relief, he nodded. Buses on Sundays never mind Easter Sunday were like flowers on the moon.

'We can take you,' he said, 'but we go slowly, OK? We have much wind.'

'Thank you.' Was all she could utter once she'd settled on the seat between them. It was as if the Devil's Wife had scoured out her insides leaving only her old dry shell to cope with the world.

'Let us hope that tomorrow will see the end of it. It's frightening.' He said, setting off once more, switching the windscreen wipers to fast, then fiddling with the radio. She didn't recognise the programme, but its cosy hum provided a welcome sense of security as the swaying journey progressed without incident until the hill town and its church loomed up darkly against the sky. The Tramontane also seemed to have rid the region of all its inhabitants. Normally even at this early hour, there'd be roads full of people going to Mass. But not today. God could hardly expect it, could he? And, sliding her cold hand inside her damp coat to touch her rosary, she begged not only for the English family's safety, but her own.

'Just listen to this, Miep,' the Dutch woman leant across her to turn up the radio's volume as they reached the town's dreary outskirts. 'It's shocking. And here of all places.'

Liliane strained to listen once the newsreader had ended his report of the Monjuste fire. 'The badly burnt body of a man has been discovered in Gandoux's main public park early this morning. Not only that, but a swastika had been carved on his forehead...'

'Lieve Hemel,' exclaimed the driver. 'I don't believe this.'

Liliane's chest tightened. A small cry escaped her lips. Could this possibly be Samson? Had he got himself into yet more trouble? Or maybe been mistaken for someone else? She wished there'd been more detail, but on the other hand, no...

'Are you alright?' the Dutch woman asked her.

'Yes. I'm sorry.' Then came further mention of Bernard Metz's death and a short interview with an elderly aunt of his in Toulouse. His one surviv-

368

ing relative, her voice choked with emotion. Such a successful man, she said. A man with so much to live for. The newsreader went on to say that although alcohol might still be a possible factor, the police were also looking for a possible careless haulier who'd not had the courage to stop. Liliane strained to listen, surprised at this official stance. Hadn't poor Mademoiselle Musset seemed fearful of being interrogated? Hadn't she felt under suspicion? Yet her name hadn't been mentioned, and when the bulletin finished with a brief account of the sculptor's life, she closed her eyes and prayed.

'Do many things like this happen here?' Interrupted the driver's wife over the squealing wipers on the now-dry windscreen. Liliane blinked, aware she was being observed through the rear view mirror.

'No, of course not. Normally bad news is scarce. If anything, life here is very dull...'

'We're looking for a farm to buy,' her husband volunteered. We want to breed ducks.'

'Ah well, you'll be spoilt for choice,' she wheezed, thinking of Belette should she already be childless. 'But sellers are getting greedy. It's the same everywhere.'

'Do you have money?' he asked, catching her by surprise while parking in a gap along the Rue St Arnac. 'I noticed you weren't carrying a bag, that's all.'

'But I have my bones,' she replied without thinking, then when she saw the puzzlement in their big grey eyes, quickly tried to correct the situation. 'What am I saying? I'm just a stupid old woman.'

'No, you're not. Here, take this. It's not much,

369

as we're saving up for our dream.' He produced a crumpled hundred euro note from his trouser pocket and pressed it into her hand. She felt her tired eyes sting with tears as this kindness only served to make her feel more alone than ever.

'Good luck, then.' The woman helped her down into the street then waved as the vehicle swayed away towards the TOUTES DIRECTIONS sign after the roundabout. Liliane stared after it till it was lost from view then hobbled through a swathe of last year's plane tree leaves into a warm boulangerie with temptingly vacant tables beyond the shop. When had she last ordered coffee like this? she asked herself, sitting down, feeling the little bones against hers under the coat. And what about a tip? In the old days whenever she'd gone out with Albert, he'd always left a generous pile of coins behind.

She crossed herself just as the waitress came towards her to take her order. Perhaps she was another student just like Natalie Musset must have once been. So young, so hopeful, and it was only by thinking of St Michael positioned behind her neck, that she kept tears at bay.

While Tom Wardle-Smith was standing with his back to the wind and wiping his eyes with his daughter's Pooh Bear handkerchief, Liliane Bonneau, warmed by the mug of coffee, kept his coat tight against her body as she crossed the Rue St Arnac which would eventually reach St Marc's church at the top of the hill. However it wasn't any house of God that she was seeking, but a simple terraced property in the town's oldest quarter.

As she waited to cross the main street, she noticed the Bishop of Gandoux's limousine glide by, bearing not the usual red and white flag on its bonnet, but a black one, already torn ragged by the wind. She wondered why black, and who of importance had recently died, but it was only Metz's name which came to mind. A man who, to her knowledge, had never knelt by any altar or rarely taken communion.

She reached the Rue des Éspoirs with half an hour to spare. Of course, this wasn't where her friend used to live in the days when he'd worked as Sales Manager at the big Renault garage on the road to Monjuste. Then, he'd had a future assured, married to Zoulika – a hairdresser – one of the prettiest black women she'd ever seen. Only from photographs, mind. The ones in the papers. They'd shown her holding their new baby, Philippe Auguste. Happiness in her eyes.

The air grew still. Was the dreadful wind easing at last, or was it because of the exceptionally narrow winding street where anything wider than a normal car was liable to hit the houses' walls? She took deep calming breaths as she passed these ugly lacerations, realising that these were nothing compared to what must surely still lie in that bereaved father's heart.

She'd seen it written all over him when they'd met up again in the New Year following Communion at St Sauveur. His appearance then still so different from when she'd first contacted him after his tragedy. Dark haired instead of fair. Thin instead of a prosperous plumpness once flattered by his working suit. He was searching for the right church to meet his spiritual needs, he'd told her. A place away from the pressures of his new job, where he could unburden his soul and find peace. Not through Confession, as he had nothing to confess, but by quiet contemplation and the sharing of the Eucharist with kindred spirits...

What would he look like now after three months? She wondered. Would she even recognise him? She'd have to wait and see, and there was still a little way to go.

The Avenue des Éspoirs seemed to represent anything but. It was where the old like her, lived out their quieter days, and even quieter nights with only the TV and busy fly-strips for company. Younger people who moved into the street weren't so settled, judging by the number of *À Vendre* signs. There was nowhere for children to play safely or ride a bike. He'd said that's why he'd chosen it, for seeing children now made him weep.

As she neared his house, her heartbeat quickened. Was it because she'd had a terrible night and was still recovering, or that he'd somehow known she was at Hibou? She wasn't sure, but as she reached his dark oak door with its intricate inlaid ironwork, she resolved to find out.

After two rings of the bell, she waited, observing his new name in smudged blue letters boxed in underneath. A name which he'd confessed had once belonged to a character from one of his old school books. A Corsican olive farmer who kept a pet pig.

After two rings came a voice seemingly from the wall until she spotted a tiny silver disc set into the door frame. Its central hole surrounded by perforations. This was new.

'Oui?'

'Liliane Bonneau,' she quickly composed herself. 'And I'm bang on time.'

'Please wait, *madame*.'

Just then the church bells from high above the town struck the half hour and she automatically touched her rosary again, at the same time offering up a silent prayer for the missing and the dead to know some kind of peace.

'Vite,' he said, holding open the door just enough for her to slip inside to the hallway. 'This isn't the best place for you to be seen, but our choice is limited. How did you get here, by the way?'

'Some Dutch tourists dropped me off...'

'Where?' His eyes darted around past her into the street. He was still as tense as ever. Nothing changes, she thought, feeling a surge of pity for such a once normal man.

'Don't worry. In the town centre.'

He seemed relieved as he closed the door behind her, and for a brief moment, she wondered why.

Within the hallway's confines, she stared at his further loss of weight which the bullet-proof vest worn over his blue shirt couldn't disguise. His eyes too, seemed to have sunk deeper into his skull, making him look at least twenty years older than when she'd last seen him in January. The black gun lodged half in half out of his shoulder holster glowed dully in what light there was. Just to see it made her shudder.

'How did you know I was still at Belette when you phoned?' she ventured, aware of a faint smell of singed cloth coming from somewhere. Perhaps he'd been distracted from ironing. She'd done that often enough herself and suffered Samson's tongue.

'It's my job.' His smile reassured her. 'Because we now inhabit a world of terror.'

'A world gone mad, more like,' she added, unsure whether to stay put or follow the black and white tiles further down the hall. 'I mean, why was Bernard Metz's poor dog killed and left on our grave if you please. Then Metz himself smashed up on the *péage?* You think Mademoiselle Musset has something to do with it all, don't you? But she's a good girl. She wouldn't hurt a fly.'

Her friend's smile soon faded. He took a backwards step, avoiding her eyes.

'Where did you hear that?'

'She told me.'

'*Madame,* I've never even met her. She must be imagining things.'

Liliane frowned. Perhaps she was becoming confused. But there was something the young woman had said about the Florentin services yesterday morning. Why, oh why, couldn't she remember?

'After all,' the man went on, 'someone may well have been driven to take revenge. Your son, if I recall correctly, was one of several citizens who objected to his Cross. This is still a strongly Catholic area, *madame*. Feelings run high about such risqué works of art.'

Her blood seemed to chill.

'You mean Samson is a suspect?'

'We'd certainly like to talk to him at some point. But please don't dwell on it. We have to

374

cast our net far and wide.'

Liliane felt unsteady. The floor's tiles under her feet suddenly seemed too black. Too white.

'And what about that poor man found in the park this morning?' she managed to continue.

'Rumours only, *madame*, let me assure you. He was either a dealer, or some pimp in trouble over his girls. We're still investigating.'

'But the swastika?'

'Easy enough to do.'

'Not my son, then?' Thinking that was an odd answer to give.

'No.'

Her rosary beads felt even colder to the touch. Why, despite his denial, did there seem to be no comfort from this, her supposed friend? She leaned back against the wall. Steadied herself with both hands on the bumpy wallpaper. It was time to confess. To lighten her load.

'Do you remember after Communion last January, I told you about my fears?'

'Certainly. You seemed to be bearing the weight of the world on your shoulders...'

'I'm sure I'd still have my husband, his brother Eric, and their parents if it weren't for him.'

'How can you possibly say that?'

'A woman's instinct.'

'Instinct isn't evidence, *madame*.'

'But it's what I feel with all my heart. It seems like only yesterday. I was folding away Eric's working clothes; wrapping his false teeth in a copy of *Éleveurs du Sud*. But I was too frightened to act. To rock the boat.'

The *gendarme* gave a small smile, showing just

the tips of his teeth. His angular face half in half out of shadow.

'You do realise there can be no prosecution after a lapse of ten years.'

'Are you sure? Even for Nicolette Metz?'

She expected some reaction at that name, but he merely nodded.

'Whatever happened then at Hibou, Belette or anywhere else, we are powerless to investigate. Besides, Samson may not have killed her or your brother-in-law after all. You said yourself at the Inquest how Eric would often go out without telling anyone where he was going. And as for your other family members, your son may be completely innocent of those crimes too. If you recall the Post-Mortems on Jean and Christine...'

'I do, of course.'

'Regarding your husband, Albert,' her friend momentarily rested a well-kept hand on her arm. 'No one could have survived a terrible gale like that at such a height. Poor man.'

She shook her head. His words meaningless. He was trying to be kind. To spare her feelings, but only she knew what those were.

'Please listen to me. Because of my suspicions, I wanted to *poison* him. I deliberately gave him mouldy rye bread for his lunches. What else could I do? I wanted him to suffer the Fire, and God forgive me, I'm his *mother*.'

She felt light-headed, as if the plug that for so long had stopped up the stew of hate and guilt had suddenly been pulled away.

'Have you confessed?'

'Of course,' she lied.

376

'That's good. God has forgiven you.'

'So you don't come to St Sauveur any more?'

'No. Pressure of work, I'm afraid. But once all this is over, I promise I will.' He took her arm. His fingers firm, even through the thick coat she wore as they passed by a room on the right whose door, bearing a key in the lock, was closed.

'What's in there?' She asked. 'A *séjour?*'

He hesitated, and let his hand rest on the key.

'No, *madame*. As you'll see, it's a very special room. And surely better for us than standing in the cold.'

He turned the key and pushed open the door to a room whose function wasn't clear until she saw how the walls and every available surface, including a pair of white wardrobes along the nearest wall, bore colour shots of his late wife and their baby. So many dusky well-fed cheeks, so many multiples of happiness.

Without warning, she began to sob and fumbled in her coat for a handkerchief that wasn't there.

'Oh la la, *madame*. Please, don't cry.' He passed her a folded tissue from his own pocket. She took it gratefully, all too aware that her friend had enough on his plate without some weepy old woman to comfort. Then she picked up one of the photographs.

Philippe Auguste's steady gaze held hers. A knowing, haunting look. What was it about babies? she asked herself, unable to focus on him any more. Because just then, he seemed to be searching her very soul. At just eight weeks old on February 12th 2000, he'd been snatched from outside the Caves de Gandoux wine shop. At the end of that same month, his mother, having left a note saying there was nothing left to live for, had gassed herself in the garage in the family's Renault. After that, the widower sold up, changed his identity and joined his brother in the local *gendarmerie* to find out what had happened to his child. Now, two years later, he'd told Liliane outside St Sauveur, he was still none the wiser. Still getting nowhere...

She stared at her sympathy card which had pride of place amongst all the others on the dresser. The purple lilies depicted on its front, matching perfectly the mood of the room. Belette was bad enough, she thought, but this was worse. More like the inside of a sepulchre, where the blue skies in so many of the photographs seemed a tasteless intrusion.

'*Madame,* those bones you mentioned earlier,' he reminded her gently. 'If you wouldn't mind.'

'No, of course. We tried to get them to you yesterday.'

'We?' His dark eyebrows raised.

'Mademoiselle Musset and me.'

'Right.'

She sat down on the seat of the only chair and, one by one, extracted all six specimens from inside her coat. He waited, tanned fingers drumming against his thighs until she handed them over, then arranged them in a circle on his outspread palm.

'At first I thought they were just bits of limestone,' she explained, 'or even part of some animal. Then I realised they might even belong to Eric, but Mademoiselle Musset said no. She thought most likely a baby.'

'I see.'

Her eyes began to sting again.

'Anyway, she was desperate to see you yester-day afternoon.'

His hand closed tight over the bones, as if the pain of his own son's disappearance had suddenly overpowered him.

'Your Mademoiselle Musset may be right.'

Her earlier coffee crept up her throat as he switched on the main light to see better.

'Rest assured, *madame*, I'll get these examined as soon as possible. We have DNA testing now, remember, so these specimens – and they do seem to be from the same skeleton – may well prove to belong to someone totally unknown to any of us. A gypsy's child maybe. Someone inhabiting Hibou illegally while it lay empty.'

'How long do you think they've been there for?'

He paused. His eyelids briefly closed then opened.

'I'm no forensic expert, but I'd say not that long, judging by their colour and lack of deterioration.'

'Babies just don't bury themselves,' she went on. 'Someone must have done it. Oh, what a world. Do you know I sometimes look at youngsters today and think what will they inherit? The Devil and all his works? Is there no more mercy? No more kindness?'

'Let me remind you, *madame*, it was *your* kindness that stopped me from joining my wife in death. Your words of hope, written every week, especially those of Kierkegaard which you included, "That in order to believe in God, we must ourselves endure suffering..."'

'You've suffered enough.'

'No. *She* has. I've betrayed her.' He then bit his lip as if he'd said too much, and Liliane was about to ask him what he'd meant by that, but the moment had passed. He was speaking again, in earnest. His eyes downcast on the bones in his hand. 'It's you we must think of. Not forgetting the soul of our departed sculptor.' He, too, crossed himself then turned the bones over once more.

'By the way,' she began, attempting to change the subject. 'The Englishwoman and her daughter have gone back to England. It's terrible...'

'My wife always vowed she'd never leave *me*. *Madame,* it's only the rocks that are constant. Only they will survive, at least until God wearies of us.'

'But I'd never have left a good man like that. Or the little boy. Just think of it. And I've a feeling they've gone for good, too.'

The man looked at her, his eyes narrowing.

'What makes you say that?'

'They didn't return to Hibou last night.'

'Oh, I wouldn't worry, *madame*. People change their plans. Do things on the spur of the moment...'

'I'm not sure...'

All at once, his mobile phone began to ring. He set the bones down on a nearby occasional table. Again in a circle.

'When?' he barked in answer to his caller, keeping his eyes on the relics. 'Not priority.' He lowered his voice, moved a step away from her. 'And the Queen?'

A pause while he listened to the answer, frowning. Liliane wondered briefly who this Queen was. France was a Republic, surely?

The call over, he left the room and she could hear the repeated click of a lock – a safe, perhaps? It didn't matter. At least she'd fulfilled her mission.

'They're secure for now as I've a busy day ahead.' Said the man on his return. He then followed her from the room, his shoes silent against the tiles.

'You will let me know the results? I mean about those bones...'

'Of course.'

'Please take care,' she said. 'And your mother and brother.'

'You too.' He rested a shapely hand on her shoulder while the other fingered the gun's holster. 'Remember, *madame*, I'm here to protect you.' A small smile followed. 'By the way, are you off home now?'

It wasn't only that question which threw her. A moment's panic as she tried to gather her thoughts. Just one look at his expression was enough. Despite his ordeals, here stood a man of steel.

'Yes I am. And if ever you're passing...'

'Of course. Thank you. But I have to say, *madame*, that's not such a good idea. There's no guarantee you'd be safe there, and while that fire's still burning in Monjuste, we can't spare anyone to keep an eye on you.'

'I don't understand...'

'Trust me. Now then, if you are agreeable, I have a plan. At one o'clock, another good friend of mine, like yourself – Louis Panet, will collect you from Belette, then drive you to over to Brive.

381

He and his wife Anouk have already said you can stay at their villa in the town until this business is all over.'

'Who's he?'

'A retired *Notaire*. One of the best.'

'What about my new friends? They'll wonder where I've gone.'

'I'll inform them. Don't worry. And remember, while you're back home, and until he calls, don't answer the telephone or the door.'

'What does this Monsieur Panet look like?'

'Tallish, grey hair and moustache. Distinguished, as you'd expect.'

She heard the bells again. It must be nine o'clock, she thought. With a Sunday bus from the market square at ten. 'I'm really most grateful, believe me. But that farm's my home.'

She felt her voice fade as that gaunt face came closer. His breath surprisingly cold against her skin. 'One o'clock, *madame*. And remember, all will be well.'

The street outside his door seemed even more oppressive then ever; the barely opened shutters of the dwellings opposite concealing too many curious eyes. Liliane willed herself to leave it as quickly as possible, all the while unsure about that plan for her to go to Brive. For a start, she'd never met this Louis Panet. Or his wife. And was any friend of the *gendarme's* necessarily a friend of hers? Secondly, gypsies would soon be heading for pickings in the region. Someone would have to be at the farm otherwise it could be stripped bare in a few hours.

The newspapers were always full of such stories, and they made disturbing reading. In one incident near Loupin, a *maison de maître* belonging to an absent Belgian, even had all its floorboards removed. Although her friend meant well, she'd have to give his proposition careful thought.

She walked away from his gloomy surroundings, missing those little bones already, and wondering where on earth her son might be. The only part of Fritz left to her, and knowing that had made her the wrong kind of mother for him. She'd been weak, over-indulgent, and what had she done when he'd started those cruel ways with his calves? Nothing.

It had taken that brave young women to curb his cruelty and now it was her turn to be strong. To trust the troubled, enigmatic Major Belassis.

CHAPTER THIRTY-SIX

The foul gag had fallen free of Natalie's face, letting a darkness of grey-black smoke and low cloud eke under her eyelids, up her nose and insinuate itself between her half-open lips. No ordinary smoke this, its acrid stink jerked her into a coughing fit, making her ribs feel like wreckage inside her chest. This was diesel.

Had she died and come back to earth? Or was that treat still to follow? And then she thought of Max and Tom. Where were they? Where was Bonneau? Why that fire? She tried to raise herself on one elbow to enable her to see more, then realised with a sickening jolt that not only were her wrists and ankles still knotted together with the same twine she'd found on Metz's poor bitch, but that her bare feet were freezing. She also noticed her diving watch was missing. Twenty weekends in Wimbledon's Spar shop had paid for that.

Roll over, she told herself. Shout. No, maybe not. Bonneau might still be around, besides filling her lungs with diesel smoke wasn't a good idea either. However, from the corner of her eye, the dark smoke seemed suddenly to coalesce into a single solid form, hovering overhead. What the hell was that? A ghost of something? A piece of fire debris borne upwards by the wind? But not until the eager croak reached her ears did she realise it was some huge carnivorous bird, ready to take its chance.

Her scream sent the thing flapping away into the murky sky. Her pulse throbbed everywhere. Hard, hurting. But she wasn't going to give up. As the minutes passed it became clear that Bonneau had abandoned her to be eaten alive. But Bonneau had another thing coming; she would survive. Then she thought of Max. Had he ended up here too, in this dreadful place with his bones hidden among the rocks somewhere, never to be found? Why him, anyway? she asked herself. Perhaps Bonneau had screwed up. Perhaps she'd been the target instead. After all, she'd helped ruin his life.

She squinted at the clearing sky between hot, gritty tears.

'If you're out there somewhere, Jesus,' she prayed, 'come and sort this out. Give me some hope, please...'

All at once, by an uncanny synchronicity, came the sound of clapping. Closer and closer...

'Natalie!'

A voice she recognised.

My God.

A blur of pink and white was coming closer...

'I killed him! I killed him! Like this,' the voice chanted, as little arms were raised up and down together. Once, twice, three times...

Max.

Oh my God...

'Max, are you sure? What happened?'

'I think I did – I hit him. Hard. He fell down and there was blood coming from his head. He didn't move. Didn't open his eyes. I threw a stone at him and he didn't moan when it hit him. Didn't do anything. Then I ran away.' He looked at her, frowning. 'He must have been dead, mustn't he?'

'Let's hope so.'

'You should have seen all the birds round him afterwards,' he grinned. 'Gross.'

Max then knelt beside her and touched something very sore on her head. She winced in pain, but nevertheless managed a tiny, weak smile.

'You're a brave boy.'

'And you're hurt.'

'I'll be OK.'

He was wet, filthy. In other words, a health hazard. His normally blonde curls were grey, his skin a mess of scratches.

'He had all your stuff in his pockets, but I got your watch back, and your phone. I don't think they're working, mind. Dad's number just made a funny noise when I tried it. And sorry, but I ate the rest of your radishes. I was starving.'

He selected a sharp piece of rock instead and began to saw away at both bands of twine, until at last, the final snap enabled her to move. But, for a moment, the will to move seemed to leave her. She began to cough, retching air. Too weak to vomit. To even give him a cuddle.

She then felt her pockets and realised that her wallet and both IDs were also missing. Her precious photo. Her credit card. And what about her knife that Belassis had taken and not yet returned? Apart from representing too much – her dad, for a start – she could have used it on Bonneau or to cut themselves free in the van...

'Ugh! Why's there so much smoke?' Max's cough interrupted her regrets as she eased herself up to a sitting position, trying to absorb what he'd told her. To gauge their bearings on that barren expanse of rock and try and find a way down.

'It's clearing already,' she tried to sound optimistic. 'But try not to breathe in so hard. We can look for your dad in a minute. I had the feeling he followed us last night. I recognised the sound of the engine.' She took his hand. A small version of his father's. Blackened, scratched. 'If you can bear to tell me, Max, what exactly happened at Loupin when we'd left you?'

'It was the giant. He took me by surprise. Asked if I'd like a drink and stuff. At first, I wouldn't budge. I wasn't sure. Then he made these glugging noises. Said he'd get me a whole bottle of Coke from the Café...'

'Was your dad's car locked when he showed up?'

386

A moment's hesitation. Uncertainty altering his features.

''Course it was.'

'So, how did he open your door?'

'He had a thingummygig...'

'You mean a piece of wire?'

He nodded. Almost too eagerly, she thought.

'Something like that. Only took him a second. He's really weird, Natalie. All the way to his farm he kept calling me his special little calf.'

My God.

Was this the reason he wanted him? Some kind of sick replacement for what he'd lost?

'I can't get my head round this. He didn't, you know, try anything on?'

'No, but he kept asking about Flora, if she had a boyfriend.'

'Ugh. He's the pits.'

'His English is rubbish, too.'

She leant over and squeezed him as tight as her aching limbs would allow. 'But you're my hero, d'you know that? This is all my fault. What can I say?'

'Why's it your fault?' Those huge eyes again.

'For reporting him about his poor veal calves. I'd no choice. They were suffering terribly. This is obviously his revenge on me. Horrible man.'

'You were right to do that, though. Dad thinks you're very brave.'

A blush reached her neck. If only Tom were here now, coming towards them out of the ether... If only...

'Let's give the mobile a try,' she said. 'You never know.'

Max withdrew her phone and the watch from his puffa jacket pocket, and handed them over to her. He was right. All the watch's functions were kaput and when she tried first Tom's then her father's number, the display stayed blank.

She threw the lot as far as she could and they disintegrated, tinkling against the rocks. Just so many bits of useless metal. Then she turned to him.

'We still shouldn't have left you alone. I know your dad's sorry too. He's still got the drink and your sweets with him.'

'It's OK.' His turn to blush now and, before standing up to survey the scene, he planted a kiss on her cheek.

'But it wasn't you the giant was after,' he suddenly began in a serious tone, keeping his head turned away from her. 'It was me. I knew from the first time I saw him something wasn't right about him. The way he kind of touched my thumb when I'd got stuck on that Cross thing. And Dad...'

'What about Dad?'

'He never took any notice of what I said. Even got him to start work on the dump...'

'Everyone's human, Max.'

'No. Not everyone.'

'By the way, how the hell did you get out of that cave?' she asked, getting to her knees, aware now of the full extent of the damage to her leathers. 'That really set him off. He took my boots after that.'

'Sorry.'

She remembered what Tom had said to her.

'No more sorries from either of us, OK?' She

smiled at Max, and he began his story.

'I wriggled like a worm, didn't I? Our teacher told us how they move, segment by segment. Anyway, he was busy doing you-know-what to you...' Here he stopped. Another blush visible beneath the dirt. 'Then I noticed the exhaust on that van. Have you seen the state of it? The edge was great for cutting myself free. After that I went and hid in it. He never thought to look there, thank God.'

He coughed again, then took her hand to help her get up.

'Ouch.' She held him for support as burning blood seemed to drain from her head.

'Natalie, we've got to move. It's too open here,' he announced, clapping his hands yet again as another winged predator zoomed in from nowhere. 'So, what do you think?'

She tried to focus. To think rationally. She was the adult, after all.

'That cave again? There were some pretty deep places in there.'

'Uh, uh.' He shook his head. 'If the giant knew of it, then other people might too. He might have told someone about taking us there.'

'He may not even be dead.' Even as she said it, a massive shudder hit her whole body. 'It's been too easy, somehow. I don't know...'

'Look,' Max faced her with a formidable expression on his grubby face. 'I tested his pulse like I've seen them do on *Casualty*. I closed his eyelids, didn't like the way he was staring. Then, like I said, the big birds got busy. I saw...' He composed himself enough to continue. 'I saw bits of him in their beaks. He didn't stop them. He couldn't...'

389

'OK, OK. That's enough. Any chance of a drink round here?'

Max cocked his head, frowning.

'Ssh. Listen.'

She did.

'I hear water.'

'You're right. Over that way.' She pointed north to the oddest range of rocks she'd ever seen. As though the Creator had simply dropped them into place, like the vast crenellations of some old castle's turret. 'It's worth a try.'

All at once she spotted something, way above these same rocks, occupying a space of pale blue sky between the hustling clouds. It was small, red, growing bigger as it slowly drew south towards them.

'Max, look!'

'It's a helicopter.'

'Are you sure?'

''Course I am. It's the cops, come to help us. Let's wave.'

'I don't think so. Quick. We've got to lie low.'

An irrational fear had tweaked her insides. Instinct, nothing more.

'Where?' asked Max. All at once, a frightened little boy. She felt sick, but couldn't let her nerves show. She had to be strong, like when she'd turned up at the abattoir at Aujac. Strong. And cunning.

'To the right. I'm no geologist, but that shadow over there might be some kind of gulley. Move.'

Despite her bare feet and the sheer pain of movement, she was first to reach the edge of a narrow channel, approximately six metres long, lying below the molten looking rock which formed the limestone pavement. Apart from some stray feathers and grey soil lodged inside, it was empty. She pulled Max down alongside her then ordered him to dig with his hands.

'Just pretend we're at the seaside and the tide's due in any minute.'

'I used to bury Flora there loads of times,' he said, frantically scooping out the dusty limestone and yelping when it hit his eyes. 'But Mummy hated any sand getting near her skin.'

That didn't surprise her. But what did was that until now, he'd not mentioned them at all.

'I used to make huge models of dogs,' she said. 'My dad had a Great Dane once, called Maurice.'

'I bet he ate a lot.'

'Bottomless pit, Dad said.'

But this wasn't, and the hum of the chopper's engine was growing louder. In fact, they'd be lucky if their shallow grave concealed even half of them. There wasn't time for any more digging. She made Max crouch down like her.

'Now then, just lie on your left side and I'll cover you as best I can. Don't move or speak.'

'Who'll cover *you?*'

'Never mind.'

'Supposing it *is* the police?'

'That's the trouble.'

Within a minute, his head nudged against hers in that makeshift double-length coffin. Stuffy out of the breeze, the soil's subtle smells reminded her of her dog's dry meal mixer, with calcium added for his bones. Reminded her of the life she'd had in Agen when her parents were still together. Without a care in the world...

The noise grew deafening. Her instinct was to get up and lie next to Max to hold him tight, protect him from what she knew she'd set in motion, just thirty-six hours ago. But she couldn't. She was powerless.

'Don't move a muscle,' she urged him, at the same time praying for the red-bellied monster passing overhead, to keep moving. To give them both a chance. However, as her prayer ended, she heard the twin engine cutting back. The draught decreasing. It was landing not so very far away.

What to do? Lie still, or make a run for it?

She thought of her dad, who'd not phoned for over a fortnight. Her mum in Southfields, counselling the whole world. Their lives would go on. New people would crowd in each day and, week by week, month by month, she, Natalie Bridget Musset, would be shouldered out of their consciousness.

And what about Tom?

He'd grieve, of course. Maybe not for her, but for Max. To lose a kid of that age must be the worst torment. But then, in a while, like her parents, he'd open up to life again. Perhaps think of Max whenever he saw a boy with curly hair, and of her if ever a black motorbike passed him by. Maybe in his declining years, he'd write a poem or two and struggle to find the right ending...

To her horror, she noticed Max stir. The pink puffa jacket beginning to show through the soil like a ripening hyacinth. She bumped her head against his and he promptly lay still.

Then, suddenly, without warning, she saw four booted legs standing at the gulley's edge beside her. They belonged to two masked watchers, dressed identically from head to toe in black. Were they two men? Or a man and a woman? It made no difference. They were there for one thing only, and before she could react or even reach out to protect Max, a voice growled, 'One for you and one for me, huh? Just like Christmas all over again.'

'Let's go, shall we, Reignet? We've not got all day.'

CHAPTER THIRTY-SEVEN

The only bus that day delivered Liliane back to the farm at eleven o'clock, but her journey had been far from peaceful. Her friend's words about being her protector had made her even more edgy. His judgement on the bones, a shocking confirmation. Nevertheless, her thoughts turned not to death, but life. The *Tramontane* had eased, leaving the vineyard workers' *camionettes* glowing gem-like amongst the rows of dark vines. The plane trees' leaves jutted, unstoppable from their pruned branches, while tiny lambs tottered from their makeshift shelters in the fields near St Sauveur. She recalled the *Anglais* children's colouring book. Abandoned now, like the rest of their new home.

All this rebirth, she thought, with newborns everywhere laying claim to the world with angry cries. The memory of Samson's own entry became suddenly overpowering. How he'd fought his way

393

out of her body leaving her torn and bruised, then let out such a roar of protest, as if she and Fritz had set him on a journey he didn't want to make. If only Fritz had lived. If only Samson had known him as a father, as a man of great tenderness, things might have been different.

She sighed. Albert had proved a good man but deep in her heart she knew he didn't consider Samson his real son. It was never spoken of. Never whispered, even in bed after a day's work, where sleep follows to soothe the most painful of problems. No, love for her son hadn't been enough. And often it had soured to hate. The kind of hate she felt for the men who'd shot her lover six times before he'd finally fallen. For the townsfolk of Pech Merle who'd taken her clothes and her hair, leaving her as bald and feeling worse than a leper. Who'd almost induced a late miscarriage. Better that she'd had one, she thought. But there was no turning back the clock now; doing things differently.

Liliane shunned the driver as she disembarked, and the women washing rugs in the public *lavabo*. Normally she'd have given each a smile, passed the time of day, but she was too suspicious now. Frightened someone would drag her away, just as Fritz had been, his boots juddering on the cobbles...

Not a soul around. Animal or human and, once the bus had pulled away from Belette, an eerie silence seemed to freeze her to the spot. In the daylight, her home of sixty years looked shell-shocked after the wind. Fallen branches now added to the mess of wire and fencing. Downpipes listed away from the walls and, worse, Samson's blood still stained the back step.

The bells struck quarter past, reminding her that Monsieur Panet would be calling at 1p.m. Well, she certainly wasn't interested in a stay in Brive, however short. *This* was still her home and her friend hadn't quite grasped that, like him, she'd lost too much already.

Liliane unlocked the rear door and listened to even the smallest sound, unwilling to risk using the *toilette* and tidying herself up a bit. God alone knew who might still be in there from when the farmhouse had been unlocked. Although Monsieur Tom's coat weighed heavily on her shoulders now the sun was up, she was loathe to shed it, as now more than ever its bulk represented security.

Suddenly she jumped. The phone inside the farmhouse was ringing. Samson, she thought. Maybe he was calling her.

Then the major's advice came to mind.

She hesitated, letting it ring. Of course he was right. She was a vulnerable old woman with an angry son out there somewhere... She picked her way along to the ruined calf barn. Albert's old wartime cuttings showed nothing compared to this. She squeezed her eyes shut as if to shield him and Eric, Jean and Christine, from the sad reality of their much-loved Belette. Now today, Easter Sunday, March 31st 2002, was the end of another era.

Liliane wiped away a stray tear with her coat cuff. Should she stay or go while she had the chance? She felt dizzy with uncertainty, as if the ground under her feet was shifting like those treacherous sands you sometimes found on beaches.

Now wasn't the time to run. She would just have to face him when the time came.

She pushed open the back door and crept over the uneven floor to the kitchen. Here she poured herself the last of some syrupy grenadine into an old glass then diluted it with the leftovers in an Evian bottle. She gulped it down, its sweetness giving her the strength to move towards the cellar door in the hall. Suddenly the hall phone rang again. She stared at it for a moment, then tentatively picked up the receiver.

Samson was alive. Monsieur Tom had just said so. She offered up a prayer, said four Aves then realised that one o'clock was only ten minutes away. Time to lie low.

She eased open the cellar door, slipped inside, taking care not to lose her footing on that top step, then shot the one big bolt across. All she could do was wait. The air was cold, clammy and the smell of the Menthe still lingered, bringing back memories of Samson. She'd done this kind of thing before, with Fritz. Anywhere they could hide. Anyone who'd have them, who could be trusted. At least, that's what they'd thought...

All at once, from the cellar's depths, she could hear knocking coming from above. Hard, insistent. Not the kind you'd associate with a social call. Then came an ominous thud. She remembered she'd not checked the front door. Had that been unbolted? If not, then whoever it was had got in. Footsteps now, heavier than even Samson's. Coming nearer. She thanked God they weren't going upstairs...

... the respectable Monsieur Panet, he
*If th*siness to intrude like this. She prayed
had *r*ouldn't hear her grating breath.
*that*ame Bonneau?' a man's voice called out
'*h* behind the cellar door. No one she knew,
fr was certain of that. 'You must let me in,
s ease...'

She felt faint and momentarily lost her balance.
The distant past lapping at her mind. The local
Resistance hot on her tail, hammering on doors
up and down the village street. That searching.
The frantic getaways, especially the last one...
She wobbled again, held out her arms for Fritz to
take her and, before night fell fast in the Forêt du
Diable, saw the pointed crowns of its black fir
trees sashaying against the sky.

'Fritz?' she murmured when she came round on
the cold damp floor. 'Where are you?' Then realised the war was over. That this was Belette and
she was on her own, struggling to right herself.
Minutes later, with the farmhouse quiet again,
she ventured up the cellar steps and pressed her
ear to the door's wormy wood as a faint breeze
reached her ankles through the crack beneath it.

That previous silence enveloped her once more
once she'd drawn back the bolt and shoved the
door open. What met her eyes made her gasp. The
normally solid, protective front door now hung
ar on one hinge while the dust from some newly
parted vehicle still hung in the air beyond.

er gaze passed round the hallway where the
e lay askew on its cradle, to the *séjour* and
en drawers in the old dresser, to Albert's

397

overturned armchair, and she knew at once outside with her few belongings, she that be coming back.

Merde.

Something she'd forgotten. With Mons. Tom's coat dragging on each step, she scram' upstairs and into her bedroom, to the one secret place she'd guarded all these years. Then to her mother's old needlework box where, thankfully a rusted needle lay already threaded with black cotton. Minutes later, with the precious bulky package sewn in place behind the coat's lining under its left arm, she went to fill her old tapestry bag with necessities; her Ashes of Violet talc, a clean nightdress, soap and flannel. Her crushed Christening spoon and her purse.

She gave a last look at Fritz's wireless and righted Albert's chair.

No buses.

Panic.

Then she remembered the Suzuki. She still had its keys.

'*Merci Dieu...*'

It took her ten minutes to reach Hibou's old shed and finally settle her bony bottom on the machine's seat. However, it wasn't until she'd started the engine and had reached the Rue des Martyrs in the midday sunshine that she noticed with a gasp the telephone wire pulled free of Belette's front wall.

CHAPTER THIRTY-EIGHT

Some smart-arse at work had once joked about how long it can take a human to die. Now Tom believed him. This wasn't only long, but an agony, and here he was, choked up with diesel smoke, half-blind with the wind and worse than any of this, he'd been too feeble to find anything to wave at that red chopper that had been and gone an hour ago.

Search and Rescue had missed him. They'd landed before circling away to the north, leaving him to the tide of stinking air, the odd evil-looking bird and torn shreds of memory teasing his mind. Max and Natalie must still be up here somewhere. He knew it. Just like he knew that, after all this, his life with Kathy would never be the same again.

He turned a complete circle to get his bearings. His wrecked-up brain no longer capable of any more deductions, any forward planning. Here he was in this last place God made, which perhaps in different circumstances, might actually be described as awesome. On a par with Glencoe or Cader Idris – respite from the modern world and the ways of men.

But it was a man who'd brought him here. A man he had to find.

He must have been overlooked by that chopper for a reason, and no way was he going to call for a second rescue attempt. He would search for Max and Natalie himself. He would find them. He would rescue them – he would be his little boy's hero.

The deadly smoke was now indiscernible amongst the leaden clouds cruising in from the south, and slowly, patches of pale blue sky appeared between each ugly mass. He prayed for any further rain to hold off. And he wasn't just thinking of himself. Despite exhaustion and repeated cramp in both thighs, he willed his legs into an even stride over one pitted slab after another.

Soon these widened, becoming smoother, more closely packed, allowing him to make good progress in the direction he guessed Bonneau might have taken. The battering wind, too, had slowed, allowing him to check yet again for any giveaway signs of human life. It was then that he spotted a scrap of white between a clutch of small bare trees. Close by stood a rocky mound, the front of which revealed a gaping arc of darkness.

Was this a cave of some sort? he wondered, his pace quickening to match his pulse as he headed towards it. If so, anything was possible. Drawing closer, he realised with a mix of elation and apprehension that he was right, and the sliver of white belonged to a 20cwt van. Even without its number plate he knew it was Bonneau's.

His feet seemed to be held fast. His nerves deserting him.

Supposing the loony thug was still around, guarding his prey? How could mere bare fists be a match for a rifle? On the other hand, with his hands already full, what if he'd abandoned that cumbersome weapon somewhere? Hidden it for later?

Suddenly, a noise.

'Max? Natalie?' Up to now he'd had to suppress more urges to bawl their names to the heavens, and even now his voice was hardly more than a whisper. Could this be Bonneau himself?

Tom listened, unsure of the sound's origins. There it was again. Some kind of animal in pain, maybe. Or perhaps a trap.

He crept into the cave entrance and almost gagged on the sour-sweet stench which hit his nose. The same as at a dog rescue place near Pirbright that Flora had made them visit to choose a mutt. Where, because of a staffing shortages, the pens hadn't been cleaned out for a week...

'Who's there?' he hollered, suddenly seeing his life as a series of snapshots now about to end. No reply, but from somewhere deep underground came the echoing sound of running water.

With one hand over his nose, he moved further in, dodging the newer half-formed stalactites twisting downwards from the cave's roof. Then he stopped. Began to back away, his legs barely able to support him. All at once the malevolent *kek kek* of a bird call was followed by a huge feathered form with an angry eye and a full beak emerging from the cave's deeper gloom. Its wing tip brushed against his face as it made for the entrance and when he lowered his gaze he noticed the body of a man lying in the foetal position, pressed up against the cave wall. His face lay half-buried in the damp soil, his eyes rolling around in what was left of his head. A black mouth bathed in blood. The veal farmer was still alive. Just. Had that bird and others been to blame for this? If so, how had he been immobilised in the first place? Was it possible that Natalie had struggled free and attacked him? Even shot him? If so, where? There didn't seem to be any visible bullet wound, and no sign of the rifle either, unless he was lying on it.

'Where's my son and the young woman? Why did you take them?'

'Not my fault...'

'You wanted Hibou, didn't you? Go on, tell me, you piece of trash. You thought that if you made life hell, we'd all clear off. Well, you've done alright so far.' He aimed a kick at the man's gut. A groan, then more incoherence followed. Only two words were recognisable.

'Not true.'

'OK, so who put you up to this?' Tom snarled at him, trying to keep the smell out of his system. 'Tell me, or I'll finish you off. Nice and private. Who's to know? Was it because of some photo of a man holding a toddler?' He edged one step further forward, but could go no closer. His nose wouldn't let him. Nor could he bend down to bellow into what had once been an ear. 'I'm waiting.'

The mouth moved, only to gargle the single word, 'red'.

'Red what? Red who?'

Then he twigged. Search and Rescue heli-copter. Of course.

'Were Max and Natalie injured?' nudging Bon-neau with the toe of his boot. 'Is that what you're trying to say?' He drew back. The guy was done for. No point in going for twenty questious now. Only one. 'Where's your rifle?'

'Van.'

Once outside, Tom heaved in great gulps of air and stumbled over to the Ford, all the while sensing that something wasn't right. Surely if that chopper had picked them up, he'd have been told? He found his phone. Punched in the Emergency Services number. Finally, after what seemed like an eternity, that same woman he'd spoken to earlier came on the line. She sounded stressed and busy. But then, so was he.

'No one went up in that wind,' she said. 'Couldn't risk it.'

What?

'What about that fire? I bet it was all systems go for that.'

'I'm not at liberty to say, *monsieur*. That's confidential. But we can re-activate Search and Rescue, if you wish. Conditions are better now.'

'Please. It's urgent.'

Then he remembered red.

'By the way, what colour are your helicopters?'

'The Cougar? It's white. Why?'

'Not red?'

'No. That's the Alouette. Used by the Police.'

He had to be anonymous. Hide his phone number and keep stumm about Max and Natalie. No cops, remember?

'To whom am I speaking?' he asked.

'Captain Tesault. Gandoux Emergency Enquiry Desk.' His French rapid. Local.

'Was one of your helicopters up on the Causse

403

de Framat an hour ago?'

'Why do you wish to know?'

His lie came easily.

'My friend's just reported one there behaving rather oddly, that's all. Thought you ought to know.'

'*Monsieur*, my records show there's no data on any such flight in that area.'

'Are you sure?'

'Absolutely.'

What the hell was going on? Either some buff flew his own chopper for private use, or the guy had lied through his teeth.

That particular supposition was too much to deal with.

He then thought of the stinking cave and its occupant.

If Bonneau was found, he'd be fingered at the drop of a hat. No, he thought, let him die where he was. But he'd keep the rifle, once he found it, just in case he needed it.

However, just to see that van's rear doors sent a shot of pain through his body. His fingers shook as they reached for the handle. Both doors were unlocked. He forgot to breathe as they squealed open, his son's brave face so real in his mind and Natalie's one brief laugh at Hibou ringing in his ears.

'Fuck you, Bonneau.'

He slammed them shut only for one to swing back and whack his arm. Next he tried the passenger door. A result, thank God. He tilted the driver's seat forward and manoeuvred the old rifle

404

free from the narrow space behind it. Was just about to check if it was still loaded when he heard an engine noise coming from the other side of the cave.

Never mind a car, more like a bloody train, he thought, gripping the rifle. Could he use it if he had to? Sure. Hadn't the rifle range been his favourite fairground sideshow since he was a kid? Hadn't he always won the biggest, fluffiest toy? Only last summer he'd won a huge blue panda when the fair had come to Wisley and, at Flora's request, had added it to Right Move's load, to help make Hibou seem more of a home...

Four rounds of ammo left. Enough surely, if he was careful... Now a voice, calling out names he couldn't catch. A female voice, definitely.

Using the van as cover, he watched as a familiar figure in a big black coat advanced into the cave. Her hair a wild tangle, her walk unsteady, yet determined. Liliane Bonneau.

He stared in amazement at how an eighty-two-year-old could have made it so far. Then glanced at the Suzuki and his one decent coat. Three hundred quid it had cost from M&S.

'I didn't know you could handle one of those,' he pointed at the parked bike.

'And you didn't say *you* were here...' she began. 'Just Samson.'

'I have to be careful.'

'What do you mean?'

'I'll tell you in a moment.' He guided her towards the cave. Her arm feeling no more substantial than a piece of wire under the coat's fabric. She looked up at him, puzzlement still in her eyes.

'It was kind of you to call me, *monsieur*.'

'It's nothing, but how did you know the way up? I had to climb.'

'There's a special route to the top that not many people know about. Samson used it when he was young. Heaven knows what he got up to here, mind...' Her breath raw from exertion. She placed a hand over her chest. 'Look, *monsieur*. Please, where is he?'

'In there.'

'Is he still alive?'

'Take a look, but first, there are certain things you alone need to know. Things which are absolutely secret between you and me, understand?'

She nodded, her eyes on his all the while as if she could read his anguish. 'Something's wrong, isn't it? Where's your son, and Mademoiselle Musset? Why aren't they here with you?'

When he'd finished his account, she clamped both her hands against the nearest rock wall, then, having righted herself but still clearly shaken, she hobbled into the cave. He followed, listening as her voice echoed in it vast space.

'Answer mc, son. What have you done with the little boy and Mademoiselle Musset?'

'*Maman?*' the farmer burbled. 'Is that you, *Maman?*'

'Never mind me. Where are they?'

Tom cocked the rifle as a precaution. The smell now worse, if anything.

She knelt down and stared hard at her son's damaged face as if trying to work out just who, or what, he was.

'You've still not answered my question, Samson.' She began to clear out his pockets, digging deep into his bleu de travail but finding nothing. Tom wanted to kick the slob lying at her feet to kingdom come. The man whose quivering semigloved hands had held his son. Brought him here. Concealed him. A man who deserved to die.

He tensed up, his grip on the rifle tightening.

'Tell your mother if you can't tell me,' he said. 'Max is my son, for Christ's sake. My son...'

'God will never forgive you, Samson,' Liliane's voice hardened. 'And I prayed so hard for you to survive, to live. Now you will die here a sinner and alone...'

Bonneau groaned and tried to move but she kept both hands pressed down on his shoulders.

'If you help us, then we'll get you to hospital. If not, then I'll do the worst thing any mother can do to her child: I'll leave you here to perish the way you deserve.'

She let go of him and waited for a response. Her wheezy gasps echoing in that stinking space while Tom poked the rifle against his head. Liliane flinched.

'Man...' he mumbled.

'A man called you? Right?'

Bonneau's great head moved as if attempting a nod.

'Anyone you knew?'

'No.'

'What did he say?'

'Bring them here... Money.'

'We must get him to hospital,' she looked up at Tom with pleading eyes. 'I believe him. I really

407

do. Once he's better, he'll be able to tell us more.'

'Don't bank on it.'

'*Monsieur...*'

He hesitated. Hospital would mean police and the rest.

'Look, I'm going round in circles here. It's one riddle after another.' He transferred the rifle to his other hand and poked the man's chest. 'Just tell me straight. *Who* called you?'

'He said, he doesn't know.'

Tom walked away to clear his head outside, aware of her scrambling to her feet, tracking him as he went. Just then, something caught his eye. Something pink. A rarity in that land of grey and more grey. It wasn't a flower, nor a sweet wrapper. This was fabric. The shiny nylon variety, and it lay just a few metres away inside an unexpectedly shallow pit.

He stumbled towards it, then picked up the fragment, sensing his pulse rate quicken. His mouth suddenly dry. 'This is Max's! He was wearing his sister's puffa jacket. He *must* have been here, at least. Look.'

Liliane came over to examine the soil at its base.

'You could be right, and if you don't disturb anything, you'll see...' she paused, staring at the obvious dents aligned with both sides, 'that there were two people here. Not one. You can see where they were lying. One of them was much taller and heavier than the other...' She touched his arm. 'Oh, I'm so sorry. So sorry...'

Tom shut her out, slotting the scrap of material into his inside jacket pocket as if it was the most precious relic in the whole world. In fact, all he had. He then charged back into the cave to where Bonneau was now attempting to move his legs.

'You listen to me, you frigging scumbag. Your time's just run out.'

That damaged head lolled from side to side. The lips drooling sounds as if he was still an infant.

Suddenly Tom felt a hand on his arm. Liliane stared up at him.

'I know you hate him. So do I, believe me. But just in case anything should happen to me, there's something else I have to tell you, *monsieur*. It's nothing to do with all this, at least I don't think so. But everything seems so much of a puzzle...'

'Go on.' Thinking understatement of the year.

'I saw Major Belassis this morning to take him those bones from Hibou, like Mademoiselle Musset said. But I don't know...' She paused. 'I'm convinced that either he, or someone connected with him, broke into Belette to try to kill me.'

Tom met her gaze and just then, the cave's interior seemed to freeze over. Was she pulling a fast one, trying to distract him from pulling the trigger on her son, or could it be true? If so, the man was showing quite a different side to when he'd called at Hibou. Besides, hadn't he still got Natalie's knife?

'What happened to the bones? Did he give them back to you or what?'

'No, no. In fact, he seemed rather keen to put them in his safe. At least, I think that's what it was. Said he'd get them checked after Easter.'

'I see.'

At Prestige People, his intuition had often earned some tidy bonuses, and not for the first time was he wondering about those strange little relics. Whose they were, and who might have left them behind.

'*Monsieur,*' she broke up his thoughts. 'Enough of me and my affairs. We need to get my son seen to. Then go the *gendarmerie.*'

'No. Remember our secret? If the police find out anything, then...'

'Then what?'

'I may not see my son or Mademoiselle Musset ever again.'

Tom looked around the desolate scene, weighing up in his mind what he should do next. Yes, he had Liliane Bonneau's agenda and yes, he had the mysterious red helicopter to think about. Was it possible it had landed for Max and Natalie? Far-fetched, he knew, but an idea all the same. If it had taken them away, then what was to keep him here? Surely he'd be better off getting back to Gandoux and, having delivered the farmer to hospital, make Didier Keppel next on his list?

Having then agonised about the risks of visiting a hospital with a made-up story about where Bonneau had been found, Tom and Liliane somehow managed to drag the farmer out of the cave and into the back of the van. The Volvo could stay where it was. Besides, who'd want a bashed-up old heap anyway? Apart from that, it reminded him of too much. His family and the life they'd shared together.

It was also unlucky.

When this was all over, he'd get a Subaru. Shining, valeted, smelling nice. Free of any associa-

410

tions. There'd be Max and Flora sparring together on a trip to the seaside. Max on his own, going to football practice. And Natalie? What about her? And then he wondered how the hell he could let her parents know...

Suddenly his imagination died...

Instead he looked at the mess the farmer had made on the van's floor and had just closed its doors when he saw Liliane remount Natalie's machine. They'd agreed to meet up at the Emergency entrance of Gandoux's only hospital. However, he suddenly thought of Didier and that film.

'*Madame*,' he called out. 'Change of plan. You're coming with us. We can hide Natalie's bike in the cave.'

'There are things in the panniers,' she argued. 'Her camera, for example.'

'I'll see to anything valuable, don't worry. Come on, now.'

She hesitated then must have seen the look on his face for soon they were on their way downhill, scraping along that same winding scree track he'd climbed, often barely wide enough and as overgrown as the land behind Hibou. Moving ever closer to what all his faculties suspected was a throbbing heart of darkness.

Suddenly his mobile began to ring. Liliane jumped in surprise beside him. The line was poor and for a moment the caller was unclear.

Ben Simiston. Not now...

His free hand wobbled on the unfamiliar wheel and his passenger cried out as the car hit a wall of thick scrub then righted itself.

'Hey, *buongiorno*, old son. How's things in *La*

411

Belle France?' the man brayed into his ear. 'Bet you've opened a few bottles by now.'

Tom could hear Una laughing next to him. The perfect wife...

'Not really, look...'

'Just to say, we'll be heading off tomorrow,' his neighbour interrupted. 'Austria, then Germany, maybe Spain. Taking it easy, as you do. Sampling all the jolly little *ristorantes* and the native plumbing as we go...'

'You never said...'

'Didn't want to steal your thunder, old son.'

'How long for?'

'How long's a piece of string? Could be a month, two months, even more. Like you, we're free agents...'

'Great.'

'Anyhow, thought it best to give you all time to settle in. Get the *fosse septique* sorted, etcetera.' His guffaw made Tom wince. 'Will buzz you for directions nearer the time. *Ciao* till then, old boy...'

Tom glanced at Liliane, too busy looking out of her window to notice how tears had sprung from his eyes.

CHAPTER THIRTY-NINE

Natalie awoke to faint sounds of sobbing, rising and falling without respite. Then, once she'd prised open her eyelids and taken in her warm airless surroundings, the noise had stopped. Who had that been, and where had it come from? she asked herself. It was truly weird.

She sat up in the single bed listening for anything else that might give her the smallest clue as to where she was. A cistern flushing somewhere; the hint of muffled voices. That was all. And Max? Where was he? Hadn't she been with him, lying in a place that, to her, smelt vaguely familiar? Why couldn't she remember any more than that? Why?

Her sore head turned to scour her surroundings and it didn't take long to realise she was alone, dressed in someone else's clothes. A pink woollen top and purple viscose bootleg pants. A colour and style she'd never worn in her life. They smelt stale, unwashed, while on her feet were scuffed black pumps a size too large. But whose?

Oh Jesus... Her empty stomach turned over as her brain repeated. This is all your fault.

Both eyes gradually adjusted to the daylight that seeped through the floral curtains, changing their orange hues to yellow, their green to lime, enhancing the eerie familiarity of the room. This was surely a Campanile Hotel somewhere because the furnishings, the tea and coffee making tray lined by a cheery breakfast mat were all typical of that commercial chain. Even 'Good Morning' translated into six different languages. Sick joke, she thought.

There were also two vinyl chairs, a gingery coloured carpet that extended up the walls to ensure soundproofing, and a pine framed watercolour of the Louvre next to the walk-in wardrobe.

She vaguely recalled staying in these places

413

while travelling with her mother back and fore to Paris, before the split with her dad had widened, become official.

Her dad...

She had to ring him. To get some help remembering what had happened. To say how she missed his voice, everything. Up to now she'd coped without worrying either parent with the ups and downs of her life. But not any more. This down was the deepest she'd ever been. She struggled to her feet to check out the obligatory desk for travelling salesmen and the like, where a stylish phone stood in its corner, under the wall-mounted TV. But where the hell was *her* phone? Her watch, her leathers? Bra and briefs?

Then she saw the strip of pale sheltered skin where her watch must have been, and a tiny red pinprick on the back of her right hand. Had she been drugged to make her sleep, or worse, to make her forget what had happened?

Time to make that call. She snatched at the desk phone and was poised to dial for an outside line, when she realised it was totally dead. But there was something else that sent another shiver of fear from head to toe: The subtle yet menacing click of a key turning in the door's lock. She replaced the receiver and backed away into the ensuite bathroom.

No towels or sheets, or even lock on the door. Just a roll of economy loo paper. Nothing with which she could take her own life or secure her safety, and the realisation dawned on her that this was not a hotel but a prison. And was this her gaoler about to come in? She moved to the bed

...orner of it as the door began to
draining away.

Two peo
masked,
ucked i
seemed
full br
man ta
mask, te

...All ...ntered. A man and a woman, both
...ing long black jackets and trousers
...calf-length boots which, to Natalie,
...rdly familiar. The woman carried a
...fast tray over to the desk, while the
...ler, thinner, with hair the colour of his
...ted the defunct phone and made a small
noise of satisfaction. Where on earth had she seen
these two before? Come on, she urged herself, as
the woman began to pour coffee from a silver
cafétière into a large cup. Think, you idiot! Think.
There was something about his eyes...

But the smells of coffee and warm croissants
only brought saliva to her mouth. Nothing to her
empty head.

'Bonjour *mademoiselle*,' purred the female. 'We
hope you slept well.'

Definitely Parisian. Not remotely deep south.

'We do pride ourselves on the accommodation
and, of course, the food here...'

'Where the hell am I? Where's Max?' demanded
Natalie. 'And what have you done with my
clothes?'

The woman looked her way. Kohl-rimmed eyes
...ming over her body.

...e'll talk later. Meanwhile,' she then indicated
...y, 'eat up, *mademoiselle*. You're far too thin.'

...s that got to do with you?'

...the questions.'

...Max?'

...time. Now then,' she brought over
...nd a plate bearing two croissants

415

oozing butter. 'If you want to be you'd better eat up.'

'What have you done with him?' N...ie yelled, knocking the offerings out of the wom...s hands. The plate was clearly unbreakable, so ...n wrist slitting wouldn't be an option. The co...e stair spread into an irregular shape on the c...et and reached those pointed boots.

A slap followed. Hard, stinging across her cheek. She fought back. Used her teeth, her voice, anything. She didn't care any more.

'Keep your din down,' growled the man backing away, rubbing his arm. 'And make sure you clear up your mess.'

With that, they both turned to leave and, as they did so, he cupped an outspread hand on the woman's rear, which she promptly removed.

'I've got friends, family,' she called out after them, even though just then, they were little more than a blur. 'You bloody wait. Bastards!'

Their reply was to silently close the door, re-lock it then move away as soundlessly as they'd arrived.

Damndamndamn...

She went over to the window in search of a way out and parted the floral curtains in the hope of finding a handle. Then she blinked in surpris... Instead of any typical Campanile setting – or town amongst dealerships and wholesal... stood an expanse of triple thickness froste... through which lay a blur of red and g... three white columns dazzling in the i... sun. So, where on earth was she?

Jesus help me...

and sat on the corner of it as the door began to open. All hope draining away.

Two people entered. A man and a woman, both masked, wearing long black jackets and trousers tucked into calf-length boots which, to Natalie, seemed weirdly familiar. The woman carried a full breakfast tray over to the desk, while the man, taller, thinner, with hair the colour of his mask, tested the defunct phone and made a small noise of satisfaction. Where on earth had she seen these two before? Come on, she urged herself, as the woman began to pour coffee from a silver cafetière into a large cup. Think, you idiot! Think. There was something about his eyes...

But the smells of coffee and warm croissants only brought saliva to her mouth. Nothing to her empty head.

'Bonjour *mademoiselle*,' purred the female. 'We hope you slept well?'

Definitely Parisian. Not remotely deep south.

'We do pride ourselves on the accommodation and, of course, the food here...'

'Where the hell am I? Where's Max?' demanded Natalie. 'And what have you done with my clothes?'

The woman looked her way. Kohl-rimmed eyes roaming over her body.

'We'll talk later. Meanwhile,' she then indicated the tray, 'eat up, *mademoiselle*. You're far too thin.'

'What's that got to do with you?'

'We ask the questions.'

'Where's Max?'

'All in good time. Now then,' she brought over the coffee cup and a plate bearing two croissants oozing butter. 'If you want to be any use to him, you'd better eat up.'

'What have you done with him?' Natalie yelled, knocking the offerings out of the woman's hands. The plate was clearly unbreakable, so even wrist-slitting wouldn't be an option. The coffee stain spread into an irregular shape on the carpet and reached those pointed boots.

A slap followed. Hard, stinging across her cheek. She fought back. Used her teeth, her voice, any-thing. She didn't care any more.

'Keep your din down,' growled the man backing away, rubbing his arm. 'And make sure you clear up your mess.'

With that, they both turned to leave and, as they did so, he cupped an outspread hand on the woman's rear, which she promptly removed.

'I've got friends, family,' she called out after them, even though just then, they were little more than a blur. 'You bloody wait. Bastards!'

Their reply was to silently close the door, re-lock it then move away as soundlessly as they'd arrived.

Damdamdamn...

She went over to the window in search of a way out and parted the floral curtains in the hope of finding a handle. Then she blinked in surprise. Instead of any typical Campanile setting – out of town amongst dealerships and wholesalers – stood an expanse of triple thickness frosted glass, through which lay a blur of red and green with three white columns dazzling in the intermittent sun. So, where on earth was she?

Jesus help me...

She must get out somehow. Back to Max, wherever he was. To Tom... But how?

Suddenly, without warning, that same masked man in black returned to her room. This time his curt tone had sharpened. He stood over her, slapping her face twice, demanding to know where the film had come from. She thought of her father. Saw him as clearly as if he was actually with her, willing her to stand firm, to bottle up her anger. Telling her the ordeal would soon be over.

'I found it in the Café de la Paix in Loupin,' she said finally. 'I was curious, that's all.' At least it got rid of him. At least she was on her own again to try and work out a means of escape. To find Max.

Having checked to see if her room door was locked after all, she became aware of a muffled tapping sound that seemed to come from the window. She parted the curtains and could just make out a small figure in blue positioned in front of her, yet so indistinct she didn't dare wonder if it might be Max. If so, how on earth had he managed to get outside and what was he up to? She yelled his name and hit the glass with her fists. But why no movement, no reaction? Surely like her, he must be able to see something. But then, maybe not.

'I'm coming. Wait.' She told herself, but who was she trying to kid? She stumbled round her room in the vain hope of finding some way out to him, but soon realised it was impossible, and by the time she'd returned to the window, the tantalising vision had gone.

CHAPTER FORTY

By half past one, with the Monjuste fire long since abated, vivid strips of cerulean sky cast the whole landscape in a much sharper light. It was as if some over-zealous cosmic picture restorer had cleaned the layer of murky varnish from the region's dwellings and churches, the crowded dovecotes, the flocks of Easter lambs drifting over ancient pastures. Such had been the *Tramontane's* brief but potent power which left the smell of diesel and blown soil in the air. It had, however, energized the clerk, driven her to make not only important decisions, but the *right* decisions. To re-evaluate her timetable, tidy up loose ends and find out what had become of her son.

Inside the master bedroom of the luxury apartment in Gandoux's quartier Louis Pasteur, even this eerie post-storm light couldn't penetrate the two sets of tightly drawn velvet curtains that shut out the functional rear of the Hôtel de Ville. For this was the world of wick and wax; of carved exotic candles set in wrought-iron sconces around the crimson walls. And in particular, those two, half-melted, on either side of the double bed. Their musky scents mingled with hers, their flames wavering as she began to sort through her clothes, which would be more appropriate for a colder climate.

However, just as she had folded a pair of leather trousers and a collection of Hermès scarves into her suitcase, she detected a small movement to her right as the main louvred door to the wall-to-wall wardrobe, imperceptibly opened.

She spun round to see a gaunt man bulked out by a bulletproof vest under his dark suit, holding a Browning complete with silencer in both hands. He was taking aim at her head. The whites of his eyes like those of a picador's horse in a bullring, his teeth showing between his lips.

Major Belassis, angry. In love.

The single shot that followed sounded no more than a gas hob lighting, or a wash cycle kicking in. She ducked, felt it fly past her hair to lodge in the wall behind the TV

Her scream lasted less then a second before he stood over her, a hand clamped to her mouth. The major then tied her wrists together with something far stronger, more discreet than twine: fishing gut. He removed the gun's silencer and slipped both parts of the weapon into his jacket pocket.

'Why, you bastard?' she lashed out with a bare leg and he smiled the kind of smile she'd first seen when he was a new recruit at the Police Annual Ball. 'What have I done?'

'*I* was next after Metz, remember? So much for your promises.'

'Major, understand this. I never promise anything.'

'Liar.'

'You infiltrated us to find out who killed your little *beur*. I didn't ask you to become...' She stalled, as if choosing the right word.

419

'Become what?'

'Obsessed.'

'Bitch.'

'You knew the rules, Carl.'

'Don't call me that. Ever.'

'You were a salesman once, remember? You're familiar with deals. And this one was simple. I took first pick with those I wanted, but you couldn't wait your turn, could you?'

'Metz wanted Musset back again, not you. Some gratitude, eh?'

The corners of her lips began to twitch. She flexed her wrists to shift the twine he'd tied too tightly. Thin red lines of indented skin were beginning to show.

'That suited you, my friend. You thought then I'd go leaping into your arms. Ha...' Her sudden laugh made him blink as he groomed himself in her dressing table mirror, slicking down his hair with both hands. Although tied up, she resolved to keep her small advantage.

'By the way, I see you've had your Jeep repaired. That's what I like about you, Carl. You always do as you're told.'

He began to click his knuckles, one by one, like he'd done at their meeting yesterday. Be careful, Pauline, she told herself. Think of Monday...

Crack ... crack...

'Didn't you hear the first time?'

'So, untie me if you don't want to hear your real name again.'

The candles by the bed sizzled as more fat waxy tears fell down their sides. A film of grey smoke filled the room.

'I said, untie me.'

By way of reply, the *gendarme* picked up the TV's remote control and clicked its red button. Immediately, the flat screen set between the two windows erupted into life with stills of Metz welding in his workshop, then the Wardle-Smith wife and daughter caught on camera in Gandoux, looking lost.

'Are our young friends still behaving themselves?' he asked, still focused on the screen.

'The boy's been pushing it. I caught him outside.'

'That's clever.' The major switched off the TV placed the remote on the bed, and walked over to the window, where he parted the curtains to allow a bright beam of light to enter the room. 'For God's sake. Anyone could have seen him.' He turned to her, his face a dark mask against the daylight. 'Why I've never been happy about using this place of yours.'

I'm not asking you to happy. Just obedient...

'It's been good enough up to now. Besides, where else is there?'

He brushed past her and into the ensuite bathroom as if to deflect from the implied inadequacy of his own home for that vital element of their mission.

'Musset claims she found the film in Loupin,' he said, turning on the mixer tap in her marble basin, using her expensive soap. 'Café de la Paix, would you believe?'

'If *you* do, you're a fool.'

'And I'm a fool to believe you'll hand over my share on Tuesday.'

421

'Believe what you like, Carl. I've told you, half will be all yours.'

'You said Bonneau was dead,' she reminded the major after he'd drunk from the tap and ruffled his hair with wet hands. 'What about his mother?'

'I got her too. Nosy little shrew.' His lips glistened with water as he eyed her breasts.

'Traitor. She deserved it.'

'And what about me, Pauline? Haven't I waited long enough?'

She sighed inwardly. The game was nearly over. All she had to do was play along...

'Three minutes. That's all.'

He snapped the fishing gut with his teeth, unbuttoned her blouse to cup her breasts together and feed her plump brown nipples into his mouth. She stood up, unstrapped his body armour, letting it drop to the floor. He moved in closer this time, and nudged her back towards the bed.

Afterwards, as she slipped on her hound's-tooth jacket – the nearest item of clothing to hand – her toe pushed the major's armour out of sight under the bed. Still dizzy from *la petite mort*, he didn't notice this significant movement and, paler than usual, dressed only in his suit trousers and shirt, with his jacket over one arm, allowed her to lead the way into the kitchen for a squeezed orange juice drink from the fridge. Meanwhile, the hi-tech Japanese waste-disposal unit taking up a sizeable portion of the nearside wall, hummed its anticipation while a red light on the operating panel, glowed intermittently.

'You wouldn't think she was five years old,' she announced, opening the fridge and pulling out an already opened carton of juice.

'She?'

'Naturally.'

Keppel lifted up the carton's pouring flap then set two tumblers in place on the granite worktop. A slow smile forming on her mouth. 'A woman of big appetites, like me.'

The light orange liquid filled their glasses. Belassis drank first. Licked his lips.

'Remember those chiropodists from Narbonne? The Biryhas?' she smiled. 'They paid for it.'

'Money well spent. Think what that kid of theirs would have cost over the years.'

'Mine costs enough.'

'Where is he, by the way?'

'At a friend's for the night.'

The major eyed her as if reading her mind. Seeing her lie.

'Didn't think he had any.'

'You don't know everything, Major.' She looked at her orange juice, suddenly without any appetite, while he lifted up the waste disposal unit's lid, and peered down at the multi-spiked drum lying in repose beneath the gaping hole. It looked pristine, barely used.

Suddenly, without warning, he closed the lid, backed away, then dug in his trouser's left pocket before placing a small wrapped package on the section of worktop in front of her.

'Take a look,' he said.

'Why? What's inside?'

'A surprise.'

Her purple varnished nails worked the kitchen towel paper free, then pulled away as six tiny human bones appeared. Bones she recognised all too clearly.

Silence, in which she regained her composure.

'I've just had them tested for DNA,' he continued before she could speak. 'Alain did me a favour.'

'And?'

'Guess what, Pauline,' a note of triumph in his voice. 'They're His and Hers.'

'Don't get it.'

'OK. Let's say, His and *Yours*.'

A sudden intake of her breath. A hand clamped to the worktop's edge as he played his advantage, toying with one bone then another, holding each in turn to the spotlight overhead. 'Shame Metz will miss out on all the fun. You should have waited a while.'

The clerk had no answer for that. He was enjoying himself too much, and had yet more tricks up his sleeve, this time in the form of a slightly battered Kodak wallet from his other pocket, which he waved in the air out of her reach.

'So, six bones, four photos plus negs,' he crowed.

'Four photos...?'

'*Voilà.*' He pulled out first one print, then the other. All sequential. Showing what happened next in his memorial room in the Rue des Espoirs. She suddenly felt cold.

'You told Alain to destroy them. I was there when you called him.'

'He's got a mind of his own. Like you.'

'What's that supposed to mean?' She was thinking of the box-cutter in her left-hand pocket.

Her colleague edged closer.

'So, where's your son?'

She supported herself against the worktop, blood seeming to drain from her face.

'I said, where is he?'

'I've not the faintest idea.'

She watched in stunned silence as he carefully re-wrapped the little souvenirs as carefully as he'd undone them and returned them to his trouser pockets.

'You get dressed,' he ordered. 'Finish packing that case and leave with me now. We'll go to America. A big country, a new life. You and me, Pauline, for ever...' Suddenly, she drew closer, placed a restraining hand over his. Her lips hot on his ear, whispering forced words of love, then, with no preamble, hate.

'In your dreams, Carl. Never in a million years. When will you ever learn? That money on Monday will be all mine. Mine. Are you listening? *That's* your reward.'

For a moment he seemed to freeze, caught between doubt and desire. Locked in that morgue of a kitchen with a woman who'd just sunk her hand into her jacket pocket. But he was quicker. Had Musset's knife and, of course, the Browning, but he chose the knife. His index finger's nail had already found the narrow niche on its five inch blade, and the man who would never possess his Queen, who'd betrayed his soul, caught her by surprise. Steel on cheek skin; a swift curved line bringing an eruption of dark blood on to her breasts.

She screamed, tried to staunch the flow with both hands pressed to her face, giving him the chance to flee the kitchen and the rest of the apartment, snatching up his jacket as he went.

'I'm off to New York anyway,' he yelled back at her. 'Away from you and your crazy life. And if you want to live, don't ever come looking for me to save your sick skin.'

After that, he was out in the foyer, then the sunlight, with the bones and photographs safe, revving up his Jeep, scorching away from the courtyard.

The marble steps took a long time to clean. What if her son should return, how would she explain the bloodstains away? Only with more bleach, more swabbing, did the marble glow clean once more.

She still wore nothing under her black jacket. Still hadn't douched him from her body nor washed her own blood off her breasts. Time to shower and get rid. Time to make a move. The water's jet seemed to clean not just her skin, but her mind. Her thoughts raced on in the same way she imagined the dying see their lives unravel before their last breath. But her own ending was quite clear now. As clear as melted snow.

Afterwards, she blow-dried her light brown hair then removed her nail varnish and the gold ring from her marriage finger, whose *vena amora* would still continue to link with her heart. She'd already fed her crucifix into the waste disposal unit, as if to symbolise the end of an era. Next, having dressed and checked on her two lodgers

426

in their sealed-off rooms, she phoned around to find out where the hell her son was.

Her cheek stung under the fifth wad of lint. Still no Didier. And why'd Belassis mentioned him in that way? She'd seen that cruel look in the man's eyes. She'd never trusted him from the word go.

How long, therefore, until he made a serious attempt on her life and other *flics* came sniffing round?

14.08 hrs. Time to check out Didier's room for clues as to his whereabouts, clear the hard drive on her laptop and feed the greedy waste disposal unit again with the contents of her briefcase and all her floppy discs plus any evidence from those two secret bedrooms. Both occupants had had far too much to say for themselves, given their precarious situation. Hadn't her old mother once croaked how silence is golden? That black-eyed raven, never quite breathing her last. Who'd insisted on Didier being named after her own father.

14.10. Not a minute to lose, and still no sign of that giveaway photograph.

Keppel secured the major's body armour under her sweater and suede coat, making sure no tell-tale bulges were visible. She and her charges would hardly attract attention wearing such everyday clothes, especially during the short trip om her apartment to the garage with her large 'tcase and the fishing gut which Belassis had d on her, invisible around their hands. They'd close together. She'd mime a conversation, at them. Such details were key. Besides, she r new box-cutter handy. Both knew that.

No CCTV, nor that nuisance concierge either. She'd seen to her earlier. Lola Couzon's demise would look like a sudden respiratory failure. These things happen, she told herself. No one lives for ever, do they?

She thanked Astarte, her personal Goddess, for tinted windows and air conditioning as she sped away from the apartments with both passengers dozing on the back seat behind her. Their smell was not very nice at all, neither was her own face, partially covered by sunglasses even though rain clouds were bowling in from the north.

Every second she checked the two for the slightest sign of protest, but no, their eyeballing had stopped the moment the second dose of Hypnosol had kicked in. Just as during the helicopter trip, with Belassis, as usual doing everything to please her. To get to her bed. And the money.

Pity not everything goes to plan.

But sometimes they do, and now Musset in particular held her attention. How sweet was revenge, she thought, taking the minor road east along the Florentin's valley to approach Gandoux from its less busy western side.

She'd done her research. Just as for Bonneau. Even visited Limoges university incognito to find for herself what Metz had seen in her. And, for the life of her, she still couldn't tell. The hair was too thick, too uniform in colour. Her nose shi*, her eyes nowhere near as distinct as her own, other words, a conventional nonentity who he'd tipped her out of his bed, had begun t* a big black bike just to get herself noticed,

428

even called round to St Sauveur on it, when she herself was pregnant. When she'd made him change his phone number and email address.

Had Musset been trying to get another glimpse of him? Hadn't eighteen months been enough for her? Whatever, he'd been impressed with the bike, she knew that much. Told her later that was one of the reasons he fancied her all over again. The black leather gear. Not cheap, especially on her meagre earnings, but worth it to keep him.

And now look at her. Sad bitch. She couldn't resist a smile, except that it hurt her wound.

She then recalled the first time she and Metz had met. He'd stormed into her office at the Hôtel de Ville eighteen months ago, dried plaster spattered over his face and overalls, waving the farmer's letters of protest about a new work of his for the Florentin service station.

His eyes had signalled passion, anger, echoing her own for mistakenly having left Paris in exchange for a life of small town affairs. A life devoid of the smallest excitement, until then. She'd read through Bonneau's vitriol while the sculptor had stood there, his presence magnetic, powerful in a way she'd never known before. While making copies for her colleagues, she'd felt the artisan's warm hand suddenly rest on hers. His body moving closer, his groin pressed against her hip.

She'd tried to explain he'd come to the wrong office. That it was really Greenbaum's clerk he should see, but that collision of desire had already gone too far. They'd met later at a bar in hors town centre where he'd told her of his als for France. How it was time the Catholic church was challenged by real visions of a pure *patrimoine*. The same as the Crusaders, whose work he regarded as unfinished.

And then, as kindred spirits, they'd made love. Made their tiny daughter, Léontine.

She stared at her sleeping fellow-travellers, repressing yet another painful smile, reminding herself to speak kindly to them. String them along...

'Only a little while now,' she said. 'I expect you'll be glad for your warm clothes. Mind you, I had a job deciding what to dress you in. I had to be practical, but at the same time, I do have some pride.'

The Grotto can be cold at night, she thought to herself as Gandoux came into view. Worse than cold, in fact, but there had to be a difference between refrigeration and freezing. For her to claim her money tomorrow, the boy must be outwardly perfect in every way. That was priority, having come so far. Having risked so much.

The journey continued without incident, although the appearance of two police vans near the next junction into town was unnerving. Not hard to guess where they were going, she said to herself, now approaching the eastern entrance to the Parc National. A different view of St Marc's church this time. In fact everything was different. The town's less public side protruded above a sheer rock face, unchanged since the fourteenth century when its first dwellings were built. Her wing mirror showed dark against dark beneath a brooding sky. The church and its gargoyles barely visible. Leontir could only be seen from the front. The last to finished, little wings and all. Now, she just war

430

to knock it down and hurl the shattered bits of her daughter's likeness at Metz's own remains in the town hospital's morgue.

Then came a thud from the back seat. She glanced in her rearview mirror and saw two other heads colliding, bone on bone. Neither woke, but the sooner she could install them out of sight the better, while she worked out a fool-proof strategy for tomorrow. A strategy where she was already moving the goal-posts...

She slowed up, then stopped to get her bearings. The Merc's headlights strobed the narrow sunken road ahead, the wall of firs beyond and then, something quite unexpected; the figure of a man and his bicycle, blocking her way.

'*Excusez-moi, madame...*' His beard moved up and down as he shouted.

Damnation.

This was the only route to the Grotto and already he was a potential witness. The stranger peered into the car with the curiosity of the ignorant. She thanked her personal Goddess again for tinted windows...

'What do you want?'

'A telephone,' he persisted, in defiance of her blatant irritation. 'Do you know if there's one nearby?'

Could he see her car phone? Her passengers? She revved the engine as a warning, but he stayed put.

'I'm sorry, *monsieur.* But I'm not from here...'

'Paris. I can tell.'

'Orléans, actually. Now if you'd kindly let me pass...'

'The Grotto's closed. Some emergency or other,' he indicated further up the narrow road. 'Not another suicide, I hope. Anyway, it's my chest. It's hurting. I think it's urgent. Help me, please...'

She could run him over, silence that furry mouth for ever. But no. The million euros was more important than a mess in the road and, with that in mind, she reversed away from him, her pulse throbbing like her cheek. Already her passengers were beginning to stir. The boy in particular, as rain spots hit the windscreen. She set the wipers to intermittent, only to realise that the peasant was following. A swerve. A spray of red earth and she was back on that Gandoux road, her pursuer now a mere speck behind her.

He'd see her number plate.

Merde.

The boy murmured in his sleep.

'Save your breath, you troublemaker,' she snarled without thinking, as she drove past the town once more to the north, bent on another idea. As plain rural dwellings gave way to flat uncultivated fields, clusters of *bricolage* depots and various *usines*, she mentally rehearsed for post-midday tomorrow when the million euros would be snug in her bag and, instead of Toulouse, she'd be on her way to the Alps – to the small but charming chalet she'd bought during her first job as PA to the FN campaigner, Ralph Dilman. As Annie Touroy, former paediatric nurse from Vierzon, she could start afresh. Run things the way *she* wanted. Away from the damaged man who might one day want to kill her. He'd made a start on her face after all. No prizes for guessing what might come next should he ever find her...

No one knew a thing about this particular impulse buy. Not even Metz or her one friend from her convent days, who'd stayed in touch with her during her early months at the Hôtel de Ville, before her other work had taken over her life and she'd cut off most ties with her past. In many ways, the Alpine village of Les Aiguilles was more her scene than this drab backwater. Its starlit streets, the icy drifts of virginal snow delivered with first light, whitening the wild wolves' black fur, cocooning for days, weeks, the hungers, the desires which had driven her so far...

Fire and ice. Ice and fire.

Fire...

Strange how things evolve, she thought, recalling her mother's favourite quotation.

You *can* have your cake and eat it.

The mother she'd not seen for years. But would she want to view that particular pile of skin and bones again, even after death? Hardly. They'd never got on. She'd been pushed into a convent for a start, then marriage, where a nightly meal on the table was to be her chief priority. And once Didier, the longed-for son, had been born, she'd had to give up work altogether for five years.

Didier...

No sign of him in Gandoux. No joy with those two schoolmates of his. He knew her mobile number, but for some inexplicable reason, had left his own phone by his bed.

More rain. The land levelling beyond the lines of plane trees which were always too near the road

433

and were decorated at intervals by bouquets for the dead. She passed one now: *Pour Julie,* set amongst wet, brown carnations.

The boy stirred.

'Mrs Keppel? Where's Didier? Where are we?'

Merde.

She turned around.

'One more word and you'll get this.' She pulled out the box-cutter from the space in the dashboard used for spare coins, and held it up. 'I'll silence you for good.'

That seemed to work, but not for long.

'Max, are you alright? Answer me?' The tart this time. Nothing wrong with *her* either, thought Keppel, as the car swerved again to cries from the back as hedgeless fields gave way to the vine. Their writhing shoots lay trained along kilometre after kilometre of wire grids. Here the upturned empty water bottle, there the makeshift scarecrow to repel the foraging boar. But these piffling devices weren't going to keep her at bay. Not with tomorrow and its bounty drawing ever closer.

CHAPTER FORTY-ONE

No kicking, no screaming. Just drowsy, hungry, and more than frightened. Natalie forced her eyes to stay open for any clue, however small, as to their whereabouts. Before the storm had broken and turned everything black, there'd been a sign advertising the Domaine de Pous, Vins de Gandoux, and posters for tomorrow's Bull Fair at Loupin. So, perhaps that village couldn't be that far away. Something at least to tell the police later on. And about the cyclist near the Grotto, who'd pressed his puzzled face to the window glass, while she and Max had been too scared too call out to him.

The sculptor had once told her how corpses used to often turn up in that deepest, most dangerous of the region's caves. And that's where this crazy woman would have taken them. But why Pauline Keppel of all people? The super-efficient clerk, role model for professional women everywhere? Max had blurted out her name then asked where Didier was. Before the box-cutter threat had silenced him.

Was she in this with Bonneau as well? That thug? It didn't add up. Nor the fact she'd entertained Max and his dad at her place only yesterday.

His dad...

She'd thought of him more than she should. When she *could* think, that is, with the drugs wearing off. Of how it would be when this was all over. Imagined his embrace. The smell of his jacket. His skin. Seeing him smile again. Then she realised this was pure self-delusion. He wouldn't want her now, not after what had happened. Her one-time association with Metz was like a poison – the slow-release kind, yet no less powerful for that. Warping his mind, stripping away any chance of a future...

Tears came that she couldn't wipe away. Nor could she reach out to the little boy next to her, wearing jeans far too big for him and a sweatshirt with the Gandoux Swimming Club logo on the front. His hair, still smelling of chlorine, lay in soft curls over his forehead. After he'd escaped from his room, Keppel had hit him, bruised both arms, then cursed her carelessness. That's what he'd said anyway. But what had she meant by careless? It didn't make sense. And what had happened to her cheek?

Natalie tried to cast her mind back to that first part of the helicopter journey, before she'd blanked out. The way the two masked black-clad figures had addressed each other. Their body language. Could this be the same woman? She certainly *sounded* similar. Even walked the same swaggering walk. But who the hell was Reignet? Whoever he was, he'd been treated like dirt. Definitely big tension between them, she decided. And maybe he'd cut her face to teach her a lesson.

She glanced again at Max. At least he was fast asleep, little snores coming with each breath, and once she was sure the bitch sitting in the Merc outside their *cabane* was asleep, she'd try and get them both out of there.

Suddenly that Limoges fortune teller's face filled Natalie's mind – half-lit, skeletal in its thinness, her dry lips spelling out her fate. A fate she'd still not paid for. She shivered, sniffed the pungent air of rotten vegetation and God knew what else. Wondered what to do next.

Her hands were tied, literally. She could only shuffle centimetre by centimetre, like Max had done in that gross cave yesterday. But to where? The one exit was blocked by the bloody car. The noise of rain hitting its roof. She thought of her apartment. It wasn't perfect, but at least it was

436

home. The new coffee maker and grey scatter-cushions she'd bought only last Wednesday. Things she'd probably never see again. And worst of all, no phone, no nothing. She'd even left her Suzuki and its keys at Hibou and that thought brought a despair even darker than the cold wet night.

'What's the time?' Max suddenly asked, his eyes still shut.

'God knows.'

'Where are we?'

'Sssh. She'll hear you.'

'I don't care. Anyway, she *can't* be Didier's mum. She was normal. This one's weird.'

More than weird...

'Where's Flora?' he asked suddenly, catching her on the hop.

'She's fine. Don't worry.'

'And Sandy?'

'The same.'

How could she say otherwise? He was just a little kid...

'You know that film he gave me?'

'Yes. But whisper, for Christ's sake. I've been saying I found it in that café in Loupin. You must, too, if anyone asks you. Promise me?'

'OK. Well, he said *he* took the photos. He'd followed his mum one Saturday night and managed to creep in behind her and hide in a wardrobe in one of the rooms. He just wanted to know what the meetings were about.'

'How odd. Did he say any more?'

'No.'

Natalie shivered again. Seven on the Richter scale.

'Where was this? Close by, or else how would he have got there?'

'He never said.' Max tried to make himself comfortable and failed. His head bumped against the ground. 'Where are *we*, anyway?'

'Some hovel or other,' she said absently, still testing her brain to recall whom Metz might have mentioned while she'd been with him. There'd been fellow artists, of course. The odd acquaintances met on his travels, but rarely anyone local, apart from the Bonneaus or Père Julien. Certainly no one else who'd seemed important to him. 'We're in the middle of nowhere,' she added. And a hovel it was too. Filthier than Hibou, and that was saying something. You couldn't get much worse, except for the Grotte de Gandoux, which had clearly been the nutter's first choice.

This dump was built of stone and was full of redundant ones, sharp enough to cut through to the bone, plus something that could have been wild boar dung. Hard lumps, anyway. And a heap of old wood, crawling with insect life. She could hear the things. Feel them creeping up inside the legs of her hideous pants. At least she'd shoved Max away from all that before she'd begun to work on an idea.

Sweet boy. She couldn't look at him now without a surge of helplessness. So what must Tom be thinking? And Kathy? And Flora? If they knew, that is. Then, for some reason, that same wine shop incident she'd recalled last night came into clearer focus. A car salesman's baby had disappeared from his pram and never been found. The family had fallen apart and, worse, the

Algerian wife had killed herself.

Think, think, she urged herself, because a name was nudging at her brain. A name she'd heard only that morning. He'd become a policeman soon afterwards...

Reignet...

'That's *it!*'

'What?'

'Tell you later.' Because all at once, she heard the car door open. Glimpsed a leg, followed by a hand, then the rest of Keppel, making a mewling noise. Good, she was in pain. But with pain comes anger...

She saw the dull glint of that cutter's blade. Heard the ominous shift of stones...

Keppel was coming nearer. Her posture stiff, as if she was wearing some kind of back support. Red lipstick all over her mouth.

'Did I hear you two colluding?'

Natalie froze. How to play it? Innocent or guilty?

'You must be mistaken. He's too frightened to do anything.'

'So will you be, if you don't shut your mouth.'

'Look, if you just let us go, no one will know. I promise.'

The woman's black eyes fixed on hers. That slim, lethal blade too close. Quivering.

'I knew someone else who made promises, *mademoiselle*. And now look at him...'

Ice everywhere. A white fear. Natalie prayed Max would keep quiet. If death was waiting, let it be hers.

The woman bent down, with some difficulty,

her sheepskin collar framing her face. The box-cutter's tip moving upwards.

'Now I'm about to change you.'

'How?'

'You'll see.'

'My God. You're sick.'

The blade had settled by her head, flicking up strands of her hair, letting them drop.

'You're not the first to say that to me, and actually, I'm rather flattered. It's you and all the other left-wing liberals that don't understand. You'd give citizenship to monkeys if you had your way. No, France must belong to the French. The *white* French. The *pur-sang...*'

Those last two words seemed to cue a sudden frenzied cutting, and soft lumps of hair fell on her face, her chest. For God's sake, she told herself, pretend you're at the hairdressers. Keep up the chat. Keep the crazy talking.

'I'm actually half Irish and proud of it...'

'I know. Maureen Bridget, née Boyd. Father an architect, mother a teacher. Am I correct?'

A deeper chill seemed to invade the *cabane* as the woman continued to air her knowledge. And yet more hair fell from Natalie's head.

'However, you do have one redeeming feature...'

'Meaning?'

'Your father was born near Moissac on 9th April 1948 to a good family. The Mussets more than made up for your mother's ordinariness. You should look them up some time, especially Grandpère Lionel. Ask your father about his stint at Drancy, *mademoiselle*.'

Drancy?

Natalie stared at her. Outrage burning her blood at mention of that infamous deportation centre near Paris. How dare she connect that shameful evil with her family? It was all lies. It had to be...

Keppel snipped one last lock from near her forehead and withdrew the blade while Natalie glanced at Max, deep in sleep again. His hands still tied together on his chest. Little did he know they were in the company of a mad woman, someone so warped, so vile, she couldn't even begin to rationalise her thinking.

'No one will look at you now, *mademoiselle,*' she said. A smirk on those full red lips. The lint bandage no longer white, curling away from her cheek. 'And to think it's *your* body on show in the church at Villefort. I'm surprised the bishop allowed it, but then who in the Church these days can resist a donation of ten thousand francs?'

Ten thousand francs?

'You mean Metz *paid* to have the sculpture there?'

'Absolutely. And I don't have to stop at cutting your hair, so take heed...'

Apart from the ignominy of a bribe, where had Metz got that kind of money from? Acid tainted Natalie's throat as the clerk retreated and, in her wake, she noticed drops of her blood had fallen on to the bare gap of her leg between shoe and trouser hem. Warm, thick. Spreading. Natalie's scream woke Max up, sending a hovering bat on its way.

'Dad ... Dad...' he seemed to be saying then blinked his eyes open. 'What was that?'

'Sssh!'

441

Keppel turned round.

'I've warned you, tart. Think of the newspaper headline: Woman's Body Found in *Cabane*. Can't you see it? Such a shame A waste of a life. All that crass sentimentality, because there'll always be more impurities where you came from...'

With that, she re-entered her car, leaving behind not only the rain's thrum on the old tiled roof, and the lingering nightmare of that March evening, but a young woman she'd underestimated. Although Natalie had viewed the odd horror flick, read de Sade and Poe, their fiction was nothing compared to this. Only Primo Levi came close. The one man whose words had changed her fifteen-year-old life all those years ago. Who'd mined the dark seam of suffering, yet offered that elusive pinprick of light.

And now, as she edged herself nearer the wall to begin the slow and painful job of loosening a few of its lower stones, she, too, was somehow going to survive.

'You OK?' whispered Max.

'Just about.'

'What's happened to your hair? Did she do that?'

Natalie nodded, aware of the cold reaching her skull. He at least had the grace to stop staring at her as if she was Wurzel Gummidge

'Hey, I've just remembered something else.' He lowered his voice to a whisper. 'That Jeep we went in to her place. The black one. I checked its number.'

'So?'

'It's the same as the one we saw yesterday, after that crash. Mum had memorised it, too, I know, but you wait till I tell Dad. And when I get the tenner he owes me, I'll buy you something really cool.'

'How about a wig, then?'

A brief tired smile, then he closed his eyes as she wondered what to do to make amends to Tom and bring Max back to him safe and sound. Every minute, every second of her thirty years seemed to coalesce into this one heart-stopping moment. The life of a gutsy nine year-old had become more precious than anything or anyone she knew. Even herself.

And then she remembered when she'd heard that name, Reignet. In the helicopter.

Jesus.

Was it possible he was a cop?

CHAPTER FORTY-TWO

Tom swore as he ended yet another fruitless call to Natalie's phone. The battery on his mobile was starting to get low and he still had no idea where Max and Natalie were.

What a mess.

Bonneau suddenly broke wind and his mother apologised for him, like she had done ever since they'd set off. Now, he just had to get to Gandoux and find the Keppel boy for a question and answer session, which might just help him reach

Max and Natalie before tomorrow.

He switched on the one dipped headlight and tried to tune the radio. Waited till the blur of sound become the newsreader's understandable words...

'...and according to the police the charred remains of a man in his early forties discovered by a cyclist in Gandoux's Parc du Lac, has yielded up one important clue. The signet ring, which survived the fire has just been identified by Marthe Greenbaum as belonging to her husband Nathan, one well-respected mayor of Gandoux, who has lived in the region all his life. The remains of a swastika carved into his forehead, gives rise to the theory among investigators that this was a racially provoked attack...'

Liliane gasped. Gripped her door handle ever more tightly as the account continued then faded, only to end with an almost inaudible reference to the Quartier Louis Pasteur, where the family had an *apartment*.

Quartier Louis Pasteur? Tom remembered those tiles, that blue water. It seemed a coincidence that he'd only been there the previous day.

His foot involuntarily lifted off the gas. The van stalled. He tried restarting it to ominous sounds from underneath and the exhaust rattling its death-throes. That drive up and down from the Causse had just about finished it off.

'Please, God,' muttered Liliane beside him. 'The hospital.'

'OK, OK. Doing my best.' He revved until a plume of black smoke appeared, then the Ford lurched forwards almost colliding with a car and trailer turning in from the Monfort road. The rifle slid from under the seat. Bonneau had shifted, too, he could tell by the van's list to the left. Each roar from his throat drowning out the radio. Tom switched it off. He was knackered, drained of everything. He'd even tried Kathy's phone, again, but no one had answered. No voicemail facility either.

He wished to God he'd been able spell it out to Flora about her little brother. But how could he? He wondered what she was doing. If she was OK. One day, he'd explain to her, try and make it up. The thought of losing both his kids made him punish the van even harder along the open road through more vineyards. Mile after mile of the same, save for the odd tumbledown *cabane* and black pointed poplars under a doom-laden sky. Steady rain diluted the remains of insects on the windscreen. Red, yellow and a smear of green...

'*Maman... Maman...*' Bonneau suddenly cried out as Tom slowed up for a level crossing.

'Shut your face, you. Unless you've something useful to say.'

Liliane touched his arm.

'Please help him, Monsieur Tom,' she pleaded. 'You're a good man.'

'Not that good.' He grimly stepped on the gas again, taking them to the outskirts of Gandoux. He remembered the way. Avenue des Acaces then a street lined with small shops. All closed, all dark. The Hôtel de Ville was behind him; the apartments straight ahead studded by blocks of light. People at home, doing homely things. He glanced at his anxious passenger and felt a moment's indecision. The hospital wasn't far. He'd make it easily in five minutes. So why wasn't he turning round, doing as she'd asked? Because he knew that his priorities were all wrong. Max and Natalie were still out there somewhere and still her parents didn't know.

Bonneau could wait.

'This isn't the hospital,' she observed in a tremulous voice.

'Tough.'

She sighed in despair before her son began bawling.

Dammit. Coppers.

More specifically, an armed *gendarme* manning the gates to the Quartier Louis Pasteur's courtyard, where three police vans already stood strewn over the tarmac. None with the 97 prefix Natalie had mentioned.

What was going on? What to do? Turn round quick and get away, or try his luck? He thought of Max.

'Is Didier Keppel here?' he asked the guy who stared into the van. 'I have to see him. It's urgent.'

'Your name, *monsieur?*'

'Bob Thomas,' he blurted out. It would do again. But not for long.

'Passport?'

He struggled to find it. Handed it over with a thudding heart. His photo under the torchlight showed a smiling successful man, taken June 8th 2001. Seven months ago.

'*Monsieur,*' the gatekeeper gestured to his younger uniformed colleague, 'we have a problem.' Then to Tom. 'Can you please explain the

446

you have two names?'

keep the law out of this, or else...

Too late now. He'd mucked up big time, and who'd be paying for it? Who?

The other *gendarme* came over. Introduced himself as Lieutenant Daniel Valon of the Serious Crimes Unit. He possessed a youthful open face. Keen expressive eyes. Someone he could confide in. Let it all out. Christ, it felt good to talk.

'We appreciate your predicament about not involving the law, but, you have to trust me,' Valon said finally, when Tom had finished.

'Major Belassis said exactly the same to me and my son yesterday.'

The two officers exchanged a glance, then, once Valon had handed back the passport, expressed his deep sympathy but also a certain optimism about the outcome, and reassured him that nothing would be done to jeopardise either his young son or the lecturer before the deadline. Any intelligence operation that followed, including contacting her parents in London and Quebec, would be covert. Likewise on the ground.

'Didier Keppel,' Tom reminded them. 'You seen him anywhere?'

'Let's just deal with your companions first, eh?' He scrutinised Liliane, who seemed unable to speak. 'Any weapons that you know of?'

'No.' The rifle hidden under the seat was his business. Then he gestured towards the frail, wild-haired lady sitting next to him, who seemed to be praying to herself. 'That's Madame Bonneau of Belette Farm.'

Without warning, a black wave of claustro-

phobia swept over him. He just wanted to t
his elderly neighbour and her son, get them as
away as possible, giving him the space to breathe
and to think and to plan, just for a moment...

'And her son's in the back. He took my boy and
Miss Musset. I was there. You've got to believe
me. He's the one...'

He watched his two passengers being led away
to the nearest van, complete with blue light strip
on top. Bonneau trying to resist, even then, sandwiched between two more cops. Walking, after a
fashion. He'll live, thought Tom. There was no
justice.

Suddenly, Liliane stopped by the *gendarmerie*
van, called out his name, then signalled for him
to come closer. Torn between this and his real
mission, he obliged.

'I know it's none of my business,' she began,
'but because I may not see you again I have to
ask you something. Tell me, Monsieur Tom, do
you love Mademoiselle Musset?'

The question ricocheted like some mad bullet
round his brain. The answer was, he didn't know.
Yes, she represented a certain longing – like that
for a summer moon, drawing up the tide of his
wretched life – yet a moon nevertheless, of mes-
merising light and puzzling shadows...

'That's private, *madame*.'

'Well, I'm just an old woman who was your age
once. I was even younger when I met the man
I...' Here she faltered, wincing as her son was
loaded into the vehicle. 'The man I loved more
than the whole world.'

'Your husband?'

'No. But this man would have been if his life hadn't been snuffed out. Maybe I'll tell you one day, if God is willing.'

'What's this got to do with me?' he challenged, more impatient than ever to find Didier.

'Everything. When you find a precious stone, you keep it. You polish it, you guard it, fearing its loss. Mademoiselle Musset is *your* treasure. Just remember...'

One more question to ask her. Something that might make all the difference.

'Tell me, *madame,* do you keep any yellow twine at Belette? Please, it's important.'

She lowered her voice.

'Yes. Eric once brought lots back with him from Spain. He swore by it. Why?'

'Just wondering. Thanks.'

When their van had gone, Tom was ushered into the foyer of the building named after François Mitterand, where a Lieutenant Alain Reignet, also part of the SCU team, and who, in more ways than one, seemed to be vaguely familiar, introduced himself. Crew-cut, late twenties, early thirties, a good colour on his cheeks. He soon ordered a clutch of journalists who'd appeared from nowhere to leave. Vultures, Tom thought, watching as their Nissan Patrol sped away through the gates.

'Too right,' said the Lieutenant. 'We're trying to keep a lid on everything. At least until Tuesday morning.'

Tuesday morning seemed like a century away. And before Tuesday comes Monday...

'Thanks. But someone needs to tell Kathy, my

wife,' Tom said. 'Apart from anything else, there's a potential money issue. I'll be honest,' he elaborated as Valon caught up with them. 'Our relationship's hit rock bottom since moving here. She threatened to withdraw her share from our account yesterday, then said she hadn't. She may well have lied to me and already done it. Now she's not even answering the phone...'

Dismay clouded their faces.

'We'll have to break the news to her as soon as possible,' said Valon. 'Once she knows what's going on, I'm sure she'll help any way she can. We'll just have to hope that she's not done what you fear. Transferring money back here again could take up precious time.'

Tom nodded slowly.

'Don't worry,' Valon reassured him. 'We've had situations like this before. Just leave it with us.' He strode away towards the foyer's glass doors and more possible trouble.

'What situations?' asked Tom, alert for any sign of Keppel's boy as he and Reignet moved further into the foyer where a police cordon surrounded an octagonal glass booth which he presumed would normally house the building's concierge.

'Like this, of course,' replied Reignet quickly. 'Lola Couzon, the concierge here was attacked yesterday afternoon sometime. And then of course there's been Nathan Greenbaum...'

The officer then guided him towards a half-open doorway behind the concierge's desk at the far end of the foyer.

'Wasn't he that mayor I heard about on the news just now?' asked Tom. 'Is that why you're here as well?'

The officer nodded and pointed in the direction of the courtyard.

'He and his wife lived in the block opposite. Terrible business.'

'The newsreader mentioned a possible racist attack.' Tom still couldn't drive Valon's final words from his mind and felt that even though there seemed to be plenty happening here, he wasn't getting the bigger picture.

'Lieutenant, is there something you're not telling me?'

Reignet stopped to run a gloved hand backwards and forwards under his chin before speaking. His earlier confident tone now replaced by something far more cautious as he told Tom of a small, exclusive ring of Gandoux's Extreme Right – four at most, including the clerk and the late Bernard Metz who'd been under suspicion for a while, but so far, with no solid evidence of any wrongdoing for arrests to be made.

Metz? My God... So what did Natalie know? Something, surely? He sensed his world begin to tilt perilously from its axis. All hope swilling away into the darkness.

'And they're the ones behind my boy and Mademoiselle Musset being taken?'

The lieutenant nodded, studying each of his gloved fingers in turn.

'Apart from Samson Bonneau, let's guess.' Tom recalled a pair of hard blue eyes; things Liliane had said...

'Could Major Belassis be involved, by any chance? After all, he called into my place with

451

Keppel on Friday night.'

Reignet stared at him in a strange way. A vertical frown bisecting his pink forehead.

'Monsieur, our Major Belassis is a committed church-goer. A man of great faith. He is as shocked as any of us by what has happened to your family and the Greenbaums.'

'Nothing's making sense. Why us? Why them?'

Reignet shrugged. He genuinely seemed not to know.

Then Tom remembered the photograph. How the hell could he have forgotten it? Because he'd been too stressed with the Bonneaus to mention it when he'd arrived, that was why.

'OK, take a look at this,' he said, as, with shaking fingers, he dug out the somewhat battered photo from his jeans' back pocket. Shared the silence while the other man scrutinised it, taking his time. 'For a start, why's the little girl got a circle drawn on the left side of her chest?'

Reignet turned away as if sickened.

'No wonder they want this back.'

'They?'

And then he thought he knew.

'My guess is – and this is off the record – it's possibly our late sculptor friend,' said the lieutenant.

'Bernard Metz? So where do you reckon it's taken?'

'Hard to say. Some gallery or other, judging by all those pictures, or whatever they are. Keep it very safe, *monsieur*,' Reignet urged, handing it back. 'We'll make copies later today, back at HQ.'

'Would you say it's recent?'

'Fairly.'

Tom stared at the image again.

'I don't get it. He didn't have kids as far as my wife and I knew. Or perhaps he'd recently adopted one? But if so, why no mention of it in the reports about his death?' These were also questions for Natalie, when he found her. 'And why's he looking so ... triumphant? Yes, that's the word.'

'I honestly don't know, *monsieur*. It may be something and nothing.'

Tom felt anger redden his neck.

'I hardly think it's nothing, given all the fuss being made about it. The fact that two innocent lives depend on it.'

'Look, I'm no expert, and I'm not defending him, but I seem to remember the prototypes for his gargoyles were originally sculpted in wax, then cast in a flexible vinyl and coloured to look extremely realistic. At least, that's what the catalogue at the time claimed. He held a small exhibition of them at the Hôtel de Ville last year. He liked to show the public his early studies. You know, drawings, maquettes, half-scale models. By the way, his place is being thoroughly searched at the moment, and hopefully we'll soon find out more. At this stage, like you, *monsieur*, we can only guess at what was going on.'

'But what you can't do is blind me with science. *That* is no lump of vinyl.'

'Keppel's apartment,' announced Reignet, seconds later, barring the way in with his stocky body. 'Number 3. Where we're focused for the time being.'

Tom saw some curious residents beginning to

group together in the foyer's darker recesses, or hover on the staircase. Their hands strangely pink against the white marble. The lieutenant, attempting to shield Tom from their stares, told them all to return to their own flats; that there was nothing to be gained by being there, getting in the police's way. Still no sign of Didier.

'We heard our concierge was attacked last night,' said one woman to Reignet. 'Is she alright? Have you caught the culprit yet?'

'Madame Couzon's now at home, recovering. Her assailant must have panicked and left the scene, but as the CCTV camera wasn't working, the incident isn't on film. Therefore, it'll take a while to establish the full facts.'

He then he turned to Tom.

'We're also trying to find out who contacted Samson Bonneau, to...' He hesitated, avoiding Tom's eyes. 'Take your son and Mademoiselle Musset.'

This is a new one...

'I hope whoever it is rots in Hell.'

'Hell's too good for people like that, *monsieur.* And in my job I don't often say such things.'

Then the officer explained how Keppel and a male companion had piloted a police helicopter to bring Max and Natalie down from the Causse de Framat. It had been carefully planned with no one in the control office suspecting a thing. 'They'd landed in the furthest part of the Parc du Lac and had driven to Keppel's apartment from there.'

Just as he'd suspected.

To steady himself, Tom leant back against the cool wall behind him. To think they'd been here just a few short hours ago, had walked through this foyer and through that door... He'd been one step behind all along. A terrible feeling.

'So if Keppel kept my son and Miss Musset in her flat, where are they now? Why aren't you finding out more?' His hand closed over the scrap of puffa jacket in his pocket.

'We can't.' The Lieutenant's voice had suddenly lost its edge.

'What d'you mean, *can't?*'

'Like you said yourself, everything depends on Monday going ahead as planned. We mustn't, how do you say? Stir the waters.'

Valon now rejoined them from his duties outside. Tom took his chance.

'But this lieutenant here told me something surreptitious could be done. Covert was the word he used.'

'Sorry, *monsieur*,' said the younger *gendarme*. 'Was only trying to help.'

Tom knew that made sense, but accepting it was another matter. That same dark wave was lurking in the depths of his soul, ready to consume him again as Reignet quickly acknowledged someone in a white coat making for the exit.

Tom caught the stranger's eye. Wondered if he really was who he seemed. Wondered, too, if he could ever trust anyone again.

'So, where's Didier?' He pressed his companions again. 'He could tell us more, surely? I mean, he may have been here with my son, after what happened on the mountain.'

Reignet laid a strong square hand on his arm. The smell of garlic reached Tom's nose. There was something so familiar about him...

'We're searching now. Maybe he's just having fun somewhere.'

'Perhaps the CCTV was working at the time he left.'

'We hope so as much as you.'

Tom felt the foyer grew cold. The evening breeze, now feeling malignant, swirled around his feet, spiralling up his body. Possessing him. For all the apartment block's lavish fitments and fittings, this was one truly evil place, and he prayed silently with all his heart that Max and Natalie and Didier had somehow survived it.

'He's a brave boy, like your son. We'll find him.' Valon was trying hard. All he could do, thought Tom bleakly. He eyed the half-open door to Apartment 3, where the forensics team was busy in the distant kitchen. Doing what exactly, he couldn't quite make out.

'I've *got* to go in there. Got to see where...' He stopped. The unsaid words like fishbones in his gullet.

'Not at the moment, I'm afraid,' said Reignet guiding him away by the elbow. 'This was just for you to get your bearings, so to speak.'

'Why? I mean, why them? Why my boy and Natalie?' Those simple words asking for so much.

'Basically, it's the money. That's our guess. These small-time organisations need it to survive. Most of them are thankfully the here today gone tomorrow variety.'

'Let's hope this one is.'

Tom stared at the scene around him. Yesterday at the pool seemed an hallucination. She, charm

456

itself. Max and Didier relaxed and happy. Then he recalled his final glimpse of the boy and added, 'Yesterday, I saw the lad's face. I reckon he was scared of her.'

The two *gendarmes* exchanged a second glance. As if to say, so are we.

Tom shivered. It was time to go. Get on with whatever he could. He couldn't just stay here, doing nothing.

They reached the empty van. He explained to them where his Volvo was, and Natalie's Suzuki. Immediately Valon was on the case, ordering recovery.

'Follow me, then,' said Reignet. 'We'll check that van over, get a statement, then sort you out. Shower and shave. Hot meal and a drink, eh?'

'I just want my son,' he protested, then remembered the rifle. And that thought triggered the memory of Liliane Bonneau's parting words. What an idiot he'd been to her. 'I need to know Natalie Musset is safe, and for my wife to know what I'm going through.'

The small crowd, now assembled outside the courtyard, stayed silent. Their faces registering the kind of fear that comes from knowing that deep within the heart of their bureaucratically run yet comfortable existence, there had throbbed such evil. Word had spread as quickly as the Monjuste fire, but speed also brought inaccuracies. Who was dead and who alive changed every time someone spoke. But when the Bishop of Gandoux drew up in his black saloon to offer his sympathy, the townsfolk edged away, suspicious.

457

Once the forensic team had placed their various white bags in the back of an unmarked van, another, bearing a team of workmen arrived to board up Keppel's apartment doors. While the repeated banging of nails into wood continued, the onlookers dispersed, and in their wake lay a line of homemade floral sprays of whatever had come to hand from local gardens and streets.

Tom lasted just ten minutes at the *gendarmerie*'s SCU room. Enough time for copies of that print to be made and for him to have signed yet another statement. He'd then gulped down some foul-tasting coffee and put his phone on to charge, before storming out in frustration, slamming the door behind him and, before the stray *gendarme* by the rear exit could challenge him, he had leapt down the steps and into the crew compound.

Thank God Bonneau's van was still there. It's key in the ignition. The rifle under the front seat.

How slack was that?

Yes, Valon had promised again they could sort the money out with the bank. Yes, there'd be armed plain-clothed personnel at the rendezvous tomorrow, but offering Tom protection was another matter.

'Protection?' he'd jibed. 'Oh yeah? Like we've had so far? Forget it.'

Now, inside the Ford, he saw the petrol gauge hovering near red. As he revved the old engine for a swift getaway, he felt his heart slow up, burn out. Empty of everything except Max and Natalie...

Natalie...

He recalled her hair, her face, that first time

they'd met. How Max had loved her, too. No, he thought, pulling out into the Avenue des Peupliers, under a darkening sky, he wasn't totally alone. Not while she was alive. *If* she was alive... After five minutes trawling the now eerily quiet streets for a garage, he located a one pump affair next to a single storey biscuit factory. Miraculously it was open till 10 p.m. The cashier's radio was on full blast, spewing out theories about the now notorious little group. How the current climate of intolerance was allowing them to spring up like wild mushrooms.

Tom paid for his fuel and two chocolate bars for Max, then realised he'd left both the cola sweets and unopened bottles of drink in the Volvo's boot. He'd forgotten all about them.

'Nasty times,' the man shouted in fluent English above the din as he handed over the change. 'But then, nothing changes really, does it?' He then studied Tom more closely, took in his haggard, unwashed and terrified appearance. 'You're not that British guy, are you? The one who's lost his kid?'

Tom swallowed. His throat suddenly dry as dust.

'How did you know?'

He indicated the radio where some Social Science expert was now expounding on the fanatical Far Right's growing influence. Turned it down to a faint buzz. 'Hell, I'm sorry.' He looked it.

'I'm not giving up,' said Tom. But after this gross breach of security, he might as well.

The cashier leaned on his counter, his wary eyes now on the open door in front of him. 'You watch your back. That bitch and whoever else will be waiting for you somewhere. You tooled up?'

'Found an old rifle.'

'You'll need something handier than that. I know a guy just round the corner who might be able to help you out.'

The garage owner passed through a beaded curtain into a back room and soon returned with his mobile phone tucked between his jaw and his shoulder.

'Cheers,' he said to whoever he'd called, then stuffed the phone in his jeans' pocket. 'Number forty-two Rue Jean Moulin. Guy called Francke. He's expecting you. Says he's got a neat Walther PPK you can borrow. Let's hope you don't need it.'

'Thanks.'

'No worries. I hope it all works out for you.'

The young man then opened a small chiller cabinet and removed a pack of sandwiches. 'Jambon et cornichons. Catch.'

Once outside in the slanting rain, Tom tore off the cellophane wrapping and crammed the food into his mouth. Then he swung the van out of the little forecourt and found the Rue Jean Moulin.

Ten minutes later, with the loaded Walther safely in the glove box, he rejoined the main road south, all the while keeping an eye on all his mirrors.

8.30 p.m. While the van laboured along the wet road towards Loupin, Daniel Valon took a breathless call from a Monsieur Jammes, who'd been cycling near Gandoux's Grotto. He'd called

out a suspicious looking female car
with detail a nasty cheek wound whom he'd
driver w ask for help. She was in a silver Mer-
stopped in such heavily tinted glass he'd not been
cedes see who, if anyone, was seated behind her.
able ate was local. He'd recorded the number.
Its

CHAPTER FORTY-THREE

Liliane had always hated hospitals, which was why
she'd elected to give birth to her first and only
child at home in Belette in their bedroom – her
bedroom now – now with that old bed landscaped
by hers and Albert's deep hollows. Its mattress
freckled by dark, ancient stains. This one however,
couldn't be more different. Pristine white. Hard
on her old bones, keeping her from the sleep she
craved. Bringing guilt, not slumber, which smothered her mind like the algae that, every spring,
turned the pond at Belette an ever richer shade of
green. A problem she'd neglected since Albert had
died. Since she'd lost the will. But now was
different. God had answered her prayers to save
her wretched son. It was her turn to come clean.

She put aside Sunday's *L'Expresse*, featuring a
photo of Pauline Keppel with her serious looking
son on its front page, and waited for her Con-
fessor.

Nine o'clock exactly. He was on time. From her
d in the Pompidou Wing of Gandoux's only
pital, she watched the ward door open and a

young officer stand and glance at the fellow patients until his gaze alighted on her. He was handsome, certainly. Not like Monsieur, but equally someone she felt she could open up to. That impression was confirmed as the young man drew closer and pulled a nearby chair up next to her bed.

'Lieutenant Valon,' he said, extending a hand which she gratefully took. It was clean, with good nails, she noticed. And, before he could add anything more about himself, she passed him the Suzuki's keys and told him where the Volvo and the young woman's precious bike could be found.

'Thank you, *madame*. They're already safe with us. But for now, I just need to ask you a few simple questions...'

'About Samson? His crimes?'

'Whatever information you can give. Then I'll ask you to read through everything and sign. Are you feeling well enough?'

'I have to be, Lieutenant. Three people's lives depend on it. By the way, could you please check that my black coat's still under my bed?'

He bent down and, after glancing under the bed, he also plugged in some machine or other – a small slim version of what Samson had in his bedroom for the accounts. 'It is.'

'Good.'

'Now, Madame Bonneau, please speak slowly while I type. There's no hurry. You've had a bad time and your doctor's told me to be brief and not to distress you.'

By nine thirty her statement was complete. Sh

been lucid and kept control of her emotions. However, she wasn't yet ready to sign it. Not by a long chalk.

'There's something else, *monsieur*,' she went on, determined to fulfil her promise to herself. 'I'm afraid I've lied.'

He looked puzzled.

'Who to? Me?'

'Yes, and to others who care for me. And if I don't confess my sins, God will judge me a sinner...'

'So tell me,' he resumed typing. '*How* have you lied?'

A young nurse came by with a medicine trolley. Started to give him a smile, but it expired as soon as she registered Liliane's face. She pulled the privacy curtain around the bed.

Mademoiselle Musset wouldn't have done that. She'd have asked if she was alright. If she needed anything. Which was why she, Liliane, had said what she had to Monsieur Tom, despite him not taking her and Samson to hospital. Despite his seeming ingratitude. But who could blame him? At least *her* son was lying in the ward beneath her.

She gathered her thoughts, all too aware of the leaping pulse in her wrist and the drip attached to her right hand. She'd suffered a minor *crise* on the way to hospital, but so far, her speech and other functions seemed unaffected. Only her soul was 'l...

'I heard Samson's van leave Belette at 5 a.m. on day morning,' she began. 'Then back he came x to check on his calves. That afternoon he to the abattoir. On the Saturday, he left early again, but this time I didn't see him until he attacked me and I left for Hibou.' She leant forwards. Lowered her voice. 'I'd found a pair of his trousers that he's not worn for years, and there was blood on them. Not human blood, you understand. And not calves' blood either, that's too pale...'

'Go on, please.' The lieutenant continued typing with a light sure touch, eyes focused on the keys.

'It wouldn't wash off so ... I burnt them.' She crossed herself with her left hand, letting it come to rest on her rosary. 'And I've also committed another crime. I was also trying to poison him with mouldy rye bread sandwiches to give him the St Anthony's Fire. I wanted to boil his skin, even boil his mind. Do you understand?'

He nodded.

'I don't think anyone will blame you, *madame*. From what we've heard, you've lived a life of terror with him and I'm sure any reasonable *juge d'instruction* – especially Felix Laurent here – would be sympathetic to your situation.'

'Thank you, Lieutenant, but there's something else again. I knew my son hated the *Anglais*. Perhaps not as much as...'

'As?' Valon looked up, curious.

'Germans.' That word so hard to say, even now. 'He badly wanted to buy that *fermette*. He resented the family being there. What I'm gettin' at, is, I believe he was *willing* to do what he w asked. Who was it that called him? Do you kno

'Yes. But at the moment, that's confidenti

'You will tell me when you can?'

464

'Of course.'

'If I'd only spoken out that I thought my son had killed Filou, then this other terrible business wouldn't have happened.'

'Who's to say, *madame?* Too may police were tied up with the sculptor's death that afternoon. Besides, there wouldn't have been an investigation till Tuesday at the earliest. And by then, your son had been approached. It's all chance I'm afraid. Out of our hands...'

Her eyes turned to the window above her bedside table where the curtains were still undrawn. Rain from a black sky slapped against the glass.

'I'm just praying Monsieur Tom, his dear little boy and Mademoiselle Musset are alright out there.'

'Don't worry.' He checked his watch. 'At least we'll be prepared for their handover at the Bull Fair on Monday.'

Bull Fair? Monday?

'What? I didn't know that.'

A small prayer came to her lips, but quickly died. She'd been to that very place just the once with Albert and Eric, leaving Samson at the farm. Never before had she seen so many people and animals all mixed up together. The shouting, the drunkenness as the day had worn on. One bull had escaped and bucked his way around the packed field until caught near the main gateway. She'd come away feeling ill and resolved never to go again.

'There's a big ransom to be paid and big problems getting hold of it. I shouldn't have told you, *madame*. Please keep all this strictly to yourself.'

'Of course, but why such a terrible place? The

little boy will be scared stiff.'

'We don't know. Now, *madame*, is there anything else you need to tell me before I go?' he asked. 'Have one last think.'

It didn't take long. That cold damp cellar was still all too vivid in her mind.

'Who was it that came looking for me today at Belette and damaged its front door?'

He seemed genuinely taken aback.

'When?'

'One o'clock yesterday. On the dot. Major Belassis had said one of his friends from Brive was coming to take me to his home. To be safe. A Monsieur Panet, he said. But, Lieutenant, it hardly sounded like anyone wanting to take care of me. If I'd not been hiding in the cellar, then...'

She shivered under her hospital nightdress. Would have liked a hot, sweet drink to steady her nerves. Even something stronger.

'And the telephone wire was pulled out of the wall.'

The young man appeared to be very concerned, and patted her hand before getting up to go.

'Is that it? Nothing else now?'

She shook her head, but as the lieutenant closed the lid of his machine, a lingering look of hatred sprung to mind; a young girl's triumphant laugh. So vivid, so clear, after all these years...

'Great,' he said, then glanced at that same nurse on her return journey down the ward. She gave him another alluring smile.

'Thank you for your assistance, *madame*. Justice will be done, let me assure you of that.'

Liliane heard someone cough and spit out the

result. She winced, telling herself that if Samson wasn't here, she'd be out of this place in a flash.

Then the lieutenant was gone, Leaving her bed curtains unparted, striding, almost running to the end of the Stroke ward. She wondered about Samson and realised with a jolt to her old heart that she'd not yet told him that Bernard Metz was dead. Besides, it was probably too late now. He'd got other demons to consider before meeting his Maker, and once she'd finished a short prayer for an end to his suffering, she began working out a plan for the morning.

CHAPTER FORTY-FOUR

While Lieutenant Daniel Valon was speeding away from the hospital, at the same time arranging a police guard for Liliane Bonneau and her son, a heavily bandaged Samson Bonneau lay half in, half out of his hospital bed in a side room – for his own safety, they'd said – off the men's ward, muttering some half-forgotten prayer...

'Deus in adjutorium meum intende, Domine ad adjuvandum me festina...' Each breath grated in his throat, in his lungs. The effort of speech bringing more boiling blood into his head.

Delirious, stupefied, he could sniff death, even feel it, and such was his condition that the one nurse and doctor who'd admitted him had seemed little more than pale disembodied spirits, stirring the air around him; their brief repartee

467

conducted in the third person as if he were already a corpse.

At least the hospital chaplain had just given him Absolution for all his sins, yet despite this forgiveness, he knew he'd failed. Not just himself, but whoever it was that had planned to make him rich. It was all the English brat's fault. He'd tried to kill him. Smash his skull. Leave him for dead. And afterwards, while pretending to have snuffed it up on the Causse, he, Bonneau had heard every threatening word the father and his own mother had spat at him.

No matter he'd tried to help. Tell the fool he'd seen that red helicopter...

That was gratitude for you. And, to cap it all, he'd had to accept the father's charity with a lift in his own van. Not that his manner had been charitable. Far from it. Now he prayed they'd all get their comeuppance. At least the foul weather would help.

Despite his imprisoning bandages, his one good ear picked up the rain's onslaught against the window. The other ear stung like the Devil while the rubber tube leading from his wrist to a contraption over the bed reminded him of milking days at Belette. But instead of milk, this was morphine on demand and it was not making the least difference to his pain.

Were they ignoring him here, letting him die? Was that it?

'Inter oves locum praesta, statuens in parte dextra...' he murmured. But that wasn't going to happen by any means. Not while revenge still burned in his soul. All at once, a nurse suddenly appeared by

his bed. He could smell her. Soap, *Cif* and arm-pits. She set a small terracotta pot filled with fake earth, silk anenomes and matching card on his bedside locker.

'What's this all about?' he growled at the blur of colour passing his eyes. The card's impossibly small type.

'Just arrived, *monsieur.* A gentleman left it for you at Reception. Said he was in too much of a rush to see you personally, but sends his best wishes for your speedy recovery.'

She began to move away, then turned to face him.

'By the way, Dr Pichaud will be calling in to see you with a police officer around ten thirty. I did explain you were still in IC, not completely out of danger, and we normally have lights out by then, but he insisted on seeing you. In the meantime, we'll see if we can't arrange a bed bath for the morning.'

Bed bath?

No good asking her what she meant, snooty bitch. And, when a bedpan trolley clattered by the Unit, he managed to raise his hand to attract the orderly's attention.

'Two things,' he rasped at the white blur in front of him. 'What's a bed bath, and can you read that card for me?'

'Sure man. A bed bath's where they wipe you all over while you stay put.' The man reached for the card then dug in his overall's pocket. 'I jus' need me glasses on me nose...'

Bonneau swore to himself.

A noir. *He'd asked a bloody* noir *to help him. Now*

there really was no hope.

'OK, you ready?' The other man held the card at eye level and began to read its contents.

> *Samson, we are thinking of you.*
> *Not long now.*
> *Jean, Christine, Eric and Albert.*

'Hey, man, sounds like you got yourself a nice family...' The man returned the card to the flowerpot and worked his noisy way up the ward.

Bonneau tried to make sense of it all. A gentleman well-wisher? But who? And why mention his dead family? Something wasn't right about this. He'd have to find out.

Think... Think...

But he couldn't. It was bad enough just trying to breathe.

He called out from his bed, but this was the busiest time of day in the Hôpital de La Sainte Vierge with emergencies and the usual end of day procedures. No one was listening. Least of all the black-frocked priest praying nearby. Nor the roughneck in a nearby bed, in the main ward, being sick into a bowl...

'Help!'

He closed his sticky eyes. Saw those pale faces again, one by one: Jean and Christine, both struggling for air under the pillow. Eric the same, turning bilberry blue, staring at him, staring... And his father clinging with hands like eagles' claws on his shoulders, terror in his eyes before he'd finally pushed him over the Florentin Bridge's guard rail.

He heard again that echoing cry, the soft *phut*

as he landed far below. His mother's wail when she'd first found out.

'Help!' he cried. Where the Hell was *she*? Didn't she care either? The mother who'd outlive him and keep Belette for herself to do with as she pleased. She was probably there now, in the *séjour* watching television with her feet up.

That same trolley rattled by again, with the orderly slapping down the empty aluminium bedpans under each bed, whistling as he went. So no one heard the first loud ticks emanating from Bonneau's locker, but when the flash came, and the force which accompanied it that tipped his bed over, pinning him to the floor, screams of terror filled the air.

'*Cor tontritus quasi cinis*
Gere curam mei finis...'

Total darkness. The sound of running feet from somewhere far away, drawing closer. Closer...

'*Maman?*' he murmured. 'Is that you?'

Then in his fading mind, as flames engulfed his body, he saw her with a young black-haired man in some foreign uniform, their arms outstretched in a gesture of love as they ran towards him.

CHAPTER FORTY-FIVE

Tom woke to grey drizzle, grey everything, after a bad night. He felt like death. His legs aching from yesterday's climb and from being stuck under the Transit's dashboard for too long. But

471

he just had to be here for the Bull Fair, good and ready. Trouble was, he'd left his mobile plugged in at the *gendarmerie*.

Dammit, dammit, dammit.

The first livestock trailers of the day were arriving at the vast level field that lay between Loupin's last dwelling and the vineyards. Already, officials clad in orange waterproofs stood holding their clipboards at either side of the main gate, unaware of the turmoil in his mind, and of what events might follow.

Four hours to go, with the stubby Walther snug in his right hand jacket pocket; wallet in the left. He'd always meant to put some photos of the kids in there at some point, but never got round to it. Now, in a way, he was glad. His stomach rumbled after a second night of inadequate food and sleep, and Kathy'd still not come to the phone when he'd rung her mother's house in Camden from a Loupin call box just ten minutes ago. Without giving him a chance to speak, Marjorie Hare had informed him with her usual clipped public school voice, that her GP had called and prescribed sleeping pills for both her daughter and granddaughter.

He wasn't to phone again, she'd said. Everything that had occurred in France was his fault and, saving the bombshell till last, added that her daughter's share of the money in the Banque du Midi account had already been electronically transferred to London yesterday afternoon. The day she'd decided to leave.

So, they still didn't know about Max.

For a moment he blanked out, then in numb shock he drove from the roadside parking area back into crowded Loupin, where he tried to ring Camden again from that same call box, all the while watching out for a *gendarme*. Any *gendarme* he could alert to this madness.

Flora answered. A miracle. His little girl's voice sounded as clear as if she was in the booth with him.

'Have the French police been in touch with your mum?'

'Yes. Just now I think.'

'Thank God.'

But still the words *double-edged sword* wouldn't go away.

'You never said Max and Natalie were missing,' Flora challenged him.

'I couldn't. Just in case...'

'Where are they?'

'I'm doing my best. OK? But tell your mum we'll need her money transferred back to the Banque du Midi in Gandoux again by eleven at the latest. No million euros, no Max. Get it?'

'She's making a fuss about paying for Natalie.'

Tom felt his stomach turn over.

'Tell her I'll pay her back. Every last euro. For God's sake...'

Silence. Then his mother-in-law's voice getting closer.

'Mrs Whiskers. She's coming.'

'Look. You've got to help us. Max's big sister, right?'

'How can I? You don't know what it's like here. I can't breathe...'

473

His heart did more than sink; it seemed to disappear altogether.

'How many miles away am I?' she asked.

'Too many.'

'So, Dad, get real...'

But the line was already dead.

Next, he called Gandoux. Apparently, Bonneau's van had gone missing from their compound, and Reignet and Valon were still at the town's hospital where a bomb had exploded last night. No, there were no more details at this stage, but the officer took his message about the ransom money problem. Promised to pass it on immediately. Tom also added he'd be at the Bull Fair field in half an hour and then asked if Major Belassis would be involved in the forthcoming undercover operation.

'He's on leave until after Easter,' explained the officer. 'Would you like to leave him a message?'

Tom emerged on to the busy pavement and, for a moment, walked the wrong way to the van. He could be fingered for having taken it. But so what? Nothing mattered now except the minutes ticking away to that impossible deadline.

He hated the place now. All these people enjoying the gloomy Bank Holiday as if they inhabited a different planet. As he restarted the engine he wondered about the bomb. Why there of all places? Surely ETA, the Basque separatists, operated further north? He also wondered if Liliane was unscathed and not for the first time felt regret that he'd been so nasty to her yesterday.

He'd phone her later if he could, but for now

there was Max, and Natalie, to think about...

What good would yelling do now? Or hitting his head against the car window? Even running round in the rain till he fell over? He didn't know, but any one of these would do.

As visitors to the village butted his wing mirrors as they passed by, he closed his eyes. Saw Max in that turquoise water and Keppel in her gold swimming costume, reaching out to him. His empty stomach turned over again. He began to drive, containing the tears and useless frustration he felt till he found a convenient grass verge near the field where he dropped to his knees in the sodden earth and cried in great heaving sobs, trying to force the pain in his heart out through his eyes and throat. It made him feel no better.

Too early to go into the field. Besides, the shabby van would be an instant giveaway amongst the local 4x4s and other more rustic vehicles. He had another plan, and continued along the busy road until he reached a campsite adjoining what looked like a closed-down *auberge*. Here, among the caravans and camper vans from the rest of Europe, he was just another tourist doing France on the cheap. Except that this crate looked a wreck. Both wings like caves and the nearside light smashed in.

'My brother's bringing his BMW and caravan later this morning,' he lied to the girl in the entrance booth who, having turned her music down, gave him a windscreen sticker and pointed to a double spot by the *toilettes*.

He recognised Westlife's 'My Love.' One of

Flora's favourites. His stomach swirled again...

'I know a panel beater if you want one,' she said. 'Looks like you've been in a scrap.'

'Thanks, but I'll sort it later.'

'Have a good holiday then,' she lit a cigarette and turned her music up again. 'By the way, d'you know about the Bull Fair up the road?'

'Sure.'

Jesus Christ.

He baled out. Used the WC's hole in the floor as quickly as possible, then bought himself a black baseball cap and a pair of shades from a dingy stall near the *poubelles*. Ten minutes later with the drizzle dwindling, he reached the Bull Fair field and stumped up 8 euros for a ticket and catalogue featuring that same poster image he'd seen with Max. As he was pocketing the change, a succession of trailers doused him with mud. Normally he'd have waved a fist, but not today. Today he must lie low. To observe, be on his guard, until the right moment. The lives of two people depended on it. He glanced around for any sign of the police. Perhaps they were in unmarked cars, being cautious, like him. He wondered if they'd recognise him. Make contact.

He'd never been to any kind of agricultural show before and soon realised that this was strictly business. There were no knick-knack stalls, no *dégustation* tables. In fact, nothing deviating from the world of the bull. He stared at the range of white marquees that stood behind the cattle pens and sawdusted parade ring. Some revealed their function – Information on AI, Farmers' unions, foodstuffs and the like. Duclerc, Vitacal etcetera.

476

Others did not. So where was Bactrix for goodness' sake? He'd have to take a closer look. No way
could he risk asking anyone. You never knew...

He loped over the muddied grass towards the
new looking pens, some already filled with the
biggest, most malevolent looking beasts he'd ever
seen, making midgets of those carcasses he'd
seen being delivered to his local butcher's in
Guildford every Saturday morning.

Guildford...

His heart more than ached for that normality of
shopping. Coffee at Starbucks, then the library
with the kids...

Forget it. Forget everything, he told himself.
It'll only drive you mad.

9.10 a.m.

Suddenly, a gentle tap on his back made him
spin round.

'Monsieur Tom. Thank goodness I've found
you.'

'What are you doing here?'

Liliane Bonneau still wore his coat, but this
time, over her hospital nightdress. Her feet in
once-white slippers initialled with *HSV* on the
front of each. Her hair pulled back into a bun.
She looked older, more frail. But not her voice.

'I couldn't leave you with all this worry, *monsieur*. And I wanted to be here in good time. A
kind lorry driver gave me a lift from Gandoux.'

'But surely, there was a bomb at your hospital?'

'In the ward below me, so I was fortunate.' She
looked away. He knew then he didn't have to ask
about her son. 'The police say it was deliberate,
but have no idea who was responsible or why it

477

happened. Anyway,' she sniffed. 'It's all over now. Can you believe that?'

Tom. shook his head, but how could he say sorry? He couldn't. In fact, he'd have preferred it if the bastard had died a long painful death.

'They say six other patients died, many are injured.'

'Someone with a grudge, perhaps? Someone who was sacked recently?' Yet his words were automatic. Normally he'd have cared, but not today.

He took Liliane's arm and walked past the latest arrivals to the pens, steam rising from their assorted flanks. The smell of meat and manure overpowering. So too the noise from the overhead loudspeakers instructing sellers to be ready for the first sale in twenty minutes.

'I heard you had problems getting the money,' she said without preamble.

'How?'

'Lieutenant Valon visited me again after the evacuation from the hospital.'

'Is he here yet, do you know?'

'I've not recognised him so far. Mind you, he'll be in disguise like the rest of them, and I've only ever seen him in uniform. By the way, I told him about Major Belassis and his so-called friend. He asked if I'd got anyone I could stay with. Somewhere preferably far away. But who is there? I'm all alone now.'

'Why suggest you go far away?'

'It's those bones, I'm sure of it. The way he looked at them, held them. I knew he thought they were significant, but, even though I pressed him with questions, he wouldn't say any more.'

...one who saw them. We all did...'

'You're ...ver under his coat. Her eyes He sa... ...rom left to right. Christ, hadn't roaming on his plate? What could he say or he got at now?

do ...once today's over, I can give you some 'I... travel, find a hotel for a while...'

cash... ...o, *monsieur*. It is *I* who should give to you.'

She undid the top three coat buttons one by one and reached inside. A slight noise, like the tearing of silk, followed. His best coat. Then she extracted a big brown paper package and, having checked no one was looking, handed it over to him.

'What is it?' for some reason he was thinking about bombs. That she may not be the only target.

'Open it and see.'

The tape that had once sealed its edges had yellowed and now peeled off easily. She watched his shaking fingers unravel the outer layers until they reached a stained inner lining paper, this time bearing the words:

An meine liebe Liliane

He frowned, hesitating, aware of her growing impatience beside him. For some reason, he couldn't bring himself to open the rest.

'We must separate now,' she said as if sensing his embarrassment. 'Certain people here know ...me. However, I'll be between the Alphalux and ...e Bactrix marquees at a quarter to twelve.'

...Bactrix?' The name sent a cold spasm through ...body. 'I've been looking for it.'

...e pointed to the longest marquee.

..., the one with the black flag. *Voilà.*'

She turned away, soon lost am
crowds. The din growing as yet
lurched and bucked their way to
clutched the parcel, still wary of
because that's what opening it would
violation of something clearly very priva

And what about those words? He knew
they meant, but why German?

Then a fresh wave of panic hit him. Who would
he be meeting here? What if he didn't recognise
anyone, or they him? What would he do then?

At least he was armed.

But first things first, he told himself. What kind
of vehicle was he looking for? A silver Merc? Some
rented van or other? Maybe there wouldn't be
one. Maybe something quite unexpected would
arrive. The Saturday night caller hadn't specified
that either, nevertheless, he kept up surveillance
both on the busy main gate and that marquee,
now only fifty yards away, as the auctioneer and
his support team mounted the improvised rostrum at the edge of the parade ring. He tested the
microphone yet again: 'Un, deux, trois,' followed
by fervent clapping. The atmosphere intensifying
as crowds gathered around the parade ring, six
deep at least. And then he realised that if Liliane
Bonneau'd recognised him, then so might others.

He slotted her parcel between his thighs,
tempted for a moment to leave it somewhere safe
until later. He had enough to carry. Enough
deal with. He stuffed the Walther and his wal
in his jeans' side pockets, then shed his jacket
rolled it up to tuck snugly under his left arm
ideal, but what else could he do? It was t

giveaway when he needed to be anonymous until the last possible moment.

His stomach roared with hunger but if he ate anything now it would soon reappear, such was his mounting dread. Then the bidding started.

'Lot number 1. A three-year-old Limousin, *Fils du Satan...*'

Not the only one, Tom thought, scouring the multitude for any sign of the most wanted people in the world. But no, there was just a sea of strangers and rising excitement as a record price for the breed was swiftly reached.

'Lot number 12. A four year old locally bred Charolais. Prince de Villefort. Property of Monsieur Armand Valon...'

'There he goes,' said a man's voice behind him. 'That's my father's.'

Tom turned to see that young Lieutenant Valon had not only cropped his hair short but wore a black waterproof over a dark pair of jogging bottoms and a jumper with the letters 'Gandoux Rugby Club' emblazoned on the front. A large canvas rucksack hung over one shoulder. He looked more like a hobby player kitted out for a training session than an armed copper.

'Big enough, *hein?*' he gestured towards the muscled beast showing his paces. Its sheer size making the ring appear smaller.

'Where's Reignet?'

'He's rather pissed off you did a bunk yesterday.' He handed Tom his mobile. 'It's fully charged.'

'Thanks. I just had to get out...'

'I know. And I also guessed you took Bonneau's

van. Where is it, by the way?'

Tom indicated the road to the left, beyond the entrance.

'In that old *auberge*'s caravan park. The rifle's still inside it. Look, I had no choice.'

'I know that,' the lieutenant smiled. 'Anyway, good news.'

Tom gripped his arm. A flame igniting in his chest.

'Go on. About Max? About...?'

'The money.'

Tom let go.

'There's no problem, Monsieur. As soon as the call from London came through, the bank here authorised an immediate bridging loan until your wife's share is transferred to your account. You see, there are always contingency plans, especially for public holidays...'

Tom thought of Natalie.

'*All* my wife's share?'

'Yes.'

Flora had done the business. What a girl.

'Because the London bank was closed, and neither your wife or her mother knew what to do, your daughter suggested they find the local MP. He then got the ball rolling, as you say.' He smiled again. 'She deserves a medal.'

'She deserves her brother.'

Silence until Valon eyed the half-opened parcel in Tom's hand.

'Who gave you that?'

'Liliane Bonneau. She's here somewhere.'

'She shouldn't be.' He pointed at the parcel. 'Why not take a proper look inside?'

Tom tentatively reached that same stained lining paper with its inscription and unravelled it until a thick wad of five-hundred franc notes saw the light of day.

'Holy Mother,' breathed Valon, taking a closer look. Although the notes' engraved portraits had faded and the paper seemed slightly damp to the touch, they were otherwise perfect.

Tom felt dizzy. Conscience money not something he was used to.

'Where did she get this lot from? There's at least half a million here.'

'The clue's in the German inscription. I'm sure you'll find out more later. In the meantime, keep it all safe, for God's sake, *monsieur*. But remember, francs are only valid till the end of July.'

'I thought she was poor. I mean, look at the state of her...'

'It's often the case.'

'But how did she know there was a cash crisis?'

'I told her. I hope you don't mind. She was extremely concerned for you. Just as I am.' The young officer scanned the surroundings, his two-way crackling from under his jacket. Then he checked his watch. 'Look, I'm going to wander. We've got six armed men with dogs at the ready. May I remind you, we don't want you taking any risks. That's our job. At 11.58 a.m. Reignet and myself will be in the Bactrix marquee. The others will be outside in a yellow Alphalux van. We were lucky to get hold of one.' Then, he transferred his half-filled rucksack to Tom's shoulder, urging him to store his jacket and the francs in it to keep his hands free. 'The euros are safely wrapped inside copies of yesterday's *L'Expresse*. God knows how they got Keppel's photo in there and about the son having vanished. We don't need that.'

'Reignet said there'd be no publicity.'

'He did his best to stall things, I can assure you. At least there's nothing about that in today's edition. Or about your family, or...'

Tom interrupted him.

'Not what I heard on some guy's radio last night.'

Valon's shrug was one of despair.

'To the media, everything is prey. We've not had time to get injunctions to stop them. By the way, you got that photo ready?'

Tom nodded. Heard a ripple of applause spread round the fair. To him, just then, it sounded obscene. The Charolais had topped 200,000 euros. So, Max and Natalie were worth five bulls...

However, Valon seemed preoccupied. The news of his father's success irrelevant.

'Did you hear about that hospital bomb last night?' he asked.

'Madame Bonneau told me.'

'I wasn't going to mention it, what with today, but I have a feeling someone wanted Samson Bonneau and his mother out of the way. That's what I've told my colleagues and my bosses.'

'Could Belassis have been involved in that?'

'We've no proof yet. But, if the threat to her life at Belette and the hospital was related to the bones found in your home, then you, too, are in danger.'

The day seemed to instantly darken.

'Natalie and Max saw them too.'

'*Monsieur*, we'll do everything to protect you and

them, wherever they are, at least until this deal is done. I doubt very much if this man of secrets will dare to be here. Everything about him is too conspicuous. I could spot him five kilometres away.'

'Have you ever had anything like this happen before? I mean, has this group tried this on with anyone else?'

'You mean, a kidnap?'

Tom nodded. The lieutenant hesitated. Was he gauging how much he knew? Or simply gathering his thoughts?

'No.' But his almost whispered answer brought no relief.

Tom saw the Bactrix tent swarming with punters as another bull stormed into the ring, dragging its handler behind him. He felt sick. Powerlessness gripping his gut.

'Don't think I'm leaving you,' said Valon. 'You are covered. Remember that.'

He sauntered towards the one snack outlet. A converted camper van selling *frites*, coffee and Cola. Tom caught up with him – the only one in the queue – waited till the girl behind the counter had moved away to fetch more cooking oil.

'Tell me something,' he lowered his voice. 'Was Natalie Musset ever a suspect in the killing of Bernard Metz's dog, or Metz himself?'

The Lieutenant stared at him as if Tom had just declared the world was flat.

'*Monsieur*, someone we're getting to know better and better has been making mischief.' Valon paid for his *frites* then, ostensibly for security's sake, moved off. 'And, as far as we know, has still got her knife.'

485

CHAPTER FORTY-SIX

The madwoman's face was wrecked. The night had done her no favours, but still she seemed determined to proceed with whatever it was she'd got planned. Her cheek wound, still bubbling, had conjoined with a red patch in the corner of her mouth. Her hair flattened at the back by the car's headrest. The three of them were on the move again in that same saloon which smelt nauseatingly of old blood.

There was too much drizzle but no sun for Natalie to judge the time of day. Morning surely, as she'd watched dawn's light reveal the true nature of their accommodation but, as the lunatic had her car clock covered over and her gold watch was now off her wrist, she could only guess.

So where now? What else was in store for them after a night that had left both she and Max chilled to the bone? Max who could barely keep his eyes open. Who'd given up struggling against his bonds. Begging for a drink... Her own fingertips sore and reddened by shifting what she could of the *cabane's* stones.

'Story time, part two,' announced their driver suddenly as she manoeuvred the C-Class down a road that Natalie vaguely recognised from last night. The plane trees, the posters... She must concentrate on all this. To be, as far as possible, one step ahead, to pounce on any chance for escape, because Keppel had still not explained *why* she, a university lecturer of thirty and a nine-year-old English boy were even in this fight for survival.

'And, if either of you interrupt or make me lose my temper, I'll stop the car and finish you off,' ranted the woman. 'Wherever we are. Final destination or not.'

Final destination? Those words had a terrible resonance to them. Where, for Christ's sake? Near here? The other end of the country? The other end of the world? Natalie saw a station sign, reading DRANCY. A railway line snaking through bleak suburbs to open country. The welcome red brick, the air touched by putrid smoke...

Then, as if the bleak daylight was the trigger, she wondered yet again how they could escape. Only to realise that to do so, was a recipe for madness. A madness that was catching.

'As I was saying, and I'd urge you to listen, *mademoiselle*,' Keppel glared at her through the driving mirror. 'It's all your fault. You see, I have something to show you, which naturally, at the time, I found very hard to stomach...'

Where was all this leading? Natalie asked herself, seeing vineyards petering out to be replaced by less distinctive fields filled with cattle. More Bull Fair signs and traffic too seemed to be building up. Mostly trucks and trailers. The kind Bonneau used.

The woman passed over a typed note on plain print-out paper. It seemed well-thumbed. Much pored-over. The address and the font unmistakable. Natalie noticed her unpainted fingernails caked with blood.

12, Rue des Martyrs,
St Sauveur.
2/1/2002
My own heart,
Please understand that I cannot be duplicitous, and please try to accept this my explanation as to why I have decided I can no longer share your bed. I realise that although my relationship with Natalie Musset ended in September, I'm still very much in love with her and want her back, if she'll have me. True, she is younger than you, but it is her innocence and openness that touches my soul. Words are never adequate, are they? In sorrow,
Regrets, Bernard.
*Our work will go on, however.

So, she's *the one I was dumped for. My God.*

And what had he meant by *our work* going on? What work?

There was no flattery whatsoever in this message.

Natalie handed it back, then heard the rest of the macabre tale about the daughter conceived with Metz while he'd been two-timing her as well. The late miscarriage just after Christmas. The phone-tapping and emails to Boisseuil intercepted. Oh yes, the clerk boasted, she'd had plenty of support and technical help in her mission to find out about her rival...

'So, *mademoiselle,* I have to punish you as well. No one, however successful they are, treats me like that. No one. It was a humiliation. I lost my self-esteem. Three kilos in weight. All for love...'

Natalie found it hard to speak. Her throat closed up. Max was thankfully dozing, hearing nothing.

'Did Didier ever know you were pregnant?'

'No. Of course not. No one at the Hôtel de Ville, either. I exercised, wore flattering clothes. When the time came after a full term, things would have been different. But, until then, it was our secret...'

Natalie's hunger turned to a raw pain. Was this true, or was Keppel lying to justify her terrible actions?

She had to save Max and herself. Fast. Engage with your abductor is the thing to do, surely? Use empathy not blame. How often had she read that in women's self-defence articles? But even though she believed that was mostly rubbish, she'd have to try.

'It's *not* my fault. That's the easy way out. Metz was a free agent, but,' she lied, 'I'd never have gone back with him. Even if he'd begged me.'

The Merc suddenly swerved. Natalie was flung against Max and together they hit the seat corner.

'You're implying he wasn't good enough for you, *hein?*' raved the driver. 'If so, what does that say for *my* judgement? My character?'

Mad cow. Mad cow... Nothing to lose then...

'So you had him killed? And his poor dog?'

Another lurch of the car and she realised that they were approaching some field in a queue of traffic. 'And who was holding that child in the photo? Was it Bernard Metz, after all?'

That hateful head nodded. Natalie choked back revulsion.

'Why like that, though? Like a trophy?'

'Couldn't you tell? It was a Kraut.'

Jesus.

Keppel smiled at the officials at the gate, keeping a hand judiciously over her scar. She could turn on the charm alright, thought Natalie, hearing cash changing hands. She raised herself to look out, to try and catch someone's eye, just like near the Grotto, but you don't always see what you're not looking for, do you? She'd soon learnt that one in her job. Damn these tinted windows. She and Max were still invisible as Keppel parked the saloon between two massive trucks facing the exit, then, from under her seat she withdrew two new number plates. Natalie noticed that both ended in 05. The department of Hautes-Alpes.

'One false move from either of you, and you get this.' The woman drew an imaginary line across her throat, then, having picked up her snakeskin bag and the plates, baled out. She manually locked the car, then crouched for a few moments near the bonnet and the boot before straightening herself and walking somewhat stiffly into the crowd. It was then Natalie wondered if she was in fact wearing a bullet-proof vest. She'd seen them in films, how they gave the wearer's upper torso a kind of boxy shape. That was it. The bitch was ready for battle...

Max began to cry. She saw how the fish gut dug into his wrists, turning the surrounding skin purple. Hers were no better. Keppel had made sure of that. Then she had an idea. She had good sharp teeth. It was worth a try. Better here than in that stinking *cabane*.

'Hold out your hands. Quick.'

He did.

'What you doing?'

'Pretending I'm a rat. Ratty from *Wind in the Willows*. Get it? Hang on.' She began to gnaw.

'Ouch.'

'Sorry. Let's try again.' But there wasn't enough give in the gut to allow her teeth to even get a grip. Never mind chew. She'd already nipped him once. 'Here, you try.'

It was hopeless. He could do no better than her.

'Isn't there anything else we can use in this stupid car?' he pleaded.

'Nothing I can get hold of. But don't worry. Come on, brave boy. We've got each other. And your dad will be here somewhere. He'll get us out.'

'I know he will.' He hoisted himself up to stare out at the scene beyond. 'Hey,' his eyes widened. 'See those bulls? He was going to tell me why their willies were so big...'

Normally, she'd have smiled, given him a hug. But how could she? The nightmare was only just beginning. If what Keppel had implied about her *Grandpère* Lionel was right, then perhaps this was her punishment.

Suddenly two figures in the middle distance caught her eye.

'Look!'

And sure enough, alongside Liliane Bonneau covered by a black coat was a man she recognised, despite his cap, his shades and that big rucksack. Just the way he moved, with his jaw stuck out. It was none other than Tom.

CHAPTER FORTY-SEVEN

Who'd taken Natalie's knife and tried to brand her a criminal, but Belassis? That name now churned around and around in Tom's mind as he approached the BACTRIX marquee, which was warm and busy, filled with the smell of its own rich bone supplement and the buzz of good-natured banter of deals being struck with the company's suited sales staff. But Tom had quite a different take on it all, as if he was embalmed in ice; his chest bound by a steel belt of nerves and expectation, which threatened to suddenly explode, while all around him, others' voices seemed eerily detached; the people like shadows merging and separating. No one he recognised. Not a soul. And all the connections he'd been trying to make from what he now knew, seemed to snap in two like those brittle branches near the Florentin services.

Two minutes to go. His pulse slowing as he hovered near the entrance, aware of Liliane now alongside. Part of him was grateful. The rest not so sure.

'Best you hide somewhere,' he could barely speak. 'Please. For your own safety.'

'I want to be a witness.'

'No. Just in case.'

Reluctantly, she crept outside. He'd not had time to thank her for the money or to try and give it back to her.

Midday.

He stared at the far end of the marquee, where the day's dull light had infiltrated the canvas overhead and turned its interior the colour of sour cream. Where tables had been arranged to display the company's brochures alongside before-and-after photographs and giveaway samples of this obviously popular product. The logo that dominated every poster, every piece of printed matter was that of a horned bull's head.

And then he spotted someone whose presence seemed to tighten that steel belt particularly around his heart. A woman with light brown dishevelled hair, whose left cheek bore a red-stained bandage. She was sitting, legs crossed, on a courtesy chair in front of the middle table, her gaze fixed on the far corner of the marquee, as if expecting someone. Although her sheepskin jacket and suede trousers tucked into fur-lined boots looked new and expensive, they nevertheless bore the giveaway creases, suggesting, like her hair, that she'd had a rough night. He moved closer. Held his breath until he could see it was her alright.

Pauline Keppel.

Her head now turned his way, black eyes roaming up and down his body, waiting for him to speak first. All part of the game, he supposed, as his right hand gripped the Walther in his jeans' pocket. There were too many punters in the way to just finish her off. Besides, he had two lots of money on his back. The bigger portion to hand over.

'Where's Max? Where's Natalie?' he demanded. A question he'd been asking for too long and now the words seemed to be coming from someone else, not him.

'First things first, *hein?* You know what I mean.'

No ring, no crucifix, no nail varnish he noticed. But a mouth smudged by red lipstick. One or two browsers stopped to stare then moved away. To her he seemed a stranger. It was as if she'd never shown up at Hibou so full of concern, so keen to help. Or ever invited him and Max to the pool...

Bitch.

'I've got the money and that photograph. But before I hand them over, I want to see my son. And Mademoiselle Musset.'

'I bet you do. Even Metz wanted to start bedding her again. Let me tell you something, *monsieur.* You won't be the only one. I know her. Her legs open like clockwork for whoever happens to turn her little key. Click, clickety click, *comme ça...*'

A sick smile tweaked her lips but didn't last long, because Tom lunged towards her, knocking over a stack of cartons and tubs which spilt their powdery contents to the floor. Then he stopped. Drew back because a box-cutter's blade was jutting from her closed, gloved fist.

The marquee's din suddenly faded. Its occupants, sensing trouble, hurried away towards the entrance as she twisted the blade to and fro in front of him, teasing him to come closer. One jab could sever an artery in his wrist. Then where would Max and Natalie be?

He had to live for them and Flora. Period.

'No see, no cash,' he tried to sound strong, in control. 'Get that into your skull.' Wondering too, where the cops were. Reignet, Valon and the rest.

All at once, scuffling sounds came from under the largest table draped in a red cloth. Then a man's voice he recognised. 'Go on, Pauline. Be a sport, eh? Then I'll be out of your hair too...'

Keppel's lips parted in shock, while Tom watched the table's fabric being jostled then raised to reveal a masked bald-headed man emerging, not on his own, but with a flushed, fearful twelve-year-old, struggling to free himself from his captor's neck grip.

'Didier? Christ...' Was all he could say. But who was the other one? Thin as a rake, brown eyes, no eyebrows. At least none that Tom could see above that sleek black velvet mask.

'Help, *monsieur*. Please, please,' the boy begged him. And then Tom saw his raw nail-less finger-tips, the bruising on his hands, his face, everywhere...

'I will. I will...' But how could he? The stranger, dressed from head to toe in black, was king. He placed the boy in front of his mother. Pushed him so they were almost touching. Keppel tried to stand up to hold him, her box-cutter skittering to the floor. Tom moved to reach it first, but the man kicked it under a nearby table. Then, as if in a slow-motion dream, Tom saw him produce a gun. Smaller than his Walther, even with a silencer attached which nudged against Didier's head. But just as lethal. Didier flinched at the sudden contact. Closed his eyes at the start of war as Keppel focused on his captor...

'You sabotaged *Le Cercle* the moment you joined. You had to be best. You had to have me. And now you've lied. So, what about your new life in America, then, Carl? You afraid of flying?' she sneered. 'That it?'

Carl?

Tom didn't get it.

A short bilious laugh followed.

'How could I go anywhere, after what *he's* done?' The man teased the gun barrel through the boy's hair, making him flinch again.

'He's my son.'

'Precisely. But at least you've still got one,' he said in a strange voice. 'For the moment, anyway.'

'We've a gargoyle each. That's quits, surely?'

'What about the fifty thousand francs I paid you to get Philippe back? Remember? That ruined us, me and Zulika. Bloody ruined us, you bitch. You kept the money *and* our kid. What kind of sick deal was that?'

'I neither made you marry a *noir,* nor did I stop you from becoming one of us. From calling me your Queen and wanting me from the word go. Wanting to obey my every order...'

Tom saw the man's hand holding the gun begin to waver.

'Give me my money back plus Bonneau's payoff if you want to save your brat. That'll be a start, at least.' Another prod of the lad's head. Tom prayed again as Didier began to cry. Kept his hand on his pistol in case the focus should suddenly swing on him. Max was waiting. Max and Natalie. He had to be careful. 'And I might even consider returning his sister's bones you buried at Hibou. The kid you had with Metz, remember?'

Tom's mind flashbacked to Kathy coming out of the *fermette* with the first little specimen in her hand, but that was all, as the man had started up again. His mouth curled in a snarl. 'Shall I tell the *rosbif* here, what you did with her first? Why you drew the circle on her chest? And all the others? Why it is you have so much energy...'

Keppel's voice seemed to have deserted her while Didier glanced at Tom. Animal terror in his eyes as he struggled to free himself. 'I tried to phone you, *monsieur* 'Tom. To tell you about the blood I once found in our waste disposal unit, and those weird bedrooms she's got. But she gave me the wrong number...'

'You were much more forthcoming with me, though, weren't you?' his captor gloated. 'Confessed how you'd followed *Maman* up to my place in Gandoux and sneaked in behind her while I was distracted in the kitchen for a moment. How you'd hidden in one of the wardrobes there. Yes, all very interesting, and thank you for that. The film case was tested for prints and guess what, my man? We found a perfect match with yours...'

Keppel tried to push her son away. Revulsion contorting her mouth into the same expression as appeared on those gargoyles. But Didier clung on now, his ragged sobs too heartbreaking for Tom's ears.

'You *made* me tell you,' the lad protested. 'Look at my fingernails. I'll show the rest as well...'

Tom looked away, powerless to help. His insides on the rampage. The rucksack on his back like a heavy useless rock.

'I wouldn't if I were you. My motives were to keep your mother in the clear with all her crimes. But was she grateful? Oh no. Not her.' He glanced at Tom. 'She's even threatened to take all this *rosbif's* cash.'

Keppel glared at their tormentor, poised over both of them like a panther. Her face now quite grey. Her cheek wound, through the gauze bandage, almost black.

'You only wanted to save your neck. Worried that my child's bones would lead to *Le Cercle* and then to you. Go, while you still can. You devil.'

'It takes one to know one, Pauline.'

A tiny click. The black-gloved hand closing around the trigger.

Didier suddenly yelled to Tom.

'Her Merc's by the exit, *monsieur!* Near the *frites*. I bet Max and your friend are in there. Go, before it's too late!'

Memory would rob him of the next few seconds. Weeks, months afterwards were to make no difference. They'd remain not merely a black hole in his psyche, but one brimming with fear and blood.

A shot filled the air, more like a wine cork un-popping. The boy fell, spraying his mother red as if he was some passing graffiti artist with a ready can. Then the Browning's gun barrel changed direction. On to him, Tom. Or, more accurately, his eyes. But he was ready. Took aim at the man's chest and fired once, twice, the force making him lose his own balance. Then he realised the masked man with the blue-black skull was invincible, even up for some more.

'*Fille ... faille ... faux ... femme...*
Aie semelle de blaude evanouie (ne glisse man...)'

A shot breathed past Tom's ear as he leapt away, treading air until he was outside. He'd not sprinted like this since an early team-building course at Ascot some years back. But he did now, with the rucksack bob-bobbing against his back. Past bewildered fair-goers and animals abandoned in their pens towards the exit.

Soon, in his peripheral vision, all hell seemed to be breaking loose. A yellow van with an ALPHALUX logo was disgorging armed police and dogs into the BACTRIX marquee behind him. Bystanders were scattering. Obstructing him. A young couple joined at the hip. An old woman he didn't recognise. Auctioneers and other officials fleeing their rostrum.

All at once he was utterly alone. The Merc with its tinted glass was in his sights, but, to his horror, as he drew closer to it, mouthing Max and Natalie's names, it began to draw away from him, swooping out into the road, almost colliding with an oncoming lorry.

No time to wonder how she'd got to it before him or how on earth he'd not noticed it in the first place. Someone was pushing him towards a black Saab. A thick-set man in jeans and a quilted sleeveless jacket. A gun belt visible underneath.

Lieutenant Alain Reignet. A red baseball cap and shades disguising his eyes.

Tom's mumbled thanks were lost in the noise of static from Reignet's radio. His lips numb. Foreboding in every pore of his body. It had all gone so wrong.

'Who was the psycho in that marquee?' he said. 'He knew Keppel. Knew plenty.'

A roaring crash of gears, from first to second. Tom's fillings rebelling in his mouth.

'All we know is the boy's dead.'

The driver slammed up into third gear. 'Suffer the little children. Sick joke that, *hein?*' Speeding now, taking bends too fast while Tom cradled the rucksack full of money in his lap. His mind teetering between meagre hope and the chasm of darkness, imagining his own son. What he might be going through. Wishing he'd just tipped the money out on the floor while he'd had the chance.

He saw the caravan park, the Transit van just visible, and toppled away from the driver as he took a sudden left before the St Sauveur turning. Still no sign of the Merc, and the cop, as if psychic, answered his silent question: why here of all places?

'A hunch. Better than nothing. We think Keppel, your son and Musset spent the night in the vineyards here. Our target may well decide to return, at least to plan her next move.' He then radioed for back-up. Gave staccato directions as to their whereabouts, listened to something for two seconds and ended by ordering two helicopters with thermal imaging devices.

So, unless this copper was a bloody good actor, that meagre hope remained.

'If Keppel's driving, how the hell did she manage to leave that marquee?' Tom asked.

'Slit in the canvas. Short cut to her car from that end. Anyway,' as the Saab branched off along more stony road between the vines, leaving cloud of red dust behind. 'May not even be behind the wheel.'

That ice again. Moving in on his heart.

'Who then?'

'We'll have to wait and see, won't we?' Reignet's tone had sharpened imperceptibly. Hardly surprising, Tom thought. He'd run out on him yesterday, after all. Maybe that explained it.

'What did she mean when she said that guy had sabotaged *Le Cercle?*'

The man increased speed. His lips tightening with tension.

'She's the wrecker,' he muttered. Tom thought that odd but let it go. He had enough on his mind to think about. To dread...

Suddenly he saw a large sign depicting a painting of a green wine bottle. Highlights, reflections, the lot. DOMAINE DE POUS. Normally he'd have remarked on it. Even salivated at the prospect of a rich glass of red...

But not now. Not ever.

Reignet glanced round to check on back-up, he said, but thick dust obscured the view, then he used his radio again. More urgency now in the directions he gave. Then stuff Tom couldn't quite make out.

Someone passing information it seemed.

A meaner path now, with dried and dead foliage snagging in the wheels. Fresher foliage bent over from the *Tramontane* crushed by other wheels. Tyre tracks in the soil, still dusty despite last night's rain. But whose? They seemed too wide apart to be those small vans the *viticulteurs* used. Another crossroads marked by a simple iron set in a lump of rock. For the second time landing at Caen, Tom prayed. Then saw a

501

familiar yellow vehicle drawing closer behind. The SCU's unlikely Trojan horse with Valon driving.

Reignet's grip tightened on the wheel. His neck muscles tensed, and Tom wondered why. Surely he'd be glad of extra support. But then maybe he'd planned on being a hero. That this one was all his.

The Saab came to a sudden halt in the middle of bloody nowhere. Been there, done this, thought Tom as Reignet unclicked his seat belt and turned to him. His face tense and drawn.

'Something you need to know,' he said, patting his gun belt. 'Keppel's dead too. Our mystery killer finished her off apparently. In the head.'

'Where's he now, then?'

'Christ knows, but I'm going in.'

The Lieutenant was already out of the Saab, checking his gun.

'In where?' Tom's brain seemed to be curdling when he needed it most of all.

'Down the slope, there. Look.'

The vines were in close-up now. Tom saw gnarled black branches, scaled and fissured like some old hag's skin. Their beginnings hidden by soil more like cremation ashes, littered with stones and pottery remnants from long-ago inhabitants. Chunks of worn brick, a battered bottle top, a lizard jerking its way over the ground and vanishing. He stared at all this before his eye was finall' led downwards to a tumbledown shack, dom¡ ated by an open doorway, guarded on the r side by two poplars, black and still, against the

'Let me go first,' he told Reignet. 'He's my

'*Monsieur.* May I remind you, you also have a daughter.'

The lieutenant nudged his arm as they set off towards the *cabane.* 'The Merc's here. Look.'

Tom elbowed him away. Shivered in the awesome silence, unable to look at the silver saloon slewed to the left of the wide track ahead. Unable even to run.

'Where *were* you all, for Christ's sake?' he hissed.

'We couldn't risk more casualties. We had our orders.'

Tom glanced back at the yellow van, now drawing closer, bringing with it the sound of police dogs barking. He, too, advanced over the dark grey dust, feeling even more weightless now, like a moon walker, pistol poised. But just then, without warning, he felt a stifling weight around his neck, pinning him next to another racing heart. It was Reignet, attempting to prise his Walther from his grasp.

He was too strong for Tom to kick against, to escape from. His breath in close-up was hot garlic. Worse than before.

Tom gripped the Walther with every last effort, as if it was Max's hand. And then, from the *cabane's* gloomy entrance some ten yards away, he saw that same bald masked man from the marquee blink his way into the daylight. And was that a glimmer of recognition for his captor? He wasn't sure.

No gloves this time, but bloodstained hands around his gun. Pointing it his way.

503

Tom tried wrenching himself from the iron grip. His throat closed on a feeble yell for Max. The best he could do.

'All yours, *monsieur*,' teased the black-clad figure, indolently cocking his head back towards the doorway. A sly smile on his lips. The glint of perfect teeth.

'And Natalie?'

A shrug. Nothing more.

'Where's the cash, *rosbif*?'

'Don't you want the photo?'

'Your souvenir, eh?'

The lieutenant behind him suddenly released his grip to allow Tom to haul the rucksack from his back. With his free hand, Tom tore the single buckle apart and threw the newspaper-covered parcel at the bald man's booted feet. The euro notes it contained scattered, beginning to lift in the small breeze, while the centre pages parted to show Pauline and Didier Keppel's faces lying uppermost in the dirt, under a heading about her missing boy

The man in black swiftly scooped up the notes with one hand and stuffed them in his pockets. Don't shoot yet. Let him take the lot, Tom told himself, barely able to look at the dark, hellish doorway that lay behind him.

But just then, a nudge from behind made him spin round to see Reignet's hand on his own revolver. But it wasn't just that that sent a trickle of fear into his heart: something in his profile suddenly looked familiar. Those same deep-set eyes, that same ice blue of someone he'd seen at Hibou and faced over a counter in Gandoux. The straight thin nose and flared nostrils. Those pink-tipped fingers...

This was the guy from the *Tabac*. Those remarks of his about the Café de la Paix and the *noirs* all making sense now. He was one of *Le Cercie*. So, who else was there?

'Max!'

Tom ran forwards, but the man at the *cabane* door took aim, stopped him in his tracks. Tom ducked, hearing two shots in quick succession. One from way behind him, the other muffled, from the front, hitting bone.

His.

Pain overflowed from his shoulder, drowning his whole body as a wounded Reignet lurched against him, almost toppling him over. Tom grabbed the pistol from his hand while Valon, quicker than the man with the money, who seemed momentarily paralysed, delivered a shot to the masked blue-black head.

'Alain? Don't let me die,' he gargled. 'For Christ's sake, get me out of here...' Then he pitched backwards to lie prone in a lake of seeping blood together with the displaced contents of his pockets. Tiny pieces of bone and several photo-graphs, half submerged in his death, while his younger brother, the amateur photographer, still twitched at Tom's side, taking longer to reach the end of his journey.

Deaf but not blind to the ensuing commotion of men and dogs, and Valon's plea that he stay put, Tom staggered over him into the *cabane's* terrible darkness. Seconds later, a murder of crows fled from the neighbouring poplars. Their startled croaks providing the bass line to his keening grief.

The air lay still. The sky an even grey as far as the eye could see. The only colour being the vivid green of tiny pleated leaves sprouting from the vine's ancient limbs. New life on the old. A miracle obscured by his tears. The *cabane* had been empty as a banished soul. But then something else to the left caught his eye. The figure of a young woman in unfamiliar pink and purple, weaving her way towards him through the plantation, dazed and disorientated, her fair hair chopped short. The ends tipped by blood. She was carrying something in her arms. Something that weighed her down, made her stumble then right herself, twice, three times...

Natalie... Max...

'He's OK. He's OK,' she burbled, her mouth full of tears as he finally took his son in his arms. 'I kept offering myself instead, but the bastard didn't want me. He didn't want me... So, when he went out of the *cabane* to get the money, I found this old bottle cap and sawed through the gut she'd bound us up with. Then we squeezed through the hole I'd started making last night...'

'Last night?'

'Yeah,' said Max finally opening his bloodshot eyes and fixing them first on Tom's face and then his wounded shoulder. 'We were in there for ages. It was really horrible. And Dad,' he asked, 'when you're better, can I have my cola bottles?'

'You bet.' Despite his pain, Tom held him tighter than he'd ever held anyone or anything before. Heard his heart strong against his own, as he reached out for Natalie with that one question he had to ask her, burning his lips. But she'd just saved his son's life, so, like most things, it would have to wait.

She leant against him and Max as five officers emerged from the *cabane* and joined them on the walk to their van. Each leaving a puff of dust in their wake.

CHAPTER FORTY-EIGHT

Trees in full leaf now. Layer upon layer of terraced vineyards crammed with dusky blue grapes turning purple under the foliage's shifting shadows. A vivid July sky broken only by harmless soft-edged clouds nudging from west to east over the Col des Sept Frères and a country road punctuated by snow markers winding up to a small village in the Department of Ariège.

With his two children safe behind him on the blue leather rear seat, Tom's new silver Subaru made light of the ascent and, following a sign for 'Les Coquelicots' Maison de Repos, soon reached the gravelled plateau surrounded by wooden tubs of miniature firs. However, once there, and parked between two new off-roaders in the shade at the side of the house, Max and Flora seemed in no hurry to get out. Instead, they examined his brand-new map bought specially for the occasion, finding out with the aid of a six inch ruler, how far they were from home. Their hair several tones lighter from the summer sun, their limbs and faces tanned from days in the new garden where he'd built a tree house.

'We'll stay in here, Dad,' said his daughter, not looking up. 'We'll be OK.'

'No. And that's final. I'm not letting anything like that happen ever again.'

Neither argued with that particular memory, and, having set the alarm and hoisted a brand new rucksack over his good shoulder, he held their hands as together they walked over the gravel towards the house, built in the style of an Alpine chalet, gleaming wholesomely in the sun. Its window boxes brimmed with colour, while the appetising smell of a meal cooking eked from the partly open front door.

'Stew,' Max guessed, sniffing the air. 'I'm starved.'

'It's not stew, it's calves,' said Flora, correcting him. 'Remember that horrible farm?'

'Hey, you two,' Tom squeezed their hands in turn. 'Let's not talk about that now.'

Indeed, a welcome aura of stability and comfort seemed to envelop them all as he checked his watch, something he did constantly. His counsellor said that and the sleeplessness, the debilitating sense of failure, would soon pass, but perhaps not as quickly as the pain from his shattered shoulder. These were normal manifestations of trauma. His new boss at Prestige People, where he'd been offered his old job back, had proved equally understanding. Unlike Kathy, now living with her mother in Camden. Refusing to even see him.

Still opposing the Court Order that had granted him full custody of Max and Flora.

The three of them now occupied a Bryant Homes new-build just outside Chertsey. Flora had become a more pensive, cautious girl, sometimes difficult to reach, but never argumentative like her contemporaries. Never once blaming him for what had happened. Rather her mother for leaving him and Max on their own. As for Max, he'd clung for a while, not letting either him or his sister out of his sight for long, but then he'd settled into a new Cubs' group and had just discovered the joys of drumming.

After the *enquête* in Cahors at the end of April, Flora and Max had exchanged letters and gifts with Natalie, hoping to see her again. To ride pillion on her Suzuki. To see their dad happy again. So Flora had said...

But never again had he wanted to see another wooden beam or a dirt floor, hike over limestone or explore a French vineyard. It had been bad enough returning to France for the first time since the *enquête*, seeing hectare after hectare of them on the journey down here, when he'd just stared straight ahead at the tarmac. Bad enough to see their adverts for wine. And as for the Simistons in Berris Hill Road, they'd totally lost touch. He'd put it down to the fact that some people don't know what to say in times of tragedy. But rumour was they were still freewheeling round Europe in their auto home with its double oven and flushing wc. He'd never returned their badly timed phone call but maybe he would once summer was over.

'Dad, listen!' Max tugged at his arm as a familiar

engine noise reached his ears from the road behind. He spun round to see a neat figure in black leathers, wearing that same blue crash helmet, dismount from her machine. His pulse rate jumped as she removed her helmet and shook out her hair, longer now, trimmed to a bob. It seemed several shades lighter, glowing above her smile which had quickly replaced her look of surprise at his appearance.

'Hi, you guys,' she said, then drew the three of them towards her. 'I've not stopped thinking about you for a moment. You look fantastic.'

Their embrace was the kind never meant to end, but when a friendly voice from the house called out, 'Excuse me, *monsieur,* but *madame* is waiting for you,' they pulled apart. Each battling with their own tears.

'Where are we going?' Asked Max, still holding Flora's hand.

Don't they know? A surprised Natalie asked Tom with her eyes.

'To see an old friend. Someone who's been good to us,' he said. 'Madame Bonneau.'

'You mean, the giant's mother.' Max announced, breaking free of his sister and running towards a full length mirror placed near the Visitor's Book. He pulled one face after another then spotted the open book filled with names and addresses from all over France – but none so far for Liliane Bonneau – and begged to sign his name. However, instead of Max Frederick Wardle-Smith he wrote *The Thumb Boy, March 29th*

'Why ever did you do that?' asked Flora, but Tom nudged her to leave it.

'Because that's what set everything off.'

No one spoke as Tom led the way further into the cool tiled vestibule, where they were met by the Home's owner sporting a crisp green overall and a smell of toilet cleaner. After the usual introductions, she asked if Max and Flora would like to use the play area specially set aside for visitors' often boisterous children.

'Can we?' his son looked up at him.

'I'll keep an eye on him,' said Flora. 'Don't worry.'

For a moment, Tom hesitated, caught Natalie looking at him, then realised how Max had changed more than he'd thought. How he couldn't keep them both in strait-jackets for the rest of their lives.

'OK, but remember, this is an old people's home, not a circus.'

Once a young woman helper had escorted them away down another corridor towards the garden, the owner began to climb the stairs, which were partially obstructed by a chair lift.

'She's so impatient to see you,' she explained, having reached the top and stopped outside a door marked number 7. 'She didn't want any breakfast.'

Nor had Tom. Not for a long time.

'I must warn you though,' she lowered her voice, 'we don't think it'll be long for her. She keeps saying her life ended that Easter Monday. Even threw her rosary away the moment she arrived here.' The kindly face grew serious. 'I'm so sorry, *monsieur*. And I have to say, I'm so ashamed of our country for what happened. The newspapers are

511

saying your ordeal has affected the numbers of British people wanting to buy in France. It's not good. The Germans and Algerians are already nervous. Now it's your turn...' The woman knocked, then opened the door. Tom wasn't expecting to see an occupied wheelchair facing the window, let alone the skeleton who sat in it, until Liliane Bonneau turned herself round to face them.

Yes, a cadaver. That was the only word to describe the old woman's transformation. Tom suppressed a gasp and Natalie reached for his hand, before going over to her chair. Eyes glistening with sorrow.

'No more tears,' Liliane said, dabbing her own sunken eyes with a lace handkerchief. 'Or you'll set me off again. And by the way, I hope you didn't mind my getting in touch. I had to see you both again before...' she hesitated, and Natalie laid a hand on her shoulder. 'Before I leave this earth.'

'Of course not,' Natalie glanced at Tom, who was digging in his rucksack for that same brown paper parcel given to him that terrible day. He winced with the effort of it.

'*Madame,* please take this money back. I insist. I've a job now, a reasonable mortgage...' He tried to place it in her lap, but she pushed it away with a surprising show of strength. 'For a start, the amount was far too much, and secondly, I bet this place doesn't come cheap. You'll need the money for here, surely?'

'It was originally destined for someone I cared deeply about, and, *monsieur,*' she fixed her gaze on his, 'in my eyes, you're the same.'

Tom's neck began to burn.

'Thank you, *madame*.' What else could he say? The gift would help pay for Flora and Max to go to decent schools and then college or University. Or whatever else they wanted to do.

'Please don't delay exchanging them for euros,' she said. 'They won't be legal currency for long.'

'I won't.' He glanced at the scattered newspapers on Liliane's table – most dating back to the case and the *enquête*. Headlines on the DNA identification of Léontine Keppel's bones buried by her mother at Hibou to incriminate Metz. Her efforts to recover them before the English family started making unwanted connections. The miniscule remains of little Ute Stenckel and other young victims in the clerk's drains below the luxury apartment – an account accompanied by some Parisian academic's reference to the Lamia and Juno myth. The awe-inspiring courage of two young boys and a university lecturer. The burnt corpse of Gandoux's mayor, and Georges Ninon who'd succumbed to a heart attack on April 2nd – the Day of Mourning at Nanterre...

Tom suppressed a sudden nausea not felt since those gruelling April days, as he shuffled the pages together, leaving more innocuous news of plans for a Mosque in some nearby town on top.

'Now then, why I asked you to come all the way here,' she continued. 'You may not realise this, but I'm now Belette's sole owner.' Tom wondered where this was leading. That farm's name almost like a curse in the pleasant, sunny room. Natalie felt it too, he suspected. She gripped his hand even more tightly as Liliane continued. 'Accord-

513

ing to French law, I can't leave it to a charity or a dog's home, but,' her eyes seemed to recover their former animation, 'I have no son to sign his permission, so I *can* sell it.'

Tom and Natalie looked at each other.

'It's yours, if you'd like it. For a pittance. A token sum.'

He felt as if a fist had connected with his solar plexus. He was stuck for words. Focused on the sun forcing its way between the open shutters, making a bright bleached oblong on the parquet floor. What he'd wanted for Hibou. Alarm bells, like those of St Sauveur's church, began hammering in his head.

'My brother-in-law's body was dug up from the big field just after Samson died. We held a blessing for him there and then, so there'll be no more ghosts. No more trouble.' She looked up expectantly. Those cataract-pale eyes glazing over. 'It would make you a lovely home, Monsieur Tom, and I'd die a happy woman, after all the grief my son has caused you.'

'But *madame,* as I said earlier, surely you need whatever money you can get to keep you here?'

She shook her head.

'I've been prudent all my life. Watching every *centime.* But I confess that sometimes I did steal from Samson. Just small amounts for a rainy day, you understand. Bit by bit, these francs added up and he never noticed. So now, after all these years, I'm quite well provided for.'

'But why come here? I mean, it's very nice, but not exactly in your area. I'd have thought prices around Gandoux would be cheaper.'

She gave both of them the strangest look.

'I don't think so, Monsieur Tom. And just now, I'm not sure if I should tell you...'

'Tell me what?'

She paused for a moment, then dipped her hand into the pocket of her beige cardigan. It looked new, neatly pressed, like the rest of her clothes.

'Here we are.' She passed him a typed note, signed Daniel Valon. Dated April 6th 2002. 'Major Valon – he's not a lieutenant any more – was kind enough to do some research for me on his computer.'

Tom read the various unfamiliar names out loud, while Natalie kept busy dead-heading the nasturtiums that trailed in from the balcony. When she'd finished, she sat down on Liliane's single bed, positioned under a pretty Monet print of a riverbank.

'Let me take you back to Wednesday, May 31st 1944.' Her knobbly fists clenched tighter on each thin thigh as she continued. 'I was in love. Deeply in love, you understand?'

Tom saw Natalie nod her head.

'The farming village of Pech Merle is about fifty kilometres north of St Sauveur and was the only home I'd ever known. Back then, both my parents were still alive and became very resourceful during the Occupation. *Papa* ran his little *boucherie* there with whatever supplies he could get hold of, while *Maman* mended clothes. She was a clever woman, full of ideas, but never educated like people are now...' Here she broke off. Her breath louder, more wheezy. Tom waited, aware of Natalie clearly deep in thought.

515

'Anyway,' Liliane went on, 'one of *Papa's* suppliers were the Bertrands. Their farm lay just outside the village near the Forêt du Diable. Oh, they were clever too, and one or two rumours began to spread as to how they managed to buy new stock. Keep two servants...'

Tom joined Natalie on the bed. He'd recognised the name on that piece of paper, and hoped his nod of encouragement would keep her going.

'Meanwhile, I'd met a man. Nothing new in that you might say, but he happened to be Fritz Brandt. A senior officer in the Werhmacht. They'd been stationed in the school there for four months...'

Suddenly the silence in the room grew stifling. The tension palpable. But nobody moved as she continued.

'He was twenty six. Three years older than me. Yes, I'd had boyfriends, just like Mademoiselle Natalie here, if she'll forgive my saying so.'

Tom saw an instant blush as she turned away.

'Some of them not always the best choice for me, but of course, at the time, you can't see it. Can you?'

Her tiny smile gave way to a trembling of the lips, her eyes now downcast.

The same as those police at the *cabane*...

'However, Fritz was my life. And I his. We were so very careful. Even now, I always look behind me in case I'm being followed. But then, it was different. Although they were dangerous times, we somehow felt as if nothing could touch us. That somehow, against all the odds, our love would survive...'

'Do please go on,' Natalie urged her after that last pause threatened to become permanent.

'I'd fallen pregnant in the January. Of course, I had to be careful, living with my mother, especially. To pretend my monthlies came, that sort of thing. That all was normal.'

Tom thought of Flora, sleeping over at her best friend's house. She'd become a young woman just three weeks ago. An odd feeling for him as her dad. Another loss, he supposed, if he analysed it. Then he listened as the story unfolded...

'And Fritz, well,' her moist eyes brightened for a moment, 'he was overjoyed. Began making all sorts of plans for the three of us, once the war was over... He'd take us back to Germany and we'd live in a cottage somewhere by a lake. Maybe even start a small farm.' She turned towards them. 'Who hasn't dreamt of such things? It's human to do so. Besides, Fritz said his father could help us. He owned a flour mill. Was prosperous and generous. He saved regularly for his only son, for when he returned from duty. Oh, and his wife kept a few cows and made the best cheese in the whole area...'

Tom now guessed where all that money she'd given him must have come from. That loving message inside the parcel from the father was for the daughter-in-law he'd never have.

'What happened next?' asked Natalie engrossed.

'On that day, May 3rd, it was wet. Too wet just to go riding around in the forest. So we'd arranged to meet in the Bertrand's old barn. We'd done that before, many times. It was the furthest building away from the farmhouse and rarely used. Full of old hay, but useful for early spring lambing and calving if the weather got too bad. Anyway, we were just getting ready to leave our hiding place when we saw the Bertrand's young daughter, Irène – she must have been fourteen at the time – just standing there, staring at us, with such hate in her eyes. Those black, black eyes... She must have followed us there, the little vixen. Must have listened in to everything we did. Everything we said...'

'So what did you do?' Natalie again, tucking her legs underneath her. Reaching out to touch Tom's hand.

'Fritz pushed her out of the way and we ran. Ran like the wind to where he'd left his motorbike in some trees at the edge of the wood. It was too noisy to bring it any nearer the barn you see.' She looked at Natalie. 'Although I took to you straight away that day I first met you, it was when I saw you on your bike that I sensed a kindred spirit. You and Fritz both had the same kind of machine. Big, black. The most wonderful invention on wheels in the world. So,' for a moment she seemed confused. 'Where was I?'

'Fritz's bike,' said Tom.

'Ah, yes. Then, we rode away into the forest, not knowing where to go, or when to come back. It was terrible, but worst of all, when I looked round, I saw the girl had run after us. She just stood there, as if casting some kind of wicked spell. I warned Fritz and he rode faster and faster into the forest. Black trees and more black trees. It was then I knew she'd betray us.'

Tom saw raw grief in her eyes as suddenly there came a knock on the door. He jumped. His nerves on edge. This time a different woman entered and introduced herself as Marie. She carried a tray on which the full dinner plate was topped by a plastic cover, misted by condensation.

'You need to eat, *madame*. It's veal today. The very best.'

'Flora was right.' Tom glanced at Natalie, but it was as if she was still back in that forest, urging her machine on to safety. Rocking backwards and forwards, her eyes tight shut.

'I can't. I'm sorry. It's the one meat I can't manage.'

'But veal's full of goodness. Everyone enjoys its flavour. Especially Madame Plessis.'

'I hope she chokes on it.'

'That's not a very nice thing to say.' The woman looked in vain for support from the visitors, then left, muttering about the waste of good food.

After another prompt from Tom, Liliane continued her story. 'We'd travelled at least a kilometre, when we heard gunshot. Not once but twice and then again. The bike keeled over. We ended up on the forest floor, Fritz trying to protect me. It was Didier Bertrand and his two labourers. They took us to Pech Merle and then next day... Next day...' she slumped a little in her chair, then recovered. 'Fritz was shot in front of me. The Resistance gave him no blindfold, nothing. He looked at me. Then faced the gun... He was so brave and wanted so much to be a father. How could I know his son'd turn out the way he did.'

'You mean Samson?' But Tom was also thinking of a different Didier. A hero.

She nodded.

Tom and Natalie stared at each other. Listened to the rest.

'Life is like the Loto, my friends. A game of chance.' She unclenched her fists. Rested her palms on her knees.

'That woman who came in just now,' said Natalie. 'She mentioned a Madame Plessis. The same as on that note you showed us...'

'Yes. When I first saw Pauline Keppel in close-up in that marquee, I recognised something deep in her eyes. Something I'll never forget till my last breath. At first, I thought I might be going mad, but the more I looked, the more I realised. You see, some things don't change, do they? Especially evil...'

'And?'

'You see, her mother, Irène, is here too. That's why I asked to come to this rest home and, despite my age, my weariness, as God's my witness, I'll tell her what I know, and watch her die. That will be my revenge.'

The room's temperature seemed to drop. Tom and Natalie lost for words, until he pushed his fingers back through his hair and went over to stand in the block of sunshine.

'In the summer of 1946, the whole family moved to a farm just south of Paris. Then, in 1964 – October 12th it was – when Pauline Plessis was just two years old, Didier Bertrand, a widower at the time, died suddenly. Someone must have shot him while he was out on his tractor. The Inquest verdict said death due to misadventure, possibly because of a huntsman being trigger-happy during *la chasse*. After that, Irène, sold the farm and moved with her husband, Charles Plessis and their young family into the city.'

October 12th

Tom noticed the challenge in her eyes. Daring him to ask if she'd been the man's killer. He thought about that old rifle. Wondered if that could have been her weapon.

'So his killer wasn't found?'

'The case was never solved,' she said. 'And nor can it be. It's over ten years old. Major Belassis told me that much. Some truth at least from the demon. I knew he had a brother, but...' Her voice faded to nothing.

Natalie stood up and joined Tom, as if sitting down made her feel vulnerable. He knew from her letters that she couldn't sleep on her own in the dark, and that a flatmate had moved in with her in Boisseuil.

'One more thing, please,' Liliane gestured for Tom to stay a moment longer. 'After you'd run off, I went back into that marquee...'

'I don't think I can deal with this.' He found himself saying. 'Can't we leave it? Talk about something else?'

'No. I do have to tell you. Painful though it is. I saw that Keppel as she was dying. Blood everywhere, just like my Fritz. She looked up at me with her mother's eyes. Said she thought I was dead.

'She tried to get her son to breathe till I told her it was useless. That no wonder she'd lost him. God's punishment, I shouted at her, before the police dragged me away. She could hear me alright, oh yes. Heard me tell her she couldn't be anything but a devil, coming from a mother like that.'

The sun had moved on further west over fir-clad mountains. The room darker now. Tom shivered. His watch said three o'clock.

'Best be going,' he bent down and patted her skinny arm. 'I've booked an hotel in Chartres for tonight, and roads round here aren't exactly straight.'

'So kind of you both to come.' She suddenly gripped his hand. Her eyes filmed by sadness. 'That sounds feeble, doesn't it? But I had to make sure you wouldn't give me that money back. And to give you first option on Belette.'

Natalie kissed both her cavernous cheeks. 'I'm sure it'll sell quickly. Then at least you'll have some peace of mind.'

'I'll never have that, my dear.' She navigated her wheelchair towards the door. 'Take good care of her and your children, Monsieur Tom. Remember what I told you that day at the apartments.'

'What was that?' Natalie asked, curious.

'Tell you later.'

'And yourself.' She gave him such a knowing look that suddenly he felt his conscience well up like water behind a sluice-gate. How could he take care of anybody after all that had happened?

Outside the front door, with Max and Flora exhausted from play and trudging towards the car, Natalie caught up with him. Their shadows stark and still on the gravel like those two poplars that had stood outside that *cabane*.

'I know what you might be thinking,' she said softly.

'That I doubted you?'

'No. Something else.' Her steady grey gaze met his and in that moment, he sensed Liliane Bonneau watching from between her shutters. If he was to have any future it was time to set his secret free.

'I lied to you,' he began. 'I lied to that enquiry, under oath. All that stuff about a piece of wire was crap... I gave Bonneau the chance he needed, didn't I? After I'd unlocked the car door for Max to stretch his legs, I had to go back into the *Tabac* to look at those bloody magazines, didn't I? How to mend your roof, deal with termites. Not how to keep your kid safe. Oh no...'

She took his hand.

'So, Max covered up for you, OK? But he would, wouldn't he? He's that kind of boy. Look, Tom, like the old girl in there said, things move on. They have to.'

He stared at her lovely face. Her eyelashes so much darker than her eyes. The first thing he'd noticed about her and never forgotten. That mouth he'd never kissed...

But that one question still remained. It was now or never.

He saw Max and Flora leaning against the Subaru, waiting for him to take them back yet somehow aware he wasn't quite ready.

'Tell me,' he began tentatively. 'Did you ever know what Metz was into? Did you have even the faintest idea?'

Seconds passed in which her grey eyes closed,

brimming with fresh tears.

'You don't know me at all, do you?'

And he knew he could never ask it of her again.

'What will you do now?' he ventured, shame-faced after she'd moved away from him to wipe her eyes, blow her nose and return, keeping a little more distance between them this time. 'Go back to work at the university?'

She shrugged.

'There's some family history I need to deal with, and,' she eyed him, as if watching for his reaction, 'seeing that veal just now got me thinking.'

'Not the League?' His heart sank. All those memories of Belette, of everything, still too real. Too raw.

'No. It's called Viva! But I can work for them from anywhere.'

'Anywhere?'

He moved towards her, aware of his children smiling, almost urging him on. He took her hand and squeezed it. Hard. His lifebelt...

'If you'll have me.'

EPILOGUE

The middle-aged couple in matching beige slacks and Pringle cotton-knit shirts trekked up the weed-lined track as the late afternoon sun slid behind the Fer à Cheval above the hamlet of St Sauveur.

It was music they heard first. The rough, throbbing kind accompanied by handclapping, then yells and screams; rocks banging together in a jarring percussion.

Una Simiston gripped her husband's arm to stall him. This didn't feel right. Not right at all. She glanced behind her and noticed their deluxe 4 berth Pilote was now disconcertingly out of sight.

'Please, Ben, let's go back,' she urged her husband. 'Tom's not here. Never was. We've got it completely wrong.'

'My dear, my map-reading's impeccable, as you know. Look, see that sign.' He indicated a hand-painted plank of wood set at an angle in the overgrown hedge. Its letters barely visible. 'Hibou. *Voilà*. Hell, I'm just staggered that out of the whole of France, this is what he chose...'

He pulled her along, their faces flushed by the dying sun and the climb. Their last spur-of-the-moment *sortie* before heading back to Guildford.

Suddenly, without warning, a massive brown sparrowhawk with an already open beak, descended from the hovel's roof and snatched at the man's medallion, glowing in the V of his shirt. Then his hair – what was left of it – then hers, styled in Loupin only yesterday. Next came the rocks. All sizes. All accurate, making short work of the intruders.

The bells followed. Louder than ever. Almost celebratory, it seemed, to the *gipsy* standing with his kids at the door. A thin black smile on his face.

The publishers hope that this book has given you enjoyable reading. Large Print Books are especially designed to be as easy to see and hold as possible. If you wish a complete list of our books please ask at your local library or write directly to:

Magna Large Print Books
Magna House, Long Preston,
Skipton, North Yorkshire.
BD23 4ND

This Large Print Book for the partially sighted, who cannot read normal print, is published under the auspices of

THE ULVERSCROFT FOUNDATION